The Millennium AFFAIR

LUCY LYONS

Published in the UK in 2024 by Twist House Books
Copyright © Lucy Lyons 2024
Cover Art by Spiffing Covers

lucylyonswrites.com

This is a work of fiction. The characters contained within its pages are wholly imaginary. Any resemblance to actual persons, living or dead, is entirely coincidental. Descriptions of Hertfordshire and Birmingham, although loosely based on real places, have been re-imagined to suit the convenience of the story. The opinions expressed are those of the characters and should not be confused with the author's own.

Paperback ISBN: 978-1-7393079-2-9
eBook ISBN: 978-1-7393079-3-6

For Sean

1

— • —

DECEMBER 1999

I ce sparkles in the headlights as I turn into the car park. Birmingham City Council had the genius idea of digging up the A38 the moment I needed it, and now I'm late for my shift.

My workplace is a futuristic, mirror-clad office block that looms over the frosty tarmac. Its panels are alive with yellow and red streaks from passing traffic. My headlights shine back at me as I swing the Audi TT next to my boss's car and leave the engine idling for a second, building up the courage to face the bitter cold.

Holding my numb fingers against the hot air vents, I snuggle into my tartan snood and glance up to the fourth floor where the National Missing Persons Helpline has its home. When my boss called, I was cuddling with Antony on the sofa. I'd like to say we were watching TV together, but Antony fell asleep ten minutes after dinner and I couldn't hear the programme through his snores. His job has worn him out to the point where I count *any* time together as precious, even if he's not conscious.

Lin said Trevor had been taken ill, and could I cover his shift. No one else was available. My first thought was to make an excuse. But I'm so close to completing my training as a Caller Support Officer, if I show willing, that has to help my chances.

The irony of working for an organisation that finds people when I have a machine that can do it isn't lost on me. Last year, Dad's invention changed my life. I felt close to him whenever I used it, almost like he'd left part of himself inside the casing.

Using the finding machine turned out to be an emotional roller-coaster. The highs I felt at finding someone safe and sound were countered by sad tales of people who didn't want to be found, or were no longer alive. The experience also led me into danger.

Antony and I discussed the risks. We both agreed the best course of action was to put the machine away in its shoebox.

Since then, I've never felt the urge to use it again. My job enables me to find people through the regular channels. It's a quieter, uncomplicated life, and I prefer it that way.

The clock on the dashboard displays 22:32. Choice FM's weather report drifts through the car speakers. *'A weather warning is in place throughout the West Midlands. A cold front pushing in from the north will bring freezing temperatures, down to a low of minus three. So, wrap up, make yourself a mug of hot chocolate, and enjoy an hour of festive favourites...'*

I switch the engine off as Bing Crosby starts crooning.

Grabbing my rucksack, I clamber from the low-slung convertible. My heel slides on a slick of ice. Cursing the idiots who forgot to grit the tarmac, I tread carefully towards the glass doors and run my swipe-card through the reader.

The lock clicks and I step into the warm foyer.

An enormous Christmas tree dominates the clean, white space, festooned with tinsel and coloured lights. The foyer is deserted apart from a lone figure on the sleek leather sofa, hunched over a plastic wastepaper bin. Trevor's black Adidas tracksuit accentuates his ghastly pallor.

I rush over. 'Trev, what's the matter?'

'Bloody *Wazzy's Kebabs,* that's what,' Trevor groans, his bald head beaded with sweat. 'I had a lamb doner earlier and it's turned on me.'

'Do you want an antacid tablet?' I say, rummaging in my bag.

Trevor groans, turns a curious shade of yellow, and retches into the bin. I hand him a box of tissues from the reception desk and stand uselessly by, patting his shoulder.

'My missus should have been here by now,' he says.

'She's probably stuck in roadworks,' I explain. 'Is there anything I can do?'

'No, you'd better get off. Thanks for covering my shift.' Trevor dabs his lips and forces his head up to meet my gaze. 'Remember, Lin's a stickler for the rules. Make sure you do everything by the book.'

'I will, don't worry.'

Trevor looks up as car headlights sweep the foyer. 'At last.'

I squeeze his arm. Ignoring the notoriously slow elevator, I run up the stairs to the fourth floor and pause to catch my breath outside the office, before pushing through the door.

The main room contains four workstations strung with tinsel, a worn sofa, Lin's office, and a tiny kitchenette.

As I shrug off my coat and sling it over my chair, Lin walks out of her office, carrying paperwork. She is a five-foot-nothing powerhouse with dark hair and piercing blue eyes. I'm three inches taller but I feel small beside her. Lin has worked for the NMPH for twenty years and is in her fifties with no signs of slowing down.

'Ah, Alexandra. There you are. Thanks for coming in at such short notice.'

'I would have been here earlier but the traffic was terrible.' I pause. 'Poor Trevor.'

'He's in for a rough night.' She lets out a sigh. 'I suggested he go to A&E, but he wouldn't hear of it.'

Lin arranges her files at the desk opposite so she can supervise me while I take calls. It's a term of my probation that will change once I pass my course.

I rub my hands together. 'Do you want a tea? Coffee?'

'Coffee, thanks.' Lin pauses. 'Just so you know, tonight counts towards your probation. If all goes to plan, you should be a fully-fledged member of the team by Christmas.'

My cheeks flush at the thought of taking calls unsupervised and having a set of keys to the office. I set up the coffee percolator and within moments, the rich aroma of ground Arabica fills the air.

Once Lin and I are settled with mugs of coffee, I log onto my computer and read through the evening's callers. Contrary to popular belief, it's not just missing people and their concerned families who call us. Runaways, sofa-surfers and the homeless also call when they need to talk to someone, or to let us know they're safe. People go missing for all sorts of reasons, and the NMPH serves them all. Our charity connects missing persons, relatives, and the police.

Pushing my long hair back, I put on my phone headset. I can't say I relish the night shift, but the satisfaction from helping callers makes up for the long, dark hours.

An hour passes, and the phone doesn't ring. If I was working with Trevor, he'd be chatting non-stop about football results and the missus, and I'd proudly tell him about my oil paintings, a passion I pursue in my spare time. But Lin is busy and the only sounds are buzzing computers, the click of the storage heaters, and *tick-tick* of the clock.

It's going to be a long night.

In the run-up to one a.m., we receive a total of four calls. Lin pauses from her work to listen in and gives an approving nod each time I put the phone down.

The phone rings again. I answer, 'Hello. You're through to the NMPH. Can I take your name, please?'

'Yeah, it's Philpot.'

Philpot, born Philip Sanderson, is a long-term homeless man in his sixties with an alcohol problem, who calls us every few days from a payphone to talk about anything and everything. He's lost contact with his remaining family and sees us as the next best thing.

'Philpot, it's Alex. How are you doing? Do you have a bed for the night?' I pray he's not sleeping rough with tonight's bitter forecast.

'Yeah, I'm at the Sally Army shelter in Coleshill. Got the last bed.' His voice slurs. 'This fella in the bunkroom told me the world's about to end. So, we thought what the hell, and went halves on some vodka.'

'The world's not going to end. Don't worry, everything will be fine,' I reassure him. With the new Millennium close at hand, the doomsayers are crawling from the woodwork. I half-listen to his incoherent rambling for a few minutes until he hangs up.

The next caller sounds young and full of beans. As soon as I've introduced myself, he says, 'Yeah, my neighbour's gone missing. His name's Mike. Can you find him?'

'I'll need some details,' I say, fingers poised over the keyboard. 'What is your neighbour's surname?'

'Rotch.'

'What makes you think Mike Ro—' I stop suddenly. 'Idiot!'

I slam the receiver down, cutting off guffaws of laughter. These kids get bored too easily. I blame Bart Simpson.

Lin gives me a narrow look. 'Alex, we need to remain professional at all times.'

'Sorry. Kids.' I log the nuisance call, colour rising to my cheeks.

The phone's ringing again. I answer it.

'My name's Sandra,' a woman says in a hurry. 'I'm here with Lin's mother. I tried Lin at home but there was no reply. Is she there?'

'Yes, I'll pass you over.' I catch Lin's eye and say, 'Someone called Sandra? She's with your mum.' I transfer the call.

'Hi Sandra,' Lin answers, pressing the receiver to her ear.

Just as I take a sip of coffee, the phone rings. *A quiet night. Give me a break!*

'Hello. This is Alex at the N—'

'They mucked me about and did a runner!' an indignant youth yells. 'Tossers!'

'Who is this, please?'

'Rashid.'

I twist the earpiece cord. Rashid's a regular who left home at sixteen after constant clashes with his traditional Muslim family. He's popped into the office plenty of times, charming us with his cheeky grin and jokes, but his life is tough. Rashid stopped attending school and spends his days hanging around the inner city with dubious individuals, and his nights squatting in the worst parts of Walsall.

My heart goes out to him. I'm about to lend him a sympathetic ear when Lin's shoulders slump.

'Birmingham City Hospital? Do you know which ward?' She jots something down. 'I'll be there as soon as I can.'

She drops the receiver in the cradle.

'Rashid, hold on a sec.' I cover the phone. 'Lin, what happened?'

Lin shoots to her feet and throws on her winter coat. 'Mum had a fall. She was putting the bins out and slipped on some ice.'

'That's terrible!' I frown. 'Is there anything I can do?'

'I'm afraid you'll have to go home. Can you shut everything down, divert the calls to ansaphone and lock up? '

I'm not allowed to work unsupervised. My soul sinks at the fact I left my nice, warm house, sat in traffic jams, and braved the cold for nothing.

'Of course,' I say. 'Leave everything to me.'

'See you tomorrow,' Lin says, rushing out.

As soon as the door swings shut I say, 'Rashid, I can't speak now, I have to shut down the office. Can you call back in the morning, after nine?'

'They took my Pumas. And my puffa jacket.'

'Who did?'

'I told you. Tigs and Benzaboy. Bloody hell, it's cold.' Rashid's teeth chatter at the end of the line.

'Where are you?'

'I dunno.' His breath comes out in huffs. It sounds like he's moving about to keep warm. 'I've been walking for ages but there's no way out. My feet are soaked. I think I'm getting frostbite.' He pauses. 'You've got to help me. My phone's nearly out of juice.'

2

I throw a panicked look at the clock. Five minutes have passed since Lin left. I'm already breaking the rules.

'Listen, Rashid, you need to ring the police. I can't help you.'

'No way, not the law.'

Closing my eyes, I try and stay calm. 'You must have some idea where you are.'

'No, coz Tigs and Benzaboy picked me up in Walsall and we rode the buses. We went out of town, then we got off at some park.'

'Which park?' I push him. 'Don't you remember?'

'Nah.' Rashid stops short. Swears under his breath. 'There's something out here! Can you hear it?'

The wind roars down my earpiece as he holds the mobile up.

'It's just the wind.'

'I'm not lying, I swear!' His voice shoots up. 'Sounded big. Like a bear.'

'There are no bears in England!' Unless he's somehow wound up inside Birmingham Zoo. I scribble notes. *Large animal – deer? Wild horses?* 'What happened to your clothes?'

'Tigs took them! We dropped some acid, but then Tigs got freaked. Said I was a space goblin with a melted face.' Rashid's teeth chatter. 'They were really tripping. Next thing I know, Tigs is coming for me. I punched him good, but then Benzaboy joined in and held me down. They took my trainers, coat, money. Luckily, they didn't get my phone coz I stashed it in my combats.' He pauses. 'I'm so cold, Alex. Can you come get me?'

7

Rashid's voice breaks, and I hear the young, vulnerable boy behind his tough shell. His mother told me he used to be a studious boy, good at maths, with a bright future ahead of him. Then he hit fourteen and started hankering after the freedoms of his non-Muslim friends.

I hear a shuffling sound, like he's moving his arms around.

'When will you be here?'

His raw hope is overwhelming. Stretching across Lin's desk, I grab the AA Big Road Map and flick to the map of Birmingham. It's one of the greenest cities in the UK, surrounded by forests and parks.

I rack my brain thinking how to pinpoint his location. Sutton Park's close enough to Walsall but it's larger than the city centre. I stare at multiple green patches on the map: Park Lime Pits, Moseley Bog, Kingfisher Country Park, and that's just for starters.

I don't see how the police can find him. He could be further out. He could be anywhere.

'Rashid, listen to me. Try and find a landmark. A statue, playground, river or a building. Something that stands out.'

'I can hear a river and—' Muffled noises follow. More curses. 'I dropped the phone. I can't feel my fingers. Hold on, there's some kind of bridge or tunnel ahead. I'll go under it. It can't be as cold as out here.'

I study the map. One or two railway lines cross green areas. Could Rashid be beside a freight line or a disused bridge?

'Is it a railway bridge, Rashid?'

'Dunno. How do I tell?'

'Are there any train-tracks, gates, or barriers?' Or preferably, a bloody train going over it.

'Can't see. There's bushes in the way. I'm pushing my way through.'

'Just watch your step. Once you get to the bridge, stay there, OK?' I gulp down the dregs of my coffee to relieve the sudden dryness in my mouth. Rashid's making himself harder to find, but what can I do? I can't ask him to stand out in the open where he'll die of exposure.

'This place...is...dark. And wet.' His voice slurs, sending a spike of panic through me. Could it be an after-effect of the acid? But he has sounded lucid so far. It's more likely to be an early sign of hypothermia. He's inadequately dressed, his feet are wet, and he's coming down off drugs. He probably hasn't eaten or drunk much all day. The temperature outside is below freezing and dropping. Cold enough to kill.

The phone rattles from his involuntary shivering. 'Are you coming to get me, now?'

'Yes, I promise. I'm getting help. Hold on.'

I reach across the desk for a spare phone, and dial 999.

A female call answers, 'Which service do you require?'

'Police, please.' With the phone to my left ear and the headset earpiece to my right, I say, 'This is Alex Martin from the National Missing Persons Helpline in Birmingham. I'm on the phone to a lost teenager suffering from hypothermia. He needs an ambulance.'

'What's the address?'

'We don't know where he is. Can you trace his mobile number?' I read Rashid's number from the display on the base unit, to the call handler. 'Rashid is slurring his speech and he's inadequately dressed for the weather. His phone's low on charge, too.'

'Do you have the nearest main road or intersection? Or a public building?'

'He thinks he's lost in a large park with animals - deer maybe - on the outskirts of Birmingham. He's found shelter under an old bridge near a river.'

I press the headset to my ear. 'Rashid? How are you doing?'

'I'm u...under the bridge. It's dark in here. C...an't t...t...alk.'

Rashid's phone goes dead.

'Rashid, hello. Hello?' I shout into my mouthpiece even though I know it's hopeless.

'Did you get that? Can you track him?' I say loudly to the police.

'I'm passing on the details,' the operator says. 'Stay on the line, please.'

'Can you track him?' I repeat.

But the operator's put me on hold.

Seconds tick past. I click the end of my pen. In my mind's eye, Rashid is slipping into unconsciousness under a dark bridge, where a week from now, some dog-walker will stumble across his frozen body. I occupy my over-worried brain by filling in the log and drumming my fingers on the desk. I call Rashid's number again, hoping his phone might have mustered enough charge to work.

Nothing.

A male voice comes on the line. 'Hello, I'm John, the senior call handler. We tried the number you gave us, but Rashid isn't answering,'

'His mobile phone died,' I say. 'Can you still track it?'

'That might be a problem. Hold on.'

In the silence that follows, I squeeze the life out of my stress ball.

'I'm afraid we can't trace the phone,' John says. 'Even if Rashid's mobile was working, he'd have to wait for the intelligence team, and they're not here until morning, so it's a no go.'

'The boy's had his coat and trainers stolen. He's going to freeze to death!'

'I understand your concern,' John says. 'But without knowing which park he's in, we'll have to search them all. Even if we had sufficient manpower, which we don't, it'll be like finding a needle in a haystack.'

'Can't you get the helicopter up?' I ask. The noise and lights might lure Rashid out from cover. On the other hand, he's paranoid where the police are concerned. He might stay hidden.

'Leave it with me,' says John. 'Ring back if you have further information.'

I hang up, sick to my stomach. Even if the police sent a thousand officers to check every bridge in every park, it wouldn't be enough to find him in time.

I stare at the ticking clock: 02:03

How can I log off and go home to my safe, warm bed? I'd only lie awake, staring at the ceiling.

Biting my lip, my mind goes to a place I didn't think I'd be visiting again. Anticipation trickles down my breastbone. If I commit to this, there will be consequences. There always are. I vowed never to use the finding machine again, but Rashid's life is in danger.

I ring home, and count nine rings before Antony picks up.

''Sup?' he says in a groggy voice.

'Antony. I need your help.'

'Whass going on?' says Antony, sleep-slurred. 'Are you all right?'

'I'm fine. It's not about me. It's Rashid. You remember me telling you about him?'

'Yeah, what about him?'

'He's under a bridge in a park somewhere, freezing to death. The police don't know where he is and his mobile's dead. We have to find him before it's too late.' I pause, swallow hard. 'You know what I'm asking.'

'Are you crazy? I have to be up for work in a few hours!' Antony lets out a groan. 'I thought we agreed not to go down this road again. Leave it to the police. It's their job to find missing kids.'

Grinding my teeth, I say, 'The police aren't going to find Rashid in time. They're not miracle workers. If he dies under a bridge I'll never forgive myself. We can help him, Antony. We can save his life.'

Antony gives an almighty sigh. 'You swore blind you weren't doing this again.'

'Please, I need you to help me. This is really, really, important.'

'Why can't you come home and do it?'

'Because there's roadworks on the A38 and it'll take too long!'

Antony lets out a strangled sound. 'All right. What do you want me to do?'

'Go to the office. In the bottom drawer of my desk, you'll find a shoebox. Get the finding machine out and ring me straight back.'

3

—·—

I throw my headset to the desk and launch myself towards the row of filing cabinets lining the back wall. The third cabinet from the left contains our client files. I delve inside the top drawer, flicking through manila folders.

AHMED, ASTOR, BLACK, CHENG, CLARKE

Cold sweat breaks on my upper lip. There are so many files. I grip the top of the filing cabinet, take a deep breath and gather my thoughts. I've seen Rashid's file often enough. I should be able to remember his surname.

It's on the tip of my tongue. His surname starts with the letter S, something like Saleh, or Shah.

Pushing the top drawer closed, I open the bottom one and flick through the alphabetic tabs to the letter S.

I find Rashid's file near the middle. SHAKIR, RASHID.

The file makes a heavy *thunk* as I drop it onto my desk. I'm not interested in the contents, just the photo clipped to the cover. Rashid smiles at me. His neatly gelled hair has a trendy, spiral pattern cut over one ear. The photo was sent in by Rashid's family. It was taken in happier times before he ran away.

I unclip his photo and place it face down on the scanner. The damn thing takes forever to warm up. When the bar of light finally starts travelling across the flatbed, I watch its progress with my finger hovering impatiently over the mouse.

Once the scan is complete, I save the file and email it to Antony.

My hands won't stop shaking. Sharing details of missing persons without their consent to anyone outside the NMPH is an absolute no-no. I don't want to break the rules, but Rashid's going to freeze to death unless I do something. I'll have to come up with a convincing explanation for my actions later.

I jump as the phone rings.

'Before you ask, yeah, it's out of the box,' Antony says. 'Took me forever to get through the bubble-wrap.'

I used five layers of the stuff and a mile of sticky-tape to stop me using the machine again on a whim.

'That shoebox is like a fridge,' he goes on. 'Your dad's machine is still freezing cold. Guess that means it still works and is still nuclear. So, if we ever decide to have kids and can't, you'll know the reason why.'

My ears prick up at the mention of kids, but now's not the time. Much as I love Antony, I wish he'd stop banging on about radiation. Dad would never have built something unsafe.

'You know the finding machine isn't nuclear, Antony.'

'I've stuffed tin-foil down my pants, just in case.'

'You are a sweetie. Thanks for doing this.'

'Yeah, you owe me big time.' Antony pauses. 'Hold on, it's not switching on. There's nothing. Just a blank screen.'

'Oh, God, I took the battery out.'

Closing my eyes, I picture Dad's invention, which is a repurposed, blocky calculator case. Where you would expect number buttons, it has a clear screen protecting the electronics: an array of analogue components including resistors, capacitors and tiny valves. The on/off switch is on the side, and the battery compartment is down the bottom behind a slide-off cover.

'OK, we need a 9-volt battery,' Antony says. 'One of those square ones. Have we got any?'

'I can't remember,' I say, with a sinking feeling. 'What about the torch?'

'That takes big C batteries.'

'Your remote-control car?'

'That went to charity last year.'

'The radio-alarm clock!' I blurt out. 'That definitely takes a 9-volt.'

A minute later, Antony gives me good news. 'OK, we're in business. There's a green dot on the display.'

Dad's dot, I like to call it. The starting point for all my adventures.

'OK. Boot up your Mac,' I tell him. 'I've emailed you Rashid's photo. You need to print it out so it fits in the machine.'

'Hello, it's me, remember?'

In the background, I hear the distinctive chime of the iMac booting up, followed by Antony moving around, clicking and typing.

I open a new window on my computer and type in: *www.geosp atialdata.co.uk.* Last year, my go-to website whenever I needed to find someone, but I haven't used it for so long I'm not sure it still works.

My breath catches in my throat when the webpage successfully loads. I click on *Find My Location,* then *Decimal Degrees,* which brings up two input boxes.

'How are you doing with the photo?' I press my hand to my racing heart.

'Printing out, now.' A few moments later he says, 'I'm attaching the clips.'

Closing my eyes, I take deep, slow breaths, visualising the machine. Two antennae sit in a slotted recess on top. They lift up like windscreen wipers and lock in place, pointing upwards. Black contact strips run from the machine's body to the antennae, ending in a pair of small crocodile clips.

Once Antony puts Rashid's photo between the clips, the magic should happen.

'Come on, Antony. You're killing me. What's going on?'

'Something weird happened. The display flashed on and off. Don't remember seeing that before.'

He goes silent.

'Antony! Come on!'

'Keep your hair on, it's working again. Got a pen? Here's the read-out. **52.562015 -1.862635**.'

'Thanks, Antony. Tell me if the numbers change.'

The machine tracks people in real time, using GPS satellite technology to locate any person, alive or dead, whose photo is placed between the clips. If Rashid moves location, the read-out will change. The GPS part is hard science. The rest is a complete mystery.

I type the co-ordinates into the Latitude and Longitude input boxes on the screen and hit *GO*.

The web page fractures into overlapping blocks before the image settles. I should be looking at a map, but all I see is a block of green. I zoom out to find an identifiable landmark, road or river.

'Where is he, then?' Antony asks impatiently.

'It's Sutton Park!' The largest park in Birmingham. Zooming back in, a white-gloved hand points to Rashid's location. To my dismay, it's nowhere near a railway line or any bridges. The teenager has ended up beside a stream in the park's south-western quadrant, north of a large body of water named Longmoor Pool.

I compare the map on screen with the AA map, and carefully mark a cross on the page in red pen.

'I told the police he was under a bridge near a railway line,' I tell Antony. 'They'll be looking in the wrong place!'

'Call them and give them an update,' Antony says. 'Then come home, all right?'

'Will do,' I say. 'Call my mobile if Rashid moves in the next ten minutes.'

'All right, ten minutes. Then I'm getting my head down. Love you.'

'Love you too.'

I dial 999. The call handler is a different person to the one I spoke to before, and can't put me through to John. The directions I give her come out rather garbled.

'Did you say south of Longmoor Pool?' she asks.

'No, north. Somewhere in the south-west area of Sutton Park. There's a small stream running north from the pool, can you see it?'

'I don't have a map in front of me,' the emergency call handler says. 'I'll pass on your directions to the search team.'

'Rashid is some way north of Longmoor Pool, a little to the right of the stream.'

God, that sounds vague!

I hang up, chewing my lip. Now I've passed on Rashid's location to the police, I have to update the log. My involvement is in the public sphere and there's no hiding it. I bullet-point my actions, typing the bare minimum: *Updated police on Rashid's location. 02:43.*

Surely Lin will understand my actions?

I replace the photo in Rashid's file, put the file back inside the filing cabinet, shut the computers down, divert the calls and turn off the lights. With the map tucked under my arm, I race down four flights of stairs and across the deserted foyer, past the Christmas tree's cheery lights.

Bitter wind whips my hair when I push through the doors into the dark and empty carpark. The frigid air makes me gasp. It's far colder than when I arrived. I slip and slide to the Audi and throw myself into the cold, leather seat. Switching on the engine, I blow into my hands and take a deep breath.

This should be it for me. The police have Rashid's location. Kind of.

I put the car in gear and drive to the junction with the main road, where I sit for a moment. Home is to my right. Fumbling in the pocket of the door, I find a Maglite torch, and slip it inside my coat pocket.

Turning left, I drive away from home to join the A34 north-bound. There's a fire in my belly, urging me to get to Sutton Park as quickly as possible.

The route is straightforward. About eight miles. At this hour, there are few vehicles around. I put my foot down, hitting ninety for a couple of miles on the well-gritted, empty main roads, slowing for the approach to the A453 turn off. The A-road peels off to the left into Kingstanding Road, and I floor it along a clear stretch to a large roundabout. The Audi's tyres squeal on tarmac as I gun the engine and haul the steering wheel to the right. Rough Road is the fourth exit, and then it's a straight-line race to Banners Gate entrance, Sutton Park.

I spot blue lights flashing at the entrance to the park, and drop my speed to the legal limit. I take a sedate left turn through the gates and pull onto the verge behind an empty police car. A pair of officers wearing fluorescent jackets walk towards me.

I step from the car, assailed by the *whomp-whomp-whomp* of a low-flying helicopter. The chopper hovers to the north-west, shining a cone of light further to the east.

The helicopter is searching in the wrong area.

'Excuse me,' a female officer calls out, heading my way. 'You can't stop there.'

'I'm Alex from the National Missing Persons Helpline. I called it in.' I raise my voice, holding up my swipe-card. I open the map and show her the red cross. 'I need to show you the exact location you need to be searching. I couldn't describe it accurately on the phone.'

She eyes me curiously. 'How do you know the boy is there?'

'One of his mates who was with him in the park earlier, called in.' It's a white lie, one she can't really check up on. I hand her the map and point to the red cross. 'Rashid's north of Longmoor Pool, near this stream. This road takes you most of the way there. I can show you.'

The officer turns away to speak with her colleague and updates the team on her radio.

She comes back and opens the back door of the police car. 'All right, jump in.'

I clamber in the back. 'Follow the road to Longmoor Pool.'

The officer drives down a winding tarmac road with blackness to either side. Eventually, a parking bay opens to the left. The car's headlights reflect on a body of dark water. A black and white metal barrier blocks the road ahead.

'We'll have to go the rest of the way on foot,' the officer says.

'Okay.' I check the map again before leaping from the car with the torch. The officer calls after me, but the thunder of the chopper drowns out what she's saying. I race to the barrier, clamber over and follow the road around the far side of the pool. My breath comes out in short huffs as I head left into the rough, my boots crunching on hard, frosty ground.

My torch-beam plays along open ground with low brush and trees. Featureless terrain. Terror shoots through me. I only have a vague idea where Rashid is, and I haven't found the stream that runs north. I glance back. A second torch-light bobs twenty feet behind. I forge on, stumbling and pushing through soggy dips in the ground. Freezing water seeps into my boots, brambles claw at my clothes as I stick close to the pond, looking for the stream.

The chugging overhead grows louder, drowning out the trickle of running water.

I slip down the bank into a soggy bog of a stream surrounded by squelching mud, and shine my light around.

Suddenly, blazing light floods the ground surrounding me, like God is watching.

I look up, shielding my eyes. The helicopter has turned its nose towards us.

'Rashid!' I yell, stumbling forwards. 'Rashid, it's Alex!'

On and on I stride, half-sliding, half-falling down an incline. Ahead is a low, concrete curve. My heart hammers against my ribs.

It's not a bridge, but a water culvert. An ugly, prefabricated drainage feature.

'Rashid!' I splash towards the culvert and thrust my arms between the undergrowth tangled in my way. My torchlight falls on a huddle in the corner.

I throw myself forward and grab the shivering boy. 'It's me, Rashid. It's Alex.'

Rashid's eyes crack open. He shudders, tears run down his cheeks. 'I...I...kn...knew you'd come...Al...Alex. I knew.'

'You're safe.'

I hug him, sobbing, telling myself over and over that I've done the right thing.

4

— • —

By the time I return home, it's past four a.m. Antony left a tea-light on the porch to welcome me home. Unfortunately, the wick has burned down and the light has snuffed out. Still, it's the thought that counts.

I sneak into bed. Antony's dead to the world, lightly snoring with one arm hanging off the side of the bed.

Sleep is a long time coming after my adventure. Thoughts of Rashid, the police, and Lin circle in my mind until a blackbird breaks into song outside the window.

I must have drifted off sometime during the dawn chorus, because the next thing I know, the glorious trilling of the birds has gone, replaced by thumping and swearing.

Through bleary eyes, I watch Antony hopping on one leg amidst discarded lengths of bubble-wrap.

'I'm dead, I'm dead,' Antony repeats the mantra while pulling on a pink, striped sock. He shifts to the other foot. 'I'm so dead.'

Antony's pale-blue shirt hangs open, framing his dark, sculpted torso. His pink tie hangs loose around his collar.

'Morning.' I prop myself up on my elbow. 'Is there a problem?'

'Yeah, I'd say so.' Antony misbuttons his shirt in his haste. 'The alarm didn't go off. You know why? Because you made me take the battery out.' He checks his watch and mouths the time like a swearword. 'I'm supposed to be briefing my team on the Razorr Energy Drink pitch in twenty minutes, and I'm nowhere near the bloody building!'

'I'm sorry,' I swing my legs out of bed, glancing at the radio-alarm's blank face. 'What can I do to help?'

'Get the car keys, and my Oxfords.' Antony yanks open the wardrobe and stands in front of the mirror rebuttoning his shirt. His gorgeous bod is a testament to the hours he somehow squeezes in at the gym on weekends. But there's no disguising the tiredness in his red-rimmed eyes, or the fact his normally short and neat Afro is starting to riot and needs a trim.

I leave him doing up his tie with swift, sharp movements and search for the car keys. The keys are where I left them in the kitchen, on the countertop by the bread-bin. Antony's Oxford shoes are on the rack by the door and could do with a polish, but like everything related to his work, there isn't time.

'I'll replace the battery, I promise.' I hand him the car keys.

'Don't bother. I'll use my mobile from now on.' He looks at me in the mirror. 'Did the police find the kid?'

'I...I found him.'

'What?' Antony pauses in buckling his belt. 'You said you were coming straight home!'

'I had to show the police where he ! They'd never have found him, otherwise.'

'So, it was worth it.'

'It was!' I say emphatically. 'I'm sorry about the clock. Rashid wouldn't have stood a chance without us.'

'Good.' Antony throws on his jacket and then grabs his toothbrush and toothpaste on his way out.

At the door he takes a breath. 'I'm sorry. Work's a nightmare at the moment.' He pulls me in for a kiss. 'See you later, OK?'

'OK.'

Once he's gone, guilt washes over me. I shouldn't have woken him last night. It was selfish of me to ask for his help when he has so much on his plate. A wave of exhaustion follows the guilt. I stagger back to bed and throw myself across the warm spot Antony just vacated, pulling the duvet over my head. I'm asleep in moments, my dreams full of dark tunnels and blazing lights.

The phone rings, snapping me awake with a start. My hand shoots out and grabs the receiver. '...lo?'

'Alex, it's Lin.'

'Hi!' I shoot up in bed, blinking rapidly. I glance at the dead alarm clock. No help there. 'Is everything all right?'

'We need to talk about Rashid.'

'Is he all right?'

'He's in hospital, but I'll have a clearer picture this afternoon. Can you come in and see me at three p.m., please?'

A wave of relief hits me, knowing Rashid's all right. 'I could be there earlier, if you want. If you can give me an hour —'

'Let's stick to three.' Lin's firm tone leaves no room for negotiation. She ends the call.

Beyond the curtains, the sky is a grey slab, with the sun nowhere in sight. I check my mobile. 11:45. Far later than I'd thought. Antony's meeting will be over by now, and I haven't stuck a leg out of bed.

I head for the shower. Under the steaming water, I rack my brain for explanations I could give Lin for my actions but discount them all. I bullet-point my strengths as an employee in the condensation on the shower-screen, but it's not going to be enough. Houdini would struggle to get out of this one.

I've been a model employee for over a year. That has to count for something. And maybe I've read it all wrong. The big boss wants to congratulate me personally for saving Rashid's life.

Yeah, right.

Throwing on a dressing gown, my hair wrapped in a towel, I head into the second bedroom, which we use as an office and art-store. Antony's iMac, my PC, scanner, fax and printer are on a long desk opposite the window. A film of dust covers everything. The finding machine is back inside the open shoe-box by my keyboard, switched off, with Rashid's photo between the clips.

He's smiling, as if to say thank you.

To me, the black plastic block of electronics is so much more than a bundle of wires and soldering. Touching it is like saying hello to my dad.

Coldness seeps from the side-vents, caressing my fingers. I've no idea if it's Freon, Puron, or a substance made by aliens. Last year, a teenager named Jason Bevin searched the dark web and discovered a mysterious organisation had built a prototype of my dad's machine. But Jason couldn't find out if it worked.

My belief is Dad made the only working version. I suspect he was a member of this mysterious group, although once again I have no proof.

A framed picture of my dad, Richard Martin, hangs above my PC. He's in our old garden in Sudbury wearing a terrible chunky orange cardigan with fake leather buttons. For many years, he was alone in the frame. But now, a small photo of his sister Lilian is tucked in the corner of the frame next to him. She's only four or five in the picture, a chubby, smiling thing. A year after the picture was taken, she was dead.

If only Dad had found a photograph of his missing sister in his lifetime, he could have found her and died happy. Last year, I completed his life's mission. Now, Dad and Lilian lie together in the Martin family plot, and smile together on my wall.

Finding her wouldn't have been possible without the finding machine. If only my boss could see it working. She'd forgive all my sins. But Antony and I made an agreement to keep its existence secret. The finding machine is impartial. It will find you, whether you're a murderer or a saint. If it fell into the hands of the wrong people, no one would be safe, not even the Prime Minister, or the President of the United States.

I remove the battery, cross the hall into the main bedroom and replace it in the alarm clock.

After gathering up the bubble-wrap littering the floor, I return to my desk and carefully repackage the machine. Once it's tucked back inside the bottom drawer of my desk, I have breakfast, tie my hair back, and dress in my most professional-looking outfit.

· · · ● · ● · · · ·

Antony took the car to work so I have to walk in. Cyclists and runners zip past me as I follow the paved towpath that runs alongside the canal, towards the city. Ducks and swans glide past on the water. In the distance, I hear the *chug-chug* of a barge.

My twenty-five-minute journey takes me past original dockside buildings that have been converted into high-end apartments with balconies overlooking the water. Others stand derelict, ripe for refurbishment or demolition. Birmingham has more canals than Venice, and thousands of interesting views to paint. I've recently completed a set of three paintings which have attracted the interest of an international buyer. One painting features the graffiti-covered bridge I'm walking under.

I'm fascinated by contrast in landscapes - the old alongside the new, the natural and the man-made. On the surface, my paintings look picturesque but include details like rust on the canal-boats, litter in the hedgerows and Victorian chimneys. And, of course, graffiti.

I leave the towpath at the next junction. My route enters the office district, along a busy road lined with advertising and design businesses, coffee shops, restaurants and banks. By the time I reach the office on Woodcock Street, my smart shoes are hurting. For once, I take the lift to the fourth floor. The last thing I want is to arrive a labouring, red-faced mess.

As I push through the doors, Trevor gets up from his workstation. He looks a little peaky, but nothing like as ill as he did yesterday.

'Alex.' Trevor walks over with a downcast expression. He slowly shakes his head, as though he's heard the most terrible news. He rubs a hand over his bald head. 'I feel responsible. For what it's worth, I think you did the right thing.'

I stutter a thanks. My mouth has gone dry.

'Chat later, yes?' he says.

'Sure.' I rub the base of my throat outside Lin's door, take a deep breath and knock.

'Come in.'

I step into Lin's small office. Lin sits behind her desk, flicking through a manilla file. She looks over her glasses as I enter.

'Sit down, Alex.' Her usual cheery expression is nowhere to be seen. She gives a thin smile and gestures to the chair opposite.

'How is your mum?' I ask, hoping her dourness is down to concern for her, and not me.

'She broke her ankle. The surgeon hopes to operate today. She should be fine.' Lin pauses. 'Interestingly, she's at Birmingham City Hospital, which is where Rashid is, too.'

'Is Rashid OK?'

'He was severely hypothermic when he arrived at hospital, and he'll have to be monitored closely over the next forty-eight hours. But when I visited him, he was in good spirits.'

'Thank God.' Sighing, I close my eyes and let my head drop. My misdeeds weren't for nothing.

Lin opens the file. Knots tighten in my stomach when I see my photo clipped to the inside cover. 'Let's get to the reason I called you in.'

She laces her hands together on the desk, her eyebrows gathering. 'I have to say, Alex, I'm gobsmacked at what went on last night. You've been an ideal employee throughout your time here. You were ready to take the next step, or so I thought.'

My words come out in a rush. 'I promise, everything I did last night, was with the best of intentions. I couldn't let Rashid freeze to death.'

'I understand that,' Lin says. 'I wouldn't be human if I didn't. But good intentions don't count when you break the rules.' She picks up a stapled booklet - the training guide for the NMPH. I know its contents inside-out and could probably read them by rote if my mouth weren't so dry.

'The rules wouldn't have helped Rashid.'

Lin presses her lips together. 'If you'd rung my mobile, I could have helped you.'

I refrain from telling her that no, she couldn't have helped because she didn't have a finding machine. I search Lin's expression for an iota of sympathy, but her expression is as unreadable as the welcome message in Urdu on the wall behind her.

Lin flicks through my progress reports, shaking her head. 'I was prepared to give you a verbal warning for continuing your call with Rashid without a supervisor present. That was before I discovered you breached our number one rule. Confidentiality.'

Scrunching my hands on my lap, I brace myself.

'When you joined us, you signed a data protection form that protects missing people and their families. Their details are not to be shared with any outside person or organisation without my approval.'

'I had no choice but to call the police.'

'I'm not talking about the police. You emailed Rashid's photograph to your boyfriend, Antony. Then you rang him, and he rang back. I presume that was to discuss Rashid's disappearance.'

'I'm sorry. I panicked.'

'That's a breach of protocol I can't overlook.'

If only I'd thought to delete the email I sent to Antony. But there's nothing I could have done about the phone records. The only silver lining in the whole mess is the phone calls aren't recorded.

Lin scribbles something on an official looking sheet of paper. Her pen is blue but the lid is black. I can't stop staring at it.

'How did you find Rashid?' she asks.

Even though I've been expecting the question, it still hits me like a blow to the gut. I stay silent.

Lin fixes me with a penetrating stare. 'I spoke to the detective who interviewed Rashid. The police were unable to track his mobile phone. Rashid had no idea where he was, and neither did you.

Yet, you managed to pin him down to a tiny area within acres of wilderness.'

My mind spins as I hold my silence. There isn't an excuse I can come up with that will make a difference.

'Alex,' Lin says gently. 'You may as well tell me.'

'Tigs called in, after Rashid's phone went dead,' I say, ignoring the burning sensation in my cheeks. I squeeze my hands in my lap and plough on. 'He felt guilty for nicking Rashid's trainers and leaving him. He told me where Rashid was.'

Lin retrieves a sheet of paper and runs her finger down it. 'Then, why isn't Tigs' number on the phone log?' Her steely gaze makes me flinch. 'The only people on record are you, Antony, Rashid and the police.'

I'm screwed. The window's only three feet away, and I briefly wonder if I can hurl myself out of it before Lin stops me.

Maybe she won't try and stop me.

'I understand a lot happened last night. But you broke too many rules.' Lin closes the file. 'I'm sorry, Alex. I have to let you go.'

'What? No! Please don't fire me,' I entreat her. 'I love my job. Helping people. Making a difference.'

'My hands are tied, I'm afraid.' Lin replaces the wrong cap on the pen. 'However, I've made a recommendation to the Board of Directors not to take things further.'

'Take things further?' My nostrils flare as my breath shoots in and out. 'If it wasn't for me, Rashid would be dead!'

'It's not what you did, Alexandra. It's the way you did it.' Lin stands up and pushes an envelope into my hand. 'This is your final payslip. Please leave your swipe-card at Reception.'

Shooting to my feet, I snatch the envelope from her hand, fighting the temptation to tear it to pieces and throw it in her face.

Through gritted teeth, I say, 'I was only trying to help.'

As I turn and push through the door, I barely register Lin's words that follow me out.

'I'm sorry. Best of luck.'

5

—•—

Trevor puts his hand out to stop me, but I push past him, rush down the stairs to the foyer and throw my swipe-card onto the reception desk.

'I won't be needing this anymore,' I tell the receptionist.

She looks up with a start, then reads my name under the photograph.

'Alex Martin?' She purses her hot-pink lips. 'I have something for you.'

While she rummages through her out-tray, my gaze fixes on the enormous Christmas tree and the perfectly-wrapped presents piled underneath. This is supposed to be the most wonderful time of the year, but by this time tomorrow Lin will have chucked my Secret Santa in the bin and scrubbed me from the Christmas party list. It will be like I never worked here.

'Here you go.' The receptionist hands me a plain envelope with my name printed on the front. 'A gentleman dropped it off this morning. He was very smart in a pin-stripe suit. Silver hair.'

'Did he have a name?'

'He said he was the Director of Operations.'

I swallow hard. He must be from the NMPH, which means it's probably more bad news.

'Thank you.' I fold the envelope and stuff it inside my pocket as I leave the building. Outside in the cold, I glance back at my former workplace. My distorted reflection in the mirrored glass resembles

28

a tortured wraith. I've lost everything - being part of a team and making a difference.

I allow myself one massive huff of despair. Then I stand straight, pull my shoulders back and walk away.

In an ideal world, I'd call Antony. When we lived in Ware, he was always there to lend me a shoulder to cry on. But things have changed. Even if I catch Antony at his desk, he won't have time to talk.

'Oy! Watch it!' A cyclist swerves to avoid colliding with me on the ramp leading down to the canal.

I walk along the verge, retracing my steps home. I'm about to pass under the graffiti bridge when my Nokia rings.

The caller's name on the display is: MUM_AGH!

There's only so much angst you can put into eight characters.

I hum and haw over answering, thumb poised over the green button. The way I see it, I'm at rock-bottom. Even she can't make things worse.

'Hello Mum.' I force a bright greeting.

'Alexandra!'

A nearby swan flaps its wings in alarm. Mum's Irish accent is all the more memorable for its incredible volume. 'I'm only calling you from my new mobile phone!'

I hold the receiver away from my ear. Mum's outdone herself. She's rung me to tell me she's ringing me.

Last year, I found out that Mum hid my aunt Lilian's existence from me, thinking she was doing the right thing. At one point I hated her, because her actions stopped Dad from finding his sister. It's been nearly eighteen months since our major bust-up. Since then, we've come to an uneasy truce.

'Mum, is there a reason you're calling?' Only millionaires call the UK from Ireland on a mobile. 'This call must be costing you a pound a minute.'

'What's that in punts?'

'I don't know.'

'What about euros? Everyone keeps going on about them, but I've yet to see one.'

'I don't know!'

'Well, I'm calling to say I sent you an email.'

Stifling a groan, I continue under the bridge, hoping I'll lose the connection. 'You don't need to call me to tell me that.'

'Emails can be tricky. Your Uncle Fintan says the attachment might be too large.'

'What attachment, Mum? Is it another church flyer?'

'Well, aren't you the telepathic one! It *is* a flyer, about our pilgrimage on New Year's Eve. We're forming a torch-lit procession up Benbulbin, following in the footsteps of Saint Columba. We're praying for the new Millennium to arrive peacefully.'

Benbulbin is County Sligo's version of Table Mountain. It's where the poet Yeats, is buried.

'Moira thinks the mountain will be a great place to see if the planes crash coming into Knock.'

'Mum, that's a terrible thing to say!'

'It's all over the news.' Mum's adamant. 'The bug-thing. You know, the whatsit...the WHYTOUCAN.'

'Y2K. It's been fixed, Mum. Nothing's going to crash.'

'Don't be so sure about that. We have to pray so we don't see a load of flames burning on the horizon. You can pray along, Alexandra. Everything you need is in the flyer.' She pauses. 'We're stopping at the Fairy Door to say a special prayer.'

Did I hear Mum right? Did she say she's going to pray with the fairies?

'Is that in the flyer, Mum? Did Father Egan put that in?'

'It's tradition. Everyone says a little prayer at the Fairy Door. Besides, I'm not going to condemn anyone for believing in the old ways.' Just as I'm thinking Mum's becoming more open-minded, she adds, 'We have to forgive the pagans, because they don't know any better. Besides, Moira says there's no harm in covering all the bases.'

'Are you sure you should be trusting everything Moira says?' I ask.

'If it helps the poor passengers—'

'Mum, I have to go.' I emerge from the bridge into daylight. 'I'm under a tunnel and I'm about to lose the signal. Bye!'

'*Slán go fóill*!' Mum gets the message. 'Let me know if you received the email!'

I end the call, wondering what me and Antony will be doing at midnight on 31st December.

One thing's for sure. Whatever it is, it won't involve my mother, fairy doors, or Moira.

· · · • · • • · • · ·

Back home, I change out of my smart outfit and into thermals, layering up with jeans, jumper, and my toastiest socks. Outside the bedroom window, the light is fading and it's starting to drizzle. I close the curtains and turn on the bedside lamp.

The bed is rumpled and unmade from morning. I resist the urge to climb in and pull the duvet over my head. There's no escaping my maudlin thoughts. If I could throw paint over a blank canvas or daub shapes in black with my thickest brush, that might help. But the artists' studio I share with local creatives is too cold to work in. I've had to stop painting for the sake of my fingers.

Now I'm unemployed, a cheque from the sale of my paintings is much needed, as there's zero chance of finding a job this close to Christmas. Antony earns good money and is happy to cover the bills, but I want to pay my share.

As I dig my final payslip out of my pocket, the envelope the receptionist gave me falls out. I hesitate a moment before tearing the envelope open.

Inside, is a white business card. The first line is hand-written. My scalp tightens as I read it:

Who is this Prudente-Poulton? How does he know about my machine? What does he want?

Nausea rises inside me. Does he know I used the machine to find Rashid?

I rush into the home office, open the bottom drawer of my desk and check everything's as I left it. To my relief, the finding machine is safely tucked up inside its shoebox and switched off.

Prudente-Poulton can't have seen my machine firsthand. It hasn't left the house since we moved here. Maybe he tracked it from a signal when Antony switched it on last night. Or, he hacked into my call with Antony and overheard our conversation. I'm pretty sure that's illegal.

If he calls or turns up at the door, I'll deny all knowledge, whoever he is.

I stare at the card for ages. Eventually, I tell myself to worry about it once I have to, and force this Prudente-Poulton character from my mind.

I tuck the card inside the cardboard box, close my desk drawer and check my emails. I ignore the one from Mum with its gigantic attachment. Far more interesting is the message from Whitewalls Gallery.

Hi Alex, one of our regular buyers has expressed an interest in purchasing all three of your Birmingham Past & Present canvases.

I stretch back in my chair with a smile. At last, the break I needed! The money for the paintings will tide me over into the New Year. I continue reading.

The buyer would like you to make the following changes to make the artworks better fit his taste: Paint out the American style spray-can graffiti on the bridge in Painting 1, the black smoke coming from the industrial tower in Painting 2, and the cigarette pack-

ets, soda cans and other litter in Painting 3. It would be acceptable to replace the litter with weeds, ensuring they are British weeds.

I hope you agree, these simple changes will make our client happy and that's what Whitewalls Gallery [Your Local Gallery] strives for.

Please note, the cost of changes to the painting and transport of canvases to and from Whitewalls Gallery is the responsibility of the artist. Regards, Mina Carduccio.

My heart sinks.

Compromising my values by making the changes is out of the question, no matter how much I need the money. I rattle off an email explaining my position, add a bit about artistic integrity, then look for alcohol.

I pour myself a glass of Rioja and wander through the silent flat, turning a blind eye to the mess that's built up over the last few months. Antony's always been the tidy one. Since his work took over, the flat has deteriorated. Even the dragon tree beside the TV looks forlorn, with brown-tipped leaves and dry soil. Hard scrubbing and a bucketload of elbow grease is required to restore the flat to pristine condition. The cleaning stuff is under the sink, but my heart's not in it.

I crash out on the sofa in front of the TV and flick through channels until I hit BBC local news.

My gaze fixes on the red banner at the bottom of the screen: *BREAKING NEWS: TEENAGER RESCUED FROM SUTTON PARK.*

Grabbing the remote, I turn the volume up.

A reporter stands amidst an overgrown wilderness, bundled up in a heavy camel coat. The concrete culvert is behind him, its base covered in brambles.

'Last night, police carried out an extensive search here in Sutton Park to rescue a lost teenager, who cannot be named for legal reasons. Two other youths, who also cannot be named, assaulted the victim and ran off with his coat and trainers. The teenager was found here, amongst dense groundcover.'

The camera pans around, showing the ground dropping away to the stream. The inside of the culvert is waterlogged and dark. I count my lucky stars I managed to find Rashid. I could so easily have walked past him.

'The police have praised the actions of The National Missing Persons Helpline, who were able to pinpoint the teenager's location. The Met Office records show that the temperature in the park dropped to minus three last night. A paramedic I spoke to told me the teenager was severely hypothermic at the scene. He is expected to make a full recovery.'

I switch the TV off and throw the remote onto the table.

The police have praised the actions of the NMPH.

I pour myself more wine and start pacing the room, then reach for my mobile, ready to call Lin and give her a piece of my mind.

What's the point? Ringing her isn't going to make things better. The day's been tough enough. I rub my chest, where a ball of angst is growing, and tell myself to calm down.

I didn't do it to get a medal. I only wanted to help Rashid. But this just isn't fair.

After another glass of wine, my anger is under control, although I'm impatient for Antony to come home. Things always seem better once I've talked to him.

My mobile phone buzzes on the coffee table.

HENRY_LO

A jolt goes through me. An image of a tall, blond Viking with ice-blue eyes pops into my mind.

I haven't heard from Detective Constable Henry Longhurst since last summer, after I found Lilian Martin's remains. He oversaw her exhumation, and my aunt was laid to rest alongside Dad in the Martin family plot.

Henry suspected I had a unique way of finding people after I found her, but I never told him about the finding machine. It was his suggestion I join the NMPH last summer. We've not spoken since then.

I set down my glass and sit up, pressing the *Accept Call* button on my phone.

'Hello. Hi!' I say.

'Alex, it's Henry Longhurst.' His voice is familiar and warm. Why am I feeling flustered? My mind doesn't seem to be working.

'Is this a good time?' Henry asks.

'Umm...sure.' I stare at a wine ring on the table.

'How are you finding Birmingham? It must be exciting compared to Ware.'

'It's bigger.' I pause, struggling to find something to say. 'It has more canals than Venice.'

'Really?' If Henry's feigning interest, he's doing a really good job. 'You're probably wondering why I called. Thing is, I could do with your help.'

6

— · —

Antony arrives home late, close to nine. I squeeze up to him in the narrow hallway before he has a chance to hang up his coat, and circle my arms round his waist.

He pulls me in for a kiss. For a brief moment, my worries disappear.

Antony is first to break away. He removes his rectangular glasses to rub the bridge of his nose. Weariness hangs in tiny creases around his eyes. I don't know how he does it - out at dawn, back late, too tired to enjoy life's simple pleasures. It's been months since we went for an evening walk, skimmed stones by the river or watched TV without him falling asleep. I can't remember the last time we had a proper cuddle in bed.

'Did you make your meeting?' I ask.

'I missed half of it,' Antony says, hanging up his coat. 'Yan tore me a new one afterwards. He threatened to pull me off the Razorr pitch in front of my team. I was two seconds from knocking his lights out.'

'What stopped you?'

'Well, let me think.' Antony tucks his chin into his forefinger and thumb. His brow rises. 'I thought it best not to lose my job, my career, everything I've worked for, and serve time for GBH on top.' He shrugs off his suit jacket and slings it over his arm. 'You might not think much of that stuff, but it matters to me.'

'It matters to me, too.'

'Sure.' Antony's usual easy manner is nowhere to be seen. He straightens with a sudden intake of breath. 'I need food. My stomach thinks my throat's been cut.'

'You skipped lunch, again?'

Antony shrugs. 'Lunch is for wimps.'

'That's your boss talking. You're going to have a breakdown if this carries on.'

I lead the way into the lounge to the low coffee table set for dinner. Two beeswax candles burn with friendly, yellow flames, creating a cozy atmosphere.

Antony follows me, sniffing the air. He loosens his tie.

'Don't you sometimes wish we'd stayed in Ware?' I ask.

'Ware was nowhere,' he says, somewhat uncharitably, considering that's where we fell in love. 'I need to be here.'

'One office is the same as another,' I say dryly. 'You could work anywhere.'

'All right, Alex. Get off my back.' Antony undoes the top button of his shirt and drops onto the sofa without his customary grace.

Food should soften his mood. I retreat to the kitchen, where the chicken pies and chips are only a tiny bit burnt. I serve them with a side-salad, then pour Antony a large glass of wine and bring it to the coffee table.

'Thanks.' Antony rolls his shirt-sleeves above his elbows. He blows on a molten spoonful of pie and makes appreciative sounds while he eats. 'I needed this. I'm sorry I'm not the best company at the moment.'

'It's all right,' I say, holding my wine glass up. We chink glasses and he smiles.

'I haven't asked about your day,' he says, as he clears his plate. 'How did it go with work?'

'Not great.' I sigh. 'Lin fired me.'

'What?' Antony's eyebrows shoot up. 'But you saved a kid's life!'

'Doesn't matter. Lin said I broke too many rules.' I flash a bitter smile. 'And I've lost the buyer for my paintings.'

'Babe.' Antony swallows hard, puts his arm around me. 'What a day.'

'We'll be all right, won't we?' I ask.

'Course we will,' he says, looking down.

One thing's for sure – now's not the time to tell him about Prudente-Poulton's card.

'The search for Rashid was on the news,' I say. 'The reporter said the NMPH helped with the search. As if Lin personally found him!'

Antony sinks against the cushions, staring at the ceiling. 'Now do you get it?'

'Get what?'

'Using your dad's gizmo is bad news.' Antony points with his fork. 'You should put it back in its box or give it to MI5. Better still, scrap it.'

'You can't mean that. My dad made it!'

I briefly consider giving up on this conversation. But if I don't mention the last thing now - Henry's phone call - I'll have to wait until tomorrow, and there's no guarantee Antony's mood will be better then.

'Hey, I was meaning to tell you,' I say. 'I've been offered the chance to use the finding machine in an official capacity.'

Antony's gaze snaps to me. 'You're joking? By who?'

'Henry Longhurst called me. Remember him?'

Antony gives a nod. 'That big blond copper from Hertford?'

'He's a detective.'

'Is he.'

Antony's flat tone makes me wince, but I plough on. 'He's invited me to Hertford for a few days.'

'Why? I don't remember you training as a detective.'

'Henry knows I have a special way of finding people. He put two and two together last year when I found Jason Bevin and Aunt Lilian. He's used a psychic before, so he's open to unusual methods of solving cases. That's what he wants my help with. Old cases.'

'Why is he asking now?' Antony cocks a brow. 'Is it because he knows you found Rashid last night?'

'He didn't say.' I flush, my cheeks heating up. 'He said he'd explain everything once I get down there.'

Henry's exact words were, *One of my cold cases doesn't look so cold anymore*. I decide not to mention it.

Antony slings an arm across the back of the sofa. 'Henry rings up after all this time? You know what that says to me? He's been thinking about you. Men and women can't be friends. Not if they're straight, anyway.'

'Rubbish! I've only met Henry twice and it was strictly business. Same as the women you work with.'

'That's different,' Antony says. 'I don't pick who I work with, whereas Henry has picked you. Where are you staying? Not at his place, I hope?'

'I don't know, yet.' I snuggle closer. 'I trust you. Can't you do the same for me?'

'I guess.' Antony lets out a breath. 'What kind of cases will you be working on?'

'They're old files, that's all I know. I doubt we're going to find anything. I'll be in an office for most of it. And, I'm getting paid.'

Antony reaches for his glass. 'How's Henry going to square that with Payroll? Is there an official code for finding machine operators?'

'When Henry used the psychic, he put him down as a CHIS. A Covert Human Intelligence Source. That's what I'm going to be, too.'

Antony splutters, spraying wine on the table. He plonks the glass down, throws back his head and laughs, a hearty sound that soon has me laughing along.

'What's so funny?' I poke his ribs.

'A CHIS is another name for a nark!' Antony wipes his eyes with the back of his hand. 'A snout, a snitch. A rat. Will Henry put that on your name tag?'

My cheeks burn and I look away. Henry made it sound respectable.

'I'm joking. Lighten up,' Antony puts an arm round me, more relaxed than I've seen him all evening.

I smile at him. 'You're much nicer when you're like this. Compared to Mr Grumpy.'

'Who are you calling Mr Grumpy?' Antony says with mock outrage. He pins me down on the sofa. 'You're going to pay for that.'

I let out a squeal as we playfully tussle. I wrestle Antony's superior strength and lose. He holds my arms above my head with one hand, then tickles my sides and kisses me, holding me just where he wants me.

'Stop, stop!' I can't breathe from laughing.

Antony pins my wrists. 'Admit my superiority. Now, give me a CHIS.'

I laugh and we kiss. Before the kissing turns into something else, I break away and ask, 'So, do I have your blessing to go to Hertford?'

Antony lets out a sigh and draws back.

'I'd rather you didn't. I think that machine is trouble. But it's your decision. Go if you want.'

I loop my arm over his shoulder and try to pull him back down. 'Can't we talk this through? We're a team, remember? This could be a great chance for me.'

'Or not.' Antony gently breaks my grip, sits up and runs his hand over his hair. 'I'm sorry. My mind's all over the place.'

He stifles a yawn, leans over to place a perfunctory kiss on my forehead. 'I have to finish up a PowerPoint presentation for a meeting first thing. If I don't do it now, I'll forget.'

He swings himself from the sofa, leaving a cold space, and heads for the hall. 'Let's talk tomorrow. Deal?'

I nod, not trusting myself to say more.

My lips still tingle. Why, oh why, did I ruin the moment by asking about Henry?

Lying on the sofa feeling sorry for myself doesn't do me any good, so I force myself to my feet and switch to housewife mode, clearing away the dishes and doing the washing-up. I run over our conversation at the sink with my arms deep in soapy water, wishing I hadn't mentioned Henry and ruined the mood.

I accept it's partly my fault, but something's up with Antony. He always used to make time for me no matter what.

When I look for Antony in the home office, his Mac is on but he's not there.

I cross the hall into the bedroom. Antony's fast asleep on the bed. Red wine dots his shirt. Gently, I remove his glasses and place them on the bedside table. Something tugs within me, seeing him at low ebb. He's always had a supreme work ethic, but no matter how much he does, it's never enough.

After removing his shoes and socks, I gently rouse him so I can get his trousers and shirt off.

Once he's snug under the covers, I set the alarm clock for six. The promise of a night of passion has evaporated. Instead, I plant a chaste kiss on his forehead like a mum putting her kid to sleep, and turn off the light.

I'm desperate for Antony to change his mind about Henry's offer.

I want his blessing. But as it's not forthcoming, I'll have no choice but to go to Hertford without it.

7

—·—

The train journey from Birmingham to Hertford should be three hours long, but instead takes five. The train driver announces a storm front is sweeping in from the North Atlantic, bringing heavy rain and flash flooding.

Passengers are crammed into the aisle. I count myself lucky to get a window seat, although I can't say I'm comfortable with my heavy rucksack on my lap. I made the mistake of packing the finding machine at the very bottom. Cold air seeps through the canvas, chilling my legs until they go numb.

Outside the scratched and rain-streaked window lies a gloomy landscape of bleak fields, dark forests and grey towns.

I left Antony a note about freezer meals on the coffee table and put lots of kisses at the end. The frosty atmosphere between us hasn't thawed since I mentioned Henry. But what does Antony expect me to do? Mope around an empty flat while he works all the hours God sends? I'll be gone four days, max. Before he knows it, I'll be back.

The rain stops as we approach Hertford East, and a ray of late afternoon sun breaks through the clouds. Passengers stare out of the windows as though witnessing a miracle.

The doors open with warning beeps. Heaving my rucksack over my shoulder, I rub my numb knees and join the flow of people leaving the train. Outside the station, the sun's glare hits my eyes. I stop in my tracks and raise a hand to shield my brow.

A shadow falls across me. Blinking, details emerge of an imposing man with arctic blue eyes and blond hair, the Viking I remember. He wears a dark suit with navy tie. Nothing to show he's working for the police.

'Alex?' Henry Longhurst's gaze locks with mine. The corners of his eyes crinkle as he smiles.

'DC Longhurst,' I blurt, putting out my hand.

'Henry, please.' He clasps my small hand in his large one and smiles warmly. 'It's good to see you.'

For some reason, I struggle to break eye contact. I catch the scent of his body spray, clean and crisp, so different to Antony. I must be befuddled after the journey. My previous interactions with Henry were purely professional, and that's how I want to keep things.

I pull my hand away. 'I didn't think anyone would be here to meet me, what with the delays.'

'Believe it or not, we're quite good at keeping track of these things.' Henry takes a quick look around. 'Not brought your team, then?'

My mouth goes dry before I notice a glint in his eye and the corner of his mouth tweaking up.

'Oh, no! They're here.' I swiftly recover. 'They're undercover.'

Henry laughs. 'You know I've got a pool going.'

I'm amazed my 'team' is still a source of fascination to Hertfordshire Police. Last year, Henry informed me his department were split into those who thought I was using surveillance experts and those who thought I was a witch.

Henry has his suspicions about my methods. On the phone, he agreed not to press me for the truth. How well that works in practice is another matter.

'Here, give me your stuff.' Henry takes my rucksack as though it weighs nothing and swings it over his shoulder.

'Please be careful,' I warn. 'It's just...'

'I get it.' Henry turns to me, his brow rising. 'All your secrets are in here.'

My cheeks flush at his lucky guess.

I should have spent more time considering how I'm going to use the machine around Henry instead of moping over Antony. I've only been off the train five minutes and I'm already struggling. I never planned to bring Henry inside the circle of trust, but it's clearly something I have to factor in if we're to work together.

'I wouldn't be much of a detective if I didn't want to know how you do it.' Henry's brow furrows. He touches the base of the rucksack. 'What's in here, Alex? A bag of ice? Frozen meals? We will feed you.'

'You promised not to ask too many questions.'

'And I'm a man of my word.' Henry gives me a quick, assessing look. 'You're full of secrets, Alex Martin. I hope I'm right about you.'

His expectations weigh heavily on me.

We wait for a bus to pass before crossing the car park. To my relief, Henry changes the subject. 'How's your art going? Still painting, I hope?'

'Yes, absolutely.'

'It's a shame you live so far away. Your show in St. Albans last year was incredible.'

'Thank you.'

Henry approaches a row of cars and presses a key fob. The hazard lights flash on a dark blue Vauxhall Astra. The car has a large dent above the rear wheel arch, and is missing a hubcap.

'This is us,' he says

Henry puts my rucksack in the boot before opening the passenger door. Pay-and-display tickets, sweet wrappers, drinks cans, and Asda plastic bags litter the footwell. The only sign it's a police vehicle is the radio slotted into a console above the gearstick. 'Sorry about the mess. It's a pool car. Some of the team are pigs and I didn't have time to clean it.'

'Don't worry about it,' I say, sinking into a comfortable, spongy seat. I kick the cans away to make space for my feet and secure my seatbelt.

Henry pulls out of the car park onto roads lined with shimmering puddles. He's a careful driver, chauffeuring me past familiar sights: old pubs Antony and I used to frequent, shops and sunlit tree-lined parks where we walked hand-in-hand. I'd give anything to have those times back again, to be a carefree couple.

I wrench myself from my maudlin thoughts and remind myself I'm not here to take a trip down memory lane.

'So, how come you're working old cases?' I ask. 'Is it a step-up for your career?'

'The complete opposite,' Henry says with a tight smile. 'I upset my boss and he thought he'd teach me a lesson.'

Raising a brow, I ask, 'What did you do?'

'Let's just say I made a suggestion the DI didn't like about an operation that didn't go great. He took it personally.' He taps the steering wheel. 'Now I'm out of sight in the cold case room, getting a lesson in manners. The DI wants me to tackle the backlog of 'misper' cases and has given me until the end of the year to prove myself. We have one of the worst clear-up rates in the south of England, and it's making us look bad. I need your help, Alex. I don't want to grow old and grey, surrounded by cardboard boxes.'

With a sly grin, I say, 'If you start solving cases, your boss might decide to keep you locked away forever.'

Henry gives me an incredulous look. 'Do you want me to take you back to the station?'

'No!' I force a chuckle, unable to think of anything worse. 'I hope I can help.'

'So do I.' He stops at the next junction, scans the oncoming traffic. 'I always had a hunch about you, Alex, and I'm rarely wrong when it comes to my instincts. When a little bird told me you'd been up to your old tricks, I knew I had to call you in.'

'What do you mean, old tricks?'

'Finding people. That teenager in Birmingham.'

I press myself back in my seat, wondering how much he knows. 'How did you find out about that?'

'Rashid gave your name to the investigating officer at the hospital, and told him a very interesting story.' Henry's knowing look freezes me. 'The boy kept saying he knew you were coming, even though he was utterly lost, with a dead phone, in the middle of nowhere. He told you he was sheltering under a bridge, but that wasn't accurate. Yet, you still found him. The officer checked your files and saw we worked together on Lilian Martin's case. He thought he'd give me a ring.'

'What did you tell him?' I ask, my throat going dry.

'I said you'd helped us in the past, and gave you a good reference. That should be the end of it.'

'Thanks.' I stare at the litter round my feet, hoping he's right. 'Did you know I lost my job over Rashid?'

'I didn't.' Henry shoots me a look. 'I'm sorry to hear that. The problem with working alone is that you draw attention to yourself. You won't have that problem with me. I've put you down as a psychic advisor. We've used them before. I've said you need peace and quiet to work which should stop too many questions.'

'Thank you.' I release a tense breath, leaning back in my seat.

Henry turns left at the next roundabout. The skies darken and spits of rain hit the windscreen as he takes the first exit, past a silver marker on the grass verge that bears the words: *Hertfordshire Constabulary* and *Hertford Police Station*. A blue and white badge shows a stag strutting across three wavy lines, signifying water.

Hertfordshire Police HQ is a 1960s block of a building with ugly blue panels. It reminds me of my secondary school. The building sits amidst leafless trees. We drive past a side-road on the left which leads to a gated compound with police cars and vans.

'That's the business end, where the criminals go,' Henry informs me. 'We're this end.'

The road continues to a parking area at the front of the building. As Henry parks up, the light shower intensifies into heavy rain that beats down on the roof and windows.

'We'll have to make a run for it,' Henry says, hand on the door-latch. 'Leave your stuff in the car. I'm just going to check you in. Ready?'

I pull the hood up on my duvet jacket and jump out of the car. Luckily, my coat's rainproof, but Henry didn't bring one. By the time he's locked the car, his hair is plastered to his head and water's dripping from the end of his nose.

We dash through puddles across the carpark and under the shelter of a flat-roofed overhang running across the front of the building. Once we're out of the rain, Henry pauses with a rueful grin and brushes soaking strands of hair back from his eyes.

Although my hair is dry, my rain-spattered jeans are clinging to my legs and my boots are soaked.

Over Henry's shoulder, I see a bald bruiser suddenly appear around the corner of the building. The top of his wet head glistens. He's dressed in black, with *SECURITY* emblazoned across one sleeve. One hand grips a leash, pulled tight by a huge, wet Alsatian.

The dog strains towards us, its large ears swivelling in our direction.

I freeze, but Henry raises his hand in greeting. 'It's OK. That's just Bruno, doing the rounds.'

Reluctantly, I follow Henry across the dog's path to reach the main doors.

'Bye, Bruno.' I wave at the dog, which continues to track our movements.

'I'm Bruno,' deadpans the man. 'The dog is Kaiser.'

Shamefaced, I slink after Henry. 'What do you need security for?' I ask in a low voice. 'This is a police station.'

'We're not immune from crime.' Henry strides towards the glass doors, which open automatically at our approach. A welcome blast of warm air hits me as I walk through. 'We've having a problem with a vandal who likes to jump the fence and spray our cars.'

I decide not to mention my fascination with graffiti. 'Don't you have surveillance cameras?'

'This guy wears a hoodie, which makes it impossible to see his face.'

I glance back to the Astra.

'Don't worry about your bag,' Henry says, as though reading my mind. 'PC Rain will keep the hoodies away better than Bruno and Kaiser.'

A woman in her forties with sepia skin looks up from the reception desk. Her orange blouse contrasts vividly with the drab walls and grey carpet tiles.

'You two are running late.' Her voice is rich with a distinctive African accent.

'Yolanda, this is Alex Martin.' Henry shrugs off his soaking jacket and blots his forehead on his sleeve. 'Yolanda's in charge of everything front of house.'

'Including no-good hoodies?' I ask, approaching the desk.

Yolanda chuckles and shakes her head. 'My colleagues around the corner deal with them.' She puts down her crochet hook attached to a fat brown woollen object. The shape looks familiar, but I can't work out what it is.

'I'm in charge of civilians and paperwork,' Yolanda says, thumping down a folder. 'Lots and lots of paperwork.'

I take a closer look at her crocheting. 'Is that...a turkey?'

'It is!' Yolanda's eyes gleam. 'Christmas decorations. I make them as presents.'

'I have four,' Henry says. 'Make sure to get on Yolanda's good side and you never know.' He leans on the desk. 'Can you sort out the forms for Alex?'

'It would be my pleasure.' Yolanda opens a file with my name on the front, and hands me a pen. 'Read each sheet and sign at the bottom. There's your CRB form. No convictions or cautions. Nice and clean, the way we like it.'

Yolanda flashes a smile. She looks so pleased, I half-expect her to give me a sticker.

I sign multiple forms, then show her my driving licence and proof of address. Once Yolanda's photocopied everything, signed above my signature and stamped each page, she hands me a lanyard. To my relief, it says VISITOR and not CHIS. Antony was right about that.

'Good to go?' Henry asks. He gestures me through a set of swing-doors into a wide corridor. 'Your lanyard won't allow you access into the cold-case room, so don't leave without telling anyone or you'll find yourself locked out.'

Police officers and civilian staff walk past, nodding to Henry. Some give me curious looks.

Steel labels mark each door. *Drugs Squad, Traffic Dept, MR4, CD6.*

Millennium Team. A yellow poster stuck to the door shows a spiky creature that resembles a microchip. *Millennium Bug, Act now!*

'You have a department for Y2K?' I pause outside the door. 'I didn't realise it was a problem.'

Henry nods. 'It's a massive operation involving thousands of officers across the UK. They'll be posted to airports, hospitals, major transport hubs. If you want to know more, speak to our tech-geek, Simon.'

He continues to the end of the corridor and swipes a card against a reader by the door. The red light turns to green. Henry pushes through and holds the door open for me.

'Welcome to the cold case room. Code name, *Operation Thaw*.'

8

— · —

The cold case room is bright and airy, not what I expected. A white board hangs on the back wall, flanked by filing cabinets, boxes and office equipment. In the middle of the room, three tables pushed together create a large workstation containing four computer terminals. A large window, streaked with rain, overlooks a drab landscape of sodden grass dotted with skeletal trees.

A young police officer with a long face and heavy-lidded eyes sits at the central computer. She removes a paperclip from a sheaf of papers and runs her finger down the first page. A stack of orange cardboard folders sits beside her monitor.

'When you mentioned old files, I thought we'd be in the basement,' I say to Henry.

'Lucky for us, we don't have one.' Henry raises a brow. 'Alex, this is Tori, head of Information Retrieval.'

'Nice to meet you, Alex.' Tori stifles a yawn. 'Sorry, it's been a long day.'

Henry heads to the filing cabinets and starts searching through one of the drawers.

I approach Tori, unsure if she wants me looking over her shoulder. 'Can I ask what you're doing, or is it top secret?'

'No, it's fine.' Tori's fingers rattle over the keyboard as she tabs through green boxes on the screen, inputting data. 'We're computerising the old files. My job is to enter all the key information such as names, dates, vehicle registrations and timelines. Investigating officers can search the files using these fields to pull up relevant cases.' She pauses. 'Are you helping me wi—'

'Alex is working with me,' Henry interrupts, placing a folder on the table. 'Remember the little chat we had earlier?'

'Sorry, boss.' Tori gives me a curious look before returning to work.

Henry beckons me to a door in the far corner of the room. I follow him into a box room containing a square desk, computer, printer, scanner and a landline.

A skinny fellow sits at the desk by a computer, fingers rattling over a keyboard. CD-ROMs and cables cover the desk. The grinding sound of the hard-drive is loud in the tiny space.

A flash of white grabs my eye. Lightning flashes outside the slot-window on the far wall. The sky releases an ominous rumble.

'Simon, this is Alex.' Henry speaks over the sound. 'We nabbed Simon from Tech Support to join Tori. He's upgrading the system to ensure we're Y2K compliant.'

Simon raises a stiff hand and glances my way, his eyes magnified behind bottle-glasses. With his slight build and ginger bowl-cut he looks every inch a computer geek. 'The update's still verifying.'

'You said it would be done by five,' Henry says, one hand in his pocket.

'That was before I ran diagnostics. This PC is a relic, but we should be ready in' —he checks his digital watch— 'twenty-two minutes.'

Henry turns to me. 'Can you work in here? Will it do?'

The door has a vertical window with a hook above it, and a thumb turn latch next to the handle. If I lock myself in and hang my coat, no one will be able to see in or come in unexpectedly.

'It's perfect.'

Simon clears his throat. 'Boss, I had a call from the Millennium Team. The servers are going down at five for diagnostics and they need my eyes on it.'

'This is the third time this week,' Henry's voice rises.

'I can't ignore this one, boss. The ACC paid the Team a surprise visit today, and he's not happy.'

'The ACC?' I ask.

'Assistant Chief Constable,' Henry fills me in. 'The big cheese. What does he want?'

'More testing.' Simon glances at the progress bar on the screen. 'The Team's panicking about the alarms, heating units, air-conditioning, even the elevators. I mean, who wants to be stuck between floors in the dark? If this stuff goes down on the 31st we are screwed.'

'Elevators?' I comment. 'I thought Y2K was to do with computers.'

Simon lets out a braying laugh.

Henry gives me a pleading look. 'Don't get him started.'

'The Millennium Bug affects dates,' Simon explains, pushing the bridge of his glasses onto his nose. 'It has the potential to mess up everything from your bank account to anti-aircraft missile systems. If dates are stored wrong, things go bad quickly. The glitches started in 1988, but no one took them seriously.'

'Yes, thank you, Simon,' Henry warns.

Simon ploughs on. 'Without intervention, computers could read the year 2000 as 1900. Airports, hospitals, the stock exchange, all these places could go into complete meltdown. And those are just a few examples.'

Tori pops her head round the door. 'Take no notice, Alex. The world was supposed to end in 1986. We're still here.'

Simon takes a pen and rolls it between his fingers. 'Y2K is a whole new ballgame. The NHS is preparing for power surges and the breakdown of primary care systems, ambulances, the works. They can't guarantee patients won't die because of the Millennium Bug.'

My mind's awhirl with disastrous scenarios involving misbehaving elevators, missile attacks and ambulances racing to the wrong addresses.

Simon continues, 'I lost sleep over the ninth of September, and that was *nothing* like this.'

'The ninth of September?' I repeat blankly.

'Don't ask,' Tori says, adding a dramatic sigh. 'Something about 9/9/99. Nothing happened then, either.'

'Okay. Enough of the doom and gloom,' says Henry.

'I'm not going out on New Year's Eve. And you shouldn't, either,' Simon says. Somehow, I doubt he's on many party hotlists.

'I can't wait for the Millennium. It's going to be amazing!' Tori exclaims. 'We get to live our lives in two centuries. Our kids won't be able to say that.'

'Hear, hear.' Henry slowly claps. I shoot Tori a smile, relieved to hear some positivity.

Tori leans forward. 'Boss, is it all right if I shoot off? I've g—'

My eyes shoot to the window as it lights up with multiple lightning flashes. The long, deep booms following the sharp thunder crack go right through me.

'You'd better get off,' Henry tells Tori. 'Thanks for your help. We're finally getting that pile down, aren't we?'

'Fifty files down, one thousand and fifty to go!' she calls back as rain lashes the window.

Henry touches my shoulder. 'Let's leave Simon to it. I want to show you something.'

We return to the main room. Henry twizzles the blinds to block out the unpalatable weather. He joins me at the long table and slides over a tattered orange folder.

'I've been through hundreds of these old files, but this is the one I want you to look at. Before my psychic retired, he picked out this file and told me something was seriously off about this case. He was insistent I look into it.'

NENAGH GODDALL: MISSING 13th April 1956

A shiver of anticipation runs through me as I look at the cover. A neat column of signatures and dates runs below the heading, with Henry's signature at the bottom.

Hopefully, with the finding machine, Henry's name will be the last.

Nenagh's black and white photo, clipped to the first page, shows an attractive woman dressed in a soft wool cardigan. Her mid-tone hair is set in curls, framing a pale face with an innocent smile. Her gaze is directed to one-side as though she's looking at someone other than the photographer.

'Nenagh was married less than a year when she went missing,' Henry says. 'She was at home that day while her husband Reginald was at work.'

'Did any of the neighbours see anything?'

Henry shakes his head. 'The couple lived on a quiet road. Neither Nenagh nor Reginald had many friends. Neighbours said they led a quiet life and valued their privacy. Hardly unusual. You can read about it in the notes. She didn't like going anywhere alone, not even to the local shops.'

Nenagh's photograph doesn't match this timid description. She looks confident with her chin tilted up.

'Was this photo taken before or after she was married?' I raise my voice to be heard over a roll of thunder.

Henry leans over and flips the photo. On the back is a date: *2nd August, 1955*.

'She doesn't look like a mouse in the photo,' I point out.

'I had the same thought myself,' Henry says. 'The problem is, we don't know what went on at home. Officers saw no evidence of domestic abuse.'

'That doesn't mean it didn't happen.'

'Naturally. But we should stick to the facts for now.'

I flip through pages of reports, forms and interviews. 'So, what happened on the day she disappeared?'

'According to Reginald, he returned from work to find the house empty. Nenagh always had dinner waiting. There were no signs of violence, no forced entry. Nothing. She was never found.' Henry stretches back in his chair, hands linked behind his head. 'Nenagh didn't have a passport and there's no record of her leaving the country. It's possible she moved away somewhere to start a new life.'

'But you don't think that,' I say. 'Or I wouldn't be here.'

'Eight months after Nenagh goes missing, Reginald sells the house and disappears. From that point on, there's no trace of him. The house was a wedding present from Nenagh's father, who was a widower. He died a few months after Nenagh went missing, from a broken heart. That's a real condition, apparently.' Henry's brow rises. 'The police couldn't pin anything on him.'

'Do you have a picture of Reginald?' I ask, a flurry of excitement building inside me.

'Unfortunately, not. He came in for two interviews but wasn't questioned under caution. There was a further informal chat at home, and that was that.'

'What else do we know?' I ask, hiding my disappointment over Reginald's photo.

'He was personable, charming. Nenagh's father liked him enough to approve the marriage, and purchase a house for the couple. Reginald seems the type to make a good impression. He worked in a car showroom in Harpenden. Apparently, quite the salesman.'

I furrow my brow. 'If Reginald owned the house and was coming into an inheritance anyway, why did he need to get rid of Nenagh?'

'It's a good question.' His expression darkens. 'One thing this job's taught me, what you see on the surface is rarely the true picture.'

Looking at Nenagh's photo again, a tingle runs through me.

Henry locks eyes with me. 'Can you help me find her?'

My head's nodding before the words are out.

'I'll give it my best shot.'

9

—·—

Simon finishes upgrading my computer, grabs his cables and discs and mutters a farewell before absconding to the Millennium Team down the hall.

Henry calls me over to the box room. 'Come through, and I'll get you set up.'

I hesitate on the threshold, debating whether or not I should fetch my rucksack from the car. Without the finding machine, I can't do anything.

A small voice in my head advises caution. Henry's spider-senses are already tingling. He wouldn't be much of an investigator if he wasn't tempted to unzip my rucksack to find out what the cold thing is at the bottom, and whether it has anything to do with my special ability. Considering we're in the heartland of Hertfordshire Police, Henry has every right to search my rucksack for security reasons.

If he does, I won't have any choice but to hand it over.

A massive boom makes me jump in my skin. A long roll of thunder follows, rumbling through the floor. The lights flicker and go out momentarily as the downpour outside intensifies.

I take a seat at the tiny desk and wiggle the mouse. The computer wakes up with a welcome chirp, just about audible over the hammering rain. Sheet lightning casts an eerie blue light across the room, flashing on and off for several seconds.

Enter your Login ID and Password.

'Allow me.' Henry comes up behind me, his arms framing mine, his cheek an inch away. His proximity makes me acutely aware of the heat coming from his body. 'I'll log you on as a visitor. You'll be able to use Word, Excel and access the internet.'

Henry types in a username and password, his hands strong and efficient. I don't realise I've been holding my breath until he says, 'The web browser's ready. If you need to use the phone, dial 9 for an outside line.'

He places Nenagh's file on the desk, along with a notepad, pen and pencil.

'That's great.' I flash Henry a smile over my shoulder. 'I'll give you a shout if I need anything.'

'Are you sure?' Henry stands by my shoulder with one hand on the back of the chair. 'I'm happy to stay.'

'It's best if I do this on my own.' My determined stare is more than a match for his hopeful one.

'You win.' Henry raises his hands and backs out of the room. 'I'm next door if you need me.'

The door clicks shut. I jump up and turn the thumb latch, then hang my coat on the hook to obscure the window. Once I'm locked inside and hidden from view, I sit at the desk, close my eyes and take slow, deep breaths, wondering how long I'll have to stay in here before Henry calls it a night.

I flick through Nenagh's file, and read the interviews and incident reports. Nenagh's sister, Avril, said Reginald could be 'controlling.'

After I've familiarised myself with the file, I wake up the computer and access the internet. The home page freezes. I reload it, chewing on a pencil.

The same thing happens again. Blocks of green and blue fracture on the screen.

I wiggle the mouse. Click the button. Hit *Escape. Return*, and random buttons on the keyboard, but nothing makes any difference. A sudden crack of thunder freezes me in my chair. Simultaneously, the screen greys out.

I unlock the door and head over to Henry whose head is bowed over paperwork. I clear my throat, and he looks up expectantly.

'My computer's frozen,' I say.

Henry nods and reaches for the nearest phone. 'Simon, it's Henry. What's going on with the internet?' He pauses, then shakes his head. 'Seriously? The whole building?'

Henry presses the receiver to his ear, rubbing his forehead.

'Fine.' He puts down the receiver, pressing his fist onto the desk. 'The storm has caused floods and power outages. Our telephone lines are down. Simon has no idea when we'll be back up and running.'

'What do we do?' I cross my fingers crossed behind my back, hoping he'll call it a day.

'Can you work without the phone and the internet?'

'Not really. I'll give it one last try.' I return to my computer and click the mouse and keyboard. It's still frozen. I nudge the door closed and open Nenagh's file.

Her hopeful smile increases my resolve. Swiftly, I unclip her photograph from the page and slip it inside my coat pocket. I return to the main room to find Henry staring out of the window as another flurry of rain hits the glass, hard as hail.

'Any luck?'

I shake my head as I return Nenagh's file. 'Sorry.'

Henry takes the file and stares into the rain. 'I know you've only just started on Nenagh's case, but we'll have to leave it for today.' He drops his hand and the blinds fall into place. 'We'll get back on it first thing tomorrow. With any luck, the rain will have stopped and the computers will be back up and running.'

And this time, I'll have my rucksack with me.

I wish I didn't have to rely on unreliable technology to find Nenagh. Maybe technical problems will become a thing of the past in the twenty-first century. One can only hope.

· · · · ● · ● · · · ·

58

I stand next to Henry in the reception area, staring in dismay at the torrential rain beyond the sliding doors. The floodlit car park is becoming a lake. Henry has slung a black trench coat over his damp suit. I pull up my hood.

'Have you never seen a bit of rain?' Yolanda says cheerily from behind the desk. 'You should visit Uganda during monsoon season.' She leaves the desk and presses a golf umbrella into my hand. 'Watch out for crocodiles.'

She gives my arm a squeeze. 'See you tomorrow.'

I open the umbrella, ignoring memories of my mother's horrified warnings about the bad luck that will surely follow.

Proffering the handle to Henry, I say, 'Would you mind? You're taller.'

Henry puts an arm around my shoulders, bringing me close as we step out into the deluge. He tilts the umbrella into near-horizontal rain and steers me past overflowing gutters and overflowing drains. By the time we reach the car, my boots and socks are soaking.

Henry opens the passenger door for me. Inside, rain drums on the roof, sending a sheet of obscuring water across the windscreen. He throws the umbrella onto the back seat before getting in.

Once the doors close, I can finally hear myself think.

'We need a boat,' I say, checking the footwell for signs of water.

Henry laughs as he drives out of the carpark. Even though the windscreen wipers are on their fastest setting, our view disappears between each wipe. Henry drives towards Hertford at a crawl, water spraying from the tyres.

'You never mentioned where I'm staying tonight,' I say.

Antony was worried Henry would ask me to stay at his place. I was more concerned he'd drop me outside a soulless Travelodge. But now I have Nenagh's photo in my pocket, a quiet room would suit me fine.

'I tried to get a hotel, but everywhere's booked solid for Christmas.' Henry gives me a brief glance. 'Don't worry. I think you'll like this place.'

Uh-oh. Maybe Henry has the sofa bed ready. That would really put the cat amongst the pigeons.

We drive around the outskirts of Hertford and head down a B-road. Further on, Henry turns down a lane dotted with handsome manor houses and pulls into a gravel drive behind a luxury SUV.

I peer through the rain at a white coach house with sash-windows and large stone sills.

A dog barks inside the house. The curtains shift by the window and a boy's cheeky face appears with his nose pressed to the glass.

'Is this your house?' I ask. 'Is that your child?'

Henry shakes his head, laughing. 'It's my sister's place. She can't wait to meet you.'

10

I grab my rucksack from the boot of the Astra. Henry holds the umbrella over us as we dash to the shelter of the porch. The front door opens before Henry has a chance to press the bell. A strong-boned woman with ice-blonde hair cuts a striking figure in the doorway. The way she stands, with one hand in the pocket of her navy suit trousers, her pale grey eyes assessing me, reminds me of Henry.

'I'm Olivia.' She smiles. 'You must be Alex. Come in.'

'Thank you.' I hesitate on the coir doormat, glancing from my wet boots to the spotless terracotta tiles.

'You can leave your shoes there,' Olivia says, pointing to a boot rack under a row of coats and jackets. 'Put your bag there, too. Marcus will take it up later.'

I'm unlacing my boots and pulling off my soggy socks, when a golden retriever bounds past.

'Hi, Ludo.' Henry leans down to ruffle the dog's fur, receiving a slobbery greeting and doggy grin in return. Then, a blur of motion shoots from a door down the hall, on a collision course with Henry.

'Here's trouble!' Henry scoops up a little boy wearing pyjamas with a pattern of rockets and stars and hoists him up until his tousled hair brushes the ceiling. 'Blast off!'

'Blast off, Uncle 'enree!' the boy yells back, waving a worn teddy bear in a pudgy fist. He pushes the bear into the ceiling. 'Snuff going to the moon!'

'Let Uncle Henry get through the door, Charlie,' Olivia tuts.

'You know what? I think Snuff just found a space egg!' Henry's eyes go wide. 'Do you want to see it?'

'Yes!' A blazing grin spreads across the boy's face.

Henry sets him down, and produces a Kinder egg from his inside pocket with a magician's flourish.

The boy puts the egg between the bear's paws and with a thank you, takes Henry's hand. 'Come and see my Lego starbase.'

Henry gives me a hapless look as Charlie tugs him through a door into the lounge, past a real Christmas tree hung with amber lights.

'See you in a sec.'

Their easy familiarity melts my heart. Below that, is something else, an unfamiliar yearning.

Olivia touches my arm. 'Come through.'

Ludo leads the way, trotting through the doorway at the end of the hall into a toasty farmhouse kitchen. Aromas of garlic, onion and rich tomato sauce make my stomach growl. A dark-haired, stocky man oversees various pots and pans on a six-ring Aga. He wipes his hands on an apron.

'I'm Marcus.' He leans over to shake my hand. 'Henry's told us so much about you.'

'Not all bad, I hope.' I force a smile, wondering what on earth he's been saying.

Marcus offers a spoonful of sauce to Olivia. 'More salt?'

She leans in to taste it, and gives a sage nod. 'Just a smidgen.'

Marcus adds seasoning, then pours me a glass of red wine – a 'Barolo', which sounds expensive - before adding a generous glug to the simmering sauce. I take a seat by the warmly lit kitchen island, a languorous feeling running through my limbs.

'That smells amazing,' I say, thinking of my sad fridge at home. 'I really struggle to find time to cook after work.'

'Oh, I have plenty of time,' Marcus laughs, taking garlic bread from the oven. 'Olivia's the breadwinner.'

Olivia pours herself a glass of wine. 'I don't have Marcus's patience. I'm far happier tackling mergers and acquisitions.'

Deep laughter erupts from the lounge and combines with Charlie's shrieks of joy. Olivia gives me a curious look. 'Henry loves spending time with Charlie. Do you like children?'

'I love kids.' The words burst out. 'I don't have much experience with them, though. My nephew Oscar lives near Seattle but I rarely see him.'

Marcus says, 'All you need with Charlie is the patience to watch *The Wheels on the Bus* on a never-ending loop.'

He removes bowls from the warmer. Ludo sits by the Aga, keeping a close eye on proceedings.

Marcus looks at the dog. 'We know all the songs backwards now, don't we, Ludo?'

Ludo's ears perk up at the sound of his name.

The ambience is so warm and welcoming. Olivia and Marcus appear to have it all – a lovely home, career success, a gorgeous child, quality time together. Antony and I moved to Birmingham for many of the same reasons, but we haven't come close to achieving them.

Marcus turns the heat to low under the sauce and unties his apron. 'This is nearly done. I'd better go rescue Henry.'

A short time later, Henry enters the kitchen in stockinged feet and slings his suit jacket over the back of a chair.

'Sorry for abandoning you,' he says. 'I had to fix the docking station on Charlie's starbase. All good here?'

I nod.

Olivia passes Henry a glass of wine before turning to me. 'Henry mentioned you're working with him. But you're not with the police, are you?' She leans over the countertop. 'Do you work for a special government department?'

Why does everyone assume I'm part of a team?

'I...well...I can't say.' I add a helpless shrug and mask my discomfort by reaching for the wine.

Henry meets his sister's eye. 'You're not supposed to interrogate guests.'

'I'm hardly interrogating her. I can't help being interested.'

Before Olivia can probe deeper, Henry changes the subject to Charlie's Lego skills and his colourful drawings taped to the side of the fridge.

Marcus returns after tucking Charlie up in bed, and we sit down to eat.

Dinner with Henry's family is like spending the evening at a lovely restaurant where you know the owner. As we sit round the kitchen table, savouring slow-cooked ragu with tagliatelle, topped with parmesan shavings, I finally relax.

Thunder booms outside, briefly interrupting our conversation.

'You're lucky you avoided the power cuts,' Henry says, putting his hand over his glass when Marcus offers more wine. 'The storm caused an outage at work. Half of Hertford's affected.'

'Anyone want the last bit of garlic bread?' Marcus asks, before claiming it. 'I heard the river flooded its banks near Stanstead Abbotts. I'm glad we live on higher ground.'

'The storm's supposed to blow over tonight,' Olivia says. 'Things should be back to normal by morning.'

Under the table, Henry's leg brushes mine. It must be accidental, yet a line of heat runs up my thigh. I glance at Henry, but he gives no sign he's aware we touched.

By the time the chocolate steamed pudding and vanilla ice-cream comes out, I'm so full I can barely move. Ludo slumbers in his dog bed by the Aga, muzzle and paws twitching with doggy dreams.

'Thanks for dinner, sis. I'd better go while I still have my wits about me.' Henry pushes back from the table and catches my eye. 'Sleep well, Alex. I'll pick you up at 8.30 sharp.'

He leans close to my ear and whispers, 'Don't feel you have to answer any of Olivia's questions. Tell her it's confidential, classified, whatever. See you in the morning.'

11

— • —

After dinner, Marcus leads me upstairs to the spare bedroom, which is almost twice the size of the one I share with Antony. The muted grey-panelled walls, Laura Ashley floral quilt and matching curtains are very chic country-cottage. Rain drums against the window, accompanied by a faint rumble of thunder.

Marcus puts my rucksack on the floor next to the mirrored dresser by the window, points out the family bathroom down the hall, and leaves me to settle in.

I throw myself onto the bedspread and stare at the stippled ceiling, mulling over Nenagh Goddall. So much time has passed since 1956, the chances she's still alive are slim. Nevertheless, if I can find out where she ended up, it's worth a shot.

Forcing myself off the cozy bed, I creep downstairs. Marcus and Olivia are talking in the kitchen, their voices muffled through the door. I retrieve Nenagh's photo from my jacket and head back to my room. I shut the door, unzip my rucksack and remove handfuls of clothes and spare shoes, dumping them in untidy heaps on the dresser.

The finding machine is a towel-wrapped lump at the bottom of the rucksack. I leave it in situ, unzip the rucksack's front flap and fold it over. This way, I can use the machine and keep it concealed at the same time.

The towel has gone stiff from cold. I unpeel it from the machine, then rummage in the rucksack's side-pocket for a pack of 9-volt batteries – purchased on the way to the station this morning.

I slide-off the plastic cover protecting the battery compartment, connect a new battery and replace the cover.

I flick the on/off switch.

Nothing.

Holding my breath, I flip the switch again.

Nothing. On. Off. On. Off.

I look to the ceiling and cross my fingers before trying the switch again. 'Come on, Dad!' I hiss.

Relief courses through me when a green dot appears.

'Thank you,' I whisper, giving the machine a little stroke and putting my hands together in prayer to cover all my bases.

Next, I extend the two aerials which terminate in crocodile clips. They lock in place, pointing at the ceiling. After offering a swift prayer to the gods of technology, I secure Nenagh's photo between the clips.

51.793183 -0.087942

'Yes!' I give a fist pump, then scribble down the numbers. The number 51 rings a bell. I tap the pencil against the dresser and think back to Sebastian the Bengal cat. Last year, I found him trapped inside a shed at my local allotments when I lived in Ware. His co-ordinates started with 51. Nenagh could be nearby.

51.793185 -0.087942

Chills travels up my breastbone. I double-check my co-ordinates.

The numbers have changed.

'Oh. My. God,' I whisper. The difference is tiny, but the significance is huge. Nenagh is moving. She must be alive!

Biting back my excitement, I reach for my phone to call Henry, picturing his astonishment when I give him the news. I press the *ON* button, and the green backlight illuminates the screen. I navigate through my address book to Henry's mobile number, my thumb hovering over the *Call* icon. Then, I hesitate. If I call him now, he'll wonder how on earth I found Nenagh too quickly. That will only lead to more questions. Better to wait until morning.

The home screen shows two missed calls from Antony, plus one more from an unknown caller.

I speed-dial Antony's mobile, desperate to share my exciting news. The ringtone repeats six or seven times before his voice recording cuts in.

'You know the drill. Only your gran leaves voicemail. Text me.'

After the beep, I press the END button and give it a couple of minutes before trying again.

'You know the drill. Only your gr—'

Throwing the phone on the bed, I pace the room, chewing my fingernails. The sound of my mobile trilling makes me jump. I grab it and jab the button.

'Antony!'

'Hi, babe, how's things?'

I struggle to hear his voice against the sound of multiple conversations and uproarious laughter. 'I'm fine. Where are you?'

'I'm with a colleague at the pub.'

A velvety female voice in the background says, 'Another glass of wine, Antony? Or, shall we share a bottle?'

'Sure thing, yeah,' Antony says.

I stop dead. 'Who's that?'

'Saskia. She's one of the designers.'

'You never mentioned her before,' I say.

'We're working late and bitching about Yan. I tried your mobile earlier. A posh bloke left a message on the ansaphone for you.'

'A posh bloke?' I pause, scrambling to work out who it could be. 'Did he leave a name?'

'Yeah, a poncy one. Jonathan Prudente-Poulton. He said it was urgent.'

I stare at the flowery curtains with my mind spinning, trying to get my head around this bombshell. 'What did he want?'

'Dunno. Didn't say.'

'Prudente-Poulton is Director of Operations for the NMPH.' I lower my voice in case the woman overhears. 'He left me a card that mentions the finding machine. He knows about it!'

'What?' Antony's tone shoots up. 'Why didn't you tell me?'

'Because I'd just been fired, and that was bad enough. I didn't want to bother you with this as well. Prudente-Poulton must have found out about Dad's machine after I rescued Rashid. I bet he wants it for the NMPH.'

'Hang on. How do you know that? Has he said as much?'

'Not exactly.'

An edge creeps into Antony's tone. 'What was on the card, *exactly*?'

'It said, *'About Your Machine.'*'

Three words that still have the power to hit me like hammer blows.

Antony lets out a massive huff. 'That could mean anything. Give him a ring. He might want to help you, Alex. Use the machine for good. Isn't that what you wanted?'

I haul in short, shallow breaths. 'What if he wants to report me to the authorities for using an unauthorised GPS receiver? What if he tries to take it from me?'

Prudente-Poulton probably has that power with his connections. I can't stop him. I stomp around the bed, chewing the inside of my cheek. I should stop using the machine until he goes away. But that's not possible while I'm working with Henry.

'What am I going to do?' I blurt out.

'First of all, try and calm down. Breathe.' Antony's tone remains brusque. 'You sound hyper.'

'I won't let him have it, I won't.' My voice cracks and I catch myself before I start crying. 'It belongs to me and Dad. It's all I have left of him.'

'Deep breaths, Alex. Just sleep on it,' Antony says. 'I think you should ring him. You could be worrying over nothing.' He pauses. 'Look, I have to go. Saskia's on a timer and we have tons to get thr—'

'You sound like you'd rather spend time with her than talk to me! You haven't even asked how it went today!'

'I'm sorry. How did it go?'

'It's no good asking me now!' I grind my teeth at the thought of Antony with this unknown female.

'I promise I'll make time tomorrow.' Antony's voice is low and steady, but the idea that he's trying to mollify me only makes me madder. 'Just not now. What with work—'

'That's all you ever do!' I yell. 'Work, work, work! What about me? Why can't you make time for me?'

'Alex, sorry,' comes a voice. It takes me a moment before I realise someone's in the room. I turn with my hand covering the receiver.

Marcus hovers in the doorway, wearing an awkward smile. 'Would you mind keeping it down?' he says in a low voice. 'It's just that Charlie's trying to sleep, and he's used to a quiet house.'

'I'm so sorry.' Blotting my teary eye on my sleeve, I lower the phone. 'Yes, of course.'

Marcus nods and puts one hand out in a placating manner. 'Good night, then. See you in the morning.'

He closes the door gently, which I take as a massive hint to shut the hell up.

Sniffing, I throw myself on the bed and whisper down the phone, 'Talk tomorrow.'

But the line's dead.

12

Saskia haunts my troubled sleep. She says, '*Shall we share a bottle?*' in a never-ending loop until Antony sweeps her into his arms and dances off with her. Before the nightmare ends, Jonathan Prudente-Poulton pops up out of nowhere and raises a stern finger. '*About your machine,*' he says. '*About your machine, your machine, your machine....*'

The beeping of the alarm clock comes as a blessed relief.

The finding machine is zipped up in my rucksack, ready to go. I grab it and head downstairs.

Marcus is in the kitchen, slicing a banana at the island. 'Sleep well?' he asks.

'Yes, thanks,' I lie. 'Where's Olivia?'

'She left early to get the train.'

I sit beside Charlie. Marcus pours me coffee and pops two slices of bread in the toaster while he makes small talk about his plans for the day - a sing-along playgroup and a visit to the swings.

Charlie wiggles on his booster seat, stacking Cheerios around his bowl. Each pile is six hoops high. I smile, watching the curve of his neck as he bends to his task. How simple life is at that age.

His shock of sandy hair and dark blue eyes are a perfect blend of his parents' features. It makes me think about Antony. If we had a child together, what would it look like? I reckon it would be an exotic mix of Hackney, Jamaica, Ireland and Shropshire, with skin the colour of autumn leaves, lustrous black hair and a charming smile. Full of sass, of course, and highly creative.

I pluck a Cheerio from the box and push it towards Charlie. 'Shall we try and make a taller tower?'

Charlie shakes his head, loops his arm protectively around his bowl and turns from me.

'He's a bit grumpy this morning,' Marcus tells me.

Maybe Charlie overheard my outburst last night and thinks I'm a weirdo. I eat my breakfast staring at my solitary Cheerio, racking my brains for the right thing to say. I know more about life on Mars than how children work.

After finishing breakfast, I thank Marcus for his hospitality and blow a kiss to Charlie, which he ignores.

I wait impatiently for Henry on the doorstep outside, huddled in my coat with my rucksack over my shoulder, blinking at the pale winter sun. Although the rain has stopped, water showers from the trees with every gust of wind.

The Astra turns into the drive.

I wave at Henry, open the passenger door, put my rucksack in the footwell and slide onto the seat.

'Good morning.' Henry welcomes me with a smile. 'How are things? All good?'

I give a short nod. 'You have a lovely family.'

'I think so. It's great you met Charlie. Adorable, isn't he?'

'Sure is,' I reply, once again wishing I'd made a better impression on him. 'He thinks the world of you.'

'He's my best buddy.' Henry pulls out of the driveway onto a winding lane lined with oak trees. The tyres crunch on fallen twigs. An intersecting lane descends steeply to the left, blocked by a red warning sign: *Caution. Road Closed. Flooding.*

'I might have something on Nenagh,' I say.

Henry's hands tighten on the steering wheel. 'Really? What is it?'

'A possible location that came through last night. I'll check it again once we get to the office.' I take a breath. 'I think she's alive, Henry.'

Henry snaps a look at me. 'What? How do you know?' He tears his eyes away to steer sharply around a fallen branch lying in the middle of the road.

I reach for the dashboard, too late. Centrifugal force throws me into Henry. The car swerves again, and Henry mutters something under his breath.

'Sorry!' Heat gushes to my face until I feel myself glow. I wrench myself upright, holding the door handle with a death grip.

Henry looks at me with a faint smile. Something flickers across his features, but it's gone before I can catch it. 'You were telling me about Nenagh.'

I struggle to get back on track. 'Once we get to the station, I just need to double-check my findings.'

'Sure thing.'

The road ahead is clear of traffic. Henry puts his foot down and the car surges forward. I grip the handle as we crest a ridge and descend towards Hertford. Once we join the main road, neat verges and rows of buildings replace the fields and trees. Rivulets of water run down the verges, carrying leaf litter over clogged-up storm drains.

Henry is clearly preoccupied with getting to the police station as quickly as possible, and speaks little for the rest of the journey to the car park.

I follow Henry into the deserted reception area. He stops by the desk to sign me in. Thankfully, he doesn't comment on my rucksack.

We head for the cold case room. Henry hits the lights and opens the door to the box room. After booting up the computer, he logs me in and double-clicks on the Netscape icon. To my relief, the welcome screen comes up without any problems.

Henry checks his watch. 'If you need technical help, Simon should be here in ten minutes.'

'Fantastic,' I say. 'All I need now is Nenagh's file.'

I load up the geospatial website while Henry fetches the paper-work. He leans over my shoulder, staring at the screen.

Turning my head, I flash him a smile. 'You don't need to stay. I'll let you know the moment I find anything.'

Henry lingers by my shoulder for a moment, then leaves.

As soon as he's gone, I lock the door, hang my coat over the window and dig out the slip of paper with Nenagh's previous GPS locations. Unzipping my rucksack, I flip the towel off the finding machine and fold down the rucksack's front flap, just as I did last night.

I fiddle with the on/off switch until Dad's dot lights up. The technical issue gives me palpitations. The machine is packed with obscure technology that's way beyond my understanding.

I insert Nenagh's picture and check the display: **51.793004 -0.089963.**

The numbers have changed again.

Swiftly, I enter the co-ordinates into the longitude and latitude boxes on screen. I lean forward with tingles running up the back of my neck as I wait for a landmark, town or road. Fractured blocks break up the image, forming an array of pixelated small squares that join together to form a map.

The map shows an industrial area beside the River Mimram, south-west from the point where it diverges from the River Lea. The white-gloved hand points to the end of Mimram Road, where the industrial estate meets the river. I can't zoom in any more, this is as accurate as it gets.

I refer back to the file. Nenagh has ended up less than two miles from her old home. Could it be feasible that she left Reginald back in 1956 and moved a short distance away? If that's the case, she's lived in Hertford for over forty years without anyone making the connection. It doesn't seem possible in a town with less than thirty thousand people.

I delete the co-ordinates and enter the first location from the previous night.

The map repositions upstream. When I repeat the exercise with the second location, the finger points further down. Her final location is farther downstream. Why would Nenagh walk along the river last night in the middle of a raging storm?

I re-check the co-ordinates but they haven't changed, which means Nenagh hasn't moved.

Why isn't she moving? I put my head in my hands.

I so want Nenagh to be alive. I should have kept my mouth shut until I was sure.

Sighing, I print off the page showing Nenagh's current location, push back in my chair and close my eyes. I switch off the machine and zip up my rucksack, then grab my notepad and leave the box room to find Henry.

Henry looks up as I approach, clenches his hand on the desk. 'Have you...?'

'I think she's here.' I hand him the print-out.

Henry studies the map with a frown. 'And she's alive?'

'I'm sorry. I thought she was, but now I'm not so sure.' I bite back my disappointment. 'We'll find out once we get down there.'

· · · · ● · ● · · ·

'I want to know where you're getting your information,' Henry asks, driving out of the car park. 'You're using the internet. What else is there to it?'

'You promised you wouldn't push me.' I turn my face to the window, my mind frantically shifting gears. 'Did you give your old psychic a grilling, too?'

'No, but there weren't satellite trackers involved.'

I shoot him a terrified look. 'What do you mean?'

'I saw the website you were on. Geospatial data. That's something to do with GPS locations, isn't it?'

Prickles run down my throat. 'You know about global positioning systems?'

'Simon mentioned it a year ago, something coming in from America.' Henry shifts gears as we cross a roundabout. 'I can't say I was paying much attention, as he tends to ramble, but I looked it up. GPS receivers pick up radio waves from satellites. Every point on planet Earth has its own set of unique co-ordinates. Then I thought, you can find anyone in the world if you have those co-ordinates. Is that how you're finding people?'

I manage a nod, willing to concede that much. 'The website converts the latitude and longitude co-ordinates into real-time locations.'

'Okay, but that doesn't explain how you know those co-ordinates relate to Nenagh, or where they come from originally.'

My eyes drop to the rucksack between my feet. 'I have a type of GPS receiver in my rucksack. Really, that's all I can tell you.'

Henry falls silent. 'All right. I'll back off. For now. I need time to get my head round this.'

Hopefully, he'll need a year.

Mimram Road is off the busy A414, on the way to Hertingfordbury. We drive into a small, mixed-use industrial estate that leads down to the river. The area is noisy and built-up. Cars line the kerb on both sides, leaving a single-lane down the middle.

We wait for a delivery van and a lorry to pass before driving on. Windows, gates, cameras and eyes are everywhere. Most businesses look car-related, offering servicing, MOTs, tyres and exhausts. As we continue, the units become older – 1960s whitewashed single-story units with old hand-painted signs.

Further down, the buildings run out by the river bank. An old, brick-built unit marks the end of the estate.

Through the trees flanking the edge of the river, I catch reflections sparkling on water.

Henry pulls over onto the verge and cuts the engine.

'We're here.'

13

— • —

I wrench my gaze away from the river. Henry unclips his seatbelt and leans towards me, pale eyes bright with curiosity. 'What happens now?'

I set my rucksack on my knee, my fingers on the zip. I haven't shown the finding machine to anyone except Antony and Jason Bevin. Henry's curiosity fizzes round him like an electric aura. He wants to know everything, and keeping him from seeing too much is becoming a problem.

Glancing around the litter-strewn footwell, I have an idea. 'Why don't you have a quick scout of the area? I won't be long.'

Henry rubs his chin, staring at the rucksack. 'I'll wait.'

'Please, Henry.' I fiddle with the grab loop on top of the bag until he gets the message.

A V-shape appears on Henry's brow. 'Have it your way.'

He gets out of the car and closes it with more force than necessary, then strides along the river bank, looking through the undergrowth and into the water.

Swiftly, I retrieve Nenagh's photo from my jacket pocket and insert it into the clip-holders. I turn the machine on and off five times before Dad's dot appears. The display lights up with Nenagh's co-ordinates. I check them against my slip of paper. They haven't changed.

I examine the strip of five LED lights below the display. Three are solid red, the fourth is flashing and the fifth is off. Five solid red lights will mean I'm within a few feet of Nenagh. I grab two white carrier bags bearing the green Asda logo, and double-bag the machine. The plastic layers conceal Nenagh's photo and the bulk of the machine, leaving the glow of the LED lights still visible.

A drumming sound makes me look up. Henry's standing by the car door, tapping his fingers on the roof.

Curling my arms around the rucksack, I open the passenger door.

'I couldn't see anything,' Henry says as I clamber out. 'I guess it's down to you.'

I reverse the rucksack so that I'm wearing it on my front like a baby sling. I've left the front flap unzipped. If I look directly down, I can see the LED lights.

The finding machine drags on my front like an icy brick as I carefully approach the river bank. Damp bracken, sodden grass and mud squish beneath my boots as I walk in a circle. A swampy smell with undertones of engine oil and sewage hangs in the air.

The third indicator light goes out every time I move away from the water.

'What's the plan?' Henry watches my strange movements, one hand on his hip.

'I'm getting my bearings. I think Nenagh's in the water.'

The River Mimram is nothing like the placid Birmingham canals I'm used to painting. Dark water surges by, broken up by churning white froth, storm debris and rubbish. The Asda bags and Gore-Tex rucksack will protect my machine against splashes, but if we go under, it's toast.

'Did you bring any waterproofs?'

Henry pats his pockets. 'Afraid not. Only a pack of sterile gloves.'

Great.

I head for the bank. Henry sticks close as I reach a large weeping willow straddling the bank. Its thin branches droop into the water. I'm about to grab one to aid my descent when my heel slips on mud.

Henry grabs my belt, stopping my fall.

'Thanks.'

'No problem.' Henry peers over my shoulder at the LED display, which show three reds. 'What are those lights? Are they to do with signal strength?'

'Something like that.' I steel myself. 'I'm going in. Don't let me get swept away.'

'I won't.' Henry removes his mobile phone from his pocket, and leaves it on the verge. He comes close behind me and hooks his arm around my waist to control my descent.

Icy water seeps into my boots, making me gasp. Taking baby steps, I shift my grip from branch to branch and then grab hold of an enormous twisting root disappearing beneath the water line.

Henry wades in behind me. As he's taller, the water only reaches his mid-thigh. If he's shocked by the cold, he doesn't show it, whereas I'm cursing like a trooper.

A few more steps and water laps up to my waist, invading my underwear. I tuck one arm under the rucksack and lift it clear. Thank God the finding machine is in my rucksack and not in my numb hands, or I'd probably have dropped it by now.

Stones shift underfoot. The current tugs at my legs, pushing me sideways. I cling to the tree with my legs braced, fearful of taking another step.

'The ground's firmer over here,' Henry says, guiding me round the bulging willow trunk.

'Can you shorten my straps?' I ask, my teeth clacking.

Henry fiddles with the straps and hitches the rucksack up until it sits under my chin.

'We're getting closer. The fourth light's gone red. Fifth one's flashing!' I call out.

Water froths round my waist. Keeping one eye out for any hazardous objects heading my way, I shift one numb foot forward, then the other like a zombie, holding the rucksack in an iron grip above the water. My jeans are stuck to my legs like they're shrink-wrapped. I'll probably have to cut them off.

My foot slips on the slick, weed-covered riverbed. As I fall, I get a flash of my father looking sadly at me, shaking his head as I drown his precious invention and myself.

Henry catches me and hauls me upright. Water streams from the ends of my hair.

'I've got you.' His strong grip anchors me in the swirling current. 'Give me the rucksack.'

I shake my head, shivering. Over on the far bank, a pair of dog walkers stop to watch. A woman with three yapping chihuahuas points out my misfortune to her friend.

'Are you all right?' she calls. 'Do you need help?'

What do they mean by help? Are they going to send in the chihuahuas to rescue me?

'N-no, I'm fine!' I fix a grin. 'Cold water's g-good for the metabolism! You should try it!'

Henry smiles and adds a wave. We grin at each other for a long, painful moment. The dog walkers move on, shaking their heads.

'No w-wonder dog-walkers find all the b-bodies,' I say. 'They must be the nosiest b-bunch alive!'

'Bless them,' Henry replies. 'They're our secret police force, like you and your machine.'

From my starting point, I wade one step out to all four compass points, but it's only when I follow the protruding base of the giant willow that the fifth light goes red. Looking down, I can't make out anything past the black water, fronds of riverweed and froth.

Henry leans over my shoulder. 'Right. Can you get back to the bank? Put the rucksack on dry land. I'll search.'

I move clumsily to the bank and wedge the rucksack safely against a fallen branch.

Henry rolls up his sleeves and plunges his arms under the water. He turns in a tight circle, the front of his shirt soaked. 'I've found something. It's heavy.'

Reaching down again, he heaves until his face turns red and tendons stand out on his neck. A long, black bundle appears on the surface with blue, plastic twine wound round it.

Henry grits his teeth, making straining sounds as he tries to drag the bundle towards the bank.

'I can't move it.' He pauses to catch his breath. 'Can you give me a hand?'

Getting back into the water is worse than before, but at least the finding machine is safe and my arms are free. I wobble on a weed-slick stretch, managing to keep my feet until I reach Henry's side. Bending over, I grope blindly for the other end of the water-logged bundle.

'Something's holding it down!' I shout.

'Keep hold of your end.' Henry crouches in the water, feels around. 'There's a rock tied to it. I need to cut through the twine.'

He pulls a utility knife from his pocket, unfolds it and feels around below the waterline. A short time later, the weight drops free and the bundle springs to the surface.

I throw my arms around the waterlogged bundle before the current can carry it away. It's long and thin, full of creases and folds. I can't feel much, but it doesn't seem bulky or heavy enough to contain a body.

Henry's lips have gone blue. He grabs the other end.

'Let's get it to the bank.'

Together, we wade towards the bank. Henry clambers out of the river first, pulling the dripping bundle to higher ground. I scramble up after him on my hands and knees and help him lay it on the grass.

The area is deserted, but it's only a matter of time before someone shows up.

The bundle is six-feet long and almost flat. The covering has a soft sheen to it, like vinyl. Breathing hard, Henry reaches into another pocket for a plastic packet and breaks the seal. He struggles to pull on a pair of disposable gloves.

'You understand, I have to check before I call it in,' he says, meeting my gaze. 'It could be rubbish.'

'It's not rubbish,' I say firmly.

Henry laces his fingers to firm the gloves, then gently works a section of the bundle loose under a fraying section of cord. He pulls a small torch from his inside pocket and shines the light inside.

After a long, agonising wait he leans back on his heels. His grim expression meets mine.

'I can't see anything except mud and stones. Are you sure about this?'

I glance at my rucksack. Five solid reds.

'One hundred percent.'

14

— • —

Henry takes my arm and helps me back to the car. I insist on carrying the rucksack, praying the finding machine isn't water damaged. I rest the rucksack on the bonnet and zip it up with numb fingers, leaving Nenagh's photo between the machine's crocodile clips. I'll have to find a way to slip the photo back into the file once we return to the station.

After tucking the rucksack in the boot, Henry opens the passenger door, takes my clammy hand and assists me inside. I sink gratefully onto the seat, shuddering from head to foot.

'You're freezing.' Henry goes round the car and gets in the driver's side. He reaches inside to start the engine and directs the air-vents towards me. Streams of hot-air blast my face and hands, but I can't stop shivering.

I clamp my teeth together to stop them chattering, while he briefs me on what to expect: police, paramedics, a police surgeon, scene of crime officers, called SOCOs for short, and a dive team.

'I checked with HQ about the coroner. They said there's no need for one without an identifiable body.'

I hug myself. I want the finding machine to be right about the bundle in the water. On the other hand, I don't want Nenagh to be dead.

Henry blows on his hands and rubs them together. His lips are still blue. 'The paramedics will want to check us over. You're a tough cookie, jumping into the water like that.'

I manage a shuddery laugh. 'I'm not tough. I just didn't stop to think it through. That's always been my problem.'

'We'll agree to differ.' He pauses. 'Listen, you'll need to give a statement.'

'I'm not mentioning my machine.'

'Agreed. Describe how we searched the river. I'll tell the detective you're on my team as a paranormal resource. Leave the rest to me.'

I bite my lip, wondering how he'll explain my involvement without sounding like he's lost his marbles.

'I have to get back. Will you be all right?'

At my nod, Henry leaves the warm interior of the car to return to the bundle lying in the grass.

The windscreen starts misting up. I wind down the window as the first police car arrives. Shortly after, officers cordon off the scene with blue and white tape: POLICE LINE DO NOT CROSS. Curious onlookers gather on the other side – mechanics in greasy overalls, trade customers, and staff.

Once the press arrives, this quiet cul-de-sac will be as busy as King's Cross Station. I remember the furore when the police recovered my aunt Lilian's body.

Half an hour later, the place bustles with uniformed officers, the police surgeon and the dive team. Henry, wrapped in a blanket, takes charge of the scene. He's in constant motion, creating a no-go zone around the bundle, directing the dive team, and briefing three SOCOs who are kitted out in blue overalls, masks, gloves and foot protectors. They start taking photos and marking the area.

A police officer gives me a curious look. He taps on my window. 'Hello, there. Can I see some ID?'

I pass over my lanyard. 'I'm working with DC Henry Longhurst.'

The officer gives my lanyard a cursory look. 'You're not police. Are you a civilian investigator? Community volunteer?'

'Sorry, you'll need to ask DC Longhurst. He'll explain.' I point him out through the window.

'He's First Officer Attending, is he?' At my nod, the officer turns away to use his radio, then goes to have a word with Henry.

Shortly afterwards, the police surgeon asks me to step out of the car and checks me over.

'Did you identify what's in the bundle?' I ask, as he takes my temperature with an ear thermometer. 'Are there human remains?'

'It's too early to say,' he tells me. 'It'll need to go to forensics.'

Once he's happy I'm not hypothermic, he throws a blanket round me. The police officer who tapped on my window beckons me into the back of his police car and takes a brief statement. I remember Henry's instructions, and thankfully, the officer doesn't ask any awkward questions.

Half an hour later, back in the passenger seat of the Astra, the number of onlookers has doubled. An uncomfortable sensation of being watched settles on me. I scan the crowd.

A man stands behind the front row. His dark gaze catches my eye. Before I can register his features, he turns and walks away.

I shudder. It's probably nothing. But it reminds me of something I've heard: murderers often return to the scene of the crime.

If I'm right about Nenagh, she didn't go for a walk one day and get lost. Someone killed her, wrapped her up, weighed her down and threw her in the river. Last night's flash floods must have dislodged the body from its original resting place and carried it downstream until it snagged on the roots of the willow tree.

I wanted Dad's machine to reunite families, to bring joy. But I don't feel any satisfaction at finding Nenagh. A bitter taste floods my mouth, accompanied by a dark feeling like the sun disappearing behind a cloud.

My chest goes tight. The difference between locating a body on a map and finding it firsthand is immense. When the police dug up Lilian, I wasn't on the scene. I never saw her mortal remains.

My thoughts go from the soggy, black bundle, to Nenagh's photo with her shy smile, soft cardigan and innocent expression. A sob escapes me, coming from nowhere. Until yesterday, I knew nothing about Nenagh.

Cupping my hands over my face, I give in to sorrow until someone opens the passenger door.

'Hey, come on. It's all right.' Henry's a blur through my tears. He leans in through the passenger door and gathers me against his chest. The top of my head fits naturally beneath his chin. I cry into his damp shirt, and my tears are lost in the wet material as he whispers that everything will be fine.

Pushing my face into the hollow of his neck, I catch the brackish tang of the river, mixing with his natural smell of spice and wood. Henry tightens his arms around me and holds me like the calm after the storm. In time, my sobs subside and I realise no one's held me like this since Antony.

I pull away, muttering a shaky thank you.

Henry wipes a tear from my cheek with his thumb and rearranges the blanket around my shoulders. 'I should have warned you. It can hit hard, the first time.'

Nodding, I wipe my eyes on the edge of the blanket.

'I rang Marcus to give him a heads-up,' Henry says. 'Tori will drive you back to the house.'

'Thank you,' I say in relief.

Tori, the female officer I met yesterday in the cold case room, opens the driver's door and slips inside. She flashes a sympathetic smile.

Henry taps the roof of the car. 'I'm in for a long day. Go home, dry off, rest. I'll see you tomorrow.'

I stutter my thanks, but he's already striding away.

· · · • · • · · · ·

'What you need is a tot of rum and a hot bath,' Tori says as she drops me outside Marcus's house.

Marcus is waiting on the driveway beside his BMW X5 with his car keys in hand.

'You'll be all right. Give yourself some time,' Tori says, touching my arm.

'Thanks.' I give a shaky smile. After waving goodbye, I squelch my way towards the front door, holding my rucksack in my arms.

'Wow.' Marcus eyes my stringy hair and sodden, mud-splashed jeans. 'You really took a dunking.'

'Henry's worse-off than me,' I say with a small laugh.

Marcus opens the front door for me, and hands me a spare key. 'You may as have this, while you're staying with us.'

'Thanks,' I say.

Ludo barks from the boot of the BMW. Charlie presses his fingers to the glass from the back seat to get a good look. His eyes widen as I sit on the front step to peel off my boots and tip water onto the gravel. My socks come off next. Water runs from the ends as I wring them out.

'Did you go swimming?' Charlie yells from the window.

'Yes.' I force a grin. 'It was lovely.'

Marcus says, 'We were just heading off to the park. Do you need me to stay, or—'

'No, go! Go!' I shush him away.

'I've left a pot of coffee in the kitchen. Help yourself to anything else you need.' He adds, 'Put your clothes in the washing machine. I'll sort them out when I get back.'

A huge sigh escapes me as I put my back to the door and shut the world out. Soggy socks in one hand, soggy boots in the other, I head down the hall to the kitchen, leaving a trail of wet footprints behind me. I place my shoes in front of the Aga, sling my jacket over a chair and drag it near the blissful warmth of the stove. It's tempting to sit down, but if I do, I may never get up again.

Marcus has left a mini-cafetière, mug and packet of chocolate digestives on the counter. I pour coffee and add two sugars, because I've heard that helps with shock. A rummage in the drinks cupboard unearths a bottle of Courvoisier with a gold top.

Marcus told me I could help myself to anything. After pouring a generous slug into the coffee, I take a second straight from the bottle. The brandy courses a line of fire into my stomach.

My mood immediately improves.

After coffee and biscuits, I take a long bath and wash my hair, soaking in Olivia's luxury lavender and honey bubble-bath. After pulling on dry clothes, I go back to my room and unpack the finding machine, examining it carefully for signs of water ingress. Thankfully, both it and the photo of Nenagh have survived the River Mimram.

With a start, I remember my phone. It's been inside my jacket the whole time.

I rush downstairs and rummage in the pockets. My Nokia feels clammy to the touch but to my relief, the screen lights up when I press the power button. An alert pops up on the home screen.

Two new text messages. The first one's from Antony:
`Boss Number 0118 4960537 xx`

The second message makes Antony's redundant:
`Please call me about your father. J.Pru dente-Poulton`

I stare at my phone with a screwed-up face, wondering if I read the message wrong or I'm going mad. It was bad enough knowing Prudente-Poulton was after the finding machine. What could he possibly know about Dad?

I pour a stiff measure of brandy into a glass and take it to my room. The house is empty, but I'm not taking any chances. I close the door and wedge the dresser chair beneath the handle.

After one more sip for courage, I dial the number.

A set of strange clicks follow like a beetle is stuck inside the receiver, before the phone makes the regular ringing sound.

After seven rings, a woman picks up.

'Hello,' she says in a cut-glass English accent. She sounds like the woman on the speaking clock, who tells you what time it'll be on the third stroke. 'Who is calling, please?'

'It's Alex Martin. Mr Prudente-Poulton asked me to ring.'

'Please hold.' The clicking sound kicks in again. For some reason, I picture an old-fashioned switchboard operator unplugging me from one socket and plugging me into another.

'Alexandra, it's Jonathan Prudente-Poulton.' His voice is re-fined and confident. 'Can you confirm you are somewhere private? It's important no one overhears this conversation.'

I peer out of the window. The driveway stands empty. The country lane is equally deserted.

'I'm alone.'

'Thank you. I'm only sorry it has taken so long.'

'You're going to have to tell me who you are.' I perch on the edge of the bed. 'You mentioned my father.'

'I worked with Richard Martin years ago. Since his death, we've been trying to locate the machine he made. The one you're using.'

15

— · —

A tsunami of anxiety hits me. If Prudente-Poulton knows about the finding machine, what else does he know? Hundreds of questions bubble up inside, but my throat's so tight I can barely get anything out.

Licking my lips, I ask, 'When did Dad work for the National Missing Persons Helpline?'

'He didn't.'

Screwing my face, I work my fingers into my furrowed brow. 'Then, how do you know him?'

'Your father was a key member of our organisation back in the '60s and '70s. He led us in directions we could never have imagined. But he kept his invention secret and built it outside of our organisation without our knowledge. We only discovered the plans after his death.'

A sudden tightness clamps my temples. 'But if you're Director of Operations for the NMPH, why would my dad be working for you?'

'You seem confused, Alex. I am Director, but not of the NMPH.'

'But your card...'

Flashbacks from the day Lin sacked me pop into my mind: the receptionist handing me an envelope. The card inside was missing the charity logo, yet I assumed Prudente-Poulton worked there. Was it my mistake or his misdirection?

'If you don't work for the NMPH, who *do* you work for?'

'I work for the Turing-Tesla League.'

Goosebumps rise on my forearms. 'I know that name,' I whisper, my heart thumping in my ears. 'I've seen it on the dark web.'

Last year, Jason Bevin got a hit while he was searching online for information. A picture of Dad's machine came up with the name of the Turing-Tesla League, but nothing else.

'Information occasionally leaks out, although we do what we can to prevent it,' Prudente-Poulton says. 'I don't need to tell you every government in the world would like to get their hands on your father's machine. We know you're using it, and it's only a matter of time before others do too.'

'How on earth did you find me?'

'We knew Richard had a daughter, so you weren't difficult to track down. When you started miraculously finding people...well, it didn't take a genius to put two and two together. Now we've found you, it's imperative that we upgrade your machine and make a copy.'

My mind spins as I try to come up with a way to get him off my case. 'But if you have Dad's plans, why do you need mine?'

'We need the original. There are certain peculiarities in the plans that have us going around in circles.'

I shake my head. 'I don't understand.'

'The components in your machine date back to the 1970s. They were never designed to last this long. After all these years, I would be very surprised if it wasn't starting to fail. Capacitor deterioration, LED failure, circuit board corrosion. That sort of thing.'

Could the temperamental on/off switch be a sign the machine is failing? When I think of all the knocks and bumps the machine has suffered along the way, it's a miracle it still works.

'But those are trifles compared to the real problem,' Prudente-Poulton continues. 'I'm afraid we're facing a time-critical situation, Alex. The finding machine contains an internal real-time clock that's destined to fail at the end of the year. The GPS system requires precision timekeeping, and the clock in your machine won't survive the Millennium turnover. The error may send the machine into a death spiral from which it cannot escape. Bring it in now, and we'll upgrade the failing components to future-proof it. We'll make a copy, or clone, of your machine, and you will get your original machine back. It's a plan that should work for everyone.'

'How do I know you'll let me have it back?' I ask, twiddling a strand of hair.

'You're Richard's daughter. Richard was an honourable man. We are an honourable organisation. We have no wish to take the machine from you, Alex. Our goal is to simply to make a clone.'

'Maybe. But you'll have to take it apart.' I picture the strange, cold gas escaping. 'What if it doesn't work again?'

'Believe me, we share your concerns,' Prudente-Poulton says. 'But we have a wealth of expertise. Just say the word, and we'll send someone to pick it up. You choose the handover point.'

Silence falls between us as I run over my options. When I made the call, I didn't think the Turing-Tesla League would want me to hand over Dad's machine straightaway.

'I'd like to, but I can't. I'm using the machine as part of a police enquiry.'

'We know.' Prudente-Poulton sounds nonchalant about something he has no business knowing. 'There will always be people to find, Alex, thousands of worthy causes. But please look at the bigger picture. We have a short timeframe to address the issues I mentioned. You wouldn't want your father's work to be lost, would you?'

'No, but—'

'You're going to ask for time to think about it. I understand. All I ask is, don't take too long. The Millennium's less than ten days away.'

· · · ● · ● · · · ·

My conversation with Prudente-Poulton heralds a pounding headache. I drop the phone on the dresser, get into bed and pull the covers over my head. Cocooned under the blankets, I squeeze my eyes shut and try to push all thoughts of the Turing-Tesla League, Y2K death spirals, and blue twine-wrapped bundles out of my mind. Eventually, I drift to sleep.

A high-pitched shriek jolts me awake. At first, I think there's been a terrible accident. Then, Charlie shouts, '*Wheels on the Bus!*' followed by rapid footsteps pounding along the hall.

The floral curtains frame a darkening sky. I check my watch. Ten past four.

Dry-mouthed, I force myself up and drag a paddle brush through my damp hair in front of the dresser mirror. Prudente-Poulton's voice repeats in my head, asking for the machine. I force it aside and pad downstairs. I find Marcus in the kitchen, adding browned cubes of beef to a cast-iron casserole, the contents of which are bubbling away on the range cooker.

'Feeling better?' Marcus asks.

'Much better, thanks. Have you heard from Henry?'

'Afraid not.' Meat sizzles as he gives the pan a shake. 'I'm making extra, in case he turns up.'

Marcus makes me a cup of tea, pouring boiling water from an old-fashioned kettle that whistles when it boils.

'Can I give you a hand? Shall I lay the table?'

'Tell you what.' Marcus glances at the door. 'Why don't you go and say hello to Charlie?'

I follow the happy refrain of *Do you Know the Muffin Man?* into the lounge, tea in hand. Fairy lights twinkle on the Christmas tree. A fire blazes within a sandstone hearth, surrounded by a cast-iron fireguard. Ludo lies between the fire and Charlie, gnawing a hide bone.

Charlie sprawls on the rug by a colossal Lego creation while the video plays in the background. The video cover next to the VHS player shows a red bus with the driver waving from the window. On TV, a cartoon baker wearing a tall white hat carries a tray of muffins down Drury Lane.

It's all rather cozy and charming.

'Hello, Charlie.' I sink to my knees on the rug. 'Soooo...I love your space station.'

'It's not a space station. It's a starbase.' Charlie corrects me without looking up. He builds long shapes from red Lego pieces and fixes them onto the green baseplate. 'These are laser turrets.'

'Could I make one?' I ask, riffling through a sea of plastic pieces.

Charlie twizzles two different-shaped turrets before my eyes. 'They have to be like this. And this, 'kay?'

I've never worked for a three-year-old before, but I decide the best course of action is to follow his design and make an exact replica of the smaller turret. I can't find a red sloping piece for the top, so substitute a brown one.

'Here you go.' I hand it over for inspection.

Charlie plucks my creation from my hands and frowns at the brown piece. 'It's wrong!'

'I'm sorry. I couldn't find a red o—'

He snaps my work in half and throws it on the pile of spare pieces, his inner structural engineer clearly offended.

'Shall I build another one?' I offer, with more generosity than I feel.

'No!' Charlie glowers. 'Uncle 'enry do it. He's better than you!'

I look across the hall to the kitchen door, but Marcus is nowhere to be seen. Charlie refuses to engage with me further, so I retreat to the far corner of the sofa and flick disinterestedly through one of Olivia's magazines - *Law Today* - while animated characters sing about spiders in the bath and rowing boats downstream.

By the time the video's end credits roll, my headache has returned. Children aren't how I imagined. It's supposed to be different when they're yours, but I can't see how managing a determined toddler is easier just because you share DNA.

Massaging my temples, I grab the VCR remote, press stop, and flick through the TV channels for something Charlie can watch that doesn't involve singing.

'Watch Wheels on the Bus again!' Charlie points at the TV. 'Press weewine!'

No way am I pressing *weewine*. Leaning forwards, I say, 'Let's find something else.'

'Not something else. Wheels on the Bus!'

Ludo raises his head from his bone and gives me a soulful stare. Charlie's mouth turns down.

'WEEWINE!'

'Just a sec!' I click past a quiz show, a cookery programme and a repeat of *Minder*.

Charlie wipes his face on his sleeve before curling into a weeping ball. His whimpers grow louder, and Ludo joins in. I flip through channels until I land on Postman Pat - a positively high-brow experience after *Wheels on the Bus*. 'Here we are! You'll like this one.'

'NO POSTMAN PAT!' Charlie rolls back and forth on the mat, perilously close to knocking his Lego starbase over.

'What's all this, then?' Marcus enters the room with a teacloth in his hand. He looks at the TV. 'Postman Pat? Aren't you watching Wheels on the Bus?'

'She turned it off!' Charlie stabs his finger at me. The sight of Dad pushes him into DEFCON 1. He throws his head violently from side to side, followed by howls of misery.

Heat rushes to my cheeks. I clear my throat awkwardly. 'I thought...he might like to watch something else.'

'I used to think that, too.' Marcus gives me a knowing look. He crouches by Charlie. 'Let's rewind the tape, shall we?'

Charlie immediately stops crying.

Marcus tips his head back to the kitchen. 'Henry's on the phone for you.'

I need no further prompting to flee the room, closing my ears to the sound of Charlie's sniffles.

Scooping up the phone, I say, 'Hi, it's me.'

'You sound better.'

'I am!' I gush down the line, overjoyed to be speaking to a rational human. 'You?'

'All good. I managed to grab a shower at the station and change into dry clothes. I'm with Simon and Tori, raking through old files for more information on Reginald Goddall. My boss won't give me more officers until forensics have confirmed the tarpaulin's contents belong to Nenagh. There's a lot to do here. I'm afraid I won't see you tonight.'

'Oh, okay.' I play with the phone cord, biting back disappointment. I cast a wary glance to the lounge as singing starts up again. 'Did you find anything out about the bundle?'

'It's early days, Alex. The dive team did a sweep of the river, and retrieved the rock and twine. The bundle has gone to the forensic pathologist, but it could take weeks to get results. The lab has to confirm the remains are human before they can try and extract viable DNA. Even if they're successful, establishing cause of death is going to be difficult with so little to go on.' He pauses. 'I had a word with forensics, and there's something we can do that should help. We'll try it tomorrow.'

Henry pauses and I hear voices in the background. 'I have to go. We'll speak more tomorrow when I pick you up. Nine o'clock good for you?'

The Wheels on the Bus starts up again across the hall. 'Come as early as you like.'

16

The next morning, I wait for Henry on the drive, my face tilted up to catch a rare burst of sunshine. Although it's still cold, the sunny weather's one of the reasons my mood has improved. The other's down to the fact I'm back in Charlie's good books.

I don't know why I got so upset over his tantrum yesterday. He's only a child. Half an hour after Charlie's meltdown, an idea came to me. I nipped upstairs to get my pencil case and sketchpad and drew cartoon characters with him until it was time for dinner. My strategy worked a treat. After his bath, he begged me to read him his favourite Meg and Mog book, and gave me a kiss goodnight.

Another reason for my good mood is the man pulling into the drive in a tatty Astra. When I'm with Henry, I feel useful. I don't have to time what I say to suit his mood. He's always available to listen to me. He never loses his cool under pressure, is always good company, and the fact he's easy on the eye is an added bonus.

I flash him a grin, put my rucksack in the footwell and climb into the passenger seat. The cabin smells fresh from his spritzy cologne. Henry hasn't found time to shave - blond stubble covers his jawline, giving him a rugged look. He's wearing a pale blue shirt with the top two buttons undone, navy chinos and black Chelsea boots. Antony has a pair just like them.

As my eyes meet Henry's, hot and cold prickles run along my skin. I'd have to be emotionally blind to ignore the attraction between us. But I can easily resist and I'm sure Henry feels the same.

'Good morning!'

'Morning. You look well.' Henry returns my smile. 'No lasting ill-effects from your dip in the river?'

'No, I'm good!' I lower the visor to block the low morning sun as Henry pulls onto the road.

'Are we going to need galoshes and snorkels today?' Henry asks with a little laugh. 'I've packed a coffee thermos, blankets and sandwiches, just in case.'

'Sandwiches?' My heart does a little jump as I imagine Henry and myself picnicking in the countryside.

'It's going to be a busy day, and we might have to eat on the run,' Henry says, dashing my daydream.

'I see.' If Henry's sticking to business, so should I. 'Did you have any luck tracking down Nenagh's husband?'

'Not yet. We worked until midnight. The problem is, after 1956 Reginald doesn't exist - on paper at least.' Henry takes the A119 out of Hertford, heading into the countryside. 'We're going to interview Nenagh's sister, Avril. She lives in Much Hadham. Ever been there?'

'Once, for a village fête.'

'I want you to sit in on the interview. Get a handle on Nenagh's story.'

'Can I ask questions?'

'Sure. You're part of the team. Still have your ID?'

I rummage in the pocket of my rucksack for my lanyard, and hold it up.

'Good.'

We travel in convivial silence as we pass familiar landmarks: Van Hages garden centre, Ware train station. I have fond memories of hopping onboard the 07:45 to London last year. That was the day Antony and I had our first kiss.

Henry's breezy positivity reminds me of how Antony *used* to be. A twinge of longing hits me. Antony's over one hundred miles away and we still haven't caught up properly. I want to tell him about my mind-blowing conversation with Prudente-Poulton, but when I tried to call last night he didn't pick up, and I'm not sure my attempt to fit the day's events into a 160-character text message was entirely successful:

```
Hi, spok 2 JPP he sez mk copy of FM. I
say no coz it myt not wrk. JPP wkd with
Dad in scrt socty. Dnt no 2 trst him. PS
fell in rvr. xxx
```

After sending the text, I was overcome with a sudden urge to rush back to Birmingham. Then I pictured the messy flat and the long, empty hours stretching throughout the day, and the feeling evaporated.

For the moment, this is where I need to be.

Henry drives up Widbury Hill, past the Green Lane Allotment Society. Sunlight winks through bare branches and gaps in the hedgerows as we follow the looping road through Wareside. I stare out of the window with my mind drifting, until Henry says something to snap me out of it.

'I have some questions about your machine,' Henry says. 'I couldn't get to sleep last night thinking about it. I know we made an agreement, but it's eating me up, Alex.'

'All right, but I'm not promising anything,' I say, bracing myself. Henry's bending the rules. I'll have to watch every word I say.

'Do you type the person's name in?'

'No.'

'Are you messing around with the space time continuum or parallel universes?'

'No!' I laugh.

'Do you say their name in a witchy voice?'

I let out a bigger laugh. 'Is that even a real question?'

'Maybe.' Henry glances my way. 'Are you a witch?'

'Yes, I am.' I wink. 'A very powerful one.'

Distract and divert. That's my strategy. I must keep Henry away from the truth, especially now the Turing-Tesla League is sniffing after me.

But Henry's just getting started. 'If a person's dead, how much of them needs to remain for your machine to find them?'

I shrug. 'We need to get the results back on Nenagh to know for sure.'

Henry keeps his eyes on the road. 'What about someone who's buried at sea?'

'I've never found anyone buried at sea.'

'Okay, here's another scenario. Someone buried so long ago there's nothing left of them.'

'That's a tricky one.' I put my finger to my chin, as if giving his question serious consideration.

'What about two bodies buried together?'

'God, this is grim. Are you going to be like this all day?'

'I'm a detective. It's my job.'

We drive by the Chequers Inn with a chalkboard sign: *Game Pie of the Day*. I'd much rather discuss lunch than the finding machine.

'What about someone who's been cremated? What if their ashes are scattered? Could you find them?'

I decide to be nice and give him something. 'Everything I've found so far has been in one place and one piece. How would you test ashes, anyway?'

'Aunt Gladys's urn is in the boot. We could try your machine out on her.'

'You're joking.' I whip my head round, mouth falling open. 'Tell me you're joking.'

Henry taps the steering wheel. 'That was *too* easy.'

'You're just like Antony!' I splutter. 'He's always winding me up.'

An awkward silence follows. This space in the car, in Hertfordshire, is for me and Henry. I shouldn't have brought Antony into it.

Henry manoeuvres the Astra around bends in the road. 'I did have another reason for asking.'

'Go on.' I settle back into my seat, latching onto the chance to rekindle the mood.

'And before you ask, this isn't another wind up. A very distant relative, my great-great-and probably-great again uncle was a cavalry officer during World War I. He was on horseback when a German shell fell and blew him and his horse to smithereens.'

'That's awful!' I frown.

'The story goes, they were buried together as no-one could tell man from beast.' Henry glances my way. 'For some reason, I've always struggled with that.'

I put my hand over my mouth to hide a smile. 'Wouldn't the hooves have been a bit of a giveaway?'

'And the lovely long tail.'

I dissolve into fits of laughter. Hot tears run down my cheeks. It's been forever since I laughed like that; it's the tonic I need.

Henry stops laughing and takes a steadying breath. 'Seriously, though, what would your machine make of it?'

Blotting my eyes on a tissue, I say, 'I have found people buried together.' Back when I was learning how the finding machine worked, I tested it on Dad and his parents, who lie in the Martin family plot. 'Their GPS locations come up as similar, but not identical.'

'But that's not a mix-up of bits and pieces.'

I shrug and brace myself for more questions, as Henry turns left down a residential close. Thankfully, we've arrived at Avril's house.

Henry puts on the handbrake in front of a chalet-style house with a steeply sloping roof. A shiny red Renault Clio sits on the drive. The front garden is neatly tended, with roses already pruned back for spring, and shaped evergreen shrubs.

'You'd better leave your rucksack.' Henry's warm smile disappears, replaced by his game face. With his professional persona in place, he gets out of the car and retrieves a slim briefcase from the boot.

'Okay, you ready?'

17

— ◆ —

Henry rings the doorbell. I stand a few paces back on the path in full sun, soaking up the winter warmth.

The woman who opens the door is slim, in her mid-sixties. She's dressed in a pink tracksuit with matching peep-toe slippers. Gold bangles jangle on her wrists. Despite the early hour, she's wearing a full face of makeup. Tiny blobs of mascara clump her eyelashes together, and lipstick bleeds into wrinkles around her lips. I guess her eyesight isn't as good as it once was.

Henry holds up his warrant card. 'Avril Grayson? I'm DC Henry Longhurst and this is Alex Martin, my assistant.'

'What's this about?' she says in a raspy voice.

'It's best if we have a chat inside. May we come in?'

'All right.' Avril's mouth forms a circle as she steps back to let us through. Stale cigarette smoke hangs in the hallway, mingling with patchouli oil rising from a large bowl of potpourri on the telephone table. I try not to breathe too deeply.

Plush pink carpet runs down the hall and through to the lounge. Avril goes through a door on the right into the lounge. Glazed partition doors, currently pulled back, lead into the dining room. A cream sofa and chairs face each other across an ornate glass coffee table with gold swirls running down the legs. Gold and pink striped curtains with tasselled tie-backs frame the window overlooking the front garden.

'Would you like tea?' Avril asks.

'Yes, please,' Henry says.

Once Avril has popped across the hall to the kitchen, Henry examines three photos sitting on the mantelpiece. One, in seventies technicolour, shows Avril on a snowy mountain, wearing plum-coloured ski gear with a pair of polarised goggles perched high on her forehead.

I examine a photo of Avril in her thirties or early forties. She's showing off her deep tan, posing in a navy and white striped swimsuit on the prow of a yacht. A middle-aged man with a paunch - wearing glasses with flipped-up, tinted visors - has his arm around her.

Henry nudges my arm and points to the last picture. I recognise the slender woman, her summer dress blowing in the breeze. Nenagh has Avril's eyes and upturned nose. She's laughing, one hand brushing her hair back from her eyes. On her finger is a large sapphire ring with a gold band. It's impossible to equate this smiling, young woman with the waterlogged bundle we found in the river.

Henry beckons me closer and runs his finger down the right side of the picture. The edge is torn. A sliver of grey intrudes across the rough edges. It could be an arm.

I look round the room for more photos, without luck.

'Here we go.' Crockery rattles as Avril enters the lounge with a tray laden with a tea service and a wooden biscuit barrel. Henry and I return to the sofa. She sets the tray on the coffee table beside a glass ashtray and a packet of Marlboro Lights.

Avril pours tea for Henry and me, then pops the lid off the barrel. 'Lincoln biscuit?'

I take a round, nobbly biscuit. Henry takes two.

'Mum used to say they were circles of cobbled road,' says Avril with a smile. 'I still think of her whenever I have one.' She pours tea for herself, 'So, what's this about?'

Henry waits until Avril has finished pouring. He leans forward, placing his hands on his knees. 'There's no easy way to say this. We found a suspicious bundle in the river near Hertford yesterday, and have reason to believe it may contain human remains. We think it could be your sister.'

Tea splatters onto Avril's saucer. She puts down her cup and clasps her hands together.

'In the river?' Her hands tremble. 'She's turned up after all these years?'

'We believe the recent floods dislodged her from her resting place upstream.'

Furrows deepen on Avril's brow as she stares into her cup. Her head shakes with tiny movements she doesn't appear aware of.

'Are you okay?' I ask, leaning across the table.

Avril presses her fingers into her forehead. 'I just can't believe it. It's been so long.'

Henry waits for her to take a sip of tea, then says, 'We haven't confirmed it is Nenagh. But you can help us with that.'

Avril looks up with a start. 'How?'

'We'd like to take a sample of your DNA.'

Avril straightens on the sofa and nods. 'I'll do anything for Nenagh. But if you need a blood sample, I'll have to lie down because of my blood sugars.'

'There's no need for that,' Henry says. 'I just need to swab the inside of your cheek. The lab will analyse the sample for familial DNA. If yours matches Nenagh's, we'll know it's her. Is that okay?'

Avril nods.

I watch with interest as Henry clicks open his briefcase and retrieves a printed form, a plastic bag and a pair of disposable gloves. He uncaps a pen and fills in boxes on the document before sliding it across the coffee table. 'Please sign and date at the bottom to give your consent.'

Avril leans forward and scribbles her name in the box.

Henry pulls on the gloves, and removes a test tube from the plastic bag. He unscrews the lid of the tube and extracts a small wand with a pad. 'Open your mouth, please.'

Avril obliges, revealing several gold crowns. Henry sweeps the wand inside her cheek. He inserts the swab into the tube and screws the lid tight. After writing Avril's name and date on the sample, he slips it into the clear plastic bag, which goes into a brown envelope. He puts the envelope in his briefcase before removing the gloves.

Avril's blue-rimmed eyes are watery. She reaches for a cigarette with shaky hands and lights up. I retreat to the corner of the sofa as smoke streams from her nostrils. 'Marlon said we should move on. But I couldn't.'

I point to the mantel, and the photo of the overweight man on the yacht. 'This is Marlon, your husband?'

Avril nods. 'We were together over forty years. We loved travelling, until his heart started playing up.' She blinks rapidly and her voice catches. 'Christmas isn't the same without him.'

Looking around the room, I notice there's no tree or decorations.

I go to the mantelpiece, bring Nenagh's photo back to Avril, and point at the ragged, grey sliver running down the photo's edge. 'Is this Reginald, standing beside Nenagh?'

Avril's nose wrinkles as though she's smelled something foul. She taps the glass with a red fingernail. 'I put Nenagh in the frame with him folded over, but I couldn't bear it, so I tore him up and put him in the fire.'

'Do you have another photograph of Reginald?' I ask.

'No, not one.'

I sink back onto the sofa, disappointment seeping through me.

'So, have you arrested him?' Avril asks. 'Reginald?'

'Not yet. We don't know where he is,' Henry says. 'Can you tell us anything about him?'

'He was a slimy toe-rag,' Avril says, lighting another cigarette. 'I never trusted him from the moment I met him. Everyone said he looked like Errol Flynn and just as charming. But it was all on the surface. He could turn it on when he wanted to. That's what made him a good car salesman. He'd come up with a clever line, but if you pushed him on it he'd change the subject. I reckon it was because he'd run out of things to say.

'My father couldn't see through him. Reg bought Dad cigars and cracked open the port. He tried to charm me, too. The first time we met, he kissed my hand and told me I was beautiful.' Avril pushes herself back on the sofa. 'I wanted to wash my hands.'

The cigarette end glows orange as she takes a drag. 'When he didn't think anyone was looking, he'd stare at Nenagh with this horrible dark look. He was always checking up on her. Once, she caught him going through the laundry bin. He said he'd lost a cufflink, but she thought he was checking what clothes she'd been wearing when he was at work. If he rang home and she didn't answer, he'd interrogate her later.

'Anything else you remember about his behaviour?' Henry asks.

'Reginald controlled the finances. He opened all the post, even letters addressed to her.' Avril shrugs. 'Nenagh never seemed happy after her wedding day. She wanted kids, but Reginald always changed the subject whenever she mentioned it. Then, less than a year later, she disappeared.'

Avril drags on the remainder of her cigarette. 'The police could never pin anything on him. He got away with it. Every time I looked at his photo, I could see him laughing at me.' She glances at the photo and shakes her head. 'Look at her, beautiful in her summer dress. He's like the devil at her shoulder.'

Henry flips the page on his notepad and asks, 'In your opinion, why do you think Reginald wanted Nenagh out of the way?'

'For the house.' Avril's eyebrows arch. 'My father gave the couple the house as a wedding present. Somehow, Reginald talked him round so only his name was on the deeds. I told Nenagh to stand up for herself. She should have her name on the deeds. But she said it made no difference. Marriage was for life.'

It's hard to imagine such greed. If Reginald is to blame, he must have a hole where his soul should be.

Avril stubs out her cigarette, grinding the filter into the ashtray. 'She was so naive.'

'Anything else you think might be relevant?' Henry prompts.

Avril nods. 'Look how quickly he put the house up for sale. It was only eight months after Nenagh went missing. That's not what a normal family does when they love someone. They wait it out and hope they come back.'

Avril drains her tea, then shuffles to the drinks cabinet and pours herself two fingers of Grant's Whisky.

'Anyone else want a nip?' she asks.

'Sorry.' Henry shakes his head. 'We're on duty.'

I shake my head too, although I could do with some whisky after hearing Avril's revelations.

Avril raises a glass to her sister, the golden liquid swaying in the glass. 'We're going to get him now, Nenagh. Don't you worry.' She knocks the whisky back in one.

Henry asks, 'Did you see Reginald after Nenagh went missing? Do you know where he went?'

'We weren't on speaking terms. The last I saw of him was when the *For Sale* sign went up. He was mowing stripes on the lawn like nothing had happened. I gave him a right piece of my mind. I'll never forget what he said. *She's dead, Avril. She's gone. You know it and I know it. I can't stay, I have to let her go.* It was such an act, he should have been on EastEnders!'

Avril pours herself another drink. 'Nenagh's disappearance broke my father's heart. It was the death of him. Reginald was to blame for Dad's death and my sister's. Write that down.'

'I have,' Henry assures her, closing his notepad and slipping it inside his jacket.

Avril picks up Nenagh's photo and blinks away tears. 'Promise me you'll get him?'

I reach for her hand and gently squeeze. 'We'll do our best.'

18

— ◆ —

We say goodbye to Avril in the hallway. Henry gives her his business card. 'If you think of anything else, don't hesitate to give me a ring.'

Avril grips the card in one hand, cigarette in the other. 'When will you know the results about the DNA?'

Henry draws in breath through his teeth. 'I'll try and get the process fast-tracked, but I can't guarantee a quick result. What with Christmas and the New Year, we'll be lucky to hear anything before mid-January.'

'I've waited over forty years,' Avril says wryly. 'A few more weeks won't hurt.'

Avril takes the news much better than me. I had no idea these things took so long. Injustice burns within me. I have to find out if Reginald killed Nenagh before I return to Birmingham. Henry and I are only getting started.

I step from the house into crisp fresh air. Taking deep breaths to drive out the smell of cigarettes, I head towards the Astra.

Henry catches me up. 'You took off suddenly. Is everything OK?'

'It's nothing,' I mumble absently.

Henry's eyes search my face. 'You want to tell me?'

I look down at the band of sunlight falling across my boots. 'I thought we were getting somewhere. But if we have to wait weeks for the results to come back—'

'These things take time, Alex.' Henry places his hand on my shoulder and gives me a gentle squeeze. 'We're making progress.'

'So, this is normal?' I ask, some of my tension releasing.

'The waiting? Yes.' Henry says as he unlocks the car and puts his briefcase in the boot. 'Anyway, this case won't hinge on DNA alone. We need to find our main suspect, and you can help with that.'

'I think I might have seen him.'

'What?' Henry's gaze locks on me. 'Where? When?'

'By the river. I felt someone's eyes on me. When I looked up, I saw a man staring at me, but he walked away before I could get a good look. It sounds crazy, but I think it was Reginald.'

'Interesting. If you're right, he could still be local.' Henry opens the passenger door. 'Don't worry, you're safe with me.'

Relieved, I sink into the passenger seat and run my fingers through my hair. 'My hair smells like an ashtray.'

Henry leans closer and sniffs. 'It's not that bad.'

I crack open my window as Henry drives back along the winding roads to Hertford. The stream of cold air bites my cheeks, but it's infinitely preferable to stale fags.

My stomach grumbles as we pass the Chequers Inn again. I stare at the sign advertising Game Pie. It seems an age since breakfast.

I fish my phone from my pocket and switch it on. A message goes *ping*. It's a text message from Antony:

```
Wots up? Y did U fall in rivr? Hope U
didnt drnk the water. Ecoli, cynyde & toxc
chems r lrking in thr. BTW wot woz Hnry
doing? Watching?
```

It takes ages to type a reply. Each number button represents three or four letters. I have to press each one multiple times to get to the correct character. I'm new at texting and keep going past the letter I want, which makes the process agonisingly slow. Why do people like texting? Calling is so much easier.

Henry takes the bends carefully, but staring at a tiny screen while the car swings from side to side makes my stomach turn somer-

saults. A cold sweat breaks out on my forehead. I force my eyes
from my phone and stare at the horizon until the road straightens.
Once I'm feeling a little less green, I return to my task:

`Dont worry I no drnk watr. H got soked 2.`
`Was team effort`

A minute later, my phone pings again. Antony's a demon at
texting:

`If H put U in dnger, Im coming down 2 ave`
`a wrd. When R U home? Youv done yr bit. We`
`need 2 talk about JPP and FM. Wot you need`
`is collateral. ILY XOXO`

A spark zips up my breastbone. It's been a long time since
Antony told me he loved me. On the flip side, I'm sensing a little hostility towards Henry. It must be Antony's protective side
coming out. Thankfully, he's over a hundred miles away, so I'm
not too worried about him making good on his threat. Besides,
he's too busy with work to settle imagined scores. I press buttons
laboriously:

`B home soon, prob L8 2moro or nxt dy. B4N`
`ILY2! XXX`

The exclamation mark is a nice touch, I think, as I slip the phone
into my pocket and tilt my face towards the open window. The
rushing wind soon settles my stomach.

Henry gives me a curious look. 'All good?'

'Yep. Well, no, not really. It's about my machine.' I rub my
forehead. 'It's old and has technical problems. An organisation has
offered to fix it, but I'm not sure I trust them.'

'Why don't I ask Simon to take a look?' Henry jumps in, clearly
sensing an opportunity to find out more about the lump in my
rucksack. 'He's brilliant with technical stuff.'

'No offence to Simon, but this is above his paygrade. It's extremely specialised. The organisation has the technical know-how
to help. Antony says I need collateral, but I'm not sure what he
means.'

'Collateral just means leverage. It's a bargaining chip, a key piece of information that the organisation you mentioned wouldn't want anyone to know.'

I fall silent, wondering what I could use as collateral, but haven't thought of anything by the time we arrive back at the police station.

As Henry turns into car park, a flash of green catches my eye. Yolanda, wearing a bright lime dress, is chatting with three civilian staff beside a silver Jaguar sports car in a Reserved space near the trees.

Henry parks the Astra. I open my door to the sound of barking from the treeline. I spot the security guard, Bruno, on patrol with Kaiser. The dog sniffs the grass by the perimeter fence as it pulls him along, barking repeatedly.

Henry grabs his briefcase and a black gym bag from the back seat and locks the car. I get my rucksack and follow him.

Yolanda saunters over. 'You missed all the excitement. Bruno nearly caught his man!' She rubs her fingers against her thumb. 'He was *this* close.'

'Isn't that the ACC's car?' Henry takes a closer look at the Jaguar. 'He's not going to be a happy bunny.'

The letters *PI* have been spray-painted on the driver's door. Red paint drips from the sill.

'What does *PI* stand for?' I ask Yolanda. 'Private Investigator?'

'You are a funny girl!' Yolanda chuckles. She puts a chunky arm around my shoulders and steers me around the front of the car to the passenger door.

PIG SCUM

'You see? He was not finished.' Yolanda gives me a squeeze.

'Who's to say it wasn't a girl?' a female staff member says. 'How can you tell when they all dress the same – in joggers and hoodies?'

Yolanda retorts, 'The culprit was six foot tall and walked like a wide boy.' She puts on an angry face and strides forward, dropping her shoulders and moving with a slouchy, loose-swinging gait. Her colleagues reward her impersonation with laughter, and I can't help but join in.

The staff drift back to work, and Henry accompanies Yolanda through the sliding glass doors. I follow them to the reception desk. Henry sets his briefcase on the counter, clicks it open, and hands Yolanda the envelope containing Avril's DNA sample.

'This needs to go to Forensics. It's urgent.'

'Leave it with me.' Yolanda takes the envelope with a nod.

Henry leads the way to the cold case room. As he pushes through the door, from a stack of cardboard files and smiles at me. 'You look tons better!'

'I followed your suggestions, drank lots of brandy and had a hot bath. It worked a treat.'

Simon turns from his computer, his glasses reflecting the screen.

'Greetings.' He stiffly raises his hand. For a split second I think he's going to do the Star Trek Vulcan salute. 'Were your endeavours successful?'

'I think we're making progress,' I say.

Henry adds, 'Reginald is still our prime suspect.'

While he fills Tori and Simon in on the interview, I slip inside the box room and put my rucksack on the desk. Nenagh's file is missing which is troubling, as I need to return her photo. I search the desk drawers but the file's not there.

I return to find Henry clearing a space at one end of the long table. He unzips his bag and unpacks a thermos, a selection of Marks & Spencer sandwiches, a tub of mini muffins and a pack of melon slices.

An appreciative gurgle escapes my stomach as my eyes roam over the feast.

Simon opens the thermos and takes a sniff. He makes a face.

'Ugh. There's nothing worse than bitter, oxidised coffee. I'll make a fresh pot.' Halfway to the kitchenette, he turns and points to the sandwiches. 'Bagsy the All-Day-Breakfast.'

Tori pauses, in the process of tearing open a triangular packet. 'You're not bagsying that sandwich! I'll go halves with you. I'm starving.'

'As long as I'm not left with tuna,' Simon says dolefully, putting a new filter into the coffee maker.

Tori bites into a sausage, egg and bacon sandwich. 'Thanks, boss!'

The four of us sit around the table for our working lunch. I tear open a sachet of sugar and stir it into a mug of freshly percolated coffee.

'Let's start with you guys,' Henry says, eating a sandwich from the packet. 'Any updates?'

Tori nods, brushing crumbs from her mouth. 'Forensics rang about the bundle. Nothing on the contents yet, but they've discovered something interesting about the fabric. It's a vinyl car cover, or tarpaulin. A small square has been cut out and patched with a different fabric.'

'Our guess is an identifying mark went there,' says Simon. 'Possibly a logo or a badge.'

Henry goes to the whiteboard on the back wall and removes the lid from an erasable marker pen. Nenagh's timeline runs along the top of the board, marked with her date of birth, marriage, the day she went missing, and yesterday's discovery in the river. He draws a line from the river timeline and writes, *CAR COVER LOGO?*

'Anything else?'

'A small matter of administration.' Simon raises a cardboard file above his head. 'I went through Nenagh's file yesterday. Her photo is missing.'

'Sorry, sorry!' I raise my hand, an excuse ready. 'The photo's in the box room. I took it out of the file when I was researching Nenagh, and tucked it away in my drawer for safekeeping. I'll get it.'

Before anyone says anything, I dash into the room with my rucksack and rummage inside for Nenagh's photo. I open and close a few drawers loudly, then return to the office and hand the photo to Simon. He slips it inside the file, tutting.

Henry tears apart a muffin and pops half into his mouth. 'How did you get on with your cold case searches? Find any similar cases with Reginald's hallmark?'

Tori waves a dot-matrix printout. 'I looked for unsolved misper cases involving Hertfordshire women from 1956 onwards. The problem is, there are thousands of them. Reginald's records show he never moved out of the area, so we're searching locally.'

Henry and I swap glances. My possible sighting increases the chance he's living nearby.

Tori continues. 'I narrowed my search to Hertfordshire women who went missing in the first two years after marriage *and* whose husbands worked in the automotive industry. There are only a handful of files to go through. Maybe Alex could help me, boss?'

'I'd love to,' I jump in.

'Fine by me.' Henry nods. 'Let's see what shakes loose. Simon, how are you getting on with the sale of Nenagh's house? Did you find the deeds?'

'Yes, and it's not good news,' Simon says. 'Reginald gave the address of a boarding house, which is now a private residence. I couldn't find any houses sold to Reginald Goddall within the following two years either.'

A thought comes to me. 'Reg sold cars for a living. He would have needed a driving licence.'

'Good point,' Henry says. 'But Reginald never renewed his original driving licence when it expired in 1963. He may have stopped driving, but colleagues' statements show he was a workaholic and loved cars. I'm inclined to think he changed his identity.'

I say, 'If Reginald, or whatever he's calling himself these days, is local, a few of his old customers must have run into him.'

'True, but they wouldn't know about Nenagh, or that he was up to no good,' Henry says. 'I like the way you're thinking, though.' He returns his attention to Simon. 'Do you have the background info on Reg?'

Simon retrieves a blue cardboard folder from his desk and flips through the contents to a yellowed birth certificate.

'Did you find a picture of him?' I ask.

'Unfortunately, not.' Simon shakes his head. 'Reginald Conrad Goddall, born 8th February 1934.'

I do the maths. 'So, he'd be sixty-five now?'

Simon nods. 'His mother was Mary Goddall. The father is listed as George Stirling. He was a ship's electrician with the Royal Navy. He came and went depending on when his ship docked at Portsmouth.'

'Reginald took his mother's surname and not his father's,' Henry says, making notes on the whiteboard. 'That's interesting.'

'Mary and George never married,' Simon continues. 'We discovered from social records that George provided limited financial support during Reg's early years, and Mary struggled to make ends meet. She took in piece-work for a garment factory but didn't earn enough to provide for Reginald properly. They rented a single room, and Mary moved from place to place until Reginald turned eight.' Simon pulls out a document. 'A social worker had noted that Reginald was underweight and malnourished. Mary received coupons for orange juice, medicine and food staples, but it wasn't enough.

'There's a record of the social worker asking Reginald about his eighth birthday. George had sent him a parcel containing a toy car and half a crown. Mary took the money and confiscated the present.'

'How horrid!' I exclaim. 'I can understand she needed the money, but why not let him keep the car?'

'Mary might have been so angry at George, she didn't want anything to remind her of him,' Tori suggests.

'But Reginald wouldn't have understood,' I say. 'She must have ruined his birthday.'

Henry asks, 'What about George? What happened to him?'

'His ship was torpedoed in 1944 in the South Pacific. His body was never recovered,' Simon informs him. 'Mary contracted tuberculosis when Reg turned nine and died four months later. Reg was put into a care home in Welwyn Garden City. He was fortunate to be fostered by a wealthy couple and appears to have settled in well until he was eleven. But then, his foster father died in a road collision and, as a result, his foster mother suffered a nervous breakdown.'

'Reg went back into care. Sadly, he was too old to attract a new foster family, and ended up in an institution until fourteen, when he ran away. We don't have any record of him after that until his marriage to Nenagh.'

I sip coffee, thinking there's a lot in there for a psychologist to get their head around.

'Reginald grew up in poverty,' I say. 'That could have made him fixate on money and might explain why he was obsessed with getting Nenagh's house.'

'Maybe his mother's behaviour gave him a distorted view of families and women?' Tori adds, helping herself to a slice of melon.

'Reginald didn't want kids of his own,' I remember. 'He might not have wanted Nenagh to be a mother because of the way his own mum treated him.'

'It must have been hard for Reg, being dumped in a care-home,' Tori says.

'If I may make a point.' Simon raises his hand. 'Lots of children have gone through the care system. Very few turn out to be murderers.' He rustles through his file again. 'Additional point of interest. Mary Goddall is buried at Hertford Cemetery.'

'Reginald stayed local his whole life,' Henry says, brushing crumbs from his hands. 'If he's still alive, there's every chance he's living nearby.'

I catch Henry's eye.

Get me Reginald's photograph. And let's find out.

19

After we've cleared away the empty sandwich packets, Henry leaves the room to update his boss on our progress. Meanwhile, Simon continues his search for any more information on Reginald.

Tori hands me the dot matrix printout. 'Can you hunt down these case files? They're stored in date order.'

'Sure.' I get into my Zen space and go from box to box, pile to pile, hunting down the five cases on the printout. Each folder has a photograph clipped inside the cover. The missing women's smiling faces serve as a powerful reminder of their families' long years of uncertainty and sadness. I pause. My gaze goes to the box room door.

I have the means to locate these women and end their families' years of waiting. But I can't help everyone. Besides, it always gets complicated, and we don't have time for distractions now. I must focus my efforts on Reginald.

My thoughts go to the Turing-Tesla League. If the League makes good on its promise and copies my machine, in theory, it could produce them in their thousands. We could live in a world where no one would go missing for long. The more I think about it, the more Jonathan Prudente-Poulton's offer makes sense. The finding machine shouldn't be in the hands of an amateur like me, but a credible organisation like the police or MI5.

But I can't hand over the machine yet. Not until we find Reginald. Having come this far, the case feels like my responsibility. I deposit the five files in a neat pile on Tori's desk.

'Well done,' Tori says, gesturing to her vacated seat by a computer. 'Can you input data while I go through the files?'

'Typing is one of my fortes,' I say, happy to be useful. Since I no longer have a job, and no one wants to buy my paintings, I'd better keep my hand in.

Tori opens the first folder. It's thin and contains only a few pages. The photo shows a sturdy woman with short, dark hair and a no-nonsense look in her eye. She's neither glamorous nor pretty, and something tells me she's not Reginald's type.

'Can you input this information, Alex? Case number HA26/8419/2-D. Mrs Jane Goddall went missing on 30th March 1963. Married to Alan Goddall.'

I enter the details into the table and ask, 'Did you choose this file because Jane has the same surname as Reginald?'

Tori nods. 'The chances of Alan Goddall and Reginald being the same person are slim, but it has to be worth a look. It's easier to slip into a new ID if you keep your first or last name. Plus, Alan worked in automotive parts sales.' She flicks through the few pages in the file. 'Jane went missing early morning, walking her dog in Broxbourne Woods. A neighbour found the dog in the road trailing its lead and brought it home. Alan informed the police, who undertook a huge search with local volunteers. They found nothing.'

'Strange she wasn't found with so many people searching.'

'When I started this job, I thought that, too, but search teams can miss a body by a few feet, no matter how thoroughly they look.'

'But Jane wasn't far from home. If I went into the deepest, darkest wood and had a lie-down, a dog walker would find me within five minutes.'

Simon looks up from the phone, cupping his hand over the receiver. 'That's statistically improbable.'

Tori shakes her head with a grin. 'Let's take a look at the husband. Alan Goddall worked in sales.' She hands me a photograph of a large man in overalls. He's bald with a boxer's nose and a square jaw. I can't think of any circumstance under which anyone would compare him to Errol Flynn.

'He's thirty-eight in this picture,' Tori says.

Alan looks about fifty.

Tori continues reading. 'Alan never moved from the family house after his wife went missing. We have his complete work record. He's been listed on the electoral roll as Alan Goddall since he turned eighteen. He can't be our Reginald.' She tucks the picture back inside the file. 'Can you type that in the notes?'

'Absolutely,' I say, my fingers flying over the keyboard.

Tori opens the next file. 'Phoebe Bennett, wife of Reginald Bennett, who was an auctioneer at Letchworth car auctions. She went missing in 1980.' She flicks through the contents before saying, 'There were rumours of another man who lived in France. Phoebe was last seen with a suitcase in hand, boarding a train at Hitchin. She and Reginald rented a house and had significant debts. It doesn't match our Reginald's M.O. at all. It's another no, unfortunately.'

I look up from the computer as Henry pushes through the door, mobile phone in hand.

'I've just spoken to the forensic pathologist,' he says, approaching the desk. 'The technicians have had a preliminary look at the contents of the package. There are bone fragments, but they're tiny and badly deteriorated from being underwater for so long. The chance of extracting a complete DNA profile is slim. Pathology can't guarantee they can identify the bones as human, let alone *which* human. They're going to test other samples, but we'll be lucky to hear back before Christmas.'

My thoughts go immediately to Avril and her hopes resting on the results. 'What does this mean for the investigation?'

'The package is still suspicious,' Henry says. 'But our case drops down the priority list. Major Crime are up to their necks in active cases, so we're on our own with limited support. We have to find more evidence. The tarpaulin, maybe, or something new.'

'Or, Reginald.' I prop my elbow on the table and rest my head in my hand.

Henry reads the latest updates on Tori's screen. 'How are you getting on?'

Tori gestures to the third file. 'Case WS88/2113/8-X: Delia Carstairs, wife of Reginald Carstairs, who went missing on 8th October 1988. Reginald and his wife lived near Puckeridge where he worked as a used car salesman. In 1988, Reginald was fifty-six years old.'

I tap numbers into a calculator. 'Our Reginald would have been fifty-four back in 1988. It's close enough.'

'Reginald Carstairs was an active member of his local church at Watton-at-Stone. The vicar wrote him a reference.' Tori shows us a handwritten letter on quality paper and reads: '*Reginald is swift to step in if a bench requires mending or the groundskeeper needs an extra pair of hands. Nothing is too much trouble. An exceptional volunteer.*' A glowing reference, if ever I saw one.'

'He's good with his hands,' Henry says, leaning on the corner of the desk to listen in. 'What happened to his wife, Delia?'

'She disappeared one day.' Tori rustles through a pile of paper before pulling out an old certificate. 'Delia and Reginald had been married less than a year, a happy couple by all accounts. She was a regular church-goer and active in the community. After she went missing, the church community rallied around Reginald. If you read the police statements, no one suspected him.'

'Did Delia and Reginald own their house or rent?' Henry asks.

Tori checks through the notes. 'They owned it.'

'And did Reginald continue living there after Delia went missing?'

'It says here, when police followed up on the case a year later, Reginald had moved. So, I assume he sold up.'

I swap glances with Henry.

Henry calls over to Simon, who is off the phone and going through paperwork.

'Can you make a note to check with The Land Registry about this Reginald Carstairs?' Henry asks. 'We need the date the house was sold.'

'I'll do my best, but it'll take time,' Simon replies. 'HM Land Registry have only just computerised their records from 1995. If you want to ask about older deeds, we'll need to put in a request.'

'Can't we visit the current owner of the property?' I suggest. 'They might have the old title deeds.'

'Yes, we can.' Henry gives me a loaded look. 'This is a lead worth pursuing. The timelines make sense, and so does the geography.'

'Got a photo,' Tori says, holding up a picture of Delia wearing a pink and white chequered dress with a wide cinched-in belt that shows off her curvy figure. A broad-brimmed hat and white gloves accentuate her elegance. She's attractive and stands with poise.

'Any of Reginald?' I ask with eternal optimism.

'Afraid not.'

After I've updated the notes, I catch Henry's eye. 'Do you mind if I take the file into the box room?'

'Take copies of what you need. We have plenty to keep us busy.'

I run the photograph of Delia under the colour copier, along with a few other pages for appearance's sake, before returning the file to Tori. I bring my haul into the box room, lock the door and cover the observation window with my coat.

Grabbing a pair of scissors from the desk-tidy tubes, I cut out Delia's photo. With lots of loving words and silent prayers, I insert her image into the machine and switch it on.

Nothing happens. I flick the switch up and down repeatedly before walking in tiny circles behind the desk, biting my knuckles. I try again with no luck.

The display remains dead.

I bring my hand back and smack the side of the case.

51.853318, -0.109726

'*YES!*' Making a fist, I draw it down as though I'm pulling a chain, then swiftly scribble down the co-ordinates on a Post-it. It's a good thing I do because the display goes blank a second later.

Handing the machine over to the Turing-Tesla League is rapidly becoming the wisest option. I can't keep slapping the machine to get it to work.

The location on the desktop monitor is a green square around an L-shaped building in a churchyard. It's St. Andrew and St. Mary at Watton-at-Stone, the same church where Reginald Carstairs worked. The white finger points to the centre of the graveyard.

I chew the inside of my cheek, considering the facts. Could Delia have returned after her disappearance, died and been buried there years later without the police knowing? It's possible, but unlikely. There would be a death certificate, a tombstone with her name on it, and some kind of paper trail.

I print out the map and mark an X as accurately as possible on the graveyard, before removing the photo and zipping up my rucksack. Then I call Henry in. Once the door closes behind us, I hit him with my news.

He rubs his jaw with a frown. 'Are you sure?'

'As sure as I was with Nenagh. She's in the graveyard. We don't have a death certificate for Delia, do we?'

'I'll ask Simon to check with the General Register Office in Southport to confirm,' Henry assures me. 'This looks good, Alex.'

'Can we visit the churchyard? Do some digging?'

'I hope you mean that figuratively.' Henry rubs his forehead, staring at the X on the map. 'If we don't find a headstone with Delia Carstairs carved into it, it'll turn into one hell of an awkward conversation with the priest.'

'If St. Andrew and St. Mary is Church of England, it'll be the vicar.'

'Him, then,' Henry nods.

'Could be a her,' I add.

'Let's find out.' He pauses with his hand on the doorhandle. 'Grab your stuff.'

20

— · —

Henry and I cross the carpark and walk past a white van emblazoned with the slogan: *'Chips Away!'* The van is parked alongside the vandalised Jaguar. A technician in blue overalls kneels by the Jaguar's driver-side door, dabbing at the red paint with a special solution and soft cloth.

'I hope he can get it off,' I say to Henry.

'These guys are the best,' Henry assures me. 'Yolanda has them on speed dial.'

Once we're in the Astra, Henry slips on a pair of Aviator sunglasses and pulls out of the carpark. The parish of Watton-at-Stone lies five miles north of Hertford. The village is more-or-less on our doorstep, yet I've never heard of it until today. It's entirely possible that Reginald could have lived a new life there under an assumed name without anyone recognising him.

Within a few minutes of leaving town, the houses fall away, replaced by fields separated by drystone walls. The Astra hurtles through a dark corridor formed from the interlacing branches of twisted oak trees. I blink against the afternoon sun as we emerge on the other side.

'Where's this graveyard then?' I say as my mood lifts. 'The dead centre of town?'

'Very good.' Henry's mouth twitches up. 'From what I've heard, everyone's dying to get in.'

Within fifteen minutes, we pass a wooden sign welcoming us to the village, bearing a carving of the old parish church.

White-washed cottages and timber-framed pubs flank the main lane through Watton-at-Stone. We turn into Church Lane, a narrow road bounded on both sides by high hedges. The road steadily rises to the church atop a hill.

A long lay-by on the left serves as the church's car park, with magnificent views over countryside. I grab my rucksack and follow Henry into the grounds of St. Andrew and St. Mary. Redwoods, yews and magnolias dominate the churchyard. The crenelated stone tower has a clock set on each face. St. George's Cross whips in the breeze from the top. The building looks Norman, similar to St. Gregory's Church in Sudbury, where Dad and Lilian are buried.

A neat path leads around the left side of the church to the graveyard. The first and oldest headstones we pass lean at odd angles. More than a century of rain, wind and frost has weathered away the inscriptions, leaving pitted stone patches coated with lichen and strange yellow blobs. Over time, the roots of an enormous redwood have shifted the ledger slabs closest to it, causing one to crack down the middle.

On the far side of the plot lies a green shed with its door open. Outside, a stocky old man wearing denim overalls works on a large petrol lawnmower lying upended on a plastic sheet. From his casual, unhurried manner I'd say he's a volunteer, or someone who's worked here a long time.

'I need to get my bearings,' I say, stopping to look at the map I printed earlier. Turning it this way and that, I orient myself. The red cross marking Delia's location lies farther out from the church. I wind my way between the oldest plots, noting the dates on the headstones. The graves become more modern further out, with machine-cut headstones made from polished granite in various colours. The inscriptions are crisp and easy to read. Some are inset with colour photographs and poems.

Henry saunters behind, examining the graves. Half-way along, his phone trills in his pocket, and he turns his back to answer it.

I duck behind a redwood tree and unzip my rucksack. I have wrapped the finding machine back up in Asda carrier bags to conceal Delia's photo and the machine's display from Henry. I flick the on/off switch repeatedly but nothing happens. Sitting back on my heels, I glare at the machine. Is this game over?

I really don't want to do this, but needs must. I smack the machine, harder than before.

51.853318, -0.109726

The co-ordinates blink out seconds later, but four red LED lights come on, visible through the plastic.

I can work with this! I sling the rucksack over my chest like I did at the river, and make my way over to Henry.

'Anything?' I ask.

Henry shakes his head, stares at his mobile phone. 'That was Simon. There's no record of Delia Carstairs's death.'

'She's here.' I give my rucksack a squeeze. 'I have four lights on the machine.'

Henry's eyes light up. He stays at my shoulder as I circle the redwood, trying to peer into the rucksack. Thankfully, he can't see much except four glowing red dots through plastic.

The fourth light flashes when I step towards the church, but stays red when I move away. I'm in the right row. I take two steps to the south, and arrive at a white gravestone.

Five solid reds.

I test the accuracy of the reading by moving to the graves either side, and the rows in front and behind, but the fifth light starts blinking each time, confirming my first hit was the right one.

'This is the one?' Henry asks.

'Yup.' I crinkle my forehead as I read the gold inscription set into white granite.

DOUGLAS [DUGGIE] HALL
Beloved by all who met him.
Life's a game of cricket. Yet, Death has hit my wicket.
Went out to Bat 1905, Left the Crease 1988

Henry tucks his forefinger and thumb round his chin. 'For some reason, this isn't screaming 'Delia' to me.'

I show him the display. 'The machine doesn't lie.'

Henry rubs the back of his neck. 'My boss will need more than a promise from my psychic to justify digging up Duggie. Are you absolutely sure your machine isn't playing up? You said you were having technical issues.'

'Getting it to start is the problem. But once it's working, it always gives the right location.'

Henry reaches inside his jacket pocket and retrieves a digital camera. The camera beeps as he photographs Douglas's headstone from different angles. Before I can protest, he lowers the camera into my rucksack and snaps the five red lights glowing behind plastic.

'You aren't going to show that to anyone, are you?' I frown, zipping the rucksack shut.

'This one's for me,' Henry says as he pockets his camera. 'If I lose my job over this, I want a souvenir so I remember why.'

'You won't lose your job,' I say, pushing aside a growing sense of creeping doubt. The machine's never let me down before. I have to have faith.

I read the epitaph again: *Left the Crease 1988*.

'What date did Delia Carstairs go missing?'

'8th October, 1988.'

'Same year as Duggie,' I point out. 'I wonder what date he was buried.'

'I was thinking the same thing.' Henry tilts his head towards the church. 'Shall we see if the vicar's in?'

We head towards a wooden, arched door set into the base of the clock tower. Henry turns the iron handle and the oak door creaks open. Inside, the scents of polished wood and incense take me straight back to my childhood, and the Sunday service at St. Gregory's.

A large advent candle stands by the altar with a beautifully-crafted Nativity in front. The stable is over five feet wide, made of wood and filled with straw. Mary and Joseph kneel by Jesus in the crib, with shepherds and wise men watching over them.

'Hello!' Henry calls out. His voice and steps echo as he strides beneath the transverse arches that intersect the nave.

I take a pew near the front and soak up the ambience. To my left is a closed wooden confessional. Reginald Carstairs must have walked past it countless times. I can't help but wonder, if he was to blame for Delia's disappearance, was he ever tempted to unburden his guilt?

Henry returns a few moments later, phone in hand. 'There's no one here. I left a message with the rectory.'

We retrace our steps to the entrance. Henry holds the door open. As I walk outside, the phone rings in his pocket. I stand by the church porch and breathe in crisp air while he answers it.

'That was Marcus,' Henry says, pocketing his phone. 'He has a school reunion tonight. Olivia has to stay late at work and can't babysit Charlie. Could you do it? I'd volunteer, but my hands are full with the case.'

Conflicting thoughts flash through my mind. I can hardly refuse, having enjoyed Marcus and Olivia's incredible hospitality. The problem is, I'm not sure I have the skills to deal with Charlie if he kicks off again.

'Honestly, it's no big deal,' Henry says. 'I heard you had Charlie eating out of your hand when you drew cartoons with him.'

'That was *after* he hulked out because I wouldn't let him watch his favourite video.'

Henry chuckles, shaking his head. 'Charlie's going through a phase. He won't be begging for *Wheels on the Bus* for much longer.'

I put my hand on my hip. 'Are you sure about that? My brother had an old stuffed doggy he took to Uni! Let's hope that video doesn't break.'

'So, you'll do it?'

'Okay.' I nod in resignation. I mean, reading a book to a three-year-old. How hard can it be?

We both turn at the roar of a petrol lawnmower starting up.

Henry looks at the groundskeeper. 'Let's go and have a word.'

21

The groundskeeper fiddles with a lever on the mower and increases the throttle. The green beast lets out a deafening roar. The old man's focus is glued to the mower, and I have to wave my arms like I'm signalling an aircraft coming in for landing before I catch his attention.

Henry flashes his warrant card, and the old man kills the engine. The lawnmower cuts out with a series of half-hearted sputters. Spanners, oilcans and various tools lie on the grass by the shed. Through the open shed door, gardening tools hang on hooks above bags of grass-seed, compost, and stacked plastic plant pots.

'First time I've been pulled over with my lawnmower,' the groundskeeper says, grabbing an oily rag from one of his many pockets. He looks to be in his early seventies with a creased, friendly face topped with wisps of white hair that blow around in the breeze.

He wipes his forehead and then uses the same rag to clean round the petrol cap. 'That's Matilda serviced for winter. Just need to drain the fuel before she goes into hibernation.'

'My uncle had a Suffolk Punch,' Henry remarks, casting an eye over the contents of the shed. 'Temperamental beasts, aren't they?'

The groundskeeper nods. 'Not surprising, consid'rin' her age.' He puts out his hand. 'I'm Bill.'

Henry shakes his hand, saying, 'DC Henry Longhurst, and this is my assistant, Alex Martin.'

Bill shakes my hand, leaving grease on my palm. 'So, what's this about?'

'We're making enquiries into a woman who went missing back in the '80s. Were you working as a groundskeeper back then?'

'Oh, I've been here nigh on forty years.' Bill's white brows rise. 'You lose count at my age. The vicars come and go, but old Bill's always here. I'm part of the furniture.'

'You must have known a few people buried here,' Henry says.

Bill nods. 'I make it my business to chat to 'em whenever I mow my way past. I tell 'em all the goings-on. Some of the guests don't get many visits now. But I'm always here for them.'

'Are you a member of the parish?' I ask.

'Not strictly,' Bill replies. 'But it's me who looks after parishioners when it's their time. Me and John, who works part-time.'

'I don't suppose you remember Douglas Hall?' Henry asks.

'Ah, Duggie.' Bill's face lights up. 'Local legend, he was. Helped win the Hertfordshire League twice. A gentleman, too.'

'Sounds like you knew him well,' Henry says. 'Can you show me his final resting place?'

'It's this way.' Bill walks us to the grave.

Henry asks, 'Did you prepare this plot?'

Bill nods. 'Duggie's was a tough one. Lots of roots. It's not enough to dig a hole. It has to be square and tidy.' Bill nods to the nearby redwood. 'I'd have this beast cut down but the green brigade won't hear of it. In fifty years, half of these graves will be six feet up instead of six feet under.'

'Did you dig Duggie's grave alone?' Henry asks.

Bill shakes his head. 'You need more than one man to do it quick enough. Two at least. Course, nowadays they use mechanical diggers but we can't get one of those up here.'

'Who helped you dig?' Henry asks casually.

'That'd be John. Never says much but a real grafter.' He pauses, mouth forming a circle. 'Oh, there was Reggie, too. He was often here, helping out around the church. Said it made him feel closer to God. He lent a hand the day before a funeral.'

At the sound of Reginald's name, my mouth goes dry.

'What was Reggie's surname?' Henry asks.

'Now that, I can't remember.'

Henry stares at Douglas's grave, giving nothing away. 'Did you dig this grave on the day of the funeral?'

Bill shakes his head, looking slightly bemused. 'We dig them all the day before, cover them up with boards and a tarp, and weight the lot down with stones until morning to keep the water out. We can't leave it until the day of the funeral. There's no time.'

'So, the grave is left unattended overnight?'

'Suppose,' Bill says.

'And it's definitely Douglas in there?' I can't help blurting out.

Bill chuckles. 'I'd say so, considering it was an open casket for the service. Duggie was dressed in his whites, holding his cricket bat signed by the team.' He gives me a curious look. 'Why do you ask?'

Henry says, 'We're trying to track Reginald down. What do you remember about him?'

Bill puffs his cheeks out. 'Reggie? Lovely man. He dressed proper and was...how do you say...cultured. He must have been a lady-killer in his time. His day job was somewhere in Stevenage, I think. He sold prestige motors, top badges like Mercedes-Benz and the like. And he had a lovely wife. Now, what was her name?'

'Delia,' Henry says.

'Yes, lovely Delia. She went missing.' A look of consternation crosses his face.

'We're just getting some background information, Bill,' I say with a smile. 'Do you remember when Delia disappeared?'

'Sorry.' Bill shakes his head.

'Anything else you remember about her disappearance?'

'Only how terrible it was. Reggie put on a brave face, I'll tell you that. The police did what they could but she was never found. Then he moved away.' Bill tucks his oily rag into his pocket. 'You can understand why, can't you? Everyone kept asking how he was all the time. Giving him sympathy. He wanted none of it. Just wanted to move on.'

'Do you know where he moved to?' I ask.

Bill shakes his head. 'Reggie was angry at the man upstairs. With all the work he'd done for the parish, he couldn't understand why God would punish him by taking Delia away. He just left one day. Never even said goodbye.'

'Thank you for the information,' Henry says, handing Bill his card. 'If you remember anything else about Reggie, give me a call.'

'Will do.' Bill returns his attention to the mower.

Henry and I head back to the car, walking under giant redwoods to rejoin the main path.

'It sounds like Reginald, doesn't it?' I say, practically skipping with excitement.

Henry nods. 'He certainly had the opportunity to hide Delia at the bottom of Duggie's grave the day before the funeral.'

'That's so awful.' I shake my head.

'*If* that's what happened.'

'But it is!'

'We have to prove it.' Henry raises a brow. 'Reginald's old house isn't far away.' He refers to his notebook for the address. 'Let's pay it a visit.'

Once we're back in the Astra, Henry reaches into the door pocket for an AA Big Map and checks the route before we set off. We pass back through Ware and Wodson Park Leisure Centre, heading through the villages of Thundridge and Wadesmill. It's barely three o'clock, yet the sun's already a burning orange glow brushing the treeline.

Puckeridge High Street could be a film set for a Jane Austen adaptation. Handsome brick buildings with sash windows sit next to cottages bearing brightly-coloured renders. Wooden beams, rickety tiled roofs and black iron railings add to the charm. The refurbished Victorian streetlights come on as we drive through a deepening half-light. In the distance, the tops of the trees are starting to blend with the darkening sky.

Reginald and Delia's old house has no number. Instead, a slate sign hangs by the front door - *School Cottage*. The whitewashed house has a large chimney, black-painted windowsills and a blue wooden door that is slightly ajar. The modern UPVC windows look ugly against the cottage's original features. Outside, an estate agent's sign lies in the grass.

The narrow, concrete drive is blocked by a builder's van and a yellow skip full of plasterboard, old kitchen units and piping. Banging hammers, drilling, and loud music drift from an open upstairs window.

Henry knocks on the door and rings the bell. He flicks the letterbox, calling, 'Hello!' until a builder appears in the doorway, covered from head to foot in plaster dust. He pushes his safety goggles onto his forehead, revealing rings around his eyes in the dust. In one hand, he carries a drill with a long spiral bit.

'I'm looking for the house owner,' Henry says, showing his ID.

'She's at work,' the builder says.

'When will she be back?'

'Dunno. She's never here when we clock off at five.'

'Will she be here tomorrow?' I ask, remembering it's Friday today.

'Dunno. All I know is we won't be here. We don't work weekends.'

'That's very helpful, thanks,' Henry says, without an ounce of sarcasm. 'In that case, I'll need the homeowner's phone number.'

After a prolonged shouting exchange up the stairs, Henry gets the number. Seconds after, the ear-piercing shriek of the drill starts up.

Away from the deafening racket, Henry examines the scrawled name and number.

'The owner is Sharmilla Mehrotra. I'll give her a ring, see if we can pay her a visit first thing tomorrow.'

I'm supposed to be returning to Birmingham tomorrow, and while I'm looking forward to seeing Antony again, my anticipation is spoiled by all the work left undone here. I feel pulled in both directions.

Deep in my bones, I sense a breakthrough coming, and I can't bear the thought of being a hundred miles away when it lands.

'Can I come?' I ask. 'I can get a later train.'

'Of course, you can come.' Henry takes my hand - so naturally - it takes a moment to hit me. Work colleagues don't hold hands.

Henry gives my fingers a gentle squeeze before letting go.

I tuck my hands in my pockets, telling myself it was nothing.

'What time will you pick me up?' I keep my tone casual.

'Nine,' Henry says, unlocking the car. 'You can tell me all about your quiet night in with Charlie.'

22

Marcus stands in the lounge doorway, checking his jacket pockets. 'Thanks for doing this, Alex.'

'No problem,' I say breezily from the leather sofa. 'How long has it been since you've seen your schoolmates?'

'Twenty years. It'll be interesting to see how life has treated them. We're at the Bull's Head just down the road in Turnford.' He hands me a scrap of paper with his mobile number. 'Call me if you need anything. I should be back sometime after ten. Olivia's working late. I don't know what time she'll be home.'

I put the slip of paper on the coffee table. 'When should I check on Charlie?'

'Give it an hour or so. He's in bed. You shouldn't hear a peep out of him.'

'And Ludo?' The golden retriever pushes through the lounge door and looks up at Marcus with his tail slowly wagging, a squeaky hamburger in his mouth.

Marcus reaches down to ruffle his fur. 'He's had his walk. If he needs to go out, you'll hear him whining by the back door.'

Ludo looks up at his master with adoration in his large, brown eyes.

I smile. 'I'll see you later, then.'

Marcus gives me a wave before leaving the house. Moments later, I hear tyres crunching on gravel. Apart from the crack of flames in the fireplace, the house is silent. The massive Lego starbase looks out of place in front of the elegant Christmas tree and oak furniture.

I turn on the TV. My finger pauses over the remote. A reporter stands in a shopping mall that looks vaguely familiar. When the camera pans round, I recognise the steep bank of escalators at The Pallasades in Birmingham.

The photos of two teenage girls appear on the screen. They went missing after school yesterday and were last seen in Sock Shop. The familiar sense I should be doing something hits me, before Prudente-Poulton's words of warning resound in my head. I can't save everyone.

I flick through channels, settling on an episode of *Jonathan Creek*. Jonathan's familiar windmill house in the countryside and trademark duffle coat draw me in, even though I've missed the start.

Sipping a glass of Diet Coke, I glance at my watch. It's only seven-thirty. Marcus left a plate of lasagna by the microwave, but I'm not hungry. Nervous flutters run around my stomach. I don't know whether they're signs of homesickness, or sadness at the fact I'm leaving tomorrow.

Pushing myself off the sofa, I call Antony on my mobile phone, hearing the ringtone repeat. I pace the room, wondering what he's up to. Photos on the oak sideboard show Marcus and Olivia beneath a wooden lych-gate on their wedding day, showered with confetti. Olivia with baby Charlie in her arms, Charlie on the beach wearing a blue, floppy hat, eating ice-cream, and Ludo as a puppy.

A deep yearning grows within me. Will Antony and I have similar pictures above the fireplace with confetti and churches, babies and pets? It's doubtful, the way things are. Antony's job has sucked the joy from our relationship. He used to lavish me with affection. Whenever we were together I thought I'd won the jackpot. I want the old Antony back but I fear he might be gone for good.

Another scenario pops unbidden into my mind, one with Henry in the frame. I touch my lips, banishing the thought.

'Where's Daddy?' A small voice comes from behind me.

Charlie stands in the doorway, clutching his worn teddy bear, Snuff.

'Daddy will be back soon,' I say, jabbing the *End Call* button.

'I want Daddy.' Charlie pops his thumb into his mouth and presses the bear against his cheek. Ludo pushes through the door and gives me a solemn look. I get the feeling the dog's assessing me for weakness.

'Daddy will be back *very* soon, I promise.' I check my watch.

Damn. 7.45p.m. Marcus won't be back for ages.

'Tell you what, why don't we go upstairs, find your favourite book, and I'll read it to you.' I raise my hand for a high-five. 'Deal?'

Charlie ignores my hand and clambers onto the sofa. He plops himself at the opposite end, his little legs barely reaching the end of the cushion.

'Watch TV with you.'

This is going to take expert negotiation. I throw him a winning smile. 'Let's do a deal. We watch TV for ten minutes, then I read you a story.'

Charlie points at the TV. An old woman sinks into a comfy chair draped with a tartan blanket and starts reading a book. The scene is a slow one, but my hope that Charlie will lose interest, fall asleep, or go back to bed is dashed when he says, 'Watch Wheels on the Bus!'

'Wheels on the Bus is for daytime.' I put my foot down. 'Night-time TV is for grown-ups. Your daddy promised you would be a good boy and stay in bed.'

'Watch now!' Charlie jumps off the sofa, rummages on the shelf below the TV and thrusts his favourite video into my lap. 'This one!'

Charlie wiggles his bum on the cushion and crosses his arms.

I'm flummoxed. How can this tiny person be calling the shots?

Ludo puts his paw on my knee and gives me a pleading look. He's trying to tell me something, but I haven't a clue what it is.

The dog suddenly jumps onto the sofa between us, forming a furry barrier between me and Charlie.

'Down, Ludo!' Charlie waggles his finger at the dog. 'Bad dog!'

Ludo gives a great yawn and slumps across my lap. With my swiftly-developing cynical eye, I deduce the dog is faking tiredness to solidify his position. My theory is confirmed when he lowers his head on my legs, effectively pinning me down.

I lean round the dog to catch Charlie's eye. If I don't nip this uprising in the bud, I might end up strangling him.

'Daddy will be very sad if you don't go to bed.'

'Do the thing!' Charlie thrusts his arm out, pointing to the TV. He gives me suspicious sideways looks, clearly wondering why I'm not leaping into action.

'While Daddy's not here, guess what? I'm in charge. Come on, up we go.' I go to stand, but Ludo shifts his considerable weight on me and tries to lick my face.

'Get off get...off!' I splutter.

Charlie's mouth opens wide. A horrendous sound comes out, starting low and rapidly jumping up all the major scales.

My Nokia buzzes on the arm of the sofa. The screen lights up. ANT_MOB

I press the green phone button.

'Antony!' I yell, turning my face aside from the slobbering dog.

'Sorry, I missed your call. Everything OK?' He pauses. 'What's going on? Is that an air-raid siren?'

I cover my other ear and raise one arm to ward off Ludo's tongue.

'I'm babysitting,' I say. 'Everything's fine.'

'Are you sure? The kid sounds pretty upset.'

Clenching my jaw, I take a breath. 'Charlie won't go to bed.' I pause. 'Any ideas?'

Antony huffs. 'I don't know. Take the kid for a drive? Doesn't that make them nod off?'

'That would be brilliant if I had a car!' I raise my voice over a screaming Charlie.

'If it was me, I'd take him to the kitchen, raid the cupboards for sweets, and promise he can have some once he's in bed.'

'Are you nuts? If I give him sweets he'll never sleep. Besides, I can't get up. The dog's pinning me down and I'm getting licked to death!'

'Push the dog off. Sort Charlie out, then ring me back.'

'You've been a great help. *Not!*' I ring off, bridling at Antony's lack of empathy.

'Bad man!' Charlie throws a Lego block at the TV.

I glance at the television, expecting to see the old woman nodding off in her chair. Instead, shadows dance around a dark stairwell. A creepy figure ascends the stairs and enters the old woman's bedroom. Wind billows through the curtains to the unsettling score of high-pitched violins.

'Don't look, Charlie!' I yell, searching desperately for the remote control.

Charlie's gaze locks onto the TV. His eyes go wide as the figure enters the bedroom. The camera slowly zooms in on a white-slatted wardrobe where the old woman must be hiding.

I glance at the coffee table but the remote isn't there. It must have slipped down the sofa. I shove my hands under Ludo's belly and shove him out of the way.

'Move, you lump!' The dog thumps down on the floor, knocking against the table and sending my glass of Coke flying. The glass shatters on impact, sending brown liquid across the rug and polished floorboards.

'No, Ludo!'

The man on screen reaches the wardrobe. To my horror, he's holding a dagger.

'Don't look!' I shout.

Charlie ignores me. His thumb drops from his mouth.

Deep between the sofa cushions, my fingers close round the cold, plastic remote. I stab the red *off* button as the creepy man reaches for the wardrobe knob.

The TV won't switch off. The volume buttons don't work, either. If the situation wasn't time-critical, I'd slide off the battery compartment and roll the batteries round.

The dog starts licking Coke from the floor.

'Stop that!' I lean over and grab Ludo's collar, manhandling him towards the lounge door before he hurts himself on the broken glass. The dog fixes me with a sorrowful look loaded with judgement as I shove him through the door and close it, ignoring his whimpers.

'I don't like it,' Charlie whines.

The man on TV turns to face the camera. His grey, scarred face has one central eye.

'One eye man!' Charlie wails. 'One eye!'

His renewed bawling drowns out Ludo's muffled whimpers.

Hopping over broken glass and puddles of Coke, I reach the TV. It's a brand-new flat-screen with no visible buttons. A green light shows it's on. That's all.

'Switch off!' I wail, as desperate as Charlie.

'Make it go 'way!' Charlie's high-pitched screaming reaches volumes that the neighbours must be able to hear, as the cyclops raises his dagger and yanks open the wardrobe.

Desperate situations call for extreme measures. I crawl around the back of the TV, grab every plug I can see and yank them out.

The screen goes black.

'Look, it's gone. Everything's okay now!' I say breathlessly.

'I want Daddy!' Charlie howls.

'It's OK, it wasn't real.' I crouch before him, careful to avoid the glass. 'That was a man in a costume, like the ones they have on Hallow—'

'He had one eye!' Charlie's lower lip trembles.

'It was a mask, just a mask.'

I wipe strands of blond, damp hair from his hot little face. His subsequent howls reach record-breaking decibels, broken only by juddering breaths, where he stores energy for the next round. I get my arm round him, promising him ice-cream and his favourite video if he stops crying.

As I grab his hot clammy body, he thrashes his arms and legs ferociously.

I try again to lift him. He arches his back and kicks his legs like an Olympic swimmer, catching me square in the jaw. I stumble back against the Lego starbase, which snaps in a jagged line down the middle. Turrets, look-out shelters and landing bays shatter as they hit the rug.

Charlie is shocked into silence. He gulps a few times while I hold my throbbing jaw, standing in the middle of the devastation.

A shrill ringing makes my heart leap in my throat. For one horrifying moment, I think I've set off the fire alarm.

It's the doorbell. My racing mind pictures a concerned neighbour or the police. I really don't want to answer the door, but the bell keeps going and then I hear a thump of a fist banging the window.

'Alex, are you in there?' Henry's voice shouts through the window.

'We're fine!' I shout back. 'Everything's fine.'

'Open the door.'

23

— · —

Henry strides past me as soon as I open the door. 'Where's Charlie?'

'In the lounge,' I say, following him across through the hall to the lounge door. 'Be careful, there's glass on the floor. Ludo knocked over my drink, and then Charlie kicked me and I fell onto his starbase.'

My excuses sound so lame, I wish I'd kept my mouth shut.

Henry pushes through the door. He steps over glass shards, crouches by the sofa and brushes strands of blond hair from Charlie's sweaty forehead. 'Hey, buddy.'

Charlie's crying instantly subsides and he loops his arms around Henry's neck, pressing his clammy forehead to his cheek. My face falls, seeing the way they instantly connect.

Henry stands and lifts Charlie onto his hip. 'How about some hot chocolate?'

As Charlie blinks at his rescuer, his ragged sobs subside.

Henry carries Charlie into the kitchen and sits him on the counter. Ludo pads over and sits at Henry's feet, forming a family unit with me on the outside.

'Thank God you're here.' I hover in the doorway, hanging my head. 'Charlie came downstairs and wouldn't go back to bed. I didn't know what to do.'

'We'll talk about it later,' Henry says, cuddling Charlie. 'Would you get the milk from the fridge?'

Charlie giggles at something Henry says.

I fetch the milk, feeling a complete failure. 'Where are the cleaning things?'

Henry gestures to a tall, white cupboard next to the pantry. 'Everything's in there.' He pauses. 'I guess you didn't hear Ludo whining?'

Uh, oh. My gaze goes to the exterior door and the small yellow puddle on the terracotta tiles. I put my hand to my mouth, only now remembering Marcus's warning.

'I thought Ludo was whining because Charlie was upset,' I say.

Inside the white cupboard, I grab a mop, bucket and plastic crate full of cleaning equipment.

Charlie touches his uncle's brow. 'I saw a man with one eye, 'enry.'

'And I saw a man with five ears!' Henry says and tickles him, getting a belly-laugh in return. Charlie's laughter releases a tension knot in my stomach. I feared I'd scarred him for life.

I sweep up glass, use kitchen towel to blot Coke from the wooden floor and the rug, and brush fur off the sofa. In the kitchen, I hear Charlie happily babbling away. As I work carpet shampoo into the rug, pushing Lego pieces into the middle, I ponder how Henry got the situation under control so quickly. It's as if he and Charlie share a secret language.

Sitting back on my knees, I stare at the dwindling flames in the fireplace. It has become painfully obvious that I'm not cut out for motherhood or pet ownership. I wouldn't trust myself to look after a goldfish.

After blotting the rug, I return to the kitchen to deal with Ludo's accident and find the room empty. Charlie's empty mug is on the kitchen island.

Sighing, I clean up the puddle by the back door, put the cleaning supplies away and retreat to the lounge. Maudlin thoughts occupy me as I push back the curtain and stare into the dark.

I sense someone behind me.

Henry puts his hand gently on my shoulder and I turn to face him. He holds out a glass of red wine.

'Thought you could use this.'

I force a smile and take a large sip, releasing a breath I didn't realise I was holding.

'Thank you.' I force myself to meet Henry's gaze, steeling myself for judgement. To my surprise, his gaze is open and friendly.

'How's Charlie?' I ask.

'He fell asleep on page two of Meg and Mog. You shouldn't hear a peep from him.'

'That's what Marcus said.' I touch my brow, my gaze dropping to my feet. 'I'm so sorry. I don't know if I can face Marcus and Olivia after what's happened.'

Henry leans forward. 'Why don't you tell me what happened?'

After another fortifying sip of wine, I recount the gory details.

'Ah, so *that's* why Charlie kept poking my forehead.' Henry rolls his eyes.

'I don't think he's ever going to forgive me for that cyclops,' I say forlornly.

'Charlie's tougher than that.' The corners of Henry's mouth rise slightly. 'You're not the first babysitter he's tried to break, you know. He built a prison out of blankets for his last victim, and made her stay inside all evening.'

'Now you tell me!' I say, feeling marginally better.

'We all have a blind-spot where Charlie's concerned.' Henry pauses. 'But then, it's a miracle he's here at all.'

At my questioning look, Henry says in a low voice, 'Olivia had a series of miscarriages before Charlie. He was lucky to make it. That kind of thing changes you. Every moment you have together is precious.'

'I'm sorry. I didn't know.'

Henry's disclosure puts everything in a new light. The family barely knows me, yet they trusted me with their treasured child, which only makes me feel worse.

I move over to the sofa, slump onto it and drain my glass.

'You have an amazing bond with Charlie,' I say. 'I'm not sure kids and me go together.'

'Give it time. You've only just met him. Besides, I've heard it's different when they're yours.' Henry sits next to me with his leg touching mine. Heat rushes to my face at the intensity in his gaze. It must be the wine.

'But what if your child gets the worst parts of you?'

Henry flashes a grin. 'What if they get the best?'

I stare at my hands, trying to work out what my best parts are. 'I'm not so sure I'd be a good role-model. I can't hold down a job. No one wants my paintings.'

'Hey, you found Nenagh and Delia and uncovered an extremely dangerous man.'

'My machine did that,' I say glumly. 'Even then, we have no case.'

'We have no *evidence*,' Henry corrects. 'We'll find it. I have every faith in you.'

'What if we don't?' I lean back on the cushions, releasing an exasperated sigh.

'You're too hard on yourself.' Henry captures my hand. His thumb brushes my knuckles. 'When I heard you saved Rashid's life, I had a lightbulb moment. If anyone could help me, it would be you. Guess what? You proved me right.' He pauses. 'With your talent for detective work, you should seriously consider joining the police. Please think about it.'

I lift my chin to meet his gaze. 'You really think I've helped?'

Henry nods. 'And your heart's in the right place. If other people can't see that, they must be blind.'

As Henry trails off, my mind goes to Antony's moody, distant behaviour.

Something burns behind Henry's guarded expression. He brings my hand to his mouth and presses his lips to my folded fingers.

Prickles run up and down my skin as our eyes meet. His face glows in the dwindling firelight, accentuating his cheekbones and the curve of his lips.

'Alex...' His breath hitches.

A remote sensation swims inside my head until I feel I'm no longer on the sofa, but floating outside my body. Without thinking, I raise my hand and cup Henry's cheek. His stubble prickles against my fingertips. I lean closer until his blue eyes blur. Something has me in its spiralling grip and I can't stop myself.

I press my lips to his.

Henry encircles my waist and draws me closer. He's bigger than Antony, but we fit well as we kiss. Desire stokes long-dormant embers back to life as we melt into each other. Heat rushes to my face and my lips. I lock my fingers through his hair as the kiss deepens.

Then, Henry pulls away.

My eyes flutter open. Henry releases his grip and faces forwards with a shuttered expression, arms resting on his knees.

'Forgive me, Alex. I don't know what came over me.'

The remote feeling vanishes. Hot and cold bolts shoot through me. I push myself from the sofa and take refuge by the window, touching my guilty lips. Cupping my hot cheek, the skin feels tender from Henry's stubble - a testament to the intensity of our embrace.

My heart races and I'm hit by nagging guilt. I've created another mess and I don't know how to fix it. I can't allow one moment of weakness to ruin everything. My mind gets stuck in a loop, replaying the kiss with Henry. I think of Antony with growing shame. What will I say to him? What excuse can I possibly give?

'I'm the one who should say sorry,' I say. 'I haven't been thinking straight these last few days.'

'Neither have I.' Henry's Adam's apple bobs in his throat. He shifts on the sofa to face me.

'I'm with Antony,' I whisper, rubbing my forehead.

'I know.' Henry's voice drops.

'What happens now?'

'You're leaving tomorrow.' Henry shrugs. 'Problem solved.'

He pushes himself from the sofa to the rug. Sitting cross-legged by the ruined Lego starbase, he starts rebuilding the shattered sections.

My thoughts are so muddled, I don't know how I feel. Regret mixes with longing as I push back the curtain and stare at the empty drive, willing Marcus to come home.

'Can you give me a hand?' Henry asks, his tone neutral. 'I need red blocks for the turrets.'

I kneel on the other side of the starbase and shift through piles of Lego for red pieces.

'I didn't think this was fixable,' I say, hoping my face doesn't look as red as the Lego in my hand.

Henry gives me a tight smile. 'Charlie and I built it together. I know where every brick goes.'

'Thanks for fixing it. You've saved me, yet again.'

We work in silence until Marcus gets home. He walks into the lounge, carrying a glass of wine.

'Hey!' I leap up. 'How was your reunion?'

'Bloody awful,' Marcus says. 'Guys boasting about their careers and the girls stuck together in a ball. I left before they all started dancing around their handbags.' He plonks himself in the arm-chair and tips his glass to us. 'Cheers, you two! I hope you're enjoying my vintage San Giuseppe Reserva.'

'That's on me.' Henry glances up. 'I saw it on the counter and thought it was up for grabs.'

'Well, we may as well finish it now it's open.' Marcus takes a sip and swirls the glass. 'God, it's good to be home. How's everything been?'

'Yeah, good.' Henry fixes the last block to the Lego starbase. 'All done here. I'd better make a move.'

He stands and checks his watch before glancing my way. 'Pick you up at nine?'

'Sounds great,' I say quietly.

24

I enter the kitchen at seven-thirty the following morning, bleary-eyed. Charlie sits in his booster seat, banging the table with a spoon while eating toast soldiers and scrambled egg with his fingers.

'Morning,' Marcus greets me, shaking a frying pan on the Aga. 'Sleep well?'

'Great, thanks.' I sit opposite Charlie and force a breezy, 'Good morning, little man.'

I brace myself for accusations or tears. Instead, Charlie raises the spoon and says, 'Mornin', Alex!'

I'll never understand children.

'This should set you up for the day.' Marcus presents me with a plate laden with eggs, bacon, hash browns, fried bread, tomato and black pudding. My stomach gurgles, reminding me I haven't eaten since yesterday lunchtime.

'This is amazing, thanks.'

Charlie sings, *Row, Row, Row Your Boat*, as I pick up my knife and fork and tuck in.

Marcus sets two mugs of coffee on the table. 'Olivia's sorry she couldn't be here to wave you off. We'll miss having you around.' A chuckle escapes him. 'Though, not as much as Henry.'

Prickles run down my chest. I stop chewing.

'You're welcome to stay with us if he asks you back.' Marcus gives me a knowing smile and stirs sugar into his coffee.

Will I be back? My thoughts have been preoccupied with Antony and sorting out our relationship. I never considered the added complication of returning to Hertford.

After breakfast, I pack my rucksack and stand on the doorstep with Marcus and Charlie, who is determined to wave me off. I huddle into my coat while dark clouds roll overhead, heavy with the threat of rain.

'Uncle 'enree!' Charlie waves and jumps up and down as the Astra pulls onto the drive.

Henry waves and smiles behind the windscreen.

'Thank you everything,' I say to Marcus. He pulls me in for a hug. I lean down to give Charlie a kiss. To my surprise, he flings his arms round my neck and makes a smacking noise with his lips.

A fluttering sensation grows in my chest as I approach the Astra. I climb into the passenger seat and put my rucksack by my feet, trying my best to act natural. Breathing in Henry's cologne triggers a flashback to our kiss on the sofa. I force it from my mind as I sink into the tartan seat.

'Hi!'

'Hello.' Henry's tone is neutral. He puts the car in gear before I've secured my seatbelt and reverses off the drive.

'Charlie slept well,' I say. 'You should have seen him at breakfast, all bright and breezy like nothing happened.'

'That's good to hear.' Henry cuts me a glance. 'How about you? Did you sleep well?'

I pause. 'Not really.' I can't think of anything to add that won't lead to places I'm unwilling to go.

Henry is preoccupied and doesn't make small talk, even about the case, until we reach *School Cottage,* the old house where Reginald used to live. Henry parks on the concrete drive beside the yellow skip.

'Sharmilla's expecting us,' he says, getting out of the car. He locks the Astra after me and walks to the blue front door.

I stand beside him. Gusts of wind push me in the back.

Henry knocks on the door. A moment later, the door opens a crack before catching on the chain. A young Asian woman wearing a colourful scarf peeks out with the wariness of someone expecting a cold caller.

'Sharmilla Mehrotra?' Henry asks, showing his warrant card.

'Ah, DC Longhurst.' Sharmilla's expression softens. She un-latches the chain and opens the door. 'I've had so many suspicious characters knock on the door since I moved in, I keep the chain on.'

'It's the skip,' Henry says. 'It advertises the fact you're having work done. Once that's gone, the callers should stop.'

Beyond Sharmilla is a dusty room coated in terracotta plaster with steel props supporting the ceiling. The lounge and kitchen have been knocked through, giving line of sight to the back of the house. Newly-installed French doors allow light to flood the space.

'It's lovely and airy,' I say.

'And dusty!' Sharmilla laughs. 'Hopefully, it'll be worth it.' She retrieves a manilla file from the bottom of the stairs. 'I dug out the paperwork from the sale of the house. The deeds should be in there somewhere.'

She offers it to Henry.

'Can we take a quick look at this inside?' Henry asks, as wind billows through his coat.

'Sure.' Sharmilla moves aside to let us in, and closes the door on the blustering weather. She leads us through to the kitchen area. The empty shell of the house has been stripped of its original character. It's impossible to imagine what the place looked like when Reginald Carstairs and Delia lived here. The only furniture is a workbench with an angle-grinder at one end.

'Sorry, there's nowhere to sit,' Sharmilla says. 'I'm living upstairs at the moment.'

'It's OK,' Henry smiles. 'We're good here. I'll give you a shout when we've finished.'

After Sharmilla retreats upstairs, Henry opens the file on the workbench.

I sidle up alongside him. 'Remind me what we're looking for again?'

Henry puts his arm around my waist. My heart skips a beat before I realise he's moving me away from the angle-grinder's serrated blade.

'We want the dates Reginald Carstairs bought and sold School Cottage, whether he is the sole name on the deeds, or if he owned the house jointly with his wife,' Henry says.

We look through pages of drainage and environmental searches, boundary diagrams and correspondence with estate agents and solicitors. I spot a typed sales document, brown at the edges.

'School Cottage sold in June 1959 for the princely sum of £2,650,' I read quietly. 'I bet Sharmilla wishes she'd paid that for it.'

Henry raises an eyebrow.

A paper sleeve tucked three-quarters of the way through the file contains two stapled sheets. The top one has TRANSFER OF DEEDS printed at the top.

'This looks interesting.' Henry points to the name REGINALD CARSTAIRS in capital letters. 'This is dated February 1988.' He flicks to the second page, labelled *Deed of Trust*. 'Delia's maiden name was Spring. She assigned the deeds to Reginald on their wedding day.'

I glance back at Henry. 'Didn't Nenagh do the same?'

Henry nods. He points to a passage, half-way down the page. 'Reginald gained the beneficial interest in the property. Delia gave up her legal rights of ownership, although it stipulates she was entitled to live in the house as long as she was married.'

I shake my head. 'This is the '80s, right? Women's lib, equal rights, independence. Why would she give up her rights?'

'Delia might not have been a modern woman.' Henry shrugs. He takes his digital camera from his pocket and snaps the pages of interest.

It makes me wonder whether Delia was similar to Nenagh, a mouse of a housewife who rarely ventured far from home. The behaviour pattern fits – in both cases there was a controlling husband who did not allow either wife a stake in their shared assets.

'The timescale between both women going missing and their houses being sold, are similar,' I say.

'Indeed they are.' Henry calls up the stairs to Sharmilla, asking her to come down. Once she's returned, he shows her the relevant pages.

'Could you email these over? We may need the originals as evidence.'

'No problem,' Sharmilla says. 'Should I be worried about anything?'

'Not at all,' Henry reassures her. 'Our enquiries have nothing to do with your ownership of this house. Thank you for your help.'

'Good luck with the renovations,' I say on the way out.

Inside the Astra, I buckle my seatbelt and ask Henry, 'What do you think? Is it enough to dig up Duggie?'

'I hope so.'

I bite back my frustration at having to leave Hertford, with new discoveries coming to light.

Henry goes to turn the ignition key, then pauses.

'Listen, Alex. About last night...' The intensity of his look sets my heart racing. 'I didn't mean to step out of line.'

'It's okay.'

Henry rubs his hand over his face. 'No, it isn't. I get that you're with Antony. If you just want to be friends, I understand.'

'I...I honestly don't know what I want.' I shake my head.

'No pressure. It's fine.' Henry starts the engine. 'Let's get you signed out.'

We arrive at the police station, and after a blustery walk to the main building, Henry accompanies me to the reception desk. I return my lanyard to Yolanda.

She hands me a time-sheet with a grin. 'Sign at the bottom, or we won't pay you!'

I sign my name, happy to know I'll have money to tide me over Christmas.

Then, Henry fetches Simon and Tori.

Tori gives me a heartfelt hug. 'Have a great Christmas! Operation Thaw won't be the same without you.'

'See you on the other side,' Simon says, raising his hand in farewell.

I give the Vulcan salute. 'Live long and prosper.'

Simon's eyes widen. 'Peace and long life!'

Yolanda surprises me with a present wrapped in silver paper before pulling me into her ample bosom for a bear-hug. 'You come back and see us.'

'I will.' I clutch the featherlight package with tears welling up at the warmth of the farewells.

Suddenly, I don't want to leave. I'll miss being part of this team, investigating cases alongside Henry, and my warm and comfortable lodgings with Marcus and Olivia. I'm even starting to miss Charlie.

Once we're outside, Henry stands in my way. He leans forward and gently grasps my shoulder.

'I'll let you know of any developments.' V-shapes form on his brow.

I clutch my time-sheet and shift on the spot, unsure whether to smile, hug him, or kiss him on the cheek. Our once-easy friendship has become uncomfortable - a stand-off between Henry's expectations and my messed-up emotions. I want us to be friends. But I also want more.

Before I can decide how to act, Henry moves past me and unlocks the car. The five-minute drive to Hertford East station passes in the blink of an eye. Henry pulls into a drop-off bay and turns off the engine.

'So, this is it,' he says, patting his thighs.

We stare at each other. Electricity hangs between us waiting to strike, but neither of us makes a move.

I lift the rucksack onto my lap. 'Good luck with both cases.'

'Thanks,' Henry says, matter-of-fact.

My fingers fumble on the doorlatch. The first drops of rain hit my coat as I step out of the Astra. The wind whips my hair.

'Merry Christmas, Alex.' Henry leans across. 'Stay safe.'

'I will.' With my rucksack secured on one shoulder, I give a wistful smile and swiftly walk away.

25

— · —

I call Antony's mobile to let him know I'm on my way as the train leaves Hertford East and *click-clacks* past red-brick buildings. The call goes straight to voicemail. I try him again somewhere between London and Birmingham without any luck.

As the train rattles north, I tell myself what happened with Henry was a mistake, a one-off. If he hadn't swept in to save the day, I would never have kissed him. He caught me off-guard when I was feeling at an all-time low, and boosted my confidence with his flattery and chiselled good looks. Above all, he told me he liked me simply for being me, and what woman wouldn't want that?

But one kiss isn't enough to justify giving up Antony.

During the long hours of travel, I concoct a plan to revive my relationship with Antony. I need to be more positive and understanding. I know he loves me; he's just having a hard time at work.

He should be pleased when I tell him that I intend to hand over the finding machine to the Turing-Tesla League. This will spare me further awkward conversations over taking unnecessary risks. Wading into the river Mimram was bad enough. Who's to say next time the machine doesn't lead me down a mine or off the edge of a cliff?

I've gone back and forth regarding the pros and cons of trusting Jonathan Prudente-Poulton, but the machine needs to be fixed and no one else can do it. Besides, if the League was good enough for Dad, it's good enough for me.

The train pulls into Birmingham New Street station just after three p.m. Even though Antony's at work, I still look for him as I walk past carol singers collecting for charity. Their joyful singing follows me out of the station and into drizzle. I pull my hood up. A couple walk hand-in-hand a few steps ahead, sheltered under the canopy of an umbrella.

Antony has some much-needed time off over Christmas, which means we can cuddle, laugh, relax, and rediscover our happy place.

By the time I reach our block of flats, ominous, grey clouds are gathering overhead. The ground-floor window to the side of our front door is dark, and the Audi is gone from the parking bay. Turning the key in the lock, I cross the threshold.

'Hello!' My voice echoes down the empty hallway. I kick a pile of flyers and junk-mail out of the way and close the door, dump my keys in the bowl on the hall table, and wander into the lounge.

The sofa-cushions are flat and need plumping. My eyes go to the ailing dragon tree beside the TV. Last December, we moved the dragon tree aside to make room for a tiny fir, strung it with fairy lights, and piled our presents underneath. This year, we haven't had time to go out and choose one.

Memories of the fabulous Christmas tree in Marcus and Olivia's house, the warm Aga, home-cooked meals and fine wine, are fading fast. I push away images of Ludo padding down the hall and Charlie's excited shrieks as he flings his arms round Henry's neck.

In the kitchen, there are crumbs and coffee-rings on the work-tops along with glasses containing droplets of red wine. A stack of dirty dishes sits in the sink. I resist the urge to flop onto the sofa.

I close the slatted blinds, turn on the lights, advance the central heating, and pull on my yellow Marigolds.

For the next hour and a half, I blitz the kitchen and lounge, hoovering, cleaning, washing dishes, dusting, and thumping cush-ions. I feed and water the dragon tree, pick off the dead leaves and place it on the south-facing bathroom windowsill. Returning to the lounge, I get on my hands and knees and scrub old wine stains from the carpet. This is the second time I've cleaned the floor in twenty-four hours. I should consider a new career working for Molly Maid.

By the time I'm finished, my fringe is sticking to my sweaty forehead.

I gulp down a glass of water over the scrubbed, gleaming sink before moving on to the second stage of my plan. I dial Jonathan Prudente-Poulton's number while pushing aside any misgivings about global threats and security issues. The finding machine has the potential to do an incredible amount of good. I can't keep it to myself forever.

Like last time, peculiar clicking sounds come down the line before the woman with the plummy accent picks up on the seventh ring.

'Hello,' she says. 'Who is calling?'

'It's Alex Martin. I need to speak to Jonathan Prudente-Poulton.'

'Please hold.' Another click and silence.

I jump when Prudente-Poulton's refined voice breaks through the quiet. 'Hello, Alexandra. It's good to hear from you. All well?'

'I'm fine.' I gaze at the photo on the mantelpiece of Antony hugging me tight, and remember his warning. I need collateral. 'I've come to a decision. I'm happy to hand over the machine on three conditions.'

A long pause follows. 'Which are?'

'The first condition is, I bring the machine in to your headquarters so you can explain exactly how it works and what's inside. Secondly, you make me a member of the League. Lastly, you guarantee the date I get it back.'

'That's four conditions,' Prudente-Poulton says. 'I will respond to your last condition first. I'm afraid I cannot give you a date. The upgrades are far from straightforward. Making the copy will be a complicated and time-consuming procedure. Both machines will require rigorous testing. Please be reassured, the finest scientific minds will work on your machine around the clock.'

'You must have some idea how long it will take. A week. A month. A year?'

'The simple answer is we won't know until we start work.'

I sigh. 'I'll want regular updates.'

'Of course.'

'What about my other conditions?'

'Explaining the technical aspects of the machine is problematic. The League has a code of absolute secrecy. The workings of the machine and its plans will make no sense to you, yet a single glimpse could put our organisation at risk. It could make us discoverable. On that point, I must say no.'

'Hold on a minute. This is supposed to be a two-way thing,' I splutter. 'I let you borrow the machine, and I get something in return. Knowing how it works is important to me.'

'Our rules are quite clear,' Prudente-Poulton says brusquely. 'Nobody outside the League can have access to our secret knowledge.'

'That's why I want you to make me a member.' I pause. 'An honorary member.'

'Alex, this is not—'

'Do it in honour of my dad. I'll sign any forms you want to guarantee my secrecy.'

The following silence is so long, I think Prudente-Poulton has hung up on me.

'It would be easier for everyone if you just hand the machine over.'

'Look, I have real world experience using it. My knowledge could help you.'

'That's not the point. What w—'

Gripping the phone harder, I talk over him. 'I have the machine. It's right here. You have nothing.'

Prudente-Poulton starts to speak, then catches himself. More silence follows.

My pulse beats in my neck. I remember to breathe.

'Let me call you back,' he says, and hangs up.

The next half hour is an agony of waiting. I take the phone into the office and throw myself into a frenzy of silent cleaning. I dust my PC, keyboard and desk, tidy paperwork, clean the inside of the windows and take a dustpan and brush to the carpet.

When my mobile rings, I drop the contents of the pan in my haste to answer.

'I'm here,' I say breathlessly.

'The League is prepared to make you an honorary member,' Prudente-Poulton says. 'This way, you can bring your machine to our headquarters. Our members would be happy to meet Richard Martin's daughter.'

My lower lip quivers at the mention of my father. Seeing where Dad worked will fill in many blanks about a part of his life he kept secret.

Prudente-Pouton says, 'Do we have a deal?'

'We do,' I say, excited at the thought of seeing the League's HQ.

'Please ensure the machine is switched off and remove the battery before you deliver it,' Prudente-Poulton says.

'No problem.' I give a light laugh.

'Please double check. Whenever the switch is on, the machine leaves a trace.'

My mouth drops open. If that's true, the Turing-Tesla League may have been tracking me since the night I rescued Rashid!

I say, 'I'll put it in a lead-lined box if you want.'

'That won't be necessary. Just switch it o—'

'—off and remove the batteries. I've got it.'

'It goes without saying you mustn't tell anyone. That includes Antony Eastwood and DC Henry Longhurst.'

'O...kay.'

Prudente-Poulton clears his throat, jolting me back to the moment. 'Memorise this address. Red Croft Lodge, Church Walk, Bletchley, Milton-Keynes.'

I haven't a chance of remembering the address. I scrabble in the kitchen cupboard for a biro, grab a pizza flyer from the recycling bin and begin scribbling.

Prudente-Poulton asks, 'Can you bring it now?'

I pause with the biro stuck to the paper. 'No, I don't have the car today. The earliest I can make it is...Boxing Day.'

A pause. 'Boxing Day it is. Ten am.'

Why did I say that? My mind races as my plans for a relaxing Christmas break with Antony disintegrate.

'See you then, Alexandra,' says Jonathan Prudente-Poulton. The line lets out a series of staccato clicks and goes dead.

Dropping my phone on the sofa, I tear the address from the flyer and take it into the bedroom. Despite Prudente-Poulton's warning, I don't trust myself to remember it. I fold the paper into a tiny lozenge and tuck it into a pair of sports socks in my bedside cabinet.

Unzipping my rucksack, I lift out the finding machine.

Feeling its familiar cold weight, I slide off the little black cover and remove the battery.

26

After a blistering hot shower, I blow-dry my hair and pull on my classiest Merino V-neck jumper and skinny jeans in preparation for Antony's return. The scrape of a key in the lock makes me jump as I'm applying mascara, and I nearly jab myself in the eye. Dabbing my lashes with a tissue, I rush into the hall.

Cold gusts of air stream past Antony as he squeezes through the door and into the narrow hallway, with three bulging Waitrose bags and a long white box.

'Hey, stranger!' Antony's face lights up.

'Hey!' I swiftly take the box from his arms before it scrapes the wall and lean it against the radiator. I tilt my face for a kiss.

'You taste nice,' Antony says. 'Let me put this lot down.'

He leans on the door to shut it and pulls me close. I hesitate, but his earthy scent mixed with jasmine and amber aftershave pulls me in. I melt into him, revelling in the way we fit together. The kiss is the promise of a new start, I tell myself.

Antony breaks the kiss and nibbles my earlobe until I squeal. He takes my shoulders and examines every inch of me as if he's forgotten what I look like.

'I've really missed you. Are you back for good?'

'As far as I know.' I draw my hair over my ear. 'How's work? Still manic?'

'Not so bad. I've made a few changes for the sake of my sanity.' Antony picks up the carrier bags, ushers me into the lounge, and drops them on the table.

'What kind of changes?'

'I don't answer my mobile if Yan calls outside office hours. That pillock has taken his pound of flesh. He's not getting any more.'

'Is he cool with that?'

'He wouldn't be happy if I took a sleeping bag and camped in the office. He's such a knob.'

'Good for you.'

Antony shrugs. 'I want to work to live, not live to work.'

I suppress the urge to jump up and down at the old Antony making a comeback.

Antony rummages in the bags and takes out a plastic bowl of Caesar salad, a French stick, and a white, foil-coated bag. The bag releases a roast chicken aroma that makes my mouth water.

He cocks a brow. 'Rotisserie chicken and salad good for you?'

I give an enthusiastic nod before dashing into the kitchen to fetch the butter dish, plates and cutlery. Antony unpacks the rest of his booty: a bottle of red wine, a New York cheesecake, and a box of Ferrero Rocher. I fetch the corkscrew and uncork the wine, watching with interest as Antony opens the long box.

Whatever's in there is a tight fit, but with brute force and some cursing, Antony drags out a three-foot artificial Christmas tree. He gives me an apologetic look.

'I know you'd prefer a real tree, but an artificial one is less hassle. Now Santa's got somewhere to put the presents.'

'It's perfect.' Dropping to my knees on the carpet, I slot the plastic base together and open out the bristly branches. I slide the tree into the space beside the TV and plug it in. Colourful fibre-optic lights sweep through the tree, casting a merry glow across the walls.

'Hold on,' I say, dashing to my office to grab Yolanda's present. I hand the silver packet to Antony. 'If you met Yolanda, I know you'd love her. Go on, open it.'

Antony tears the paper, and two crocheted turkeys fall out. One is beige, the other made from dark brown wool. His eyes light up as he dangles them by their wool loops.

'Is this one supposed to be me, and that one you?' He smiles. 'Cute.'

We hang the turkeys on the tree.

'Now we can enjoy Christmas,' I say.

Antony slips his arm round me and draws me close. 'Props to you, Alex. The place looks great.'

The living room is warm and cozy. Flickering beeswax candles rest on polished wood stands, our books sit in neat rows in height order on the shelves, the furniture is gleaming and dust-free. Even the carpet is fluffed-up and fragrant.

'I feel bad I let things slide,' Antony says. 'I'm going to make more of an effort from now on. The cleaning shouldn't fall on you just because I'm working more.'

A warm glow burns through me as we enjoy a convivial glass of wine. We eat our supermarket dinner from trays sitting close together on the sofa. It might be the best dinner I've ever eaten.

I'm itching to tell Antony my news about the Turing-Tesla League, but a promise is a promise. Instead, I give him a pared-back version of my exploits with the Hertfordshire Constabulary, and mention Tori and Simon as much as possible, so it doesn't sound like I spent the whole time with Henry.

I tone down the episode where I fell into the river and omit the creepy moment I felt someone watching me from the crowd. I have no proof, but I *know* it was Reginald. At least I'm safe, over a hundred miles from a suspected murderer. Antony doesn't need to know that, either.

Despite my sanitised account, Antony gives me a grave and censorious look. 'You said you'd be in an office, not falling into rivers and examining graves! Where's Henry in all this? He was supposed to be looking after you.'

'He was looking after me.' I come to his defence. 'I made the decision to go in the river.'

'I still don't like it, or the risks you're taking.' Antony clicks his tongue, putting my back up.

'You just don't like me spending time with Henry!' I say huffily.

'That's because you're with him more than you're with me.'

'I've only been in Hertford a few days. You're the one who's always working!'

Antony's drops his cutlery, making me jump. 'Back off, Alex. I've got enough of my plate.'

'All right, all right.' I put my hands out. 'You'll be pleased to know I won't be helping Henry anymore. The finding machine keeps glitching.'

'I can't say I'm sorry to hear that.' Antony picks up his fork, and spears an iceberg lettuce leaf. 'But I know what you're like. Just promise me something. Tell me if you decide to use it again.'

'Deal.'

It's an easy pledge to make. In a few days' time, the finding machine will be out of my hands.

Antony clears his plate and stretches his arms behind his head. 'Now you're back, have you thought about what you're going to do for work?'

I shake my head, deciding now's not the time to tell him Henry thinks I'd make a good detective, and that I should join the police down in Hertfordshire.

'What about your paintings?' he says. 'Can you find another buyer for them?'

I put my fork down. 'The buyer who pulled out wanted pretty canal paintings. Not the graffiti or the grime, or any of the details that make my art unique. I don't know if I can be commercial.' I pause. 'I wish I could make a living from art, like you.'

'You'd hate it.' He clears his plate. 'I'm tied to deadlines, client briefs, company policy, and I work for fools.'

'You sounded like you were having fun when you were in the pub with Saskia.' The words blurt from me.

'Are you serious?' Antony reaches for his wine and takes a long, slow sip. He gently grips my wrists and turns me to face him. His dark brown eyes search mine. 'You can trust me, Alex. I know I can trust you.'

My cheeks flush. 'Fine. But if you hate your work that much, maybe you should try something new.'

Antony casts his eyes up to the ceiling. 'See that roof over our heads? I'd like to keep it.'

'I'm not saying you should walk out tomorrow. Just, sometimes things need to change.'

'Now you've lost your job, it's even more important I keep mine.' Antony wipes his mouth on a triangle of folded kitchen towel.

'Are you having a dig at me?'

'Look, saving Rashid was brave. It was noble. But you were the one who lost out. That's the problem with your dad's machine. You can't explain your actions. And that gets you into trouble.'

'You've made your point.' I sigh. 'I won't mention work if you stop talking about the finding machine.'

Antony releases a breath, leans forward for a kiss. 'It's a deal. Let's start again.'

He stacks our plates and takes them to the kitchen, returning with slices of cheesecake. We stick to safer topics such as where we're having Christmas dinner, laying bets on my mother calling from Ireland the moment we start carving the turkey, and how Antony's sister, Trianne, is getting on at Leeds University.

The mellow conversation trails off when Antony leans over and runs his thumb along my jawline.

We kiss and end up tangled together on the sofa. I break away, breathless. Antony stands and takes my hand. 'Come on. Let's have an early night.'

'What about the dishes?' I say, like an idiot.

'Forget them.' Antony silences me with a kiss.

'We have to blow out the candles,' I say.

Antony whispers, 'We'll do one each.'

27

— ⋅ —

CHRISTMAS EVE

I wake to Antony's alarm and the white noise of the shower running. I stretch languorously across the warm, empty bed, then kick off the duvet and pad across the hall to the bathroom. Antony stands by the sink, freshly showered and brushing his teeth.

'Come back to bed.' I take his hand and attempt to pull him away from the sink. When that fails, I run my hand inside his shirt. 'Remember what you said last night? Work to live, not live to work?'

'Ahwsssh,' he replies through a mouthful of minty foam. He pulls his hand free from my grip and rinses his toothbrush, then applies a dash of aftershave. 'You'll have me all to yourself from tonight.'

Biting my lip, I make a mental note to prepare an excuse for Boxing Day, when I'm taking the finding machine to the League.

Antony checks his watch. 'It's eight forty. I'd better get my arse in gear.' He gives me a kiss, grabs his fleece-lined jacket and heads for the door.

'What about breakfast?' I ask, knowing Antony can't function without his morning dose of coffee.

'Sorry, babe. I'll grab a coffee and one of those muesli pots on the way. I'll be back before seven. Promise.'

I huddle on the front step with my arms wrapped around myself as Antony crosses the carpark to the Audi. He waves and gets inside the car. I brave the chill until he's driven past.

Shuddering, I close the door, get dressed and look for breakfast. Our cupboards would give Mother Hubbard's a run for their money. The fridge contains two cans of Red Bull, the leftovers from dinner, a sliver of cheese, a bottle of tomato ketchup and a jar of mustard.

After a meagre breakfast of black coffee and buttered toast, I head out to get supplies from the Tesco Express around the corner.

I take a basket and fill it with milk, cheese and ingredients for a lasagna. I'm eyeing up a trifle when someone calls my name.

Trevor, the football coach from the NMPH, waves from the end of the aisle and walks over, basket in hand. He's wearing a royal blue Birmingham City shirt with white stripes, under a bomber jacket.

'Hey, Alex! Good to see you.' He gives a small smile. 'How are things?'

'Not bad,' I say. 'I'm just back from Hertford. I've been helping the police with old missing person cases.'

'Good to hear your talents aren't being wasted.' He casts a look over his shoulder. 'Look, I'm sorry about what happened with Lin. I never thought she'd fire you. I called her out on it after you'd left.'

'Thanks, Trev.' I blink up at him, heartened to know someone had my back.

'For what it's worth, I'm not the only one in the office who thinks Lin treated you poorly. You should have received a medal instead of the sack. By the way, the new girl's rubbish compared to you.'

I try and swallow the lump in my throat.

'Rashid's still your number one fan,' Trevor says quietly. 'He keeps ringing the office, asking for you.'

'Haven't you told him I was fired?'

'Company policy is not to say why you left,' Trevor says, rolling his eyes. 'Rashid thinks you're a miracle worker. He says you can find those missing girls.'

'Missing girls?'

'Sorry, I forgot. You've been away.' Trevor rummages in his basket and passes me the Birmingham Evening Mail.

DAY THREE AND STILL MISSING. WHERE ARE OUR GIRLS?

The smiling faces of Maisie Sellors and Amneet Sidhu are on the front page. A sick feeling lands in my gut. I recognise them from the news report I saw in Hertford. The last place they were seen was the Pallasades shopping centre.

Working for the NMPH taught me the first forty-eight hours are crucial. After that, the odds of a safe return drastically reduce.

'The parents of both girls ring daily for news, but we've nothing to tell them.' Trevor blinks and looks away. 'My daughter's only a year older than these two.'

I skim-read the article. The two fifteen-year-olds covered for each other, saying they were staying over at the other's house. The rumours are, they went to an illegal rave.

'There must be other kids who were there,' Trevor says. 'But no one's saying anything. They're probably underage and worried about getting into trouble. These raves can take place anywhere. Fields, disused warehouses.' His shoulders rise. 'Where would you even start to look?'

My gut knots as I look at the girls' happy faces. Would anyone remember these two amidst crowds pressed together in the dark, with pumping music and blinding, flashing lights?

'Three days,' I say in a small voice.

'What can we do but hope and pray?' Trevor pushes the paper into my hands when I try and return it. 'Take it. Maybe you can think of something, like Rashid said.'

At the till, I pay for the newspaper along with my groceries.

Someone must know where they are and call the police.

But it won't be me.

I stop by a litter bin on the way home, and hold the Birmingham Evening Mail over the jumble of drinks cans, fag ends and food containers.

It's not my job to find the girls. Besides, I promised to let Antony know if I decided to use the finding machine again, which means no more risk-taking behind his back.

My hand won't let go. Trevor gave me the newspaper in good faith. Throwing it away would be the same as giving up on the girls.

I tuck the newspaper into my carrier bag and trudge home. Back in the flat, I busy myself with domestic tasks by throwing a load of laundry in the washing machine and preparing a lasagna for dinner. I head into the spare room to check my emails, hoping another buyer might have bought my paintings, but there's no word from Whitewalls Gallery.

No word from Henry, either.

The empty, silent flat presses in on me. I head for the lounge and switch on the TV. The lunchtime news features a familiar yellow banner with the cute Millennium Bug: *How Will the Bug Affect You?*

It won't!

I flick over to ITV. A couple are getting married in a shark tank at the Birmingham Sea-Life centre. It doesn't look romantic, wearing a mask and flippers with the sharks staring hungrily behind an adjoining gate, but I guess it takes all sorts.

I switch to Channel 4 and my breath freezes. A senior detective from Midlands CID is making a heartfelt appeal to the camera with a phone number scrolling across the bottom of the screen.

'We believe Maisie and Amneet attended an illegal rave in Birmingham on the 21st December. Were you there? Did you see them? If you have any information, please call the number below in confidence. We need to get the girls home to their families for Christmas.' The detective stares directly at me. 'Help the girls. Do the right thing.'

28

—·—

Chewing on my fingernails, I turn off the TV and grab my phone. The urge to run for the finding machine is overwhelming. But that's what the old Alex would do. The new Alex keeps her promises.

I ring Antony's mobile. Unsurprisingly, he doesn't pick up. I change tack, dialling Antony's workplace - Apex 3000. I ask the receptionist to connect me to his office landline. It rings and rings.

If the mountain won't come to Muhammad...

Grabbing my jacket and keys, I set off at a brisk pace for Apex 3000. On the way, I pop into the nearest trendy deli to buy two chargrilled chicken and veggie wraps. I can't wait to see the look on Antony's face when I turn up with lunch.

The most direct route to Antony's office runs alongside the B4100. The unrelenting roar of traffic accompanies me past warehouses, run-down estates and converted dockyards. Twenty minutes later, I cross a large, pedestrianised shopping precinct that comes out on Newhall Street.

Apex 3000 is an uber-cool block, six-storeys high, amidst similar futuristic black and chrome offices that give the street a New York City vibe.

I push through a heavy revolving door into a large marble foyer. An enormous, white Christmas tree dominates the entrance. The tree is painfully chic, with black baubles dangling artfully from its branches. A curved ebony reception desk runs along the back wall, with a chrome sign above it: *Apex 3000 – The Pinnacle of Design.*

I head for the desk, brown paper bag in hand.

The receptionist tilts her chin and gives me a long, assessing look. Her scraped-back hair is twisted into a perfect chignon, without a single hair out of place. The counter space is spartan, with an open visitor's book and neat stack of guest lanyards by her keyboard.

'I'm here to see Antony Eastwood,' I say. 'Can you tell me what floor he's on?'

The receptionist checks a list. 'The third floor. What's your name?'

'Alex Martin.'

The receptionist dials his number. She taps her midnight-blue, acrylic-tipped fingernails on the desk, waiting for an answer.

I turn my back on her to watch the stairs and main door for any sign of Antony.

'I'm sorry. He's not answering,' she says. 'I'll try again.'

A delivery driver wearing DHL overalls thumps a heavy box on the counter.

'Here, love. Got a delivery.' He flicks through the paper on a clipboard. 'Supplies for a Mr Cosgrove. He thumbs back to the revolving door. 'You need to check the load and sign for it.'

The receptionist raises a finger. 'Just a second.' She puts the phone down and catches my eye. 'No answer, I'm afraid. Do you want to wait or leave a message?'

I've worked in enough offices to know I can't argue my way up to the third floor without someone giving the okay from above.

'Don't worry ab—' I say, as the delivery driver cuts in.

'Sorry to interrupt love, but the lorry's parked on double yel-lows. If you could do us a favour?'

'All right, I'm coming.' The receptionist leaves the desk and trots after the driver in high-heels.

I watch until she's left the building, then hurry to the stairs and race up three flights without pause, thankful I'm wearing jeans and sensible boots. I couldn't do this in stilettos and a tight skirt.

At the top is a glass door leading to an empty reception area.

As I pause to catch my breath, the door clicks and three young execs wearing slim-fit suits and bright-coloured shirts push through with hands in pockets, laughing. I press my back against the chrome railing as they pass me without a glance. Without heels, lipstick, or a designer suit, I'm invisible.

I rush through the door before it swings shut.

Phones trill endlessly. A corridor runs past the reception area with doors lining both sides. An open-plan area lies further down, partitioned by waist-high dividers into work cubicles with designers at each one, eyes glued to their screens. It reminds me of a call centre.

To my right is a glass-fronted meeting-room. A frosted wave design obscures the bottom half of the glass. It's stylish, but doesn't give the occupants complete privacy. Inside, four men and one woman pore over large sheets of paper covered in graphic designs. Antony's not among them.

I walk on.

A woman appears from a side room, wearing a baby-blue trouser suit and four-inch heels. With her flawless, tawny skin and Disney eyes, she looks like a model. Her bright red hair is cropped short in a daring style that she and maybe only two other women in the country could pull off.

'Hello,' she says. 'I'm Tilly. Can I help you?'

'Hi Tilly.' I crick my neck to meet her eyes. 'I'm Alex, Antony Eastwood's girlfriend. I brought Antony lunch.'

Shaking the bag, I try and sidle past, but she stands in my way and looks furtively around as though I've said a dirty word. I'm not sure if it was *girlfriend* or *lunch*.

'Antony popped out.'

'Do you know where he went?'

'No clue. But we've got a team meeting at two, so he'll be back by then.' She thrusts her hand out. 'I'll make sure he gets his lunch.'

'It's okay, I'll leave it on his desk.' I clear my throat. 'Where does he sit?'

Tilly rolls her eyes. 'Come on.'

She moves with surprising speed in her heels to the only empty cubicle at the end of the corridor, by a window.

'Thanks.' I fix a grin, taking a pen and a Post-it from Antony's desk.

Tilly stands behind the iMac with arms folded and keeps her eye on me as if I'm about to steal the pen. I shield my note with my arm as I write a message. The last time I hid my work from prying eyes like this, was in primary school.

'Tilly, can we get a coffee!' a man's voice calls from the meeting room.

'Coming!' Tilly calls in a bright voice before adding quietly, '*Tosser.*'

A brief laugh escapes me.

Tilly uncrosses her arms and flashes a conspiratorial smile before striding off.

I sink into Antony's swivel chair, tapping the pen against my teeth. A flash of gold catches my eye. Behind the iMac monitor is a bottle of Veuve Cliquot champagne with a gold bow and a card tied around the neck: *'Antony, you're a star. Let's do lunch, my shout! Oriel xx'*

A box of Charbonnel et Walker truffles leans against the bottle. I slide the box toward me and unpeel the sticky circle to have a peek. An intense cocoa aroma hits me, making my mouth water.

A small, glossy card beneath the lid bears the message: *'For turning my dreams into reality. Melissa Curtis xx'*

I deserve compensation for having to read something so cheesy. I pop a truffle in my mouth and open the top drawer.

I shouldn't go through Antony's stuff, but now I've started I can't stop. An A5 calendar lies beneath the stack of hand-written cards. December has a stock photo of two businessmen shaking hands. Under today's date Antony has written: *Lunch, S.*

On four separate occasions through December, including the evening I called him from Hertford: *Drink, S. Meet, S.*

A lead weight settles in my stomach. The letter *S.* One name springs to mind.

A pub catch-up with wine, meetings, lunch? Antony's words from a week or so ago pop into my head: *Men and women can't be friends. Not if they're straight, anyway.*

Stupidly, the next thing that comes to mind is if Antony's having lunch with Saskia, he won't want his chicken wrap. I dial his mobile number, but he doesn't pick up.

My hand shakes as I write: *Antony, I have to use the FM. It can't wait. Please understand xxx*

That's my side of the bargain done. I grab the brown lunch bag and head for the exit.

As I pass the meeting room, a man pops his head out of the door. Sweat shines through his thinning, combed-back hair. His pink shirt is stained dark under his armpits.

'Who are you?' he booms.

Stopping mid-stride, I say, 'Antony's other half.'

The man looks me up and down, face twitching in micro-expressions of disapproval.

'Do me a favour, Antony's other half. When you see him, tell him to cut short the lunches.' He taps his watch. 'I need him here, pulling his weight.'

He closes the door in my face.

That must be Yan. What a charmer!

Saskia could be lending Antony a sympathetic ear. But something about her still niggles me. What if she's more than just a colleague?

I make a hasty exit down the stairs and push through the revolving door, stopping only to dump Antony's still-warm wrap in the nearest bin.

29

I head home through a bone-chilling wind that bring tears to my eyes, turning passing cars and people into shapeless blurs. I eat my chicken wrap as I walk, forcing it down without enjoying a single bite. Antony told me lunch is for wimps. But he found time for Saskia.

Back home, I walk into the lounge, past the Christmas tree adorned with crocheted turkeys. I pick up the picture of Antony and me by the river in Ware, our arms wrapped around each other, our eyes sparkling with love. What happened to that happy couple who used to spend every waking moment together? These days, I'm lucky if Antony has time to say hello.

Pull yourself together! Things will be different over Christmas. Antony has promised to make time for me. Hopefully, by the New Year, we'll have reconnected and found our happy place again.

I replace the photo with a hopeful smile.

The Birmingham Evening Mail lies on the coffee table. I grab it and head for the office. Pulling open my bottom desk drawer, I open the shoebox lid.

I hesitate. I always get more than I bargained for when I use the finding machine.

The girls' faces smile up at me. They can't wait any longer.

I lift the finding machine from the shoebox.

'Please work,' I whisper to the cold, black case, before flicking the on/off switch.

Dad's dot appears.

'Thank you!' Grabbing a pair of scissors from my stationary tube, I cut out the photos of the girls and fit Amneet's between the clip holders.

The display blinks on and off rapidly as I struggle to scrawl down the numbers in the margin of the newspaper. I write the first part of the longitude and latitude co-ordinates. Then, the display corrupts.

52.47492 becomes **52.#####**

I switch off the machine, insert Maisie's picture, and try again.

52.##### -1.899??

The last two digits flicker. I catch a split-second glimpse before the display dies on me. I'm pretty sure they were **99** or **55**.

A cautionary voice inside tells me to switch off the machine and stop this madness. But I ignore it. I'm the girls' only hope. If there's the slightest chance Amneet and Maisie are still alive, I have to take it.

52.47492 -1.89999 or **-1.89955**

The display died on me when I searched for Delia in the churchyard, but I was able to use the five location lights to pinpoint her location. If I start in the right area, and that part of the machine still works, trial and error should lead me to the girls.

I boot up my PC and find both locations on the geospatial website. The numbers ending in **99** bring up Birmingham's central road network, close to the Chinese Quarter. It's one of the main routes into the city, where the B4127 and A38 meet at Holloway Circus Roundabout.

Zooming in, the white finger points to the edge of the roundabout's central hub. The roundabout is in full view of passing motorists and pedestrians. I can't imagine an illegal rave going unnoticed in such an exposed and open site. Anyone driving past would have noticed it. The second set of co-ordinates mark a large curved building directly east of the roundabout. A more likely location for the rave.

I formulate a plan to head for the roundabout first, then cross the road to the curved building.

A fire burns inside me as I unzip my rucksack and place the finding machine at the bottom on a blanket. Rummaging in the kitchen cupboards, I stash four bottles of Evian water into the rucksack's side pockets for the girls, pack a Maglite torch and my mobile phone before checking the finding machine's display one last time. It's dead.

I leave the flat and head for the heart of the city. The roundabout is a mile away along the main road. It shouldn't take more than twenty minutes to reach it. I walk beside the dual-carriageway, half-deafened by the roar of traffic.

A hundred yards down, workmen are resurfacing the road. Red and white barriers force me to take a diversion across a set of temporary traffic lights. On the other side, a solitary oak spreads its bare branches in front of a row of boarded-up shops. With no pedestrians in sight, I pick up my pace, passing dilapidated Victorian buildings, boarded-up houses, pubs with faded signs, and an Asian supermarket with a plastic banner above the door, displaying English and Chinese characters. Tower-blocks form the backdrop to a part of the city that last thrived back in the '60s.

Eventually, the roundabout comes into view. The central hub is an oasis of shrubs with a tall, stone pagoda standing proud at the centre. There are no pedestrian crossings, no obvious way to get across. I shift impatiently at the edge of the road, waiting for a gap in the traffic.

Motorbikes and scooters zip in and out of lane. A leather-clad motorbike courier tears through narrow gaps in the traffic like Evel Knievel. Once he's gone past, I see a gap and make a dash for it.

I run across, just as a zippy little sports car hurtles round the inside lane and cuts over to the middle lane. The driver slams on the brakes and stops two feet from my knees. An HGV squeals to a halt with deafening horn blast and hissing brakes, narrowly avoiding rear-ending the car.

I stop dead in the road with my heart hammering.

'What the hell do you think you're doing?' The lorry driver shakes his fist out the window.

'Sorry!' I throw an apologetic wave to him and the sports car driver, race to a low wall and clamber over the railing.

I lean on a nearby tree to let my heartrate drop. Two East-Asian women with shopping bags sit on a stone bench, chatting. A manicured lawn with trees, ornamental borders and a pair of stone Chinese dogs mounted on pedestals surround the pagoda. The layout appears very feng shui, but the constant low rumble from the A38 and the underpass beneath my feet spoil the illusion.

Close-up, the forty-foot-high pagoda resembles an oversized garden ornament. A brass plaque commemorates the gift to the city of Birmingham in 1998 by the founders of a local Chinese supermarket chain. I make a mental note to come back with my sketchbook. I would love to give the Pagoda the attention it deserves by painting it. But that's a task for another day.

I unzip my rucksack, ensure Amneet's picture is firmly between the clips, and switch on. The display is blank. I switch off and on until, eventually, two LED lights flash and stay on.

Slowly, I turn three hundred and sixty degrees, searching the office blocks across the road for the building I saw on the map. To the north-east is a grey curved concrete slab with most of the ground floor units boarded up. That must be it. Yellow signs are tacked across the first-floor windows: *To Let*.

I'm working out how to get across the roundabout again without being squished when a woman pulling a tartan shopping trolley emerges from a path concealed behind bushes. Intrigued, I follow the path, which is flanked on one side by a colourful glass mosaic depicting a horse fair. Green hoarding replaces the mosaic, before the pavement descends a gently curved ramp and disappears into a pedestrian underpass.

I follow the sloping path into the bunker-like tunnel, hit by the acrid smell of stale urine. Covering my nose with my sleeve, I enter the gloom. Industrial lights cast yellow pools between the shadows.

A third flashing light appears on the finding machine.

Echoing footsteps stop me in my tracks. Turning my back to the tiled walls, I scrunch the rucksack shut. A suited businessman strides past and gives me a slight nod.

I hurry towards the square of light at the end, where a staircase ascends to ground level. The roar of traffic increases as I emerge beside the concrete building. An overhang casts a shadow over eight aluminium framed doors, secured with chains and padlocks. Once, this must have been a busy place.

Three solid red lights.

Stepping under the shadow of the overhang, I cup my hands round my eyes to peer through the glass. Beyond the doors is a reception area. Dim light falls onto a red, brown, and orange carpet with repeating circles that run along the floor and halfway up the support pillars. The decor couldn't be more '70s if it tried.

At the far end is a long counter with empty display cabinets on either side. Framed posters hang on the wall.

COMING TO AMERICA.

GODZILLA.

The cinema must have shut in the late '80s when those films were released.

I test the chains wound round each pair of square aluminium handles. The first three are chained tightly, but the fourth padlock has some give in it. I pull at the hooped shackle and it swings free from the body of the lock.

I detach the lock, unwind the chains from the handles, push the door inwards, and slip inside.

A damp, musty smell hangs over everything. Grimy carpet silences my footsteps. I creep past a poster of Eddie Murphy wearing a crown, and another showing the irradiated eye of a monster, to a wide staircase that descends into darkness.

Three red lights and a fourth flashing.

A movie banner hangs by the top step: *DIE HARD. COMING THIS JULY.*

My heart speeds up as I stare into the gloom.

Bruce Willis stares past my shoulder, gun in hand, ready for action. I wish I could send him down the stairs instead of me.

Swallowing hard, I rummage in my rucksack for my torch. Twisting the rim activates a narrow beam of light. Then, with one hand on the metal handrail and my rucksack over my chest, I descend to the lower foyer and into darkness.

30

— • —

I shine the torch around the stairwell. Framed posters appear out of the dark, advertising Odeon season tickets and intermission snacks. When I was a kid, my local cinema kept the intermissions until the late '80s, even though the projectionist no longer had to change over the reels. Dad always treated me to a tub of mint-choc-chip ice-cream.

All traces of the Odeon's former glory have gone. Black mould lurks in the corners of walls and ceilings. The smell of damp increases with every step. It's like descending into a dungeon. At the bottom of the stairs is a low-ceilinged, rectangular foyer with folding tables and chairs stacked against the walls. Grey and mustard-yellow ticket stubs litter the floor.

My torch illuminates five large display boxes inset with red letters in the wrong order - D O N O E - that once blazed outside the cinema. The cracked white glass reveals rows of dirty lightbulbs.

Plastic crunches under my feet as I pick my way through piles of litter. Sweet packets, supermarket bags and muddy strips of cardboard are strewn across the carpet. I sweep the torchlight over fizzy drinks and water bottles, some half-full.

My throat goes dry. I rummage inside the rucksack for water, before stopping myself. The girls will need it more than me. They will be alive. Please, let them be alive.

The machine display hasn't changed: three lights on and one flashing.

Signs for Screens 2 and 3 hang above closed double doors to my right and left. Both sets of doors are chained and padlocked shut. I try them, but they won't budge.

At the end of the corridor, a final set of doors lead to Screen 1. The doors squeak when I push them, opening into a pitch-black auditorium.

Four red lights. I hesitate on the threshold with my heart pounding in my ears.

Light from my torch lands on a bank of switches on the wall by the doors. I flick each one in turn. Nothing.

The *Fire Exit* emergency lights on the ceiling are also dead.

My flashlight beam reveals rows of red cinema chairs along the left and right walls. Each chair has an ashtray fixed to the back. Narrow aisles separate each row from the main seating block in the centre of the auditorium.

I head down a sloping aisle towards the stage, wading through the detritus of a rave. I stumble over a Nike trainer. There's no sign of the other one. The amount of rubbish generated over one night is astonishing. Spent glow sticks, discarded T-shirts, jumpers and hoodies drape across seats and on the floor.

I imagine all the sweating teenagers partying down the aisles to pounding dance music under strobe lights. None of these kids would admit to being here. Maybe it was due to the damage they caused, fear of being blamed for the girls' disappearance, or simply because they're just kids.

The cinema is built like a bunker and surrounded by thick concrete. No one outside the Odeon would have heard a thing. Late at night, there would have been very few, if any, passers-by in this run-down part of town.

I thread my way through gaps in the seating where chairs have been ripped from their mountings and thrown aside. It looks like things got crazy.

Reaching the stage, I shine my torch into every corner. Heavy red velvet curtains form a backdrop that covers the screen. Two tables sit end-to-end in front of the curtains. Bunches of wires hang over the tables like dead snakes, trailing to a giant speaker lying on its side with its insides torn out. This must have been where the DJ ran his sets, probably using a portable generator to power the decks, speakers, and the lights.

I clamber onto the platform and push past the curtains to the dead screen. Behind the screen is nothing but a ten-foot-high solid concrete wall. I check the finding machine's display.

The machine's lights have gone out.

'Damn. Come *on.*'

Gripping the torch between my teeth, I reach inside my rucksack for the machine. Jiggling the on/off switch doesn't help. I resort to smacking the machine. Then, I raise the rucksack a few inches and let it drop with a thump.

Cursing, I zip-up my rucksack and sling it over my back, before methodically checking every inch of wall for an exit, trapdoor on the stage floor, or a secret door. I hop from the stage and work my way back up the sloping aisle towards the back row.

'Amneet! Maisie!' I call, my voice muffled by the walls. 'Are you here?'

A pair of cinema chairs block the aisle. The chairs are solidly built, bolted together as a single unit. I climb over and sweep torchlight along the back wall.

I stop short as my light hits a dusty glass pane above the back row.

When Dad took me to the cinema, he would always stare over his shoulder at the projectionist's window, not wanting to miss the moment the beam of light shone through the glass to hit the screen.

I move the light down the wall. The top half of a doorway is visible behind a row of four displaced cinema chairs and two aluminium tables, forming a barricade.

'Amneet! Maisie!' I shout, forging forwards.

Silence.

I grab one of the tables and yank at it until it slides to the carpet with a crash. As the other table shifts, the edge bashes my lip.

Cursing, I taste blood and let it fall, then drag both tables down the aisle and out of the way.

I return to the row of chairs. Each seat is bolted to its neighbour and won't budge. I try the door handle, but the seat's top edge is wedged underneath, holding it fast.

As I pause for breath, faint banging comes from the other side of the door. A fresh bout of energy surges through me as I manhandle the chairs.

'Maisie! Amneet! I'm coming!'

I grunt and strain, trying to rock the seats free, but they won't move. A primitive urge fires through my veins, fuelled by desperation. I let out a war cry that echoes around the auditorium, and pull the seats with every fibre of my being.

The pounding from the other side of the door increases.

The bank of chairs shifts a fraction. Then, a tiny bit more. I stumble backwards as the chairs pull free. Grasping the handle, I open the door.

White fingers appear around the door's edge like spiders.

I step back and stifle a scream with my hands flying to my mouth.

A thin, pale figure with blonde rattails hanging over her face, shuffles forward and falls. I rush to catch her. Sour breath hits my face as she collapses into my arms.

'You're safe now.' I hug her.

A terrible dry sound escapes her, as she puts her mouth close to my ear. 'I'm...M...Ma.'

'You're Maisie, I know. Sit here.' I guide her into the aisle to a spot relatively free of rubbish. 'Is Amneet with you?'

Maisie nods with a shiver, hugging her knees, and lets out a croaking, ragged sob.

I crouch and put my arm around her. 'I need to find Amneet. I promise I'll be quick. Keep strong, Maisie. I'll be back in a flash.'

'D...don't leave me...alone.'

I grab a water bottle from my rucksack and twist off the cap. 'Here. Try and take small sips.'

Maisie puts the bottle to her lips and splutters. She coughs, then drinks eagerly, slugs of water dripping down her chin.

I slink through the door into a small room dominated by two huge projectors. An unpleasant smell mixed with mould and stale chemicals hangs in the air.

My heart thumps as I shine the torch past projectors, a rack of old film-reels, granola bar wrappers and two sports bottles. Moving the light closer, I spy a small pink backpack next to a shivering bundle.

'Amneet,' I drop to my knees beside her and shine the light into her eyes. A shuddering breath escapes me when her eyelids crack open. 'You're safe now. Can you sit up for me?'

Amneet shifts position with a croaking groan.

I jump as Maisie's hand touches my shoulder.

'Give her this,' Maisie croaks through chapped lips, giving the half-empty water bottle back to me. 'We ran out of water ages ago.'

'You finish it.' I tell Maisie. 'I have more in my bag.'

Maisie sticks close to me, her gaze glued to the torchlight. I help Amneet into a sitting position. Her skin is sallow and drained. Dark hollows sit beneath her eyes.

I pull another bottle from my rucksack and tip it to Amneet's lips. She grabs it between shaking hands and drains half the contents before she's overcome by racking coughs.

'It's all right,' I comfort her, rubbing her shoulder. 'Take your time.'

Maisie's empty bottle drops to the floor and rolls. 'Do you have more?'

I hand over the rest of the water, then sling Amneet's arm around my neck. She's only fifteen but her weight makes me stagger, and I need Maisie's assistance to get her to her feet. With some manoeuvring, we squeeze out of the door.

With the torch in my free hand, I shine a light down the back row to the exit.

'How did you find us?' Maisie asks, moving at a snail's pace.

'I was passing by the cinema and noticed a chain was hanging off one of the doors,' I say, sticking to a simple excuse.

'Thank God you came.' Amneet sniffs and wipes her eyes with a grimy hand.

'We didn't think anyone would find us,' Maisie says, shuffling along. 'Our parents must be so worried.'

'The whole of Birmingham is worried.'

The girls are already headlines in the local papers. By tomorrow, they're going to be national news.

We reach the swing doors leading into the lower foyer. I shoulder the door open and hold it for the girls to pass through.

Late afternoon light filters down the stairs. It does the girls no favours, with their puffy red eyes, matted hair, cracked lips and vacant zombie expressions.

Amneet lifts her gaze to the light.

Maisie perks up at the sight of freedom. She stumbles through the foyer to reach the stairs. I let her go ahead and lend Amneet my arm. She leans on me with one hand holding the stair rail. We ascend one step at a time, following Maisie towards the orange-carpeted foyer.

We're nearly at the top when Maisie halts with a gasp and sways back.

I let go of Amneet and leap forward to catch her before she falls.

A silhouetted man stands at the top of the stairs, flashlight in hand.

'It's okay, you're safe,' he says in a soft American accent.

He extends his hand towards Maisie, takes her arm and guides her into the foyer before helping Amneet up the last few steps.

He turns back to me.

'Thank you, Alex. We'll take it from here.'

31

I rush up the stairs. A woman with a shock of flame-orange hair, wearing combat trousers, boots, and a black ski jacket steps forward. She helps Maisie and Amneet sit on the carpet and hands them bottles of water. The girls shudder and hug their knees as they sip from the bottles, staring vacantly into the distance.

The woman nods at me, then dials 999 on a flip-phone.

'All right love,' she says in a Brummie accent. 'I need the police and an ambulance.'

I follow the American through the foyer to the exit doors. He's over six feet tall, sharply dressed in a midnight-blue suit. He holds a mobile phone to his ear and keeps to the shadows, watching the street outside.

'Yeah, we got here in time,' he says into the phone. 'Leave it with me.'

He turns to assess me with slate-grey eyes, slipping his phone into his pocket. His skin is a coppery tone, lighter than Antony's. Silver peppers his receding hairline, sideburns and sculpted beard.

'Who are you?' I ask, dabbing my stinging lip. 'What's going on?'

'Alex, it's good to meet you. I'm Marshall.' The American pulls a handkerchief from his pocket and hands it to me. 'You've got something on your lip.'

I take the handkerchief and dab blood away.

Marshall says, 'I work for the League.'

The cogs in my mind slowly turn. My gaze goes to the redhead.

185

'Her, too?'

'That's right.' Marshall tilts his head towards the exit. 'We need to leave before the police arrive.'

I shake my head. 'I'm not leaving until the girls are safe.'

'My colleague will look after them, don't worry.' Marshall opens the door. 'Come on. My car's outside.'

I step back, shaking my head. 'No thanks. I can walk home.'

Marshall sighs, lets the door swing shut. 'I get this is a lot to take in. Jonathan said you're one of us, right?'

'I guess so.'

'So, if you're part of the team, we need to work together.' He pauses. 'That means we have to leave now.'

I squeeze my eyes shut, hoping by some miracle that when I open them, I'll know what the hell is going on.

Marshall takes a breath. 'You can't be found here with these girls, Alex. We covered for you with Rashid but we can't cover this.'

I rub at a sharp twinge shooting through my temple. 'Go back a second. What do you mean, covered for me?'

Marshall glances back to the door. 'We stopped your photo from landing in the papers. The League decided your boss should take credit for Rashid's rescue. We thought it prudent that you leave your job before you compromised us further.'

His words hit me like shotgun pellets. 'It was you? I was fired because of you?'

'Wasn't me personally.' Marshall presses his hand to his chest. 'Those decisions are above my pay grade.'

'But it was the League, and you work for them.'

I swallow my rising anger. I blamed Lin for losing my job. But evidently, neither she nor I had any choice in the matter.

'Look, the League wants you safe.' Marshall keeps his tone soft. 'Stay here, and the police and press will have a field day with you. You'll be the centre of a media storm.'

I've been on the receiving end of unwanted media attention before, back in Ware. Never again.

Sirens wail in the distance.

'Are you two hearing that?' the redhead asks, getting to her feet. 'Half the West Midlands emergency services are on their way here.'

I swiftly go to the girls and squeeze their hands. 'You're safe now. You'll be fine.'

'Thank you,' Maisie says, pressing her lips together. 'What's your name?'

'It's Susan,' Marshall says over my shoulder, before whispering in my ear, 'We need to go, *now*.'

Marshall pushes the door open and I step outside into bitter wind. The street-lights are starting to come on as daylight fades. The sirens sound like they're coming from all directions.

'This way.' Marshall heads left. A sudden cross-wind flings back his jacket as he turns down a narrow alleyway running down the side of the cinema.

I hesitate, looking back to the main road. 'I'll walk from here. Seriously, it's only a mile.'

'Look, I'm here to help.' Marshall rounds on me, his patience clearly wearing thin. 'I wouldn't be doing my job if I let you walk home alone.'

'I only have your word for that.' I tighten my grip on my rucksack. 'You say you're with the League, but how do I know? You could be working for the Russians.'

'Do I look Russian to you?'

'You could be part of a sleeper cell.'

Marshall lets out an incredulous laugh. 'Are you for real?' He pushes his jacket back and places a hand on his hip. I half expect to see a holstered gun, but the only thing beneath his suit is a pink shirt covering the beginnings of middle age spread. 'Let's rewind a second. My name's James Marshall Jones, but everyone calls me Marshall. Jonathan recruited me from the US Secret Service in '92.'

'You came all the way over here for Jonathan?' I ask.

'I sure didn't come for the weather.' He slides a hand into his pocket. 'We're based out of the Red Lodge out in Milton Keynes, about a mile from Bletchley Park.

He pauses, watching for my reaction.

'The place Alan Turing worked.'

'And?'

'Alex, the people you've rescued and the risks you've taken tell me something. Your values align with ours. We want your father's machine used for good. You want that, too, right?'

'Of course, I do.' I take a breath, my shoulders drop. 'Can I see some ID?'

Marshall reaches inside his jacket, pulls out a wallet and flicks it open, holding it out.

In the fading light, I check the details on his international driving license. The face and name match.

'All right.' I nod.

I follow Marshall down the alley into a service compound behind the cinema. He walks over to a black Lexus saloon and unlocks it. 'This is us. One last thing. I need you to remove the battery from your machine.'

'It's dead.'

Marshall glances inside his jacket. 'It's still giving a signal. Flick the switch to the off position and take out the battery.'

I reach into my rucksack and do as he says.

'Thanks.' Marshall gives me a nod and opens the rear door. I slip into the leather interior, resting my rucksack by my feet.

Marshall presses a button and the engine purrs to life. He heads for the roundabout.

As we join the stream of circling traffic, flashing lights outside the cinema catch my eye. A yellow ambulance mounts the pavement with a bump and halts outside the foyer doors, blue lights strobing. A paramedic jumps from the cab.

A police car cuts in behind us with lights flashing and siren blaring. My pulse races and I shrink in my seat.

Marshall steers the Lexus closer to the kerb. The police car changes lanes and roars past.

'All good back there?' Marshall glances at me in the rear-view mirror.

'I thought that was for us.' I give a nervous laugh.

'Don't worry, we're good. And the girls are safe, now.'

We exit the roundabout. Marshall stops as the next set of traffic lights turn red. 'Mind if I ask you something?'

'All...right.' I draw out the words, my defences rising.

'Why don't I run the machine up to the League right now? It would give the tech guys a head start. You can still come by on Boxing Day like you agreed. What do you say?'

Marshall's suggestion is logical. But I can't go along with it. I need to see the League's HQ for myself. I push my toes under the rucksack, feeling its familiar weight.

'The tech guys say Y2K could stop your machine working for good,' Marshall says. 'The more time you give them—'

'I know what you're saying, but the machine stays with me.'

The lights turn green, and the Lexus pulls away. Marshall must know the area well, because within minutes we're turning into the car park by my flat.

My soul sinks when I see my front door and dark windows. Another night in alone. I can't face it. Not after the day I've had.

Marshall puts the transmission in Park. As the engine ticks over, my mind shifts into overdrive. Finding the girls today makes me realise how many people need help. Marshall's suggestion I give the League more time to fix Dad's machine is a good one.

'I've changed my mind,' I say.

Marshall turns in his seat. 'Go on.'

'If you take me to the League, I'll hand over the machine.'

'Hold that thought. I need to make a call.' Marshall turns the engine off and steps out of the car.

I get my phone and compose a text message to Antony. I don't want him worrying when he returns to an empty flat or, heaven forbid, calling the police.

```
Had 2 pop out 4 Xmas mission don't worry
back b4 Santa comes down chimney. Lasagna
in fridge 180C 50 mins CUL8R xx
```

The tone's just right – casual and a bit mysterious.

I hit *SEND* and turn off the phone to conserve the battery.

Marshall opens the door and sinks back into the driver's seat. 'It's a go.'

He pulls out of the car park and onto the main road. Sighing, I lean back on the cushioned headrest, noticing the luxurious interior for the first time. A wide leather-coated armrest divides the rear seats. My fingers brush a chrome catch.

I lift the armrest, revealing a chilled compartment with two cut-crystal whisky glasses, cans of soft drinks and miniature bottles of Absolut Vodka, Gordon's Gin, and Glenmorangie single malt.

'Help yourself,' Marshall says, glancing in the mirror.

I pour two fingers of whisky into a tumbler and knock it back. Smooth warmth slips down my throat and into my stomach. Snapping open a Coke, I drink half the can in one go.

The Coke's icy chill quenches my thirst. Stifling a contented burp, I settle back in the leather seat, pour another measure of whisky and add the rest of the Coke.

Warm air circulates around the car. Marshall sets the radio to Classic FM. The gentle sounds of strings and mellow clarinet waft through the luxurious interior. I put my glass down as my eyelids droop.

Marshall puts his foot down as we join the motorway. The Lexus purrs along. Rows of sodium-lights zip past the window and start to blur...

· · · · ● · ● · · ·

'Hey, Alex. Wake up. We're here.' I open my eyes. Slowly, I sit up and flex my elbow, rubbing pins and needles from my hand. My head feels groggy. I wipe my eyes to bring the American into focus.

'You okay?' Marshall looks round from the driver's seat. 'You were out like a light.'

'I'm sorry.' I rub my forehead.

'Nothing to be sorry about. Let's head inside and get some coffee.'

Marshall opens my door. I grab my rucksack and step from the car. It feels late. I glance at my watch, but it's too dark to see the hands.

An impressive red-brick villa fills my view. Globe lights in the porch illuminate the doorway and part of the drive. Five cars are parked beside the Lexus, a mixture of basic runarounds and executive saloons.

This must be the place I wrote on the pizza flyer and stuck in my drawer. Red Croft Lodge.

I take a deep breath of chill air to drive away my fatigue. The narrow unlit lane at the end of the drive lies silent, but the faint white noise of a busy road reaches me from somewhere in the distance.

My breath plumes in the cold as I follow Marshall across the gravel drive to the front porch. He halts before the gloss-black door and stares straight ahead.

Click.

Marshall pushes open the door and walks across a square hallway tiled with black-and-white chequerboard tiles. His footsteps echo on the hard floor as I stick close behind.

The dimly-lit hall smells of furniture polish and old wood. A cast-iron radiator pumps out heat beneath a painting of an old battleship with tattered sails, floundering in a storm. The only sound is the steady tick-tock of a grandfather clock, beside a curving oak staircase laid with faded Oriental carpet.

Marshall leads me through an open doorway on the far side of the hall, into a drab corridor with wooden floorboards. Two white doors sit in deep recesses on one side. The passageway ends at a wall decorated with a painting of an old watermill.

'Over here, Alex.' Marshall beckons me into one of the recessed doorways. A three-gang light switch sits on the strip of wall between the doors. Above, is a fuse switch with a red light. The word

FIRE is hand-written on a piece of masking tape and stuck to the plastic.

Marshall says, 'Flip that switch.'

I eye the word FIRE suspiciously. 'Won't that set off an alarm?'

'Go on.' Marshall looks at me with a glint in his eye.

I flip the switch.

Something *clunks* below my feet. To my utter astonishment, a large central section of corridor moves, sinking into the ground. The wooden floorboards descend and lock into position, forming a secret staircase.

Marshall chuckles at my flabbergasted expression.

'Neat, huh?'

32

Marshall leads the way down the stairs to a sturdy metal door standing open at the bottom. The aroma of coffee and murmured conversation drift across the threshold.

I follow him into a large room, evenly lit by fluorescent panels in the ceiling. Four people sit around a wooden table in the middle of the room, sipping coffee and eating cake. They comprise three men and one woman, who range in age from eighteen to over eighty.

A TV mounted on the wall above displays an old man sitting in a comfy armchair. He leans forward, peering at us from behind the screen. Below the TV are banks of computers and tower racks blinking with lights. Lines of code and flashing blocks of data scroll across the monitors.

On the opposite wall hangs a row of photo portraits. The shelves above are cluttered with a mind-boggling array of old electrical equipment: radio receivers, chunky headphones, rotary and push-button telephones, and oscillators displaying green waves.

The conversation cuts off when I walk in.

A tall, distinguished gentleman with silver hair, wearing a smart pin-stripe suit, breaks from the group and approaches me.

'Alex Martin,' he says in a smooth, distinctive, and instantly recognisable voice.

Jonathan Prudente-Poulton shakes my hand. 'Welcome to the League.'

A spontaneous round of applause breaks out.

'Bravo!' calls an old man wearing a brown corduroy suit and paisley cravat.

I look at Marshall in bewilderment. He simply shrugs.

Prudente-Poulton waves the others to silence. 'Many of our members couldn't be here tonight. But they are grateful. The League is grateful.'

I look around the room. 'Will you introduce me to everyone?'

Prudente-Poulton lets out an awkward laugh. 'This is rather unorthodox. I'm not sure I—'

'Oh, lighten up, Jonathan,' the woman cuts in, peering at me over large, owl-framed glasses. Her grey hair is cut into a neat bob reaching to her shoulders, and she sports a large ruby brooch pinned to a soft pink cardigan. 'I'm Carmen, and I'm very pleased to meet you.'

'Pleased to meet you too,' I say.

At my pointed look, Prudente-Poulton introduces the man with the cravat. 'Francis Feldman is a retired Professor from Kings College Cambridge and a recipient of the ACM Turing Award for Computer Architecture and Engineering.'

Professor Feldman pushes his thick-rimmed glasses further up the bridge of his nose and throws me a warm smile. 'I was at Bletchley during the war. When I saw the incredible things Alan Turing was doing, I moved from mathematics to computing. During my career, I had the privilege of being part of the evolution of the computer, from the first electronic systems to the modern supercomputer.'

The Professor's thumbnail history leaves me in stunned silence.

'This is TJ, our security expert,' Prudente-Poulton says, nodding to the young lad with an untidy mop of blond hair, wearing jeans and a *Ghostbusters* T-shirt. He doesn't look old enough to be served in a pub.

TJ peers through his floppy fringe and mumbles, 'I deal with cybersecurity, firewa—'

Carmen touches his arm. 'Please speak up, TJ. Some of us are hard of hearing.'

The lad forces his head up and says loudly, 'I'm a hacker.'

'My field is Human-Computer Interaction,' Carmen says. 'I used to work with your father.'

'You knew Dad?' I lean forward, my stomach fluttering.

Carmen nods. 'We joined the League more or less the same time and worked on several projects together.'

'What kind of projects?'

Prudente-Poulton clears his throat.

'I'm afraid I can't say.' Carmen shoots Jonathan an exasperated look. 'But when we discovered the plans for your machine after his death, I wasn't that surprised. We knew about his sister, of course.'

I pinch my arm to check if this is real. Neither I nor my brother knew about Lilian until I discovered her photograph inside the finding machine, five years after Dad died. Yet, the League knew. I have so many questions to ask Carmen about my father.

'Here you go.' Marshall places a mug of coffee and a floral-print plate loaded with a slice of coffee and walnut cake in front of me. 'You want sugar?'

'No, it's fine.' The strong coffee hits the spot. I devour the cake in large bites, staring in wonder at the collective genius around the table.

Prudente-Poulton addresses the old man on the TV screen. 'Lazar Stovanović, can you hear me?'

Lazar fiddles with his hearing aids, and a slow grin pulls his sunken cheeks taut. The picture freezes a second, as he waves a shaky hand.

'Hello from New York!' His voice, amplified via wall-mounted speakers, has a heavy Eastern-European accent.

Prudente-Poulton meets my gaze. 'Lazar has been with the League since 1956. He's too humble to say, but he was instrumental in developing the microchip. And, he's the only surviving member of the League to have met Nikola Tesla.'

'Tesla lived in the hotel where I worked as a porter,' Lazar says. 'I was eighteen, and he' —his voice catches— 'he was an old man in failing health.'

'What was he like?' All I know about Tesla, was that he was both an eccentric and a genius.

Lazar settles back in his chair. 'He was a modest and charming man. We both grew up in what is now Croatia, near the Velebit mountains, and we shared a language. You might be surprised that a Serb and a Croat could get on with the recent wars, but we did, famously! Tesla trusted me and asked me to run errands for him.' Lazar smiles sadly. 'He was worried the US government would seize his paperwork after his death. Sadly, his fear came true.

'In his last months he had many admirers but few friends, and trusted almost no one. When he heard Alan Turing was on his way to New York, the news energized him! Tesla had heard rumours of Turing's breakthroughs in mathematics and computers. He had visions in which Turing built a machine that would end the war.' Lazar's eyes shine. 'Tesla saw into the future!'

I remember from my history lessons, Lazar is referring to Turing's Bombe, a machine that was instrumental in cracking the German Enigma code and ending the war early. Hearing tales of Tesla and Turing's brilliance from people who not only knew them but worked with them, is humbling.

Prudente-Poulton says, 'Tesla asked Lazar to deliver plans to Turing. We believe the plans were for your machine.'

'Tesla handed me an envelope,' Lazar picks up the story. 'In the weeks and months before, he talked constantly about his ideas for what he called a Human Drive. I have no doubt that Tesla sent plans for the Drive to Alan Turing and asked him to develop it using state-of-the-art electronics.'

'Human Drive?' I frown.

Professor Feldman jumps in. 'The Turing-Tesla League Human Drive is the official name for your machine. We call it the Drive, for short.'

Prudente-Poulton shoots Lazar a penetrating look. 'We can only speculate about the envelope's contents, since Lazar never looked inside.'

Lazar waggles a finger. 'That is true, but the plans Richard Martin used to build the Drive include handwritten annotations which match Tesla and Turing's handwriting.'

'Neither man signed his name,' Prudente-Poulton says. 'As scientists, we deal in absolutes.'

'They did not need to sign!' Lazar's voice rises. 'I recognised Tesla's writing.'

Professor Feldman interrupts. 'The plans contain elements from Tesla's patents, including the generation and transmission of messages. Tesla's concepts combined electrical engineering and quantum physics. He was fascinated by the idea of designing a thought camera, an eye into the brain, if you like. We think the Drive was an off-shoot from that initial idea.'

My poor, overloaded mind rolls the information into a tangled ball and shoves it somewhere for later.

I ask Lazar, 'So, you think Tesla developed this idea for the findin...the Drive?'

'That is my hypothesis.'

Prudente-Poulton adds, 'We believe Turing annotated the plans and made improvements. As far as we know, he did not take them further. The war effort consumed him. And besides, electronics available at the time did not have the capabilities Tesla's machine required.'

Carmen says warmly, 'However, Tesla's vision and Turing's technological know-how left us a blueprint. Your father did the rest.'

Pride surges through me. My father left a legacy that will live on and could impact hundreds, if not thousands of lives in a positive way.

'One question's still bugging me,' I say. 'Why did Dad build it in secret?'

Carmen shrugs. 'I can only assume he didn't want to share the machine until he found Lilian. But he died before he could find her, and the machine found its way to you. I'm sure he was also worried how the machine would be used. You have the same concerns, I'm sure.'

Indeed, I do. But meeting Carmen, Lazar and the others has gone some way towards alleviating them.

Prudente-Poulton gives me a knowing look. 'So, Alex. May we see it?'

33

The League members fall silent, leaving a background hum of oscillators and servers.

Swallowing hard, I unzip my rucksack and place my fingers around the finding machine. Taking a breath, I lift it from the bag and place it into Prudente-Poulton's hands.

His fingers brush the side vent with a kind of reverence. 'I didn't think it would be so—'

'—cold?' I give him a knowing look.

'Heavy.'

'It *is* an Olivetti accountancy case, like I thought!' Professor Feldman lets out a laugh, reaching out to touch the vent. 'The cold must be the effect of the spectr—'

Prudente-Poulton silences him with a glare. 'General observations only.'

Clearing my throat, I say, 'I'm one of you now. I have the right to know.'

But Prudente-Poulton is adamant. 'The science would mean nothing to you, or the plans. The gas is harmless and the machine is safe to handle. That's all you need to know for now.' He pauses. 'TJ, clear a space.'

The teenager stacks plates and mugs to one side of the table.

Prudente-Poulton sets the machine down and steps back, rubbing his hands together. I hope it's down to the cold and not because he's finally got his hands on my machine.

Carmen and Professor Feldman *ooh* and *aah* as they examine the machine. TJ crouches, hooking his fingers over the table's edge to view it at eye level.

'Show it to me.' Lazar pushes himself so far forward he looks in danger of falling from his chair. 'Hold it up. Can we see a demonstration?'

'I'm sorry, it's broken,' I say, but the others pay me no heed.

Carmen points to the tangle of electronics behind the perspex screen. 'The transistors are a definite improvement from the ones on the plans. Richard must have upgraded them.'

I leave them to it and wander over to the wall of photos. The first shows Nikola Tesla calmly reading a book during a furious lightning storm. Great white bolts of electricity fizz and crackle around him. The head and shoulder photo of Alan Turing hanging alongside appears dull by comparison. I briefly glance at three men I don't recognise, before I see Dad.

Dad sports natty sideburns, a green tweed jacket, and a grey shirt with pointed lapels. Seeing him amongst his friends and knowing his work will live on, brings on a mouth-trembling surge of emotion.

Prudente-Poulton comes alongside me and points to a closed door in the corner with a green light shining above. 'Over there's our clean lab, where the team will upgrade and clone the Drive. The space is sterile, dust and static-free, with a positive-pressure ventilation system. We can start work straightaway.'

I eye him. 'Once you've built your copy, what then? Will you use the cloned Drive to find people? To help them?'

'The League will vote,' Prudente-Poulton says. 'That's the way we do everything. But I give you my word we'll use it for the good of the country.'

Prudente-Poulton's cagey response niggles at me. What does *the good of the country* mean? The League has spidery connections to the police, possibly government. It makes me wonder where decisions are coming from. I somehow doubt the League would be interested in finding missing girls or lost teenagers. If I used my machine with the League's support, however, I could help others like Rashid, Amneet and Maisie.

I look Prudente-Poulton in the eye. 'When I get my machine back, I want to use it to find missing people. Can you offer me your support?'

'I'll put it to the League,' Prudente-Poulton says.

'There's one more thing. I'm working on a murder case. Our suspect is Reginald Goddall, also known as Reginald Carstairs. Can you use your connections to locate him?'

'I am aware of the case,' Prudente-Poulton says. 'A little bird tells me DC Longhurst will receive help from the Major Crime Division in the New Year. I'm sure these additional resources will ensure the culprit is swiftly found and brought to justice.'

There's no point asking how Prudente-Poulton knows this.

'What about the Drive?' I ask. 'How can I contact you to find out about progress?'

Prudente-Poulton hands me a slip of paper with a mobile number. 'This is TJ's phone. He's overseeing the build. You can liaise with him.'

'Thank you.'

'Now that you've seen our operations centre, I must respectfully ask you to leave us to our work.'

I glance at the table, hoping for one last look at my machine, but Carmen and Professor Feldman block my view. Prudente-Poulton sticks out his arm and walks me to the door.

Outside, Marshall waits by the foot of the stairs.

Prudente-Poulton says, 'Safe journey home, Alex. Happy Christmas.'

Before I can return the greeting, he closes the metal door behind me.

'I guess that's goodbye,' I mutter, shaking my head.

'They're just raring to go.' Marshall laughs as I follow him up the stairs to the corridor. He ushers me into the shelter of the doorway and presses the switch. The floor rises and the staircase becomes a boring old hallway once more.

We leave the Lodge.

'You okay?' Marshall asks, opening the Lexus's rear door.

'Just a lot to take in.' I slip into the back seat and hug my feather-light rucksack, feeling part of me is missing. The finding machine was old and awkward, cold and heavy, but it was my loyal companion and my last link to Dad.

'Marshall, how big is the League?'

'I can't say,' Marshall says, driving down the dark lane. 'We meet other members on a need-to-know basis.'

Instinct tells me Marshall's a good guy. Professor Feldman and Carmen were equally warm and open. My issues lie with the man at the top.

'I hope I get my machine back.'

'You can trust the League,' Marshall says. 'Jonathan keeps his cards close to his chest for good reason. With his connections, the fewer people in the loop the better.'

As Marshall rejoins the main road leading back to the motorway, I resolve to think of the League as a benevolent organisation working for good. I don't want mistrust and suspicion to play on my mind.

An unfamiliar lightness grows within me as the Lexus eats up the miles,

I'm free.

No more guilt-tripping over missing person posters, newspaper headlines or TV reports. Without the machine, there's nothing I can do. And once the League return my machine to me, everything will be different. Hopefully, the League will offer me its support, maybe even a job!

My achievements today help soften my feelings towards Antony. As we cruise up the M1, my thoughts turn mellow. Now Antony's off the clock, he'll be able to relax and go back to being the brilliant boyfriend I remember.

Christmas is the perfect time for new beginnings. The miles go by, and I ponder what a hollow, empty place my life would be without him.

By the time Marshall reaches Birmingham, I'm in a wholly positive frame of mind.

Marshall drives up to my door, checks his watch. 'It's gone midnight, Alex. Merry Christmas. Have a good one.'

'You too.' Once I've waved him off, I switch on my mobile. Four missed calls, all from Antony.

Three little tealights in amber holders cast a merry light on the porch. Hopefully, it's a sign Antony isn't mad at me for staying out late. I open the door and creep inside the flat, into the lounge.

Lights slowly pulse from the fibre-optic Christmas tree, casting a red and green glow across the wall and onto a pile of gold and silver-wrapped presents. Beside the tree, a plate contains half a carrot, a glass of milk, and a broken choc-chip cookie.

I don't see Antony at first. He's on the sofa, hidden in the dark.

'Antony?' I whisper.

He lets out a little snore. He's sitting up, asleep on the sofa in his boxer shorts with his mobile phone in hand.

Biting my lip, I pull off my boots and coat, and sneak into the office to retrieve Antony's presents from their hiding places. With the tiniest of rustles, I arrange them under the tree. Then, I change into my pyjamas.

I extricate Antony's phone and lightly shake him until his eyes flutter open.

'Alex...s'tat you?'

'I'm home, I'm safe. I love you,' I say, putting my arms around his waist.

'I didn't know where you were.' Fighting sleep, his voice slurs. 'You didn't answer your phone.'

'Sorry, I'm really sorry. I'll tell you about it tomorrow.'

I tug at him, encouraging him to get up and make the short journey into bed.

Antony collapses under the covers and I slip next to him. He turns to me, half-asleep, and pulls me into his arms. I snuggle back against his warm chest until we're wrapped up tight, and swiftly drift into oblivion.

34

CHRISTMAS DAY

My mobile buzzes on the side table. I fumble towards the sound, squinting against sharp sunlight streaming through the open curtains. Rubbing the sleep from my eyes, I press the button to accept the call.

'Hello?'

'Well, isn't this a fine day to welcome the birth of our Lord!' Mum's voice rings in my ear. '*Nollaig shona dhuit!*'

'Hi, Mum. Happy Christmas.' I breathe in the rich aroma of percolating coffee, drifting through the bedroom door. Stretching across Antony's empty side of the bed, I check the time:10:30. God, it's late.

'You sound groggy, Alexandra. Were you up late for Midnight Mass? If you weren't, you've missed the eight-thirty but you can still make the children's service if you get a move on.'

'I went last night.' I cover my barefaced lie with a loud yawn. Mum persists with the notion I'm a practising Catholic, although I've told her to the contrary on multiple occasions.

'Father Egan put on a splendid Mass,' Mum says. 'Did you have a candlelit procession? Ours was a great sea of lights, with everyone singing their hearts out. It moved me to tears, so much so that I lost my place on my hymn sheet and nearly collided with an altar server.'

'That's nice,' I mumble.

Mum continues on auto-pilot as I find my slippers. 'I wasn't sure what to get you for Christmas. I'm not up with the latest trends for PCs, mobile phones and Ninuendoes.'

'You mean Nintendos, Mum.'

'That's what I said. So, I've sent you a fifty-pound Marks & Spencer voucher.'

'Thanks for spoiling the surprise! Have you opened my present?'

Mum is notoriously judgmental about my gift choices, but I settled on a Fairisle jumper with a rose-pink pattern around the collar.

'It's a beautiful jumper, thank you. Now, how good is it with stains?'

'What have you done?' I ask in dismay.

'Nothing.' Mum sounds evasive. 'Anyway, Uncle Fintan is hosting the clan. Your cousin Orla's been practising on the accordion, so she'll be deafening us with that after the meal. I expect you and Antony will be having a nice, quiet time.'

'I hope so. Antony's been so busy at work.'

'You both deserve a break.' A long pause follows. 'Why don't you both come to Ireland for the New Year? You'd be far safer joining the procession up Benbulbin with me and Moira, than staying in the city.'

'I told you already, we can't come.' Mum's been asking the same question since August. After her last call, I checked local flights and ferries and found to my delight that every seat was booked until January. 'We're going to see in the New Year at home.'

'Well, Moira says the planes are going to fall from the sky on the thirty-first, and anyone living near an airport better say their prayers.' She pauses. 'Would you consider going into a bunker? Moira is sure you can find one if you ask around.'

'I don't know, Mum. I think you should take what Moira says with a pinch of salt.'

'But it's already started, Alexandra. Someone ate a tin of ninety-year-old corned beef because of the bug.'

'What?'

'And, there was an old lady in Minnesota who went to kindergarten at the age of 104 because the computer thought she was four.'

'That's fascinating, Mum, but I really must go,' I say, desperate to end the call for the sake of my sanity. 'I promise to stay away from cities and computers for New Year's Eve. I'll try and find a cellar to read a book in.'

'Good girl,' Mum says. 'You should be safe enough with that.'

I end the call and toss my phone on the bed, then pad across the hallway, following the sound of merry sleigh bell music into the kitchen.

Antony stands by the hob, chopping, boiling and frying while the radio plays Christmas classics. Every available bit of counter and hob space contains chopping boards, pans and trays full of food.

'Hello,' I say from the doorway, uncertain how this will go.

'Happy Christmas!' Antony stirs a pan and lowers the heat before striding towards me. He frowns. 'You cut your lip.'

'It's nothing.' I rush forward and wrap my arms round his waist. 'Happy Christmas!'

Antony stifles a yawn. He gestures to the hob and cluttered work surfaces. 'I couldn't sleep. Thought I might as well make myself useful.'

'It looks amazing! Are we expecting fifty guests?'

'Ha!' He gives me a squeeze. 'It's gonna be a good one. Despite you using the finding machine again.'

'I...' I go stiff in his arms, heart thumping.

'The girls and the cinema were all over the late-night news. I was really worried.' Antony gives me a sad smile.

'Did they mention me?'

Antony shakes his head. 'The reporter said they were rescued by a passer-by. Didn't say who.'

'Thank God.' I release a pent-up breath.

Antony releases me, his forehead creasing. 'Look, I'll give you props for saving their lives. But what you did was crazy. You could have ended up trapped in the cinema or held hostage by some psycho! Even after you got back, I kept running through everything that could have gone wrong. I wish you'd talked to me about it first.'

'I tried! I called your mobile *and* the office to let you know my plans, but you didn't answer. I even came in to see you. No one knew where you were, including your boss. At least, I think it was your boss. He had thinning hair, a sweaty pink shirt, and a bad attitude.'

'Sounds like Yan.' Antony removes his glasses and wipes steam from the lenses. 'Sorry I wasn't there. I was out to lunch.'

Tension stiffens my jaw. 'Who with?'

'Oh, a property guy. It was a business thing about office leases. Boring stuff.'

The urge to call him on it is so strong, I have to clench my teeth. Saskia's a designer, nothing to do with property leases. A sour taste floods my mouth.

If I push Antony on this, I won't be able to let go. It will ruin Christmas. All I want is a cozy few days with my boyfriend. Saskia needs dealing with, but not today.

'Did you get the note I left on your desk?' I ask.

'I did.' Antony leans in to kiss my forehead. 'Let's move on.'

We hold each other without speaking. I bite my lip. His secrets, my secrets, they're killing our trust. But before I start judging him, I need to put my own house in order.

'There's something you need to know about yesterday,' I say.

'What is it?'

'Someone from the League was waiting for me, after I rescued the girls.' I give him an abbreviated version of last night's events. Although I'm breaking my oath of secrecy to Prudente-Poulton, Antony deserves to know.

'The League got me fired from the NMPH. But they did it to protect me and keep my name out of the papers. They obviously have very high-up connections.' I pause. 'Once I get my machine back, I'm going to ask Prudente-Poulton if I can work for him. The League has the resources to keep me safe. That has to be a good thing, doesn't it?'

'I don't know.' Antony scratches his jaw. 'This Prudente-Poulton guy sounds cagey, and you don't know his agenda.'

I shrug. 'The others I met seemed decent, and Dad worked there for years. He wouldn't have done that if it was a corrupt organisation. The League could have stolen my machine or taken it by force. Instead, they allowed me to make the decision.'

'What if they don't give your machine back?' Antony's brow arches. 'You won't be able to do anything about it.'

'I'll send you in!' I warn him playfully. 'Don't bust my dreams. Not today.'

'All right. But it sounds like they're calling the shots. You want to find missing kids. Where do you fit in?'

'I don't know. Yet.'

I have to have faith the League will repair my machine and return it. Then I'll take it from there.

Antony says, 'Promise me, next time, you'll tell me before you go ahead and use it.'

'I promise.' I loop my arms around Antony's waist. 'Can we get on and enjoy Christmas, now?'

'Sounds like a plan.' Antony takes a pan off the heat and grabs a flyer from a drawer. 'If you want to do something, there's a laser show and fireworks at Edgbaston Stadium on the 31st. Want me to get tickets?'

'Definitely,' I nod, a weight lifting from me. 'Just don't tell my mum.'

Antony proudly points to a turkey crown topped with strips of bacon and a tray of fluffed-up potatoes, ready to go in the oven. He puts on a posh voice. 'Does ma'am approve?'

'Yes, she does!' My mouth waters at the thought of the feast to come.

Antony shows off a tray of stuffing. There are caramelised parsnips, buttered sprouts, pigs in blankets, and red-wine gravy.

'I'd better skip breakfast,' I say, rubbing my empty stomach.

'Nonsense!' Antony stirs a pan and takes it off the heat. 'I'm making Eggs Benedict. Start as you mean to go on, right?'

The last thing I ate was a slice of cake at Red Croft Lodge. Meeting the League seems like a distant memory.

'I suppose I could manage something,' I say with a grin, loving our easy banter and the fact the old Antony is back.

Antony brings breakfast through to the lounge. He dashes back into the kitchen and returns with a bottle of Veuve Clicquot champagne. My smile freezes as I look for a gold bow tied around the neck. No bow, but it could be the same bottle I saw on his desk, from a female admirer.

Get a grip, Alex! The champagne was a gift from a client, and Antony brought it home for us.

We sip champagne and eat breakfast. The bubbles go to my head, bolstering my sense of goodwill and festive cheer. My thoughts go to Maisie and Amneet. I hope they're home for Christmas and having the best one ever.

After breakfast, the atmosphere is light and easy and all traces of tension have disappeared. We kneel by the tree and open our presents. Antony makes all the right noises when he opens a little box containing silver cufflinks with *Zap!* And *Pow!* on them, and a multicoloured Ted Baker scarf. When he rips open his main present, his eyes light up.

'Quake III?' He reaches over and kisses me. 'Did I ever tell you I love you?'

I smile. 'It's good to know three hours waiting in line with a thermos of coffee was worth it!'

Antony laughs as he tears the film from the CD case. 'I'm gonna get serious with this. God, I've missed gaming! You might never see me again.'

'It'll be like the good old days in Ware.' I grin. 'Gunfire shaking the floorboards…the tortured screams of monsters being blasted to pieces.'

'That's my girl.' He pushes presents on me. 'Your turn.'

I open my presents in a delirium of excitement: Fortnum and Mason chocolates including violet creams, which I thought only existed in Enid Blyton books, and luxury knitted slippers. I run my fingers over the soft fleece lining before pulling them on.

Antony hands me a rectangular present. I tear it open. Inside, is a box of Winsor & Newton oil paints in unusual colours, including gold and fizzing green.

'Flesh Tint, Neon Yellow, Lamp Black.' I read the labels and throw him a sharp look. 'No artist worth their salt uses black!'

'Knew that would bug you,' Antony grins.

A thousand possibilities for new paintings come to mind, but the Pagoda is the one that sticks with me. Already, I'm imagining lush gardens brought to life with sparks of vivid colour.

'There's something else,' Antony says, handing me an envelope.

Inside, is a piece of paper headed: *Promissary Note.*

'What's this?' I ask, tingles of excitement mixing with the bubbles.

'It's a promise that when things settle down in the New Year, we'll find a warm artists' space for you to paint in. I'm sorry I haven't found one already, what with work and everything.' His brow skews, as he waits for my reply. 'Is that okay?'

'It's more than okay. I love it!' I squeal and launch myself at Antony, who spills champagne but manages to keep hold his glass.

'Tell you what,' he says. 'Let me get dinner in the oven, and we can have a Christmas cuddle in bed.'

Raising a brow I ask, 'What's the difference between a Christmas cuddle and a normal one?'

Antony slips his arms round me and lifts me up, carrying me from the room.

'You get to keep your slippers on.'

35

After our cuddle, Antony and I pile our plates with roast turkey and all the trimmings and eat until our stomachs groan. Somehow, we find room for Christmas pudding, then clear the plates away, stuff the fridge-freezer with leftovers, and tackle the washing up.

'Do you mind if I load up my game?' Antony asks. 'Or, we could watch TV, go for a walk...'

'No, go ahead.' I flick the tea towel at his bum and chase him into the office.

Ten minutes later, I listen at the door, disappointed not to hear anything. Back when we rented a house in Ware, Antony would crank up the volume to palpitation-inducing levels once the neighbours left for work. In the flat, it's headphones or no gaming. I prefer inhuman screams and shotgun blasts to dead silence. The noise reminds me that he's home.

I flop onto the sofa, throw a blanket over myself and flick through the TV channels. *The Great Escape, Home Alone, It's A Wonderful Life,* nothing grabs me. I switch to BBC, hoping for news of the girls. A reporter wearing a yellow hard hat discusses the much-anticipated opening of The Millennium Dome in London, due to take place on New Year's Eve.

Perhaps the League pulled the media reports on Amneet and Maisie. Either that, I've missed it, or it's old news already.

I switch off the TV and snuggle under the blanket with my eyelids drooping.

My mobile rings in the bedroom.

It could be my brother, Matt, calling from Seattle. He usually gives me a ring on Christmas and my birthday. Throwing off the covers, I drag myself into the bedroom and check who's calling.

HENRY_LO

Heat rises to my cheeks, along with a flush of guilt. My gaze goes to the wall dividing me and Antony.

I head back inside the lounge, shut the door, and press *Accept Call.*

'Hello, Henry,' I say quietly. 'Happy Christmas.'

'Happy Christmas, Alex. I don't mean to interrupt, but you asked me to keep you in the loop.' Henry's voice is taut, like he's holding back. 'Do you have a minute?'

'Sure. What is it?'

'Forensics came back yesterday, regarding the contents of the tarpaulin we pulled from the river.'

The memory of the Mimram's freezing water surging past my legs makes me shiver – my arms plunging under the black surface to grab the tarp.

'What did they find?'

'Well, the first round of familial DNA tests failed,' Henry says. 'The lab repeated the test on a tooth fragment and got a partial match to Avril. The result strongly suggests they're Nenagh's remains.' He pauses. 'This is down to you, Alex. Well done.'

Even though I knew Nenagh was inside the tarp all along, the news comes as a relief. It proves Henry was right to have faith in me.

'Have you told Avril?'

'Yes. She took the news well, considering, and suspects Reginald more than ever.'

'What happens now?'

'The good news is, my boss is assigning me a team from Major Crime. They start work in January.'

I listen in stunned silence. Prudente-Poulton told me Henry would receive help on the case. Things are happening just like he said.

Henry says, 'We must be doing something right because my boss has agreed to investigate Duggie's grave.'

My fingers twitch around the phone. Could this be down to the League, too? But how could it possibly know what's going on in Henry's department?

'But all we had to go on was the reading on my machine,' I say.

'Don't forget the supporting evidence,' Henry reminds me. 'Reginald Carstairs' property deeds, and the groundskeeper's account of Reginald helping him dig graves at the church around the same time Delia Carstairs went missing. The vicar checked the records for the date Duggie was buried. Reginald reported his wife missing less than a week later. Rather a coincidence, wouldn't you say?'

'It does sound more and more like he's to blame,' I say.

'We'll know more on the twenty-eighth.'

'Is that when they're digging Duggie up?'

'Yes,' Henry says. 'It will be a disinterment rather than an exhumation, as Duggie stays tucked inside his coffin. Luckily, Duggie's family has agreed to it. The vicar has also asked any parishioners with information on Reginald or Delia to come forward.'

I wander into the kitchen and lean against the countertop. 'Sounds like you have it all sewn up.'

'If only it was that easy,' Henry demurs. 'Reginald has reinvented himself at least once. As far as I can tell, he has only one weakness.'

'What is it?' I hold my breath.

'All the data regarding Reginald fits geographically within a ten-mile radius of Hertford. His mother is buried in Hertford Cemetery and she may be the reason he refuses to move out of the area.' He pauses. 'That man you saw staring at you by the river. It could have been him.'

A chill goes up my spine.

'It sounds like you don't need me anymore.'

'Actually, I do,' Henry says. 'I should have mentioned, when I visited Avril to tell her about the DNA results, she had found a photo of Reginald. It's an old photo, but one's all you need, right?'

My skin prickles, as if tiny spiders are running over me. 'What do you mean?'

'Photos. That's how you find people.'

My throat constricts. I drop the phone on the drainer and reach for the tap, fill a glass with water and gulp it down. The cold liquid sends pain shooting across my temples.

Henry's still talking when I pick up the phone.

'...know I'm right. I worked it out when I went back through the files. You found Nenagh and Delia easily but couldn't find Reginald. It didn't make sense. Then, I remembered Simon saying Nenagh's photo was missing from the file. You dashed into the box room, and hey presto, the photo reappears.' Henry leaves a long pause. 'You used that photo to find her, didn't you?'

I rest my arm on the wall and press my forehead into my sleeve. 'You promised not to push me on the machine.'

'All I need to know is, can you help?'

Pain throbs at my temples. I squeeze my eyes shut. 'My machine stopped working. Right now, it's in a workshop in pieces.'

A muffled groan travels down the receiver. 'When will it be fixed?' Henry asks morosely.

'I don't know.'

To say the finding machine is a niche, specialized device is putting it mildly.

Silence comes down the line. I drink more water, slowly this time.

'I'm still going to email you Reg's photo,' Henry says. 'Hopefully, your workshop guys can fix the machine quickly. In the meantime, if you have other talents in the psychic realm, now would be a good time to use them.'

'Can't you ask the psychic you used before? Didn't he direct you to Nenagh's file in the first place?'

'He did that as a favour before he retired to Spain. I don't know where he went, and I doubt he calls himself *Psychic Mike* anymore.'

'He's probably *Psychic Miguel*, now. You should look him up.'

Henry releases an exasperated sigh. 'I guess everything rests on the disinterment. Take a look at the photo and remember you're still part of the team. You have the makings of a good detective, even without your machine.'

I murmur thanks.

'I'll call you on the twenty-eighth. Enjoy the rest of your Christmas.'

'Bye.'

Dropping the phone on the counter, I rummage in the cupboard for paracetamol and swallow two with another glass of water. I fight the urge to bang my aching head against the wall. If only Avril had found the photo earlier!

Pacing the kitchen doesn't help. Neither does unloading the dishwasher. It's only after I've put the last knife in the cutlery drawer that I come up with a plan.

I cross the hall and crack open the office door. Antony has drawn the curtains to immerse himself in his game. His fingers rattle over the keys, eyes fixed on the screen. Monstrous combatants rush him from doorways, staircases and secret passages within a labyrinthine castle. Enemies explode as his shotgun pumps continuous rounds into them.

I sidle past him to my PC and boot it up.

'What the—' Antony jumps in his seat. He hits Pause and swivels to face me, eyebrows rising to his hairline. 'You nearly gave me a heart attack!'

'Sorry, I popped in to check my emails.' I put a hand on his shoulder. 'How's the game?'

'Great, but I'm rusty. I keep dying.' Antony slips his headphones off and turns the volume down on the tinny heavy metal soundtrack. 'I'm getting a coffee. You want one?'

'No thanks.' I pat my stomach. 'I'll explode.'

I log on to the internet and access my emails. My brother Matt has sent a Christmas round-robin instead of calling. I skim-read the self-congratulatory round-up of another incredible year of charity marathons, job promotions and exotic holidays. Their son Oscar won a scholarship to the most prestigious private school in the area, and they now have a dog. It's probably the most intelligent dog in the world.

I'll bang out a reply later, listing my disasters. That should curb Matt's smugness.

I open Henry's email: *Hi, Alex, Reginald's photo is attached. See what you can do. Catch up soon, Henry.*

I scold myself for looking for a kiss at the end, and banish my traitorous thoughts. No kiss means it's back to business with Henry. Considering my new start with Antony, that's probably for the best.

I double-click on the photo.

The black and white picture shows Reginald in a pinstripe suit and dark tie, striking a film star pose. He leans casually on a wall, cigarette between his fingers, his shiny fair hair styled with an attractive sweep at the front. A pencil-thin moustache hangs above a neat smile. Nothing in the photo shouts murderer.

Grabbing my phone, I call TJ's number. To my surprise, he answers on the third ring.

'Hey, TJ. Happy Christmas! Sorry to bother you.'

'No worries. I've done Christmas with the fam. Happy to be back at work.'

'I've just received a photo of Reginald, our suspected murderer. Can I email it to you?'

TJ pauses. 'I can't do anything with the Drive in pieces.'

'I know. But if you get it working sooner, please call me straightaway with Reginald's location. Believe me, you'll be doing the world a favour.'

'All right, send it over.' TJ gives me his email address. 'No guarantees on the timescale, though.'

'Just do your best.' I hang up.

Next, I open the AltaVista search engine and find a photo of Errol Flynn. I want to see if the comparison is accurate.

Reginald fades into mediocrity against Errol's dashing good looks. When compared against one of the best-looking men of all time, Reginald looks like the Poundland version. His chin is weak and lacks a dimple. His nose is slightly crooked, his neck too short, and his eyes too small.

But the glaring difference is Reginald's expression. His pupils are dark, and his smile does not reach his eyes. Errol's have a cheeky glint along with empathic depth. Reginald's stare is hollow and cold.

My stomach lurches. My heart picks up. It's him, the man in the crowd. I only caught a split-second glimpse. Too swift to remember, yet my mind must have logged his face deep in my subconscious to protect me.

I take a deep breath, and print out Reginald's picture on glossy photo paper. Then I search the internet for a photo of a middle-aged Errol Flynn and print that too. I grab my sketch pad, pencil case, tracing and carbon paper, and leave the office before Antony returns for another bout of monster hunting.

Someone around Hertford knows where Reginald is. They just need a visual reminder.

I kneel at the coffee table and transfer two outlines of Reginald's face, side-by-side, onto a large sheet of drawing paper. Using Errol Flynn's photo for reference, I set to work turning the twenty-something Reginald into a sixty-five-year-old.

I make his jawline sag, thin his hair, make his nose fleshier and give him larger ears. I pencil in wrinkles around his eyes and hollows in the slack of his cheeks. After an hour, I'm satisfied with the result.

My second version portrays Reginald as an older man, who has enjoyed too many pints and pies over the years. I remove more of his hair, add sagging jowls and age him badly. In both illustrations, I'm careful to capture the intensity in his eyes, although I have to watch my biased feelings and not make him look evil.

Once I'm happy with both sketches, I commit to final strokes with a 2B pencil, using a darker 4B for the pupils, shadows around the eyes and the line between his lips. Overall, I think I've done a pretty good job, but the proof of the pudding will be Henry's reaction.

Keen to find out if my illustrations pass muster, I sneak back into the office, giving Antony another jump scare. Once I have scanned and emailed my drawings to Henry, I sink back on my chair.

It's no finding machine, but maybe it will turn up something. I can only hope.

36

— · —

Antony and I spend Boxing Day lolling around in bed, eating and drinking, and watching old films. In the afternoon, I nap while he plays his game. My cares float away. I wish it could be like this all the time, but Antony only has one more day of freedom before he goes back to work.

I sense his mood drop as light falls.

'We have tomorrow,' I remind him.

'Sure.' He forces a small smile, but remains distracted for the rest of the evening.

The following morning, Antony nudges me awake at eight a.m. I peek from the duvet to find him standing by the bed, dressed in jogging bottoms, sweat top and trainers, with a CD Walkman clipped to his waistband and lightweight headphones looped around his neck.

'Hey, sleepy-head, the sun's out. Want to join me for a run?' He grips the doorframe and limbers up with some calf raises. 'I'll give you five minutes to get ready.'

'Mind if I give it a miss?' I offer an apologetic smile. 'I'm not feeling it.'

I could use the exercise, but running with Antony is a lose-lose. Trying to keep up with him will kill me.

Antony checks his watch. 'Might go for a longer run, then. I haven't done a 10K in months.'

'Knock yourself out.'

He raises his phone. 'Call if you need me.' A few seconds later, I hear the front door slam.

Once he's gone, I potter about in my dressing gown and Christmas slippers with a mug of coffee, watching the kitchen clock. Antony's absence gives me the opportunity to act on plans I made last night without sneaking around or risking his disapproval.

I fight the urge to call TJ about progress on the machine. The chances the team has already built the clone, upgraded my machine and completed testing are zero.

Henry made a suggestion that I tap into my 'psychic ability.' It's given me an idea. Entering the office, I switch on my PC. While it's booting up, I retrieve last year's diary hidden beneath paperwork in my in-tray, and flick through the pages to May, and a newspaper cutting glued inside:

Miriam, Spirit Reader, available for all messages from the nether to the NOW! Have you lost someone you want to contact, was there something important you needed to say? Do you need to know if someone has passed over peacefully? Miriam can help you, email me a photograph miriamskydiamond@tiscali.co.uk. Call me: 07700-900365. I can do your reading from a photo!

Last year, I sent Miriam a photo of my great-uncle, Victor. It was too blurry to work in the finding machine, but I suspected he had something to do with my aunt Lilian's death. Miriam gave me valuable insights into Lilian's fate, and I hope she can do the same regarding Reginald, even if he hasn't passed over.

I forward Miriam the photo of Reginald, adding he's a long-lost relative and it's vital I find him.

The next thing on my list is to call Henry. He picks up after three rings.

'Hey, Alex,' he says. 'I was about to call you.'

The inviting warmth of his voice sends tingles through me, even though he's a hundred miles away.

Swallowing, I say, 'How was your Christmas?'

'Pretty quiet. I'm having dinner with Olivia and the gang tonight. Charlie is really excited about showing me his presents.'

'Say hi from me.' I imagine the crackling fire, family meals, the tree filling the house with the smell of pine.

'I will.' Henry pauses. 'I guess you're ringing about your drawings. They're great! I don't think our police sketch-artists could have done any better.'

I release a huge breath. 'Really? You have people who do these...identikits, don't you?'

'We call them facial composites. They're useful when we don't know the suspect's identity, but that doesn't apply in our case. You've managed to keep Reginald's likeness while doing a good job aging him. Someone's bound to recognise him.'

I'm pleased to have done something to help that doesn't involve my machine.

Henry says, 'I'm putting together a flyer with Reginald's photograph and your drawings for the Hertford News and Mail, but I'm also going door-to-door. I've made a list of used car dealerships near Hertford, and local churches. My problem is I'm running on a skeleton crew until after the New Year. Simon's working for the Millennium Team until January, which only leaves Tori. Can you come down? I could use your help.'

'I'm sorry, I'm tied up here,' I say, reluctant to rush off now Antony and I are solid again.

'I understand,' Henry says flatly. 'Enjoy your break. I'll be in touch once we've looked in Duggie's grave.'

'Great, thanks.' I say, ending the call.

By lunchtime, Antony's still not back and I wonder if he's decided to run a marathon instead of a 10K. I fix myself a plate of cold cuts, followed by Christmas pudding, warmed in the microwave with lashings of double cream. After lunch, I call to check he's okay.

'Hey, babe,' Antony answers. In the background, I hear a woman laugh in the same velvety tone I remember from before.

'Who's that?' I ask, my antennae quivering. I strain to hear past traffic noise, quacking ducks and a crying baby.

'Sorry, I've moved somewhere quieter,' he says. 'What's up?'

'I just wondered where you were,' I say lamely. 'Are you with someone?'

'Just bumped into a friend. I should be back in an hour or two.'

'Is it Saskia?'

Antony pauses. An edge of defensiveness enters his voice. 'We bumped into each other by the river. What are the chances?'

Zero. 'She was in the pub last time I called. You were at lunch when I came to the office. Now you're hooking up behind my back!'

'Is that what you think?' The lightness leaves his voice.

'I want to know what you're up to!' I shout down the line.

'Just calm down.'

'I'll calm down when you tell me what's going on!'

'We'll talk later. I can't do this now.' Antony kills the call.

I drop the phone on the table, breathing heavily through my nose. If I had the finding machine, I'd track him down and find out exactly what he's up to. Without it, I'm left fuming at home while he gallivants around with this other woman!

Worry sits in my gut like a cannonball. I spend the afternoon checking my email for updates from Henry and Mystic Miriam, and looking out of the window for Antony. The feeling of being ignored and sidelined grows. By the time Antony gets home, I'm a mess of rage and frustration.

Antony enters the lounge breathing heavily with sweat stains under his arms.

'Now, can we talk?' I snap.

'Let me get in the door.' He raises a brow, eyes wide. 'I need a shower.'

'Forget the shower!' My heightened emotions instantly derail all reason. 'You used a run as an excuse to meet Saskia, didn't you?'

'No.' Antony wipes sweat from his forehead. 'I asked you to join me, remember? Saskia texted me. She was on my route, so we met up. End of.'

'I don't believe you.'

'That's your problem.' Antony stalks past me, grabs a towel from the bathroom and mops his brow as he heads into the lounge.

His casual reply hits me like a heavyweight right hook. My jaw drops. A burning sensation floods my cheeks as I front up to him. 'Are you having an affair?'

Antony crosses his arms, stony-faced. 'Cut me some slack, Alex. We already had this conversation.'

'This isn't a conversation. It's you lying to me!' Tears well up as I revert to toddler-in-full-tantrum mode. Our neighbours probably have their ears to the walls, but I don't care.

Antony grits his jaw, stares at the ceiling. 'You need to stop acting like this.'

'Like what?' I throw up my hands. 'Like it's my fault? You're the one sneaking around, hiding things!'

'And you're not?' Antony gives me a hard glare, then heads for the front door.

'Where are you going?' I chase after him like a spurned lover in a soap opera.

'To the gym. For a shower.' He pauses. 'And some peace, before my nose goes back to the grindstone. Thanks for nothing.'

He leaves, slamming the door.

Closing my eyes, I lean against the hall radiator, drawing in shuddering breaths. The four walls press in on me until I can't stand it any longer. Grabbing my coat and keys, I storm from the flat.

I walk for ages down the river, blinking back tears. Families throw bread to the ducks, couples stroll hand in hand, but no one notices me. I hoped fresh air would help clear my head, but the sick feeling of betrayal stays with me until I return home.

Antony's in the office, playing his game. When I cross the hall and pop my head around the door, he barely glances my way before returning his attention to the screen.

The evening that follows is one of the most uncomfortable I can remember. Neither of us acknowledges the other. Antony heats up leftovers for dinner and takes them into the office to eat, leaving me impotently simmering on the sofa. I eat reheated Christmas dinner. The turkey is dry, the potatoes are soggy, and the Brussels sprouts have gone an insipid shade of green. All festive joy has fled. I slather gravy over everything and shovel in the food mechanically, watching a black and white film without taking anything in.

We're at an impasse, and Antony's refusal to help us move past it makes me think it's really over.

I seek solace in the bottle and polish off glass after glass of wine while watching junk TV. I fall asleep in a drunken stupor, rousing briefly to find Antony in his pyjama bottoms, piling bedding by the coffee table.

'I'll sleep here,' he says. 'I need to get up early for work, so if you wouldn't mind...'

He tilts his head towards the bedroom.

'Antony,' I sit up with my head spinning. 'We can't leave it like this. We have to talk this through.'

'I don't have the energy,' he says dully, switching off the TV. 'I've got too much on my mind. Christmas is over.'

37

—·—

I wake in the night with a sour taste in my mouth and a pounding headache. My argument with Antony runs around my mind like a film stuck on a loop. Time and time again, his cold responses wound me. I only want the truth, but for some reason he won't give it to me.

I fumble on the bedside table for my phone and rub my blurry eyes to check the time: 2:30am.

Swinging my legs out of bed, sneak out of the bedroom and creep along the hall like a thief in my own home. I duck inside the office and softly close the door. Then, I start digging.

Last year, if someone had told me I'd be going through my boyfriend's things looking for signs of an affair, I'd have laughed my head off. Yet, here I am, poking through his desk drawer and switching on his Mac to check his emails.

In his desk, below a stapler, calculator, hole-punch and postage stamps, I find a few scraps of paper with Antony's handwriting:

I'm torn. I know you are too. Please be patient a little longer. It'll be worth it.

We will be so much more, when we're not snatching moments together.

When I think of you, I ~~can't find the words~~

Nausea sits under my ribs. I swallow it back, fighting tears. I wanted evidence, but now I've found it, I want to unsee it.

I plough on. Antony's email password hasn't changed since I met him. His inbox contains catch-ups from friends and family,

225

bank statements, insurance quotes, floorplans from a company called Your Workspace, bills, and spam. There's nothing from Saskia. I open random emails in sub-folders just in case, but everything appears above board.

I shut down the Mac, leave the office, and pad across the hall. At the lounge doorway, I stop short.

Snores drift from the sofa. Antony's arm hangs from the duvet. His watch glows in the dark, casting green light on the coffee table and the edge of his mobile phone.

My heart picks up as I advance around the sofa, feeling with my feet for trip hazards. Antony faces the table. Holding my breath, I reach for his phone, expecting his eyes to snap open.

In one smooth motion, I snatch the phone and press it to my chest. My heart races as I keep still. Antony sleeps on, and I allow myself to breathe again.

I head back to the bedroom with my stomach churning. Until recently, I've considered Antony to loyal. Burrowing under the covers, with my pillow over my head, I access his calls and text messages.

Antony hasn't covered his tracks. There are numerous text messages from Saskia, confirming meet-up times. Four of them stop me dead. I scribble them down on a piece of paper:

I found a place. It'll be a squeeze but we can get something bigger in time. Your share of the deposit is £1,200 by Friday.

If we're making a go of this, you must tell her. We can't keep it a secret any longer.

It's not fair keeping her in the dark. You're only making things worse. She knows something's going on. You HAVE 2 tell her.

Got the keys! Let's do lunch @ The Malt House to celebrate! Meet U at 1.30?

The last text sent was today at 16:08. My thumb hovers over the call button.

I dial Saskia with my heart thundering in my ears. The phone rings five times before a robotic voice cuts in: *Sorry, the person you are calling is not available. Please leave a message after the tone.*

At the beep, I lose my nerve and kill the call. I ring the number again. Once more, courage abandons me. Perhaps it's for the best. The two are meeting at the pub tomorrow. I fully intend to gate-crash their cozy tête-à-tête.

I fold the paper into a tiny square and tuck it into the inside pocket of my jacket. Slipping from bed, I return the phone to the coffee table, then sneak back under the covers. I toss and turn for hours, and jolt awake to a silent flat. Cursing, I check the time. I've slept in, and missed the chance to catch Antony before he left for work. I pull aside the curtains to check the car park, but the Audi's gone.

Dragging myself into the lounge, I spot a folded note on the coffee table and open it with a sick feeling separate from my hangover.

Antony's writing is untidy and rushed:

Alex, <u>*I'M SORRY ABOUT LAST NIGHT.*</u> *You're right we need to talk. Let's do it tonight as soon as I get home. XX*

My mouth tugs down at the edges. I touch the paper to my lips. Is this us, finished? But if Antony's about to confess all, why the big kisses? I'll get my answers at The Malt House. After taking paracetamol, antacid tablets dissolved in water, and three cups of coffee, I check my inbox. I have a new message:

Hello Alex, it's lovely to hear from you again. I have a session available at 11:00 am today if that is suitable. Mystic Miriam ~ ask, and the universe will answer.

At 11:00 on the dot, I'm ready. I'm wearing my old transcription headset attached to a micro-cassette recorder. The landline cable is plugged into the recorder, enabling me to tape our conversation.

I dial Miriam's number, then press *Record*.

'Hello, Alex.' Miriam's voice is warm like a hug. 'Shall we begin?'

In my mind's eye, I see a grey-haired ball of a woman watching *Gems TV* and drinking tea from a kitten-patterned mug. 'You're asking about Reginald, your uncle once removed?'

'That's right.' I had deliberated whether to make Reginald part of my family. But 'distant relation' sounds a hell of a lot better than 'murderer'.

'He's handsome,' Miriam says. 'He reminds me of a film star, and yet...'

She trails off, but I stay silent. The last time I rang, she told me off for interrupting the spiritual flow.

'I hope this doesn't upset you, dear, but darkness hangs over him. It happens sometimes, when an individual passes through the veil between this world and the next. But I don't think this is the case with your uncle.'

'Reginald is the black sheep of the family,' I say, a sudden chill running up my spine. 'You can be honest with me, Miriam. It's okay.'

'If you're sure.' Miriam hesitates. 'Your uncle's aura is blocking the spiritual flow. I sense that he is holding onto a great deal of pain and anger, and is unwilling to release the negativity that holds him back. Something in his childhood has caused this.'

I remember Reginald's mother, who fell pregnant young and had a child out of wedlock. His father was an unwanted visitor who never knew his son. Reginald spent his childhood in poverty with a bitter and angry mother.

'Hold on,' Miriam says. 'I see a flash of red, which can mean a sense of adventure. And yellow, indicating charm, the sort of person you want to be around.' A cautionary note enters her voice. 'But you do not want to be around this man, Alex.'

'I just need to know where he is.'

'The spirits reveal what they will,' Miriam explains, still hesitant. 'The realm through the veil is not like the mortal one. It is not as simple as asking a question and receiving an answer.' She pauses. 'Wait…something is coming through.'

I hold my breath, pencil poised over my pad, hoping it will be a telephone number, address, or landmark.

'A symbol. Silver wings, like angel wings. Does that mean anything to you?'

'No.'

'I'm getting something else…red roses on a red background.'

'Is that all?' I ask with a hint of desperation. 'What does it mean?'

'There's something…no…I shouldn't say.'

'Please, Miriam. I need to know everything.'

She sighs. 'The last time I saw an aura like this was when I worked as a prison counsellor. Most of the men were happy to talk and were trying to change their lives. The colours of their auras changed over time to become brighter and more positive. One day, I came upon the guards transferring a prisoner into solitary. When he looked at me, his aura was a black hole. I cannot bear to tell you what he was imprisoned for, but the experience left me so shaken that I left my job.' She gives a regretful sigh. 'I'm sorry to say, your uncle's aura is the same.'

An icy chill radiates across my chest.

'That's all I have, dear. This reading has taken a lot out of me. I'm sorry I couldn't help more, but I need to rest.'

'Thank you for everything, Miriam.'

I hang up and press *Stop* on the cassette recorder, then make notes. Silver angel wings: a sad reference to Nenagh and Delia's fate, or perhaps Miriam senses they are now in a better place. Red roses are the symbol for love. But Reginald never loved his wives. Both visions could mean something or nothing.

I rattle off an email to Henry detailing my conversation with Miriam. Anyone else would think me nuts for ringing her, but he is open-minded about psychics. He may have insights into Miriam's reading. My taped call is probably inadmissible as evidence, but if silver wings and red roses help catch Reginald, then it's worth a shot.

38

— · —

After a quick lunch, I dress warmly in my coat, tartan snood and gloves and head for the pub. I follow the main road into the city, the roar of traffic filling my ears. Flocks of starlings and mobbing crows dart across heavy grey skies.

I cross the A38 via a bleak concrete slipway and drop down a lane to rejoin the canal path. Narrow boats moored for winter gently bob on the water, as I walk alongside the river. I catch my reflection in a long, dark boat window and flinch at the pale and haggard woman staring back.

The Malt House is a quirky riverside pub with curved balustrades on the first floor that frame a raised seating area. A few brave souls are drinking outside in the chill wind. Antony's not among them.

I spot the Audi in the car park. Sidling up to the car, a flash of gold catches my eye. I press my face to the driver's window. A polka dot scarf is draped across the passenger seat. I unzip my pocket for my keys, which includes a spare for the Audi, unlock the car and look inside. The scarf is silk, Hermès, laced with expensive perfume. The casual way Saskia left it reeks of over-familiarity and a sense of ownership. A hot, angry flush courses through me.

Clenching my fists, I head for the pub and push through the doors. The place is buzzing with the lunchtime crowd. A thick-necked security guy's on the door, with forearms as big as my legs. He gives me a brief glance.

My eyes dart to the diners eating and drinking at tables set underneath arched windows overlooking the river. Groups of sharp-suited executives crowd the bar, surrounded by a haze of cigarette smoke. I squeeze through the dining area to a raised mezzanine at the back. A single step leads to an L-shaped area. Red leather sofas and armchairs are arranged around low tables.

Saskia and Antony are in the corner, having an animated conversation over glasses of wine. Antony's keys rest atop a sheaf of paper alongside Saskia's expensive bag, a half-empty bottle of wine, and two plates containing half-eaten Ploughman's lunches.

Bitterness floods my stomach.

Saskia's stunning baby-blue eyes, perfectly pale complexion and elegant ash eyebrows take my breath away. Everything about her oozes class, from her French manicure, Links jewellery, and Chanel blouse with gold chain design. She's the type Antony used to go for. Beautiful, stylish, sophisticated. Nothing like me.

If women were my thing, I'd be besotted. As it is, I find her beauty captivating in a begrudging, hateful kind of way. I duck behind a dark wooden partition leading to the loos in an attempt to eavesdrop, but can't hear anything over multiple raucous conversations, bouts of laughter, and the dinging Wheel of Fortune game in the corner.

Before I lose my nerve, I stride round the partition. I stop behind Antony with one hand on my hip.

Saskia looks up and gasps. Antony turns in his seat and pales under his dark skin.

'Caught you.' I bristle. The wine bottle is the closest thing to a weapon within reach. It's tempting to grab it and hit Antony over the head, but I want to say my piece before I kill him.

Antony opens his mouth, gets halfway out of his chair. 'Hey, Alex? What are you doing here?'

'What do you think?' I shoot Saskia a Medusa glare. Her eyes go wide as saucers. 'I've seen your texts.'

Antony puts up his hand. 'Leave her out of this. You have a problem with me, deal with me.'

'But it's both of you, isn't it?' I snap, throwing a slip of paper on the table with the text messages, and Antony's unfinished love letters.

Saskia pushes her hair awkwardly behind her ear. 'We're not together, Alex.'

'Yet.' To my shame, my jaw begins to judder. My head's still full of her perfume.

'Look, this isn't what you think,' Antony cuts in, gesturing to the bits of paper. 'All of this, I was going to explain—'

'What else could it be?' My voice rises an octave. 'You two have put money down on a house!'

'Where did you get that idea?' Antony asks.

'It's in the texts.'

His mouth falls open. 'You went through my phone?'

'What choice did I have?' I take a deep breath. 'It's not like you were going to tell me.'

'No! What? Jeez!' Antony forms a T with his hands. 'Time out, Alex! You've got it all wrong!'

My phone buzzes in my pocket. I ignore it. The middle-aged couple on the sofa opposite stare at us, whispering between themselves. A young man at the slot machine pauses to look around.

'Alex, please, let me—' Antony splutters.

'Enough!' I snap. 'Henry's asked me to help him, and you know what? I'm going. And this time I'm taking the Audi.'

'You can't do that! I need the car for work. And you promised not to use the...the *thing* again!'

'I'm not using the *thing,* so I'm keeping my promise,' I say, hand on hip.

Antony leaps from his seat as his mobile rings. He looks at his screen and swears.

Both our phones are buzzing as I turn and stumble away.

'*She* can drive you now!' I spit at him.

Antony shoves his chair back and yelps as he bangs his leg on the table.

Being small has its advantages. Blinded by tears, I push through gaps in the lunchtime crowd.

'Hey, watch it!' A businessman stops short, slopping beer over the edge of his glass. Two older men wearing Birmingham City football shirts frown and put their drinks down.

'You all right, love?' They see my teary eyes, then Antony, as he forges his way towards me, shouting my name. 'Is he giving you trouble?'

The City supporters block Antony's path. When he tries to barge past, one of them clamps his hand on Antony's shoulder. 'She doesn't want to talk to you, mate.'

'Mind your own business.' Antony's Hackney accent comes to the fore as he knocks his arm away. 'Move!'

'No chance, mate.'

'You're not my mate.' Antony shoves him. 'Back off!'

His friend shoves Antony into a six-foot-four bloke drinking a pint. Glass smashes, and a roar goes up by the bar. The tall bloke locks his arm around Antony's neck.

Antony bares his teeth, struggling to break free.

'Break it up, lads! Break it up.' The security guy barges past. 'You need to calm down, fellas.'

I take a last look at Antony, scuffling with the football fans, the giant, and the security guy. Saskia appears behind his shoulder, pleading with them all to calm down.

My phone buzzes again as I run from the pub, scrubbing tears away.

I reach the Audi, feel in my pocket for the keys and click the key fob to unlock the car. Hauling open the driver's door, I sink into the leather interior, snap on my belt and push the starter button.

The engine roars into life. I raise the lever to move the seat forward. Then, I put the car into reverse and shriek backwards in a tight circle, narrowly missing the wall.

A swift look in the rear-view mirror shows Antony being escorted from the pub in the grip of the security guy. He struggles and yells with Saskia close behind, clutching her bag.

Shoving the car into first gear, I stomp on the accelerator. The car jumps forward as my foot slips off the clutch. The engine stalls.

'Come on!' I restart the car and screech away. At the junction, I yank the steering wheel and accelerate onto the main road without indicating. I ignore angry beeps and screeching tyres of a sharply braking van, and speed through a set of traffic lights turning from amber to red, smoking the tyres.

Air circulates through the car vents, surrounding me in a haze of Saskia's perfume. I lower the electric window, grab Saskia's scarf and fling it out of the car. A gust carries it away like a balloon.

I hope it ends up in the river.

· · · · · · · · · · ·

Back home, I crash on the sofa and have a cry. My mobile has four missed calls from Henry and two from Antony. Through blurry eyes, I see the light flashing on the ansaphone. Once I've blotted my tears, I press Play.

'Alex it's Henry. I tried your mobile. Can you give me a ring when you get this?'

A second later, my mobile phone rings. ANT_MOB

I kill the call and sit back, staring at the last banana in the fruit bowl. It's gone black at the end. My phone rings again and I'm ready to hit the red button. I hesitate.

HENRY_LO

'Hi Alex, is this a good time? I've been trying to get hold of you.'

Henry's calm and friendly voice makes me feel strangely distant from the chaos at the pub. I rub my forehead and try to inject some life into my voice. 'Sorry, I was out. What's happening?'

'It's been one hell of a day. I'm still on site at St. Andrew and St. Mary. We removed Douglas Hall's coffin and found a body under a layer of soil, wrapped in tarpaulin.'

In all the turmoil, I'd completely forgotten about Duggie's grave. My beleaguered brain struggles to focus.

234

'Is it Delia?'

'Between you and me, I'd say so. Forensics is waiting on dental records before they can formally identify her. Interestingly, the tarpaulin has a square cut out of it like the one in the river. Hopefully, Reginald has left his DNA on it.'

Dark thoughts go through my mind. How many tarps has this psycho used?

Henry says, 'The vicar has put me in touch with a married couple who claim they met Reginald recently. I'm interviewing them tomorrow. Would you be interested in coming down to Hertford and helping out?'

'Yes, I would.' Biting my lip, I look around the flat. The idea of staying is intolerable. 'But I don't have my machine.'

'We don't need it. We'll do this the old-fashioned way.'

'Can I come now? I have the car.'

Henry hesitates. 'Okay, we'll work something out. Go to Olivia's, and I'll call you later.'

I grab my rucksack and stuff it with pyjamas, a change of clothes, my pencil case and sketchbook. The bag feels light on my shoulder without the finding machine. I never thought I'd miss that cold lump.

Leaving the flat, I climb in the Audi. I swallow a pang of longing, gazing one last time at my home where Antony and I once laughed and loved.

I drive away with my soul in tatters.

The drive to Hertford gives me plenty of thinking time. A pile-up on the M1, compounded by road-works and tail-backs, means I have five hours to analyse my situation to death. It takes the first few hours just to calm down. A little voice says I should have given Antony the chance to explain himself instead of letting my shredded emotions get the better of me. But the die has been cast, and I have to follow the path I chose.

I arrive at Henry's sister's house around eight-thirty, so tired I can barely focus. I make an ungainly exit from the low-slung car, straighten my creaking bones and massage my left thigh to relieve the cramps caused by the stiff clutch.

Marcus opens the door with a smile. He ushers me through to the kitchen. An enticing casserole aroma fills the room. My remaining tension melts away under the Aga's pulsing warmth, the wall-clock's steady tick, and the sight of Ludo curled up in his dog bed. Coming from an empty flat, the welcome atmosphere of a happy family home only serves to drive home what I've lost.

'Henry's been ringing to find out where you are. He tried your mobile, but got no answer.'

'Sorry, I switched my phone off on the drive down.' My hand goes to the lump in my pocket. I couldn't bear to hear the constant beep of Antony's messages. 'I'll call him now.'

'It's okay, I'll do it.' Marcus fills the kettle and sets it on the Aga's hotplate. 'Henry told me you were on your way. He wanted me to say, he has back-to-back meetings tomorrow morning, so there's no point going in until after lunch.'

'No problem.' I hastily cover a yawn with my hand and sink into a chair. 'Sorry.'

Marcus tells me about their family Christmas while he reheats a bowl of lamb casserole for my dinner.

'Is Olivia still at work?' I ask.

Marcus shakes his head. 'Out with friends, for a change.'

Ludo pads over and presses his wet nose against my leg. It would be nice to think he remembers me, but I suspect he's hoping a morsel of meat will find its way from my plate into his mouth. His adorable expression wins me over. I sneak him a piece of lamb under the table.

Marcus must have had enough of my yawning, because the moment I've finished eating he sends me upstairs for an early night.

I leave my phone in my pocket, as I can't face dealing with a hundred missed messages from Antony. He's probably furious I took the car. We both need time to calm down.

The combination of Marcus's generous hospitality, coupled with my hearty meal, the cozy atmosphere and sheer exhaustion, means I fall asleep instantly.

When I wake, it takes me a moment to realise where I am and how long I've slept. It's eleven a.m. and the house is quiet. I shower and head downstairs to find the house empty. After a leisurely late breakfast, I drive the short distance to the police station.

As the modern building comes into view, a sense of belonging settles on me. Hopefully, my decision to return was the right one. I park in a *Visitor* bay facing the sliding glass doors and head inside.

'Hello, Alex.' Yolanda greets me from behind the reception desk. She peers over her glasses, in the direction of the car park. 'That is a nice car. Was it a Christmas present?'

Shaking my head, I say, 'It belongs to my other half.' I can't bring myself to say he's soon to be my ex.

Her brow arches. 'You have a boyfriend?'

'Umm.' I look at a spot on the carpet, fiddling with my car keys.

Yolanda hands me a form to sign and date. Beside her keyboard are a crocheted a carrot in bright orange wool, a green pear and yellow banana. By the end of the week, her desk will have turned into a greengrocer's.

Once I've signed the form, Yolanda takes it and heads for the swing-doors at the back of reception. 'Give me a minute to find a lanyard. I'll let Henry know you're here.'

I pace the room until Henry pushes through the doors. He's wearing a smart grey jacket over a pale blue shirt open at the collar with a leather messenger bag across his shoulder. A trench coat is folded over his arm.

'Hey, you.' He gives me a welcoming smile and pulls me in for a hug.

The physical contact takes me by surprise. My chin grazes his shoulder as I stand awkwardly in place with my heart skipping a beat. I catch his familiar cedarwood scent and go to hug him back, but he's stepped away.

Seconds later, the doors swing open and Yolanda returns with a lanyard. 'Okay, Alex. You are back on the books.'

The act of slipping the lanyard over my head makes me feel professional, part of the team.

Henry puts on his coat and nods towards the exit. 'Shall we?'

Once we're away from the main entrance, he touches my shoulder to get my attention. His eyes dart from my hair to my eyes, to my mouth.

'What happened to your lip?' He asks, frowning.

My fingers brush the scab. 'Oh, it's nothing. A table-leg hit me.'

'Right.' Henry presses his lips together.

Hurriedly, I change the subject. 'How was your meeting?'

Henry looks skyward. 'Great, if you're on the Millennium Team. They've nabbed officers from every division. I've been putting in requests for more man-power every day, but I don't hold out much hope.' He thrusts his hands into his jacket. 'We can't leave it until January to find Reginald. By now, he probably knows we've looked under Duggie's grave.'

'He knows we found Nenagh.' I bite my lip, remembering the cold sensation of feeling someone watching me at the riverside, after we pulled her from the Mimram. 'Do you think he'll run?'

'I don't know.' Henry shrugs. 'Have you heard about your machine?'

'Sorry. Let me check.'

Henry's question prompts me to retrieve my phone from my pocket and switch it on. The phone emits beep after beep as text messages arrive, flashing on screen. I scroll past the low battery icon to read down the list, but every notification is from Antony.

```
Where r u? R U OK?
Pls come back we need 2 talk
Tell me where UR staying. Need 2 no you're
safe
Call me, even if UR with Henry
```

Swiftly, I scroll through all the messages. There's nothing from the League.

Seeing my glum expression, Henry says, 'Maybe we'll hear something today.'

We walk to the Astra, and Henry unlocks it. The interior is litter-free, and the carpets are clean and fluffy. Even the tartan seats look brighter. A Christmas tree-shaped air freshener dangles from the rear-view mirror, releasing a strong pine scent.

'It's like a new car!' I exclaim, settling onto the pristine seat.

Henry starts the car as I buckle my seatbelt. 'I was worried mushrooms would start growing under all the rubbish.'

Smiling for the first time in ages, I say, 'So, what's the plan?'

'We're interviewing Bob and Sandra Fitzgerald. They're parishioners of St. Andrew and St. Mary's church.'

Henry leaves the campus and drives through the outskirts of Hertford, past a park bounded by a low, stone wall.

'Are you all right?' He shoots me a sideways glance. 'You're not your usual, sparky self.'

'Just too much booze and late-night TV.' I shrug. 'I stupidly do it every Christmas.'

I expect Henry to nod, but his expression doesn't change. He turns onto a quiet street lined with tidy bungalows, and parks outside number 20. I follow Henry to an orange door, and shiver on the step as he presses the doorbell.

The door opens, releasing a wave of tropical heat. The short, tubby man at the door appears to be in his seventies. His black polo shirt accentuates his pink face and shock of pure white hair. A pair of bi-focals hangs on a chain around his neck.

'I'm Bob Brown. You must be DC Longhurst and...'

'This is my assistant, Alex Martin,' Henry introduces me. 'Are we all right to come in?'

Bob ushers us into the house. My hand accidentally brushes the hall radiator which is on full blast, and I whip my fingers away before I burn them. I like being warm indoors, but this is taking things a bit far.

I remove my coat and snood and leave my boots on the mat. Henry shrugs off his trench coat, but leaves his jacket on. He'll just have to suffer.

A lady with a blonde perm, wearing a blue dress with white flowers and court shoes, appears in the kitchen doorway.

'This is my wife, Sandra,' Bob introduces us.

'Shall I make tea?' she asks.

'That'd be lovely, dear.'

'Could I have a glass of water?' Henry asks. 'Ice, too, if you have it.'

'And me,' I say, tugging the neck of my jumper.

Sandra disappears into the kitchen and we follow Bob into the lounge. For a second, I think I've walked into a 1970s sitcom. A brown, corduroy sofa and matching armchair sink into a shaggy, chocolate-coloured carpet. The orange and brown waves on the curtains start moving of their own accord when I stare at them. The only modern things in the room are the TV and an artificial Christmas tree, twinkling with multicoloured lights.

I sit on the sofa beside Henry, sinking into the soft foam.

Bob collapses onto an armchair with an *oomph*. Sandra brings in a tray with two mugs of tea and tall glasses of iced water for me and Henry. She sits to the other side of Henry and passes round a plate of digestives. The chocolate topping is melting in the heat.

'Do you mind if I record our conversation?' Henry asks, setting a tape-recorder on the tiled coffee-table.

'By all means.' Bob says, stirring two sugars into his tea. 'I couldn't believe my ears when I heard about the fuss over Duggie's grave. I always thought I could tell a wrong 'un, but I was off the mark with Reg. He looked the type who might play away, but never murder.'

'Do you remember Delia?' I ask.

Bob's brows twitch up. 'She was a lovely lady, but shy, rarely got a word in. Reginald was the outgoing one, but then he worked in car sales and a big ego comes with the job. She always seemed happy enough to me.'

'I don't know about that,' Sandra interrupts archly. 'Ethel, our organist, said Delia and Reginald got married on the quiet. Reginald asked Ethel and the cleaning lady to be witnesses. We had a different vicar back then, very old-fashioned. Reginald wanted a quiet ceremony without any fuss.' Sandra tuts loudly. 'If it had been me, I would have wanted a fuss! Ethel felt sorry for Delia, playing the Wedding March to an empty church. It's a shame Delia didn't ask us to attend, especially as she had no family.'

Henry consults his notes. 'Her parents died in a boating accident years before. And, she was an only child.'

A tight line of anger grows within me. Delia was rudderless without family to support her. It sounds like Reginald wormed his way into the church community with the aim of finding his next victim, and she ticked all the boxes. I bite the inside of my cheek, struggling to understand how anyone could kill for greed.

'Did you talk much to Delia?' I ask Sandra.

'Only chit-chat. I did ask to see the ring. It was lovely, with a large, oval sapphire.'

I exchange a concerned look with Henry. He opens his bag and draws out a wedding photo of Nenagh.

'Did it look anything like this ring?'

Sandra peers forward, forehead creased in concentration. 'Yes, it could be the exact same one. Who is she?'

'Reginald's first wife,' Henry tells her.

Bob's brows shoot up. 'She's not under Duggie's grave as well, is she?'

'I can assure you, she isn't.' Henry flips open his notepad and makes notes. 'Can you recall what happened after Delia went missing?'

'We rallied around Reginald, took food round to the house.' Sandra puts her hands on her knees, her tone becoming sombre. 'The vicar visited every day for a week. As time went on, Reginald stopped coming to church. He was never in when we called by. Then, we discovered he'd moved away.'

'He left without telling anyone,' Bob adds. 'There wasn't an estate agent's sign outside, so no one knew the house was for sale.'

Henry asks, 'Can you remember anything else, like where he worked?'

'Sorry, no. All I know is, he sold cars, and drove a nice Mercedes coupe.'

'Do you remember the colour, registration, or year?'

'I can hardly remember my phone number these days.' Bob gives a wry smile. 'The Merc was silver, maybe light blue, but that's no help, is it?'

'You never know,' Henry says, making a note. 'Tell us about the day you bumped into him.'

Bob squeezes his eyes shut. 'It was the week before the operation on my ticker. End of May, that's it. We were in Boots to collect my medication. Reginald was with a blonde-haired woman, in the cold and flu aisle.'

Dread trickles down my breastbone at the thought of Reginald with another woman.

'His bag of medication was bigger than yours, Bob!' Sandra says. 'I recognised him straight away. He has the kind of face that sticks in your mind.'

'You mean, a handsome devil,' mutters Bob.

Sandra bats Bob's shoulder. 'He's not my type. Too smooth. I prefer my men more down-to-earth.'

Bob rolls his eyes.

Sandra wraps her hands around her mug. 'You should have seen Reginald's face when I called his name. He looked like he'd seen a ghost! He put his arm around the woman's shoulders and squeezed her tight, all protective.'

I sip water as my mouth goes dry. The way Sandra describes Reginald holding his wife sounds possessive rather than affectionate, like he was keeping her in check.

Bob takes up the story. 'I shook Reg's hand. Now I think about it, what he did was clever. He started asking about my health problems and people from church. He didn't give us a chance to find out what he'd been up to.'

'I asked him to introduce me to the lady,' Sandra says. 'Reginald said, *this is my lovely wife*. At the time, I thought it was wonderful Reginald had found love after Delia.'

'What was her name?' I ask, frowning.

Bob and Sandra look at each other blankly. 'He never did say,' Sandra says, biting her lip.

'I asked Reg where he was living,' Bob says. 'He said, *'A small place. Out of town.'* Then he looked at his watch and said they had to rush or he'd get a parking ticket. He was all smiles when he said goodbye.' Bob sets his mug on the table. 'Now I think about it, Reg set off at a fair clip. Almost like he couldn't get away fast enough.'

'That's very helpful.' Henry scribbles something in his notebook. He opens his slim briefcase, removes my illustrations, and places them on the table. 'Would you say Reginald looked like either of these sketch artist impressions?'

Sandra leans closer while Bob puts his glasses on.

'Not that one.' She discounts the drawing of badly aged, portly Reginald. She taps her nail on my second version - Reginald as a handsome, older man. 'That's more like him. But his face wasn't as lined, and his mouth goes up on one side like he's smirking.'

'Which side?'

'His left.'

Bob adds, 'And he's got more hair on top. Could be a toupée.'

'Got it.' I make detailed notes to work with later, determined to get the best likeness possible.

'I don't know if this is any use.' Sandra raises a finger. 'I asked Reginald's wife how long they'd been married. She said April, so only recently.'

Henry writes the date down, and I start counting the months. It's been eight months since Reg and his new lady got married, the same amount of time Nenagh and Delia's marriages lasted before they both died.

By the sombre look Henry gives me, he's come to the same conclusion. If Reginald is true to form, his wife may be dead. And if she's alive, she's living on borrowed time.

40

Henry and I shut the door on the tropical warmth of Bob and Sandra's house, and step into pelting rain. Wind flings my hood back. Freezing spray clings to my face and hands as I rush through the gloom to the car. I hurl myself onto the springy seat, pull my snood over my nose and hold my hands out to the air vents even before Henry has a chance to start the engine.

'I didn't realise you were *that* thin-blooded,' Henry remarks, brushing wet hair from his eyes. 'Aren't you the same girl who jumped in the river?'

'Not today,' I say through clenched teeth.

Henry turns the key and switches on the wipers. 'Give it a minute to warm up. You want my coat?'

'It's okay.' I hug myself as rain drums on the roof.

Henry turns the car around in the cul-de-sac and rejoins the main road, driving past the park. Soggy dogs drag their owners through puddles. Families with young children hurry home with their hoods pulled up.

'How long will it take you to make the changes to Reginald's picture?' Henry asks.

'An hour. Maybe less.'

'Good. That should be enough time to update the Hertford News and Mail before it goes to press. Then, we'll head out to local car showrooms and churches and get his picture under people's noses.'

'Wouldn't it be quicker to email his picture to everyone?' I say, angling warm air from the vents towards me.

'Quicker, yes, but nowhere near as effective. Police emails tend to end up in people's trash folders. Plus, there's always a chance that Reginald will see it and delete it before anyone has a chance to identify him.'

Fear grips my throat. 'God, what if we run into him?'

'I hope we do.'

My unease must be written all over me, because he swiftly adds, 'Don't worry. I'll keep you safe.'

We soon arrive back at the police station.

Henry puts his hand on the door-handle. 'Ready to make a run for it?'

Rain hammers my hood as we make the short dash into reception. Henry stops down the corridor leading to *Operation Thaw* and knocks on the door labelled *Millennium Team*. He pops his head inside.

Simon emerges from the room, carrying a dot-matrix print-out.

'Hey, boss.' He looks my way and grins, displaying wonky teeth and a significant amount of gum. 'Hi, Alex.'

Henry says, 'I know I sound like a broken record, but is there any way you can spare us a few hours? I have a list of forty-five locations where Reginald could be hiding, and I don't have the manpower to cover them all.'

Simon draws breath in through his teeth. 'I'm up to my neck with Y2K. Have you asked Major Crime?'

'They're rammed. They've offered to man our hotline, but nothing more until after New Year.'

'I'd help if I could, but my department's working flat out on the Y2K problem.' Simon stares dolefully at the printout. 'Our casefile system keeps glitching. Timecards aren't fixed yet. Do you know how many timecodes are recorded in our incident response vehicles and logs?' He frowns at Henry. 'Thousands.'

'I thought you'd have this sorted by now,' Henry says.

'That's the problem. Everyone thinks that.' He thumbs over his shoulder. 'It's chaos out there. Visa and the NHS are already suffering system failures. Software problems are causing shut-downs at nuclear power stations. The US is worried their satellites will stop working.' He drops his voice. 'The NHS has built an emergency mortuary the size of an Olympic stadium near Heathrow Airport.' He taps his nose. 'Word to the wise, stay indoors tomorrow.'

My mother's warnings run through my head. Planes falling from the sky. Fireballs and the end of the world.

Henry's shoulders drop. 'You'd better get on then.'

'Thanks, boss.' Simon ducks his head and hurries into the photocopier room.

As we continue down the corridor, I whisper, 'Are things that bad?'

A flicker of amusement crosses Henry's face. 'You're talking about a guy who thinks *The X-Files* are factual documentaries. In his world, everything's a conspiracy.'

We reach the door to *Operation Thaw*. 'Do you reckon Simon's going into a bunker tomorrow night?'

Henry throws his head back and laughs. 'Probably!'

He pushes through the door.

Tori throws me a wave from the desk. 'Hey, Alex, welcome back. You'll be pleased to hear the department is even more understaffed and undervalued than before!' She points her biro at Henry. 'Any good news, boss?'

Henry says, 'Afraid not, Tori. Anything your end?'

Tori flings herself back in the office chair, rubbing the bridge of her nose. 'I'm trying to get Delia's dental records so we can match them to the body. But the dental surgery is closed until January and the dentist isn't answering his mobile.'

'Keep trying.' Henry opens his briefcase, returns my drawings of Reginald, then heads to the kitchenette to fetch us coffee.

I sit at the desk, fingers wrapped around the heat of my mug, as Henry updates Tori on the interview with Bob and Sandra.

Tori straightens at the news of Reginald's latest marriage. 'Wow. Who's the unlucky lady?'

'That's what we need to find out.' Henry flashes a rueful smile. Can you get onto County Hall and check their marriage records for April?'

'Sure thing, boss.'

While Tori makes the call, Henry updates the case files and I make the changes Sandra and Bob suggested to Reginald's portrait. Drawing always puts me into a contemplative state, and my thoughts go to Antony.

I think of the good times when we first moved to Birmingham: shopping hand-in-hand for our unfurnished flat, eating takeaways from the carton while watching our favourite films, and smoochy lie-ins at the weekend. The memories make me smile. No matter what Antony's done, I miss him. But when I try to pick apart the Antony and Saskia situation, my brain fizzes into overload.

Forty-five minutes later, I pass the completed drawing to Henry.

'I'll get this to the newspaper,' he says, putting the image under the scanner. 'I need to update my boss, and ensure the border agencies know about Reg, in case he tries to flee the country. Give me half an hour.'

I take the empty mugs to the kitchenette. Leaning on the counter, I retrieve my phone, steeling myself for a flood of missed calls and texts. When I turn it on, the screen flashes green before going blank. I try again, but the Nokia's battery is dead.

I swear under my breath, waiting for Tori to finish her call. She puts the receiver down with a huff.

'How's it going?' I ask.

'County Hall is useless, and they're closing at five. God, if only we could access their bloody records online.'

'I'm sorry to hear that.' I approach her and put my mobile on the table. 'I don't suppose you have a phone charger? Mine died.'

Tori peers at my mobile. 'Nokia...mine's a Siemens, sorry. It uses a different connector. What about Henry?'

'His is an Ericsson.' I take the phone back, slip it in my pocket. 'Don't worry. I'll have to buy a new one.'

'Hold on.' Tori pulls open a drawer. 'There might be something in here. This is where electronics go to die.' She dumps a tangled ball of accessories and cables on the desk. 'Be my guest.'

Tori turns away to redial County Hall, leaving me to search through the mess of electronics. I find two chargers amongst the chaos of mouses, portable floppy drives and old pagers, but they all have the wrong kind of connector.

I sneak into the box room, and use the phone on the desk to call home. The ansaphone cuts in after seven rings. I leave a message for Antony, saying I'm fine but my phone's out of charge. Antony has no way of contacting me, and I can't remember his mobile number. The only option is to look up Apex 3000's number. I call them and ask to be put through to Antony's desk.

A woman whose voice I vaguely remember picks up and answers, 'Hello, Tilly here. Can I help you?'

An image of the Disney-perfect model with bright red hair pops into my mind.

'Hi, Tilly, it's Alex, Antony's girlfriend. Is he there?'

A pause, followed by crackling as she puts her hand over the receiver. 'Don't you know?'

I frown. 'Know what?'

'Antony's gone. He had a one-on-one with Yan this morning, cleared his desk, and left.'

'What?' I grab the back of the chair as my head spins. 'Did he say where?'

'Sorry, you'll have to ask Antony.'

'Have you got his mobile number?' I ask. 'My phone's run out of charge and I can't look it up.'

'I don't have it. Sorry,' Tilly says.

After mumbling thank you, I put the phone down and stare at the wall with my mouth dropping open. Was Antony's decision spontaneous, or did he plan it? Is he running away to start a new life with Saskia? The idea wrenches at me. Antony's betrayal is one thing, but leaving his job without telling me is another. The strength drains from me.

'Alex, everything all right?' Henry stands in the doorway.

I raise my eyes and force a smile. 'Sure. What's happening?'

'We're in luck. The paper has updated the flyer and it's going to press this evening.' Henry beckons me back to the office and points out the phone on the end on the desk. He sticks a red dot on the receiver. 'This is our hotline for Reginald. Calls come through here. If no one answers, they'll be diverted to Major Crime.'

Tori stares at the silent phone. 'God, I hope someone rings in.'

'They will.'

Henry makes photocopies of the flyer, grabs his coat, and the golf umbrella.

'Come on,' he says, looking at me. 'Let's go find him.'

41

— · —

I put up my hood and walk through the rain with Henry, sheltered under his umbrella.

A beam of light moves back and forth by the perimeter fence, accompanied by the occasional muffled bark.

I catch Henry's arm. 'Is that Bruno over there?'

Henry peers into the dark. He nods and unlocks the car. 'The vandal attacked another car yesterday.'

'I hope my car will be all right.' I slide into the passenger seat, glancing back at the gleaming Audi.

Henry folds the umbrella and throws it on the back seat. 'You're parked in front of the main entrance. It should be fine.'

As Henry turns on the heat and drives away, I look back at the bobbing torchlight until the cascading rain obscures my view.

'We know two things about Reginald,' he says. 'He's a car salesman through and through. And he met two of his wives through the church. So, there's where we'll concentrate our searches.'

Our first port of call is a used car dealership five minutes away. It's low end, with the sales office operating out of a portacabin. The concrete yard is nose-to-tail with family runarounds: Fords, Vauxhalls, Toyotas and Mazdas, along with Transits and small panel vans. Most of the vehicles look at least five years old.

'How do you feel about asking the questions?' Henry says, climbing the portacabin steps to a scuffed metal door.

I halt on the bottom step, my mouth dropping open. 'I wouldn't know what to say.'

251

'Just ask about Reginald.' Henry glances back with a reassuring smile. 'I often learn just as much standing in the background as when I'm taking the lead.'

He knocks and holds open the door for me. Stepping inside, I squint against the harsh glare from the fluorescent strip lights on the ceiling. Water drips from my hood onto a slippery vinyl floor covered in muddy footprints. A portable heater rattles in the corner, emitting the pungent odour of burning dust. I wrinkle my nose.

A tall man with a bad comb-over, cheap grey suit and pink tie stands behind a desk covered in take-away flyers, unopened letters, tax discs, telephone directories and photos of cars. It looks like the last place Reginald would work.

He puts out his hand, waves us to a pair of moulded plastic chairs. 'Welcome to County Car Sales. I'm Terry. What can I do you for?'

After we shake hands, Henry shows his warrant card and Terry's smile falls from his face.

He flumps into his chair. 'What's this about?'

We stay standing. Henry quietly steps to one side, glancing at the sales charts and posters pinned to a corkboard.

Swallowing, I hand Terry a flyer. 'Do you know this man? He goes by the name Reginald, but he might be using an alias. He's worked in car sales for a long time. Over thirty years. And...and...we think he's local.'

Terry glances briefly at the picture. The corners of his mouth turn down. 'Nah, never seen him.'

'Could you take another look?' I clear my throat and attempt to inject an authoritative tone into my voice. 'Reginald is in his mid-sixties and dresses sharply. He comes across as smooth and charming.'

'You've just described a used car salesman.' Terry gives a thin smile and adjusts his tie. 'Good luck with that.'

I keep my expression neutral and push on. 'Maybe your colleagues would recognise him?'

'It's just me.' Terry shrugs. 'Look, the dealers and traders around here are a tight bunch. If this guy was on my patch, I'd have heard of him.'

'Where else might he be working?'

'Anywhere. New cars, prestige motors, car auctions?'

Terry falls silent. I rack my brain for more questions, but nothing comes to mind.

'We'll follow up on that, thank you,' Henry breaks the silence. 'Please keep the flyer. The hotline number is at the bottom.'

'Yeah, sure,' Terry says, dropping the flyer on top of the mound of paper rising from his desk. It slides down the pile where it will no doubt be lost for all time. The phone rings somewhere beneath the mess.

We leave Terry talking to a customer about a tasty hot hatch and descend the slippery steps.

'You did well,' Henry says as we hurry across the forecourt, heads bowed against the rain. 'He wasn't the easiest subject to interview.'

'Do you think he was hiding anything?' I ask.

'I doubt it. There was no sign of Reginald anywhere, and the mess tells me Terry works alone. He made a good point about the prestige market, though. We should concentrate on that.'

In the car, Henry takes a pen to his list, marking a Jaguar dealership on the other side of town, and a place called Bentley Prestige Sales. 'Let's try these two.'

The Jaguar showroom is on the A414, near a busy junction. A row of *New* and *Approved Used* cars faces the main road. Inside the showroom, sleek new cars gleam on the polished tiles. The sales staff examine the flyer.

'I might have seen him,' says a young guy with a thin goatee and skinny suit, rubbing his beard. 'Not here. Can't remember where.'

'Call the number as soon as you remember,' Henry says.

We drive to an industrial estate on the outskirts of Hertford. Bentley Prestige Sales takes up a large lot at the far end. The forecourt boasts flashy sports, executive, and classic cars protected by a security fence and solid metal gates. The glass-fronted showroom is dark inside.

As we walk to the entrance, a red Ferrari with its engine burbling pulls out of the electrically operated gates. A man wearing a camel coat and striped, silk scarf jumps from the low-slung car and secures the gates with a hefty chain and padlock. He's in his thirties with tousled, blond hair.

Henry intercepts him before he climbs back into the car, introduces himself, and asks his name.

'Julian Debrett, sales manager,' the man says in an upper-class accent. 'How can I help?'

Henry shows him the flyer. 'We're looking for this man. Do you recognise him?'

Julian examines the picture as spats of rain darken his tie.

'Sorry, don't know him. I'll ask the team tomorrow. If anyone's seen him I'll get them to give you a call.'

He folds the flyer, tucks it into his pocket, then climbs into the driving seat. He closes the door with a solid *thunk*. The Ferrari accelerates away with a roar, the engine audible long after the car has disappeared from sight.

'Nice car.' Henry casts his eye over the showroom and forecourt before making a note on his list. 'Let's visit these two churches before the next dealership.'

The first church, St. Mary's, is closed, and so is the parish office next door. I slip a flyer through the letterbox for the attention of the vicar. All Saints Church is also closed. We ring the vicarage doorbell, and the parish secretary answers. She tells us the evening vigil service is starting in an hour if we want to speak to the vicar.

We drive through rain to a Mercedes dealership, but have no joy. Our last automotive stop of the day is South East Prestige Car Sales in Bengeo, a small area north of Hertford. The sales staff are closing up the showroom when we arrive. When I show them the flyer, I draw blank stares.

We walk past gleaming Mercedes, BMWs and Audis to the Astra. The light is fading, but the rain has stopped. I lean on the car and thrust my hands into my coat pockets. 'What do you think? That guy from Jaguar might have recognised him.'

'Something will happen,' Henry says. 'Until then, we keep trying.'

As the business day draws to a close, Henry and I return to All Saints. The small church is open in advance of the evening service. A thurible, suspended from chains beneath the stone arches sends out plumes of pungent incense. Early worshippers pray in the pews as the vicar lights candles by the altar.

He greets us warmly. He nods at Reginald's picture and says it might ring a bell, and promises to make discreet enquiries to trusted members of his congregation. We visit one more Anglican church but it's closed. I post a leaflet through the door, struggling to work my numb fingers in the chill wind.

'You look frozen,' Henry says, blowing on his hands. 'Why don't we grab something to eat out of the cold and discuss progress?'

'Sounds great.' The thought of a warm restaurant puts a spring in my step on the way to the car. Henry drives into the historic centre of Hertford and parks on Fore Street across from Pizza Express.

Warmth and delicious aromas hit me as we walk into the restaurant. A smiling male waiter in a black uniform and red apron grabs two menus and leads us through past diners and a semi-circular bar with wine glasses hanging upside down from a wooden rack. He halts beside a table by the window overlooking Fore Street.

'I'd rather sit there.' Henry points out a tiny table tucked against the back wall. He takes the chair facing the main door, a habit he shares with Antony.

I remove my coat and hang it over the back of my chair. The amber festoon lights strung across the restaurant, soft buzz of conversation, chink of cutlery on china, and smell of garlic and fresh-baked dough, induce a languor that roots me to my chair. Waiting staff scurry between tables, carrying platters of pizza and bowls of steaming pasta.

Henry smiles across the candle-lit table. A charged undercurrent fills the space between us, as though we're on a date. I feel like I'm walking a tightrope between friendship and something deeper. At the moment, I'm wobbling somewhere in the middle.

We order two Cokes and a large pepperoni thin-crust pizza to share. The waiter returns swiftly with our drinks.

'To never giving up.' Henry raises his glass and gives me an intense look that makes my cheeks flush.

'To catching Reginald,' I add, keen to keep the conversation on the job.

Henry hooks his arm over the back of his chair. 'Now Reg is in the local paper, someone's bound to spot him. I'd happily miss out on the New Year's celebrations if it means collaring him.'

The waiter arrives with our pizza which is scattered with rocket leaves, a bowl of parmesan, and a tall bottle of chilli oil. Henry loads his pizza half with parmesan, then tears off a slice and devours it in three bites.

He wipes his mouth with a serviette and pauses, seeing my wide-eyed expression. 'I skipped lunch.'

'Same.' I take a slice and bite into it. The combination of hot, sour-sweet pepperoni, melted cheese and crispy base is perfection. Suddenly, I'm ravenous. We eat in contented silence.

'Can I work with you on New Year's Eve?' I ask, licking tomato sauce from my fingers.

Henry pauses mid-chew. 'I don't want to ruin your plans.'

'I have no plans.' *Not anymore.*

Antony booked tickets for a laser light show, but the idea of us going seems as far-fetched as Simon's belief in nuclear meltdowns and alien landings. It's hard to believe how solid Antony and I once were. We loved and laughed like it would last forever, and then it just stopped.

But there's no use dwelling on the past. Though I can't turn back the clock, I can make my actions count now. Instead of spending New Year's Eve drowning my sorrows in Olivia's spare room, I can help catch a killer.

I drag myself from my thoughts to find Henry staring at me, his face unreadable.

'Sorry, I'm a bit distracted.' I put down my last half-slice of pizza.

'You can work with me. That's not a problem.'

'As long as it's okay with Marcus and Olivia. I don't want to outstay my welcome.'

Henry chuckles. 'I very much doubt that. But if you think it's a problem, you can always stay with me.' On seeing my mouth drop, he swiftly adds, 'Don't worry. I'll take the sofa.'

Henry's suggestion sends my thoughts in a thousand directions. My throat goes dry. Before I can say that's not such a good idea, he puts his hand over mine.

'The offer's there. That's all.'

With a start, I realise we're leaning towards each other. The nape of my neck prickles and my palms go clammy.

Images of Saskia and Antony pop into my mind. I sit back with a leaden sense of unease. Antony would make the same assumption I did if he saw Henry and me together right now.

The waiter appears at my side with a broad smile. 'How is every-thing for you?' His enthusiasm is out of step with the charged at-mosphere hanging over the table. 'Ready to see the dessert menu? Or would you like coffee?'

'Just the bill.' Henry removes his hand from mine and assesses me across the table like we're playing a game of poker. He turns a coaster over, end to end.

An awkward silence hangs between us until Henry pays and throws on his jacket.

'Thanks for dinner,' I say, forcing myself to meet his eye.

Henry forces a smile. 'No problem. I'll drive you back to your car.'

I step out into the cold, winter gloom. The dark hides my flushed cheeks, and the cold whips away the lingering heat that has nothing to do with the warmth of the pizzeria.

We cross the road to the Astra parked beneath a Victorian wrought-iron lamp. Henry leans against the car. The orange streetlight casts shadows under his brow, concealing his expression.

'Would you let me hold you?' he asks.

I freeze in place with a thousand conflicting questions whirling in my mind.

'Look, you're obviously going through some stuff,' he says. 'You look like you need a hug.'

I don't know whether it's a good idea or not, but he's right, I do. I step into his embrace and he draws me close, the length of my body snug against him. Enveloped in warmth, the scent of his aftershave has long worn off. A woodsy, earthen scent mixed with notes of garlic replaces it.

My brain sends out a barrage of conflicting messages telling me simultaneously to break away, stop and talk it through, kiss him and damn Antony. The last is a dangerous path leading into the unknown.

'I'm here if you need me,' Henry breathes into my hair.

Something crumbles to pieces inside me. Henry's a handsome, one-in-a-million guy. My scruples are killing me. I pull away from his embrace and stare at the street lamp with my hand over my mouth.

Shaking my head, I say, 'I'm sorry. I'm trying to sort things out, but it's all a mess at the moment. I don't want to do anything I'll regret. Can you understand?'

Henry sighs. 'I get it.'

He unlocks the car door, breaking the spell.

Uncomfortable silence hangs between us on the way back to the car park. My messed-up feelings are ruining our friendship, but I can't stop thinking about Antony.

Henry switches on the radio to an easy-listening music station. I glance across the dark interior and see him staring at the road, lost in thought.

My hasty actions caused this. If I hadn't fled the pub before Antony had a chance to explain, I wouldn't be stuck in this no-man's-land between two men. A wave of shame joins my regret. I try and find the words to tell Henry how I feel, but we arrive at the police car park before I can collect my thoughts.

I fumble for the seat-belt release button.

'Thanks for the lift,' I say over the music. 'What time do you want me in tomorrow?'

'I'm meeting Major Crime in the morning, then the DCI for updates and briefings. It's best if you come in after lunch,' Henry says, matter-of-fact.

'Okay, see you.' I force a smile before leaving the car, and Henry does the same.

42

—·—

NEW YEAR'S EVE

When you sleep on a problem, by morning it's supposed to have shrunk. But when my alarm goes off at six o'clock, the Henry-Antony situation remains a big old mess.

After a quick shower, I leave the quiet house and drive the short distance to Ware while it's still dark. I zig-zag through narrow residential streets past cars and vans parked nose-to-tail beside the kerb. The Victorian terraces are narrower and untidier than I remember, with postage-stamp front gardens and bins cluttering the paths.

Luck is with me, and I find a parking space a few doors down from the house I used to rent with Antony. I stand at the gate, hands plunged into my pockets. I look past the blue Ford Ka parked on the drive, to our old house. It hasn't changed; if anything, it looks more run-down than ever, with water dripping from the broken gutter onto a muddy gap between the paving, and my bedroom window sitting wonkily in its frame.

I stare at the flaking windowsill, waiting for a flash of inspiration, a memory to jar free, a sign to show me what to do next. Sadness pools inside me, remembering the lonely days I spent behind that ill-fitting window, transcribing documents for a faceless agency and painting pictures I wasn't brave enough to show the world. I lived a half-life until the day the postman rang the doorbell and handed me a parcel wrapped in brown paper.

A spring and summer of adventure followed, the greatest of which was finding love with Antony. It didn't matter if we were in Ware or Birmingham; my happiest times were with him. But now, my unhappiest times have been with him, too. I turn away from the house without looking back.

After driving into town, I park by the river and trudge along the canal path until the shops open. After buying a replacement charger for my Nokia, I return to Marcus's and find both cars gone from the drive. I use the spare key to let myself in.

I eat toast as my phone charges, glancing at it every few moments. Ten minutes later, the screen comes back to life. There are no new text messages or voice mail. Bitterness makes my breakfast stick in my throat. Looks like Antony's given up on me. I call his mobile but get no reply. My only leverage is, I'm holding his car hostage. If he wants it back, he'll have to call me.

I call TJ at the League.

'Hey, Alex,' he answers. 'Before you ask, we're making good progress, but it'll be a while before we're ready for first and second-stage testing. We may be able to try the photo later, but no guarantees. Sorry.'

'Just message me as soon as you know, okay?'

'Of course.'

I hang up. What more can I do?

After midday, I drive to the police station. The way Henry and I left things was awkward, but I'm determined to stay professional. I collect my lanyard from Yolanda and walk the corridor to *Operation Thaw* with butterflies in my stomach.

At my knock, Tori opens the door with a welcoming smile, a half-eaten sandwich in her hand.

I step into the room with more confidence than I feel. Despite the hour, the overhead panel lights are on. Through the picture window, stripped trees frame banks of dark clouds. It's a dour end to the twentieth century.

Tori heads for the kitchenette. On the counter is a lunch platter with neat triangle sandwiches, sausage rolls and muffins.

'You want some lunch? Henry's treat,' Tori says. 'I've just made a fresh pot of coffee.'

'I'd love some. Where's Henry?'

Tori pours coffee into a mug. 'He's out, ticking businesses off his list. I think he mentioned Letchworth car auctions.'

'Does he want me to meet him there?' I stir milk into my coffee and eat an egg mayo sandwich.

'No, he's coming back for you around two.' Tori brushes crumbs from her hands into the bin.

A weight lifts from me. I fortify myself with a good lunch and coffee. After we've eaten, I ask Tori if she needs help with anything.

She hands me the hotline phone log. Fifteen calls have come through since yesterday, most of which were answered by Major Crime. A few have red marks next to them. The months I spent working for the Birmingham missing person's helpline weren't a complete waste of time: I recognise them as hoax calls. One joker called after midnight, identifying our suspect as Reg Varney, whom he'd seen 'on the buses.' Another clever clog named him Reggie Kray. There's a Chinese takeaway order and one recording of teenagers giggling.

Ten calls remain, of which six are vague sightings with unspecified times in Harlow, St. Albans, and Bishop's Stortford. One woman saw a man in his sixties steal two tins of soup from the local Kwiksave, and thought that warranted a call. A man heard someone call 'Reginald!' on her way to the corner store but didn't lay eyes on the man in question.

Tori puts a cross beside two recent calls. One is from a female parishioner from All Saints, a church we visited yesterday.

'Can you chase up these leads and answer the hotline? The questions you need to ask are on the call sheets.' She places a stack of blank forms by the red-stickered phone at the end of the desk. A dark grey phone is beside it. 'Use the grey phone for outgoing calls, all right?'

'Got it,' I say.

'Fab. I have to ring forensics. They promised me results on the tarpaulin.'

While Tori makes her call, I take a deep breath and pick up the receiver. The first lead is Andy Weaver, who used to work with Reginald. I dial his mobile number.

'Yeah, Andy here,' a man answers. Wind buffets his phone, along with the sound of shrieking children.

'Andy Weaver, It's Alex Martin from Herts Police. I understand you have some information on our suspect?'

'Oh, yeah,' he says. 'I had no idea he had a dark side. To meet him, you'd think butter wouldn't melt.' He suddenly yells, '*Emma, don't climb up the slide, use the steps*!' After a pause, he says, 'Sorry about that. Yeah, old Reggie. He was a top-class salesman. We worked at a place called *Top Automarkt* in Harpenden.'

'Did you know Reginald's wife, Delia?'

'That's the thing. He never told me he was married. Hold on. *Emma, we don't take other children's elephants, give it back!*'

'Do you know where Reg works or lives now?'

'Sorry, I haven't seen him since he left *Automarkt*.'

'When was that?'

'Late eighties, maybe early nineties.'

I check my notes. Delia went missing in 1988.

'Can you think of anything else?' I ask, pen poised over the form.

'Reginald loves his cars. I was happy pootling about in my second-hand Ford Orion, but he chopped in his Merc for a top of the range Porsche 911. If he's still working, I'd bet you anything it'll be with top-end motors.'

I hang up, and write up my notes. Andy's information about sports cars lines up with what Portacabin Terry said yesterday.

At the far end of the desk, Tori gives me the thumbs-up, the phone receiver pressed to her ear.

'You have a partial print on the inside of the tarp?' she says. 'Excellent!'

A knock comes at the door and Simon walks in. He sidles up to Tori and taps his watch.

Tori wheels her chair away and finishes up her call. She narrows her eyes. 'What is it, Simon? Is the world about to end?'

'That would be physically impossible.' Simon half snorts a laugh. 'The DCI's called everyone across the hall for a Millennium Ops meeting. There's a serious shortfall in officers needed for tonight. Word from above is, they're worried about chaos breaking out at all the major traffic hubs with the countdown to midnight. Problems with trains, planes—'

'—and automobiles?' Tori flashes a smug smile. 'Sorry, I'm working with Henry.'

'The DCI says this takes precedence.' Simon awkwardly glances my way and smooths down his fringe. 'I'd ask you, Alex, but you aren't authorised to help.'

'You can't do this,' Tori's voice rises. 'We're about to catch a murderer, Simon. A real-life bad guy.'

'Don't shout.' Simon glances nervously at the door.

'I'm not spending New Year's Eve stuck on the motorway or at the airport!' Tori drops her biro on the desk. It bounces over the edge and hits the floor. 'Can't you tell them I'm out of the office?'

'You want me to lie?' Simon walks to the door and holds it open. 'No-can-do.'

Tori glares at him with a huffy face. 'Oh, all right!' She surrenders and gets to her feet, shooting daggers at Simon before turning to me. 'Can you wait here for Henry? He shouldn't be long.'

'I'll hold the fort,' I assure her.

The door swings shut behind them, sealing off all noise from the corridor.

The empty office brings back uncomfortable memories of the night Rashid called the NMPH. Worry worms through me. I wasn't supposed to be in that office unsupervised either, and I ended up getting fired.

Yet, there's work to be done. Pushing my inner niggles aside, I ring the All Saints parishioner.

'Hello, Pole-Baker residence?'

'Is that Rose?' I ask.

Once she's confirmed her name, I introduce myself and say, 'I understand you have information regarding Reginald?'

'Hold on, let me turn the radio down.' After a pause, she says, 'I think my friend Colette might have got herself into trouble with the man in the picture, but he wasn't called Reginald. Colette introduced him as her friend, René.'

'What else can you tell me?'

Rose says, 'Colette used to attend the ten o'clock service every Sunday. It must have been April or May when she turned up with him. Handsome he was, meticulously attired. She brought him to church over the next few weeks and I was happy for her. Colette was widowed and never thought she'd find love again.'

Electricity zings through me as I make notes. 'What happened then?'

'Colette stopped attending church. I dropped round her house several times, but she was never in. She sent me a letter in April, saying she was newly married, they were moving, and she couldn't be happier. I wanted to write back to congratulate her, but I only had her old address. I wrote, but didn't hear back.'

'What was Colette's surname, before she married René?'

'Her maiden name was Stanwick. Colette Stanwick. I must sound like a terrible friend, not knowing her married name, but she broke contact so suddenly. I did wonder if she had left the country, as her new beau looked the moneyed, jet-setting type. My René, she called him.'

'Thank you so much. If you remember anything else, please call back.'

'I will,' she promises.

I spend the next ten minutes typing up detailed notes before the hotline trills, making me jump. I grab the receiver.

'Hello, Hertfordshire Police Hotline. May I have your name, please?'

'Yeah, it's Barry Morgan. I saw your poster in the paper and reckon I've seen that guy before.'

'You have?' I grab my pen and a fresh call sheet. 'Where did you see him?'

'I'm in the motor trade, and I—'

A hand lands on my shoulder. I let out a yelp. The pen flies from my fingers.

'Alex, sorry to interrupt,' says a female officer. 'Henry sent me to get you. Someone's messing with your car.'

'What? Uh...' I get control of my tongue, 'Mr Morgan, I'm putting you through to a colleague who will take down your details. Hold on.' I dial the extension for Major Crime, transfer the call, and slam the receiver down.

I get up, thrust my arms into my coat and push through the door after the officer, then run down the corridor and through the swing doors into the empty reception area. Muffled barking and raised voices carry through the main glass-fronted doors. A huddle of admin staff on the path outside, including Yolanda, blocks my view.

The main doors slide open at my approach. A blast of cold air and a wall of sound hit me. Blue lights strobe from a police car on the kerb. I spot Henry amidst the commotion.

'Excuse me!' I say, pushing past people to reach him.

Bruno struggles to keep hold of Kaiser on the grassy strip dividing the pathway from the car park. The Alsatian is up on its hind legs, straining against the lead and spewing saliva with each bark. White fluff sticks to its bared, yellowed canines. A man lies curled up on the grass a few feet from the dog. He wears a black puffa jacket over a hoodie that conceals his face. Foam strands spill from a large rip in the padded arm. A bulging rucksack lies a few feet away.

Two uniformed officers are on their knees, restraining the guy in the hoodie. One holds his legs, while the other wrestles his arms behind his back. His resistance spurs Kaiser into savage bouts of barking.

'Stay still,' the officer warns, handcuffs in one hand.

Yolanda stands with hands on hips, rolling her eyes at Bruno. 'I am telling you, this is not the culprit! He does not have the same walk, and he is too short!' She turns on the uniformed officers. 'Let the man up so he can speak!'

'Cuff him first, and check him for weapons.' Bruno insists.

I ask Henry, 'Has he damaged my car?'

'You need to take a closer look.' Henry turns to the security guard. 'You can call the dog off.'

'*Kaiser! Halt!*' Bruno commands. The Alsatian's demeanour switches from full-on aggression to passivity in an instant. His forefeet drop to the ground, and it licks its chops. Kaiser whines, looking dolefully at the prone man.

'This man approached the Audi with intent,' Bruno states. 'He crouched by the car and looked in his bag, I assumed for spray cans or a knife. When I challenged him, he ran towards the main building. I considered him a threat and released the dog.'

'I was looking for my car keys when you set that damn animal on me!' The man shouts. 'Of course, I bloody ran away!'

The familiar voice makes my heart catch in my chest. I break away from Henry, race over to the man and drop to my knees beside him. Leaning over, I push the hood back from his face.

'Oh my God!' I cradle his face and throw a horrified look over my shoulder at Henry. 'It's Antony!'

'You know him?' a uniformed officer asks.

'We live together! This is our car. He's not a criminal!'

The officers take their hands from Antony. He sits up, releasing heavy, shuddering breaths. I fling my arms around him, oblivious to the ogling bystanders. Putting my mouth close to his ear, I whisper, 'Are you all right?'

'Yeah, I think so.' Antony gingerly squeezes his arm through the shredded material. 'The dog didn't bite into my arm, thank God. Better call 999 for my jacket, though.'

I release a breathless laugh as relief floods my veins.

Antony squeezes me tight. 'I only wanted to shove my stuff in the car. I didn't plan on making an entrance.'

'Up you get,' says a uniformed officer. He puts his hand out as an offer of help.

Antony ignores the proffered arm, grabs his rucksack and scrambles up using me for support. I stagger under his weight. He swears, brushing mud and nylon fibres off his hands and clothes.

The officers run a swift check on the Audi and ask to look at Antony's driving licence. Satisfied everything's in order, they leave their details with Henry and return to their duties.

Henry approaches, staring at the carnage of white fluff and shredded fabric on Antony's arm. 'If the dog bit you, you'll need a tetanus shot.'

'I'm good.' Antony straightens and looks Henry in the eye. 'Thanks for calling the dog off.'

'No problem.' Henry's icy stare doesn't thaw. He averts his eyes from me, directing his gaze above Antony's head. I'm suddenly aware of my arms wrapped tight around Antony's waist, his hand snug against my ribs.

'You'll need to make a report,' Henry tells Antony. 'Yolanda will give you the forms.'

With the excitement over, the staff drift inside.

'My apologies,' Bruno says from six feet away. Kaiser sits quietly beside him, long pink tongue lolling out. 'It was an honest mistake.'

Antony glowers. 'Your dog could have ripped my throat out!'

'Kaiser's not trained to do that,' Bruno says and leads the dog away.

'That doesn't mean he wouldn't have!' Antony shouts after him.

Yolanda touches Antony's arm and gives him a warm smile. 'Bruno will be filling in lots of forms, don't worry. Let us give praise that it ended well.' She eyes his damaged jacket. 'Come inside, and I will make you a cup of tea. If you will allow me, I will also try to sew up that rip.'

'Yolanda's amazing with a needle,' I whisper to Antony. 'She made our crocheted turkeys.'

'That's great.' Antony puts his arm around my shoulders and squeezes me tight as we walk towards the glass doors.

He lowers his mouth to my ear. 'We need to talk.'

Conscious of Antony's proximity, I look for Henry, but he's gone.

43

— · —

I sit in the interview room as Police Constable Jane Smyth makes notes at the desk. Antony shifts position on his plastic chair opposite, looking as uncomfortable as any suspect. The storage heater in the corner is set to *MAX*. Sweat dampens my back under stuffy waves of heat, but the sweltering conditions aren't the only reason I can't sit still.

It has taken over an hour and a half for PC Smyth to take Antony's statement, complete the paperwork, and inform him of his legal rights. Antony declined to press charges against Bruno's security company. Understandably, he wants to put the ordeal behind him.

I sip tepid tea, struggling to maintain my inner calm. It's impossible not to think about Colette Stanwick and whether there have been further developments while I've been in the room with Antony.

Antony checks through his statement. The multicoloured, crocheted scarf Yolanda looped around his neck in case he got cold without his jacket now hangs like a rainbow snake over the desk. He's slung his hoodie over the back of the chair and sits in his white T-shirt. The thin cotton clings to his defined physique and induces a wave of longing. Antony is the complete package of looks and brains. Saskia's his perfect match, *and* she makes him laugh. I haven't done that since Christmas.

Satisfied with his statement, Antony signs at the bottom.

'Thank you, that's everything.' Smyth gathers the documents and stands up.

I ask, 'Is it okay if we have a few minutes to catch up?'

Smyth nods. 'I'll leave you to escort Antony out.'

Once she's left, I move into her vacated seat. 'What now?'

Antony presses the flesh around his knuckles and releases a pent-up breath. 'I guess we'd better talk about us. You, me, and Henry.'

I'm about to add Saskia to make it a magic foursome, when he jerks his head up to meet my eye.

'Henry likes you. I can tell.' Antony tilts his chin up. 'He wouldn't look me in the eye, and he didn't like it when I put my arm around you.'

Beads of sweat break out on my brow as I squirm under his scrutiny.

'Are you seeing him?' he asks.

'Of course not!'

Antony pushes back in his chair, a muscle pulsing in his cheek. 'I listened to his message on the ansaphone. It's like every time he calls, you come running.'

I clear my throat, fighting a sudden urge to cough. 'I'm here because they're short-staffed and Henry thinks we're close to catching a murderer. What's your excuse with Saskia?'

Antony frowns. 'If you'd heard me out before you stormed out of the pub, you'd know.'

'I couldn't see the point in staying.' I press my fingers into my wobbling chin, swallowing a lump in my throat. 'Saskia's beautiful. When I saw you together, I knew you were an item.'

Antony draws air in through his teeth. 'For the last time, Saskia's not my girlfriend. I'm not seeing her!'

My mind spins as I pick at the edge of the mouse-mat. 'What about the text messages? The lovey-dovey notes?'

Antony's voice snags. 'The notes were for you! I couldn't face telling you I'd mucked everything up. I wanted to make it right, but I couldn't find the right words.' He slumps in his chair, rubbing his forehead. 'Saskia wanted me to tell you everything, but I was too proud to admit I'd failed.'

'Failed? What do you mean?'

Antony closes his eyes, takes a breath and leans forward with his hand shielding his eyes.

'I'm sorry.' A shudder travels through him. He clenches his jaw, shaking his head from side to side. 'I'm so sorry.'

Antony hunches over, his posture that of a defeated man. Seeing him at such a low ebb, I have a sudden urge to rush around the desk and throw my arms around him. Instead, I stay rooted to my seat, steeling myself to hear his side of the story.

'I should have told you ages ago, but couldn't face it. I ballsed up big time, Alex.'

'How?' I ask. 'If it's not to do with Saskia, what is it?'

Antony wipes his face with the heel of his hand. 'Apex. The company played me for a mug.'

I tuck my hands on my lap, fingers laced tight. 'What do you mean?'

'I was screwed from the day I went in for my interview. Apex put on a show. They wowed me with their glossy pitch. It was all smoke and mirrors. Fact is, I've been on minimum wage since I started, which I lied about. I'm really sorry.'

'But you told me the pay was great.'

'My wages were supposed to shoot up after the trial period. But Yan kept extending it. He made excuses and fobbed me off by promoting me to head of the Launch Team.' He pulls at his lips. 'I was trying to be a good team player and show loyalty, even though I was working for peanuts.'

My mind spirals with Antony's revelations. I pass him a tissue from a box on the desk, remembering his frustrations with work, the insane hours. All that time, and he wasn't even getting paid properly.

Antony says dolefully, 'The whole point of moving to Birmingham was to make you proud. Truth was, I could have flipped burgers at Wimpy's and made more money.'

I lean forwards. 'I could have helped, if you'd told me.'

'How?' Antony wipes his eyes. 'You lost your job. Your art buyer pulled out.'

'I could have found work. We're supposed to be a team, always there for each other.'

Antony puts his head in his hands. 'How could I live with myself, knowing I'd forced you back into admin work and temping? I know how much you hate it.'

He takes a deep breath and straightens on the chair. 'I'm thirty-two. I should be at the peak of my career. Flying high, not scraping by.' He leans his arms on his legs and hangs his head. 'I was trying to make it right before I told you.'

His eyes search mine, but all I see are secrets swirling behind them. 'You told Saskia.' I lick my dry lips.

Antony looks up at the polystyrene tiled ceiling. 'I bumped into her on the stairs at work one day. She'd just handed in her notice, and we had a rant about Apex. She said I didn't know the half of it and invited me for a drink.'

'Just like that?'

'Just like that.' Antony nods. 'Saskia had seen behind Apex's facade. She told me the company works on the *hire-break-fire* principle. They recruit designers on short-term contracts, promise them a raise, string them along and work them to death. There's always another fresh face eager to be hired in their place and make a good impression.'

My voice goes tight as I ask, 'Why couldn't you just find another job?'

'And let another company own me? No way. I was determined to find my own way out of this mess.' He draws air in through his teeth. 'Saskia told me she could help.'

The gears in my mind turn. 'So, if the texts aren't about you and Saskia moving in together, what do they mean?'

Antony fumbles in his coat pocket and produces the scrap of paper containing the text messages I transcribed from his phone. He points at one: *I found a place. It'll be a squeeze, but we can*

'The deposit was for office space,' he says. 'We're setting up a design co-operative made up of former Apex designers. There are four of us so far. We stay self-employed, but we split the work and the costs. No one else gets a cut. It's just us.'

His honesty ignites a spark of hope. I remember phoning him when he said he was meeting a property guy about office leases. I thought he was lying. The truth in his words make my throat go tight.

'When Saskia invited me to join the co-operative, I felt like a prisoner who'd just been offered their freedom. All the meetings were to set up the new venture.'

'Why didn't you tell me then, instead of meeting her behind my back?' Our blazing argument after Christmas springs to mind.

Antony takes my hands in his.

'I hadn't planned on meeting her that day. I was running along the canal when I saw her on the path. It was a total co-incidence. I'm not proud of how I behaved when I got home, but I was up to my neck with Apex, you didn't trust me and I was worried about the way you kept using the finding machine.'

I meet his gaze, my heart yielding a touch. Antony was in dire straits for most of December, yet he hid it. Not because he was having an affair, but because of misplaced pride.

Antony dips his head. 'I'm sorry.'

My words catch in my throat, thinking of the pain his pride has caused.

'I thought you didn't love me anymore.'

Antony's eyes widen. 'I've never stopped loving you. You're my beautiful, brave, awesome Alex. And now you're helping the police catch a killer. I couldn't love you more.'

He clutches my hands tighter. 'Can we give it another go? We can make it work, I know we can.'

Even through the relief, the fact he hid so much from me leaves me struggling to find the right words. My mind's all over the place.

I'm torn between flinging myself into his arms and running down the hall to Henry.

I shake my head. 'I can't...I need to get my head around this.'

'I understand.' Antony half-stands, his voice breaking. 'If you want to go off with Henry or some other guy who isn't a total loser, I won't stand in your way.'

'Wait!' I grab his wrist. 'Please.'

Antony pulls away. 'I'll wait in the car.'

The burden of Antony's expectations clash with my mixed-up feelings for Henry and my desire to help with the case.

'It's not that,' I say. 'I need to be here.'

Antony's gaze falls to the floor. 'I guess it's goodbye, then.'

'No! Come with me to the cold case room. We'll talk to Henry.'

Antony pulls his hand free. 'You can't be serious. Henry won't want me anywhere near him.'

He has a point, but I'm counting on Henry's professionalism and focus. Henry and I have put everything into finding Reginald and getting justice for his wives. Simon's been reassigned, and we may have lost Tori.

We desperately need more manpower to finish the job. I know it's a big ask, but maybe Antony can pitch in.

'Please, come with me.' I walk to the door and hold it open.

Antony gazes at the ceiling as though mustering strength, grabs his rucksack, and then follows me down the corridor.

As we approach the door to the cold case room, I fill Antony in on Reginald, and pray Henry doesn't make me choose between him, Antony, and catching a murderer.

44

— • —

Taking a deep breath, I knock on the door to *Operation Thaw*. The urge to turn and run is overwhelming.

Peering through a small window in the door, I see Henry standing by the table, talking on the hotline phone. Untidy log sheets, a notepad, and computer print-outs cover the desk. He ends the call, then walks across the room to open the door.

His gaze falls on Antony, his expression blank.

Antony and I walk into an office ten degrees cooler than the interview room.

'How are things?' I ask in the brightest voice I can muster.

Henry returns to the paperwork on his desk. 'Tori's only been gone a couple of hours, and it's already chaos.'

'I thought she was coming back.'

Henry shakes his head. 'Traffic nabbed her, in spite of my best efforts. We're so short of officers, I should count my blessings I'm still here to hold the fort. And Simon's stuck with the Millennium Team until tomorrow.'

'Ready to jump into a bunker at a moment's notice,' I say in an attempt to lighten the mood, but the joke doesn't register with Henry, and Antony doesn't know what I'm talking about.

Henry's usual warmth has fled. He glances back at Antony who is pulling on his hoodie. 'Still here, then?'

'Antony wants to help.' I brace myself. 'I was thinking he could answer the hotline while I make follow-up calls.'

Henry's mouth tightens into a thin line. He looks at Antony as if he's an alien.

'Alex said you were short-staffed, so I thought I'd make myself useful,' Antony says in a friendly tone, which is some achievement considering he'd rather be a hundred miles away. A glow goes through me. He meant what he said about being a team.

Silence fills the room.

'There must be something he can do,' I say into the void.

Henry shuffles paper. 'He hasn't had the proper background checks.'

Antony puts one hand in his pocket and jingles change. 'The officer ran a DBS check in the interview room. My sheet's clean. Besides, Alex can vouch for me.'

'It doesn't work like that. Friends can't vouch for friends. There's protocol to follow.'

'You could put me down as a psychic,' Antony says.

Cringing, I give him a swift elbow in the ribs and add, 'Could he be a CHIS like me?'

I'm aware of what I'm asking. Henry wants Antony out of the picture. Instead, Antony has invaded his territory. It doesn't help that he made a terrible first impression, rolling on the ground in a hoodie with Henry's colleagues restraining him.

Antony steps forward. 'Alex said you're chasing a suspected murderer. If she's going anywhere near this lowlife, I want to be there. Hasn't this guy already killed two women?'

Henry gives me a serious look and says, tight-lipped, 'That's confidential information.'

'I'm sorry,' I say. 'But Antony deserves to know.'

Antony adds, 'Especially if you're heading out at night to catch him.'

'I would never put Alex in danger,' Henry says, thumb looped behind his belt. 'As soon as we have eyes on the suspect, we'll pull back and call in the Response Team. But there's still work to do.' He gives me a pointed look. 'Any luck with your machine, yet?'

'I'll check again.' I pull my mobile from my pocket and autodial TJ.

'Yeah, hello.' TJ answers, sounding flustered. 'Look, we're at critical testing. Can I call you back?'

'Just let me know as soon as you've located Reginald,' I say before hanging up. 'Sounds like they're close.'

'But not close enough,' Henry says.

I throw my hands up. 'It's maddening, but what can I do?'

'We could drive up to the League's headquarters,' Antony says. 'They might have fixed it by the time we arrive.'

'And they might not,' I say. 'We'll have wasted hours rushing north on a whim.'

Antony throws me a loaded look. 'I don't see how you can help Henry without the machine.'

'I've been helping loads!' I protest.

'Sorry, that came out wrong.' Antony closes his eyes and takes a calming breath. He puts his hands up defensively. 'I didn't mean you haven't helped.'

'Alex is a very good investigator.' Henry tilts his head towards the desk. 'This afternoon, she generated two new leads, and found out Reginald's new alias and the name of his wife.' He gives me a nod. 'Well done.'

'Thanks.' I smile, but not too much in case I upset Antony.

'That's amazing, Alex.' Antony shrugs.

'Thank you,' I say, then meet Henry's eye. 'So, can he help?'

Henry briefly closes his eyes before giving Antony a level look. '*If* I can clear it with my boss, and if I do, you'll be answerable to me.'

Antony nods. 'Fair enough.'

The tension in the room lifts a touch. I point to the paperwork on Henry's desk. 'Any news on Colette or Reginald, or is it René? I don't even know what to call him, now.'

'His birth name is Reginald, so let's stick with that.' Henry retrieves a computer print-out. 'I'm concerned about Colette. I called her old house and spoke to the owners, but they don't have a forwarding address for her. Unfortunately, County Hall's closed until the third of January, which means we can't access their marriage certificate. That would have shown Reginald's new name and address.'

'Is everything on hold?' I ask, deflated from the lack of progress.

'Not everything.' Henry fishes a blue and pink sheet from the pile. 'There are two bits of good news on Delia. Tori tracked down her dental records, and by tomorrow we'll know if they're a match. Forensics also emailed a partial fingerprint found on the inside of the tarp Delia was wrapped in. If it belongs to Reginald, it would link him to Delia's murder and by association, Nenagh.'

'Have you run the print?' I ask.

'No joy, I'm afraid. There's no match on the system.' He hands me a Post-it note with an extension number. 'Can you call Major Crime and request a printout of the calls we missed?' He heads for the door. 'I need to see my boss about clearance for Antony.'

Henry leaves the room.

'Do you mind if I have a sandwich? I'm starving,' Antony asks, walking to the lunch platter on the kitchenette counter.

'Help yourself.'

Antony eats curling cheese and pickle sandwiches in front of the picture window. Outside, a forest of dark branches criss-crosses a graphite sky. Orange streetlights glow beyond the perimeter.

'I never thought this is how we'd be spending the Millennium,' he says. 'Stuck inside a police station, helping the rozzers.'

'The what?'

'You know.' He nods to the door. 'Rozzers.'

'Don't call them that!' I hiss. 'Why do you always talk about the police as if they're the enemy?'

'Gee... let me think.' He pulls up his sleeve, displaying bruises visible against his dark skin, and shoots me a pointed look.

I fold my arms with a harrumph. 'Look, that was down to an over-zealous security guard. The police are different. They're here to protect and to serve.'

Antony throws his head back and laughs. 'That's the U.S. cops! You've been watching too much TV. Jeez, Alex!'

'Whatever.' I pick up the grey phone and dial the extension for Major Crime.

A woman answers. 'Major Crime. Zoey speaking.'

'Hello Zoey, it's Alex Martin again, from Operation Thaw. Do you have the call log from this afternoon?'

'Give me a minute and I'll email it over.'

'Thanks.' I put the handset down and move to the general office computer, checking the emails until a *ping* sounds. I double-click on the new file and press print. The laser printer in the corner whirs to life, and Antony performs his first task for the Hertfordshire Constabulary by fetching the hot sheet of paper.

Three calls were diverted to Major Crime while the office was empty. Two are vague sightings, but the one from a Barry Morgan makes me straighten like someone's zapped my spine.

Henry enters the room. He motions Antony over to the desk and hands him a lanyard, along with some forms. 'You're in luck. Yolanda likes you. Sign in the highlighted boxes, and you can tag along.'

'Great.' Antony signs the forms, and hangs the lanyard labelled OBSERVER over his neck. The police insignia, all-black clothing and muscular physique make him look like a special ops agent.

Henry holds out Antony's puffa jacket. 'She's also fixed the rip.'

'Cheers. I must thank her.' Antony examines the arm of his jacket and runs his finger over the fine stitching.

'Guys, come and look at this.' I wave the print-out to get their attention. 'Barry Morgan bought a used Porsche from a salesman named René two weeks ago, at Bentley Prestige Sales.'

Henry takes the sheet. 'Bentley Prestige? Hold on. Didn't we see those guys yesterday?'

'You spoke to the sales manager. Julian something or other,' I say. 'He had a Ferrari.'

'Julian Debrett,' Henry reads from his notes. 'He said he didn't recognise Reginald's picture.'

'Sounds like Julian's a bit of a fibber.' Antony says, examining the flyer with Reginald's photo and my drawings. 'And if Reginald sees his mug on this flyer, he's gonna do a runner.'

Henry arches a brow. 'Why do you think we're working late?'

He turns to his monitor and swiftly accesses the police central database. I glance over his shoulder as he types JULIAN DE-BRETT into the search boxes and hits ENTER.

Green text populates the screen.

Henry leans forward and rubs his chin. 'Julian has form. Intent to supply Class A and B drugs, two cautions, and a suspended sentence.' He prints out his details. 'Something's off with Bentley Prestige. I want to go down there and take a closer look.'

'Gotta be better than sitting here for New Year's Eve,' says Antony.

Henry eyes Antony. 'Let me make one thing clear. When we're in the field, you're strictly an observer. Understand?'

'Understood,' Antony nods.

'Good. Let's go,' Henry says. 'Something's about to shake loose.'

45

I break into a run to keep up with Henry's ground-eating strides as he crosses the flood-lit car park. Antony is one step behind.

Henry reaches the Astra and unlocks the doors.

A pained expression flashes on Antony's face. 'This your ride? I thought you'd have an M-series Beamer or an AMG Merc.' He nods at the Astra. 'If Reggie does a runner in a sports car, we're stuffed.'

'There won't be any car chases,' Henry says archly. 'We're doing this without drama.'

Antony glances longingly at the Audi.

I hide a smile and climb into the passenger seat. Antony opens the back door and squeezes into the rear of the car. 'Can you move your seat forward, babe?' he asks.

I fumble for the lever under my legs and shunt the seat forwards. A charged atmosphere hangs amongst us as we secure our seat-belts.

Henry pulls out of the car park and drives towards Ware. He crosses the railway tracks, the bridge over the river, and drives up the high street. We pass five lads dressed as nuns, their black habits billowing in the wind, a bunch of women in spangly hats, and groups of locals out for the night. Every restaurant, takeaway, and pub we pass is warmly lit and thronging with punters.

'Can't believe it's nearly here,' Antony breaks the silence. 'The twenty-first century. A new Millennium.'

Henry's eyes flick to the rear-view mirror. 'Do you expect to-morrow to be any different to today?'

'Yeah, I'm collecting my hover-car.' Antony laughs.

'They never get the future right, do they?' I say, finding the small talk a welcome distraction from the nervous tension inside the car. 'On TV and in films, they always predict the next big thing way too soon.'

Henry briefly glances my way. 'I think your machine could be the next big thing.'

'I'm not so sure.' Much as I'd love to see lots of finding machines saving lives and rescuing people, there are too many corrupt governments, criminal organisations and bad guys who would want it for the wrong reasons.

'Watch this space,' Henry continues. 'Machines like yours, computers, and artificial intelligence are going to be game-changers. If what they're saying is true, I could be out of a job soon.'

'Join the club,' Antony says.

I look round and we share a swift smile.

'Quick question.' Antony leans forward and grips the back of my headrest. 'When you've collared Reginald, is he sitting back here with me? Or is he going in the boot?'

'No!' Henry lets out a short laugh. 'We'll sling him in the back of a wagon.'

I never thought I'd be spending New Year's Eve with Henry and Antony. Not in my wildest dreams. The thawing atmosphere loosens the knots in my stomach. I pray it lasts.

Henry takes the first exit at the roundabout at the end of the high street and follows Watton Road towards the Westmill interchange. A burst of pink shooting stars explodes in the sky above the treeline. I stare wide-eyed through the window as a flurry of fireworks go off with multiple bangs. Sparks twizzle outwards in gold starbursts, glittering stars fade against the black sky.

It looks like we're in for a noisy, colourful night.

Henry flicks on the indicator and turns into the small trading estate we visited yesterday. A display board at the entrance lists the companies in situ. Bentley Prestige Sales is last on the list.

Sodium streetlights shine on the single road running through the estate. Floodlights illuminate empty forecourts. All the single-storey units we drive past are closed for the night. Metal shutters cover their windows and the gates are locked.

Henry follows the deserted street past empty forecourts until we reach the last bend in the road. Bentley Prestige shines like a beacon at the end. The glass-fronted showroom is ablaze with multi-coloured lights.

An amazing array of cars is parked by the kerb, including top-end BMWs, Audis, Rolls-Royces, Maseratis, a classic gullwing Mercedes, and my brother's all-time Top Trump favourite – a Lamborghini Countach.

Henry performs a three-point turn and parks in front of a black Porsche 911. He switches off the engine. Thumping music, shrieks and laughter carry through the night air.

He turns in his seat and keeps his voice low, despite no one being around to hear. 'Let's get closer and see if Reginald's inside.'

My mouth goes dry as we leave the car and approach the showroom via a shadowed path running by a chain-link fence. The chill wind tousles my hair, but I barely notice it. Electric gates close off the forecourt, leaving a small side-gate open for pedestrian access.

Powerful security lights shine onto cars for sale beyond the gate. Julian's Ferrari is parked in a space at the end, marked *Staff*.

Antony dips his head close to my ear. 'You can get me one of those for Christmas next year.' He admires a classic Ford Capri parked next to the Ferrari, with gold stripes along the black coachwork. 'Wouldn't mind one of them, either.'

Henry interrupts. 'Do you think we could focus on the reason we're here?'

There must be at least fifty people inside the showroom. Their silhouettes merge under the party lights, making it difficult to see their faces.

After a few minutes, Henry says, 'I can't see Reg. You?'

'Nothing,' I add, scanning the crowd.

'Nup.' Antony says.

'Right, it's time to go inside and have a word with Julian.' Henry catches Antony's eye. 'You stay here. Tuck your lanyard away. Watch everyone coming and going. If you see our suspect, come and get me.'

Antony puts his arm around my shoulder. 'Promise you'll look after Alex.'

Henry nods. 'You have my word.'

A swift squeeze, and Antony retreats into the shadows.

Henry looks to me. 'Ready?'

I nod and follow Henry through the gate and into the main showroom. The smell of leather, car-polish and cigarettes mingles with a heady wave of perfume and booze. I squeeze past a group of women beside a towering Christmas tree festooned with ice-blue lights. A barrage of raised voices and laughter clashes with eighties pop music. The party classic, *Walk the Dinosaur*, sounds weirdly off-kilter with our serious mission.

The well-heeled guests sip champagne and bottles of lager. I check the faces of a group of party-goers helping themselves at the buffet table. Their plates are piled with vol-au-vents, smoked salmon sandwiches cut into tiny triangles, chicken skewers, and crisps. Farther down, the table is laden with ice buckets filled with champagne, bottles of beer, cider, wine, and soft drinks.

The showroom's focal point is a white Lotus Esprit Turbo. The car is mounted on a revolving podium, cordoned-off by a red velvet rope. A James Bond poster sits by the driver's door.

At the back of the room, lights strobe over a small dance floor with a DJ behind a mixing desk. Only one person is dancing: a tipsy middle-aged man. From his paunch, awkward dad-dance, and wine stains on his shirt, it's not Reg.

Henry and I thread our way past a woman in white stilettos and frizzy blonde hair laughing hysterically at a young guy with a loud tie and even louder voice, cigarette in hand, and a couple smooching by the door leading to the loos. My heart thumps as I search each face.

Is he here?

Henry glances and nods towards an office door. A man in a black shirt stands beside it, sniffing and wiping his nose on the back of his hand. Henry steps up close and surreptitiously shows his warrant card.

'Hello, Julian.'

Julian shoves both hands into his pockets and sniffs again. He doesn't look as sophisticated without his Ferrari and camel coat. He has squeezed himself into a shirt that's one size too small with the top two buttons undone. His thinning blond hair is loaded with copious amounts of gel.

'What's this about?' His eyes dart between Henry and me.

'Remember me? I'm DC Henry Longhurst, and this is my assistant Alex Martin. If you recall, we spoke yesterday.' Henry points to the door. 'Let's talk in there.'

He gestures me to go first. I open the door to a darkened room, feel on the wall for the light switches, and flick them on. Panel lights flicker and illuminate a spartan office with three metal desks. On the back wall, a whiteboard displays October, November and December sales figures. The salesmen's names form a column on the left-hand side:

JULIAN, MARTIN, DIANA, RENÉ, STUART.

The figures by each name are astounding, running into the tens of thousands. After a swift calculation, I estimate Reg has sold over one-hundred thousand pounds worth of cars in October alone.

Henry closes the door behind us, stares at the chart and frowns. He turns to Julian. 'Yesterday, you told me you didn't know René.'

Julian runs his finger around the inside of his collar. Red and white blotches rise on his neck and jaw. 'You didn't ask me about René. You asked about some guy called Reginald.' He leans back against the nearest line.

Henry's lips form a tight line. 'Where is he?'

'I don't know.'

While Henry distracts Julian with questions, I sidle up to the desks. Two are clear of clutter, their monitors black and dead. The last desk on the right contains a Rolodex and switchboard phone. With the nail-varnish, blue glitter pens, and cuddly bee stuck on top of the monitor, I'm pretty sure this is the secretary's domain.

I lean over the chair and sneakily nudge the mouse, but nothing happens. A pile of paperwork sits in the in-tray. I cast my eye across invoices and receipts, MOT certificates and V5 ownership documents, but there's nothing with René's name on.

Henry moves closer until he's looming over Julian. 'Cover up for him, and you'll go down with him as an accessory.'

'I'm not covering for him.' Julian struggles to look Henry in the eye. A sheen of sweat rises on his forehead. 'I don't know where he is.'

Henry fixes him with a steely stare. 'I've been watching you. You've had your left hand stuck in your pocket the whole time. It makes me think you've got something in there you shouldn't. How about I drag you into the showroom, kill the music, turn the lights back on, and search you in front of your guests?'

'You can't do that.' Julian runs a shaking hand through his stiff hair.

'I can and I will if you don't tell me where René is. I've seen your priors, Julian. It looks to me like you're back to your old habits.'

'I'm clean, I swear.'

'Do you want to spend New Year's Eve in the nick?' Henry asks.

'No.' Julian flushes. Sweat trickles down his cheeks. 'Look, René's his own man. He comes and goes as he pleases. I don't know where he is. For real.'

'When did you last see him?'

Julian gives an exaggerated shrug.

'What's his surname?'

'M...Moreau.'

Henry takes out his notepad. 'I need his address, car registration, make and model, mobile and landlines, everything you've got.'

'I've got his mobile.' Julian reaches into his jacket. 'I don't know his address. My secretary deals with that, and she's on holiday.'

'His car?' Henry demands.

'René owns several. He also borrows cars from the lot. We all do. It's a perk of the job.'

I peek over the top of the monitor. 'What about a payslip?'

Julian shakes his head morosely. 'I haven't a clue where Stef stores that stuff.' He retrieves a flash black clamshell phone from his back pocket and flips it open.

Henry looks on impatiently as Julian searches for the phone number.

I pull the Rolodex and casually turn the knob on the side to rotate the cards to the 'M' tab. I flick through each card.

MAINWRIGHT, MG, MORAN, MOREAU.

'Here's the number.' Julian turns his phone around.

Henry takes the phone and writes the number in his notebook. 'I'm seizing your phone. I believe it contains information relevant to our investigation.' He slips Julian's phone into his pocket.

'You can't take my phone!' Julian's jaw drops.

'I can, to prevent you destroying incriminating evidence.' Henry takes a business card from his jacket and scribbles something on the back.

The door flies open, and Antony barges in.

'There you are!' He hangs onto the door handle, breathing heavily. 'I've seen him. Out the back in an Aston Martin.'

'Are you sure?' Henry straightens like he's been stunned with a cattle prod.

'Alex's picture was spot on. It's gotta be him.'

Henry glares at Julian, who steps back until he hits the desk. 'I didn't know he was here, I swear!'

Henry pushes the business card into Julian's clammy hand. 'Here's the receipt for your phone. You can expect another visit from us.' He gestures to me before following Antony through the door.

I pull Reg's card from the Rolodex and follow them.

<h1 style="text-align:center">46</h1>

I squeeze through the inebriated crowd, following Antony and Henry to the main doors, and earn an outraged 'Oi!' when I accidentally tread on someone's foot.

Outside, exhaust plumes from a silver Aston Martin DB7 on the forecourt. The idling engine emits a deep-throated rumble as the driver waits for the electric gates to slide open. Brake lights blaze in the dark, illuminating the emblem with a blood-red cast: a pair of silver wings.

I gasp, remembering Mystic Miriam's reading. She saw a pair of silver wings. At the time I thought they might be a reference to angels or death. I suppose, in a way, they still are.

I tug Henry's coat. 'That's Reginald. It's him, I know it!'

Henry nods, striding forwards.

The performance engine roars. The Aston Martin shoots through the gates and disappears around the corner.

'Come on!' Henry races towards the Astra.

We thump across the tarmac and throw ourselves inside the car. I buckle my seatbelt as Henry swiftly drives off. Antony ignores his seatbelt completely. He leans forward, gripping my headrest.

'Can you catch him?'

Henry shakes his head. 'There's no point in trying. We'll keep our distance. I want Reg nice and relaxed and thinking no one's on his tail.'

'He may have spotted us in the showroom,' I say. 'Or, Julian could have warned him.'

Henry says, 'All the more reason to keep our distance.'

Around the bend, the Aston Martin has stopped at the T-junction.

Henry hangs back until the sports car turns right and speeds away. He accelerates to the junction, swiftly looks both ways, and pulls out behind a minicab.

Ahead, the sports car's large brake lights flash as it crests a hill in the distance and is lost from view.

Clearing my throat, I say, 'Guys, I think I know where he's going.'

Henry shoots me a surprised look.

'I took Reg's details from the secretary's desk.' I hold up the Rolodex card, using the streetlights to read by: 'The Vicarage, Marshalls Lane, High Cross, Ware. That's in this direction, isn't it?'

'It certainly is. Good work, Alex.' Henry picks up the police radio. 'Victor Hotel from Bravo Whiskey 45, over.'

The radio crackles to life. *'Bravo Whiskey 45, this is Victor Hotel, over.'*

'I'm on the Westmill Interchange tailing a silver Aston Martin, registration Romeo-Two-Zero-One-Yankee-Victor-Victor. I need to know who it's registered to. Can you do a PNC check and put out an APB to all units?'

'Yes, Yes, Bravo Whiskey 45. Repeat your exact location, over.'

'I'm on the A602 heading towards Tonwell. I'm looking to effect an arrest and will require backup once the suspect has stopped. Over.'

'Be aware that all available units are currently attending incidents. Are you in immediate danger? Over.'

Henry shoots me an exasperated look. 'Negative. I intend to hang back and wait for support. Thanks for the update, Control. Any luck with the car? Over.'

'Stand by.' A long pause follows. *'Bravo Whiskey 45, the car is registered to a trade owner, Bentley Prestige. Over.'*

'All Received. Out.' Henry slots the radio into its cradle and shakes his head. 'The car's not registered to him.'

Henry drives over the hill and checks for oncoming traffic. He eases the Astra out and peers around the minivan that shields the Aston Martin from view. The Astra's tyres rumble briefly over the raised centre line before he slips back into lane.

'He's way ahead, must be doing over ninety. With any luck, he'll get pulled over for speeding.' Henry glances in the rear-view mirror. 'There's a map and penlight back there, in the pocket behind my seat. I need you to locate Marshalls Lane and give me directions.'

'I'm on it,' says Antony. Paper crackles as he unfolds the map and clicks on the slim light. 'Marshalls Lane, Marshalls Lane. Grid reference G4.'

Henry flicks on his indicator and swings into the oncoming lane to overtake the minicab. I look around as Antony curses and topples to one side. Loose change spills from his pocket. He leans forward to fish coins from the floor and stuffs them back into his pocket.

'Forget the money.' I glare at him. 'Put your seatbelt on and read the map!'

'Yes, boss.' Antony's finger traces down and along the page and stops. He grabs the armrest as Henry swerves back into lane. 'Mate, unless you want a load of undigested cheese and pickle sandwiches all over the back seat, you need to stop swinging the car round!'

'Bend coming up,' Henry warns, changing down a gear before handling the turn like a Formula 1 driver.

'Blooooody hell! You said it wasn't a pursuit!' Antony yells, thumping into the door.

I glance back to see him clinging to the armrest with an ashen face.

'I need to keep Reg in view. I strongly suggest you put your seat belt on.' Henry floors it over a hump in the road. My stomach swoops as we leave the road. The suspension creaks as we bounce down, the shock of landing making my teeth clack.

Antony fumbles with his seatbelt, eventually securing it with a click. Although he's having a rough ride, from where I'm sitting Henry's driving feels controlled and precise. He slows for the corners, sticking tightly around each bend before accelerating away. I have faith we'll get there in one piece.

'Antony,' Henry says tightly. 'I need those directions.'

Antony's torch beam swings wildly over the page. He keeps his finger stolidly fixed on the map.

'The road makes a long loop through Tonwell,' he says. 'Then it's a right onto Sacombe Pound.'

'We've gone through Tonwell,' Henry says. 'Sacombe Pound must be up ahead.'

'It's there, THERE!' I stab my finger at a signpost partially obscured by shrubs, pointing down a dark lane.

Henry wrenches the wheel over and executes a sharp right turn that makes the tyres squeal. I cling to the door grip, praying all four wheels stay on terra firma. Thankfully, we come out of the bend unscathed, and Henry guns the engine down the unlit, country lane flanked by low hedges.

Antony says, 'Found it! You want Sacombe Green Road. It's farther up...another right turn.' He groans, winds down the window. 'Think I'm gonna be sick.'

'Give me the map and the torch,' I say.

Antony thrusts them into my hand before slumping against the door.

The Astra hurtles down the narrow lane. Over the fields, fireworks explode in a kaleidoscope of colours. I find G4 on the map and get my bearings.

'Take a right at that sign.' I point out a white marker post stuck into the verge. 'It should be Sacombe Green Road. It turns into Marshalls Lane.'

Henry turns sharply onto a pitch-black, winding lane. As he navigates the turns, an oncoming car races around the corner, its headlights blazing.

I throw my hands up to shield my eyes.

Henry squints and hits the brakes. He takes avoiding action and steers into a drainage ditch. Gravel crunches under the tyres. Sticks and branches scrape down the side of the car with a screech like nails down chalkboard. The sound shoots through my skull.

'Dip your lights!' Henry yells out the window as a monstrous 4x4 roars past, music thumping, and clips the Astra. The wing mirror topples from its housing and is left dangling by a wire. 'Bloody Chelsea tractors!'

The tyres spin as Henry drives out of the ditch and continues down the lane. He flicks from dipped headlights to full beam. Farther on, we drive past a whitewashed cottage, a modern stable-block and a barn.

The damaged mirror bangs against the door as Henry brakes at a small crossroads with a tiny grass island.

I say, 'Follow the road round to the right. It'll take you to Marshalls Lane. The Vicarage should be along this road.'

Henry follows my instructions. White picket fences demarcate wide, private driveways leading to grand houses set back from the road. There must be at least fifty yards between each property. There are no streetlights or house numbers, only fancy names carved into logs, wooden signs, stone boulders and slate plaques on the verge.

Henry slows to a crawl. 'Keep your eyes open for The Vicarage.'

I read out the names. 'Whistle's End...Down Farm...Fairisle...c an't see a name on this one.'

A ten-foot-high ornamental hedge blocks the next house from the road as effectively as any wall. Golden light from a lamppost straight out of *The Lion, The Witch and The Wardrobe* falls on a paved drive leading to a handsome manor house with a double garage.

The Aston Martin is tucked away behind the hedge.

Antony lets out a low whistle. 'Nice place.'

'It's amazing how far you can get up the property ladder by killing your wives,' I mutter darkly.

Henry pulls onto the verge behind the hedge. He turns off the engine and lights, then picks up his radio.

'Victor Hotel from Bravo Whiskey 45, over.'

'...*Brav... Whis... you are brea...u.... Over.*'

'Control, you are barely readable.' Henry speaks louder. 'I've got a sitrep at The Vicarage, Marshalls Lane, High Cross, Ware. The time is now 11:35 p.m. I require a response team to effect an arrest.'

'*Bra... Whi..., rep... a... add... Y... a... break... u... O...*'

Henry gives the address again and adds, 'I need backup and transport for the suspect. Over.'

'*I ca... re... y....*'

Henry swears, gives up on the radio. 'This place has the radio reception of a black hole.'

He reaches in his pocket for his mobile. 'Let's do it this way.' He dials the emergency services, puts the phone to his ear. 'It's still engaged. Can you two give it a go?'

Antony and I dial the emergency services, but can't get through.

'The world must be going crazy tonight,' I say, ending the call.

'I'll try the radio outside the car,' Henry says, stepping outside. He walks up the road with his hand cupped over the radio.

The ornamental hedge is a dark wall to my left. To my right, a tangled thicket bounds a field dotted with trees. Instead of pavement, there's a mud gutter. Over the field, white rockets *whoosh* into the sky.

The driver's door suddenly opens, making me jump. Henry slips behind the wheel. The radio gives a last crackle before dying. He slots it into its cradle on the dash.

'I can barely hear them, and it's the same on their end,' he says. 'We must be in a valley. I tried again on my mobile but the lines are jammed.'

I look at him in alarm. 'What's standard procedure in a case like this?'

'There isn't one.' Henry gives a rueful laugh. 'Control would advise me to wait for backup, but from the sound of things we could be waiting all night.' He sighs. 'I could kick myself for not giving them Reg's address. No one knows where we are.'

I feel the cold truth in his words. Not a single car has gone past since we've been here.

Henry pulls the door latch. 'I'm going to take a closer look. You two stay here.'

'Hold on, mate,' Antony leans forward with a frown. 'What if Reg is lying in wait? We need backup, right?'

'I agree with Antony,' I say, curling my fingers into fists.

'I'm surveiling the property from a safe distance, that's all,' Henry says. 'I won't be long.'

Henry leaves before Antony or I can protest further. He creeps along in the shadows by the hedge and pauses at the corner where it meets the driveway.

Antony leans forward between the front seats. 'Your eyes are massive. You're making me nervous.'

'We can't sit here like lemons,' I say.

'Yes, we can!' Antony puts his hand on my shoulder. 'Henry's a big boy. He doesn't need a jobless web designer and a typist putting their oar in.'

'I'm more than a typist! I'll have you know, I'm a valuable addition to the cold case team!' I grit my teeth. 'I'm going to take a look. Are you coming or not?'

Antony's hand slips from my shoulder as I step from the car. He clambers from the back seat with a resigned look.

'This is a really bad idea.'

I hurry over to Henry who is peering around the hedge at the corner of the drive. It's quiet, except for the *tick-tick-tick* of the Aston Martin's cooling engine and distant popping fireworks. The Vicarage's porch light is on. Curtains are pulled across all the windows. An orange sentinel light blinks on a burglar alarm fixed below the apex of the roof.

'Anything?' I ask Henry.

Henry glares at me. 'I told you to stay in the car.'

'See?' Antony whispers to me. 'Let's go back.'

Henry shushes us and points to a bay window to the left of the door. 'I just saw movement.'

As we watch from the shadows, a hand thrusts aside the curtains. A blonde woman in a white dress appears, her face pale and drawn. She mouths something.

I inhale sharply. My scalp prickles and icy tendrils skin down my spine. 'Oh my God. She looks like a g...ghost!'

'Stop creeping me out,' Antony hisses. 'Ghosts don't breathe. She's misting up the glass.'

The woman shakes her head and pulls back from the window. The curtains fall back into place before I can work out if she moved of her own volition or someone yanked her.

'That didn't look good,' Antony mutters.

'It's Colette, it has to be.' I throw Henry a beseeching look. 'We have to help her.'

'The front door doesn't look shut. I'm going in,' Henry says. 'You two, knock on doors, ask to use a landline, and stay on the phone until you get through to the police.'

I raise my hand, a question on my lips, but before I can ask it Henry is running for the door. He steps onto the porch and reaches up for the iron bell handle, then hesitates.

I hold my breath as he lowers his hand and slowly pushes the door open, revealing a glimpse of wall and an orange glow further down.

He slips inside and disappears from view.

Minutes tick by. Foreboding curdles in my gut. I chew my fingernails, staring at the door, willing Henry to appear with Reginald in cuffs.

Come on, Henry! Where are you?

The front door starts to move, the rectangle of hallway narrowing to a sliver as an unseen person closes it.

The door clicks shut.

My heart goes into overdrive. Rummaging in my pocket, I grab my mobile and dial 112.

Still engaged. I cock my head, hoping to hear police sirens, but there's nothing.

Antony touches my shoulder, making me jump. 'We need to get help. Let's knock on doors.'

I draw breath in sharply. 'I've got a better idea.'

I speed-dial the League with shaking hands.

TJ answers. 'Alex, we're nearly there, but we need mo—'

I cut in, keeping my gaze fixed on the front door.

'Forget that, TJ. We've found Reginald but we're in trouble.' I take a shuddering breath. 'Henry's in danger and the emergency lines are engaged.' I give him the address. 'You need to call the police and send them here.'

'I'll try. But if you can't get through, I won't be able to, either.'

'You can if you keep trying. Please don't let us down.' I hang up, swallowing hard, and exchange a worried look with Antony. 'The police will be ages. It's up to us.'

'Up to us?' Antony's mouth drops open. 'I promised to keep you safe.'

'Henry's in there. We can't stand here and do nothing.'

'Come on, Alex,' Antony implores me. 'Henry's a big guy. He's a trained officer. He can handle himself. We don't have the skills for this.'

I face the house with a dangerous fire smouldering inside me. Of all the dilemmas the finding machine has led me to, none have been this dangerous. Reginald robbed Nenagh and Delia of their lives. We can't let him do the same to Henry and Colette.

'This is a big house,' I say. 'Reg can't be everywhere at once.'

An intensity comes into Antony's eyes. I stiffen, terrified he'll refuse to help.

To my very great relief, he leans forward and kisses my forehead.

'All right, what's the plan?'

47

Antony and I creep to the front door. The first part of our plan is easy – peek through the letterbox. The iron flap makes a tiny squeak as I lift it and cautiously look through.

A metal, barred cage is fixed to the back of the letterbox to catch the post. The dimly lit entrance hall leads to a closed wooden door.

'I can't see or hear anyone,' I whisper, closing the flap.

'Let's try around the back.' Antony gestures to the garden gate attached to the end of the house. We skulk along like thieves, ducking beneath a large bay window and then a tiny window with patterned glass, probably a downstairs loo.

Our journey comes to an abrupt end at a barred iron gate topped with ornamental spears. The gate adjoins the house on one side, and a matching, spiked iron fence on the other, with thorned pyracantha bushes in front. A narrow patio on the other side adjoins a dark patch of lawn that wraps around the back of the house.

I depress the latch and push. The gate rattles in its frame.

Antony stills my hand, pointing to a sturdy combination padlock looped through the iron latch.

We retrace our steps past the front door and the window where we saw Colette, to the garage. A metal, hinged security post is set into concrete in front of the garage doors. When upright and locked in place, the post stops the doors opening. It's currently unlocked and folded down.

The garage doors are wooden, painted white, with black metal handles.

'The garage might lead into the house,' Antony whispers.

'It's worth a try,' I answer. 'I can't see another way in.'

He takes the handles and gives the doors a tug, making them wobble. He runs his thumb over a simple rim lock on the right-hand door.

'Just a sec.' He reaches inside his jacket pocket for his wallet and removes a credit card. He yanks on one of the handles to increase the gap by the latch enough to slip the card inside. He wiggles the card around until, after several attempts, the door judders open.

'Where did you learn that trick?' I whisper.

'From hanging around the wrong crowd in Hackney.' He glances nervously at the alarm.

The orange light maintains its steady blinking. Thankfully, our unauthorised entry hasn't set off any warning beeps or sirens.

Antony ducks inside and I follow, leaving the door ajar. The garage smells of oil and contains two cars covered in tarpaulins.

I pull the penlight from my pocket, switch it on and sweep the beam of light around. The tarpaulin nearest me bears a Mercedes-Benz star dead-centre of the bonnet. The second tarpaulin has a custom logo in the same place: Herbert Cooper Performance Cars. The position of both logos matches the missing squares from the tarps wrapped around Nenagh and Delia. I'm about to point it out to Antony when I realise it won't mean anything to him.

Henry would realise the significance. A flash of worry suddenly hits me like a drench of cold water. I can't bear the thought of him coming to harm.

Antony waits by an unpainted door in the back wall. 'Switch off your torch.'

Once I've extinguished the penlight and dropped it into my pocket, Antony depresses the handle.

The door cracks open.

A parquet-floored corridor leads to my right. It passes two rooms and forms a junction with the entrance hallway. Directly across from me, a red-carpeted staircase rises to the first floor.

A joist creaks overhead, accompanied by slow footsteps.

We glance up. 'Let's do this quickly,' Antony whispers, 'If there's any trouble, we do a runner, okay?'

'Got it.'

We creep down the corridor and pause by an open doorway. I peek inside, my throat dry. A polished oval dining table and eight dark wood chairs dominate the room.

Antony tries the door opposite. He shakes his head.

We continue to the T-junction. I steel my nerves and peer round. The front door is where I expect it to be. The entrance hall leads to the room I saw through the letterbox.

'See if you can open the front door,' Antony whispers.

I rush to the door and twist the thumb-turn latch. It won't budge. My gaze drops to an old-fashioned keyhole beside the pad-locked letterbox cage.

A sinking feeling comes over me. Reginald has the place locked up like a fortress. I pad back to Antony and give him an empty shrug.

Antony walks to the door at the end of the entrance hallway and puts his hand on the brass knob.

He pushes the door open. A pair of stately brass lamps cast ovals of warm light across the lounge. A floral sofa and matching armchair – also in red, like the staircase carpet - face each other across a coffee table with its feet sunk into a Persian rug. Wooden floorboards lead to a set of French windows overlooking the garden.

A grandfather clock slowly ticks in the corner: half past eleven.

A limp hand pokes out behind the foot of the sofa.

Stifling a gasp, I rush around the furniture to find Henry in a crumpled heap on the floor. His eyes are closed, and blood mats the back of his head. An iron fire-poker lies beside him, the end gleaming wet under the lamp light.

'Oh God. No. Henry.'

I crash to my knees and press my fingers against Henry's neck.

As I feel for a pulse, Henry lets out a croaking sound and his eyes
flutter open. He stares blankly at me, waves his hand until he finds
my wrist. His grip is weak.

'Alex...grouss...himhe...pleess.'

'Henry, lie still. We're going to get you out of here,' I say, placing
a hand on his forehead.

'No points for guessing who did this,' Antony says, casting a
nervous look over his shoulder.

'Can you carry him out?' My words tumble out in a panic.

'We shouldn't move him at all.'

'We don't have a choice!'

Antony puffs out his cheeks, staring at Henry's six-foot-four,
muscular frame. He switches his gaze to a Persian rug by the stone
hearth. 'I'll drag him on the rug.' He nods towards the French
windows. 'Check if they're open.'

I stride over to the windows, rattle the handles, but they're
locked and the key is nowhere to be seen. Spying a phone on the
side-table, I rush over, lift the receiver and dial 999.

Click. Click. Click. I try again. *Click. Click. Click.*

'There's no dial tone. It doesn't sound like the landline's con-
nected.'

Antony tucks Henry's arms close to his body, then drags him
onto the rug, baring his teeth from the effort. 'Go into the hall and
see if the coast is clear. Keep your eyes on the stairs.'

I trot over to the doorframe and peer both ways, my tongue
sticking to the roof of my mouth.

Antony lifts one end of the rug and hauls it towards the doorway. He grunts with effort for the first few steps before establishing
momentum on the wooden floor. He drags Henry around the
corner, following me back to the garage.

Keeping watch a few paces ahead of Antony, I frantically look
left and right, left and right, like a lollipop lady on speed. My heart
jack-hammers loud enough to compete with Antony's laboured
breathing, the creaking floorboards, cracking radiators and stately
tick of the grandfather clock.

Henry moans, and I jump in my skin.

Antony hauls Henry past the dining room, glancing back every few seconds.

We're eight feet away from the garage, then four.

Before I reach the door, a trim figure wearing a Panama hat, carrying a coat over one arm and a large briefcase in hand, moves from the shadow of the stairs.

I freeze, my hand on the door handle. For a split-second I debate diving into the garage, but I can't abandon Antony and Henry.

Reginald drops his coat and briefcase, reaches into his pocket and withdraws a black, miniature pistol. He points the gun at me.

'Stay where you are.'

48

I thought I knew fear, but that was before Reginald pointed a gun at me. The tiny barrel aimed at my chest freezes me in place as effectively as Medusa's stare.

Reginald looks every inch the Bond villain in a pressed linen suit, navy blue cravat, and gun. He's only five foot eight or so, shorter than I expected, but the specks of blood on his suit prove he's no less dangerous for it.

I survey my desperate situation with a curious sense of detachment. Although my pencil drawing of Reginald was pretty accurate, he appears younger than my best guess. I assumed a man in his sixties must have lost his looks, but he's done an incredible job of holding onto them. He has a neat pencil moustache peppered with grey, suspiciously thick, tawny hair, prominent cheekbones, and well-toned skin. I suspect he's had a face lift.

His eyes are cold and soulless, devoid of compassion or an inkling of humanity. Even if I had the finding machine, I'm not sure it would find him.

'Drop the rug, leave the officer and move back into the lounge,' Reginald tells Antony. His smooth voice has a hard edge to it. 'That goes for you, too,' he addresses me. 'Do as I say, and I might let you live.'

'Please let us go.' My hand drops from the garage door.

'You shouldn't have stuck your noses in,' Reginald says between gritted teeth. 'You've forced me into this.'

Antony moves in front of me. He squares his shoulders, sizing Reginald up. He gives the pistol a long, hard stare.

'That ain't real.' Antony's Hackney accent is twice as strong as usual. 'I had one just like it when I was a kid. Used to take those little red caps.'

'What are you doing?' I hiss through clenched teeth. The pistol is tiny, but looks real enough to me.

I glance at Henry, willing him to leap up and take control of the situation. He groans, his fingers twitching and eyes fluttering.

'It's no toy, I assure you.' Lines appear on Reginald's brow.

Antony dips his head. 'Then it must be one of those trick lighters.'

Reginald's eyes narrow. 'Certain of that, are you? Enough for me to test it out on your thick skull?'

Antony licks his lips as his bluster runs out.

I squeeze next to Antony. Bravely meeting Reginald's eye, I point at poor Henry. 'He needs an ambulance.'

'You should be concerned about your own skin rather than his. Get into the lounge. No sudden moves.'

A pulse beats in Antony's jaw. He grabs my hand, pulls me close, and walks me away from Henry and into the lounge.

Reginald points the gun at the floral sofa. 'Sit.'

We perch on the edge of the padded, silk-stitched cushions. The red floral pattern is a mixture of crimson and scarlet. Ideal for hiding blood stains. To my horror, I notice the pattern is red roses. Just like Mystic Miriam saw.

Reginald says, 'I need to know how you found Nenagh and Delia. I thought I'd taken care of everything.'

My mind races. We have to keep him talking until the police arrive. 'You were unlucky with Nenagh. The flash flood washed her from her resting place and carried her downstream.'

Reginald says, 'Nenagh was in the water over forty years. There should have been nothing left of her.'

'Well, there was.' I press my lips together.

'And Delia.' Reg's eyes bore into me. 'How did you find her? No one knew I'd put her in the bottom of Duggie's grave. There were no witnesses.'

'She said you were unlucky, mate.' Antony steps in. 'Leave it.'

'Where's Colette?' I croak, struggling to make my voice work.

'Yeah, where is she?' Antony asks. 'Did you hit her with a poker, too?'

High spots of colour appear on Reginald's cheeks.

I blurt, 'The police know all about you, René or Reginald, or whatever you're calling yourself. They're on their way.'

'That's not what I heard.' Reginald's eyes widen fractionally. 'You see, I was listening to the police channels on the scanner while driving home and the only thing that came through was static. Nothing about you.'

'The police *are* coming,' I repeat.

'Yeah, you're stuffed, mate,' Antony blusters. He takes my hand and gives it a squeeze.

Reginald's lips twist into a smile. 'I'm afraid you're clinging to false hope. The emergency services don't know you're here. This village is a dead zone and the radio reception isn't worth a damn.' He arches a caddish brow at Antony. 'So, I'd say you're the ones who are *stuffed*.'

'You're crazy if you think you can get away with this,' Antony says, his fingers tightening around mine. 'You're getting nicked and going down for life. Ponce like you, the other cons will eat you alive.'

'At least I'll be alive.'

Our situation looks bleak. I remember touching the glass on the French doors. If Reg shoots us and hides our bodies, at least my fingerprints will prove I was here.

The grandfather clock slowly ticks: eleven forty-two. The chances of Antony and me making it into the twenty-first century are looking slimmer by the second. My heart leaps as a flurry of fireworks bang and pop outside. Reginald couldn't have picked a better night to get away with murder.

I grip Antony's hand extra-tight and attempt to swallow but I can't. 'The police know you killed Nenagh and Delia,' I say, in a last desperate attempt to make him see sense. 'They know Colette's in danger.'

'Then, a couple more deaths won't make much difference.' Reginald pulls the hammer back on the pistol with a click.

Antony puts his arm across me, as if that will stop a bullet. He says thickly, 'Do what you want with me, but let her go.'

'Well, it appears chivalry isn't dead,' Reginald says, transferring his aim to the centre of Antony's forehead. 'I have a remedy for that.'

'Stop!' I beg, my lower lip uncontrollably trembling as I fight back a sob. 'Please don't do this. I know about your traumatic childhood and how you suffered, the things your mother did to you. But it's not your fault.'

'My mother?' The pistol barrel drops a fraction. 'What could you possibly know about her?'

'I've seen the social worker's files.' I press on, anything to buy us time. 'It's there in black and white, how you grew up in poverty. Your mother traumatised you by sending your father away when you were eight. She took the birthday presents he brought and burnt them in front of you.'

'What a load of old tosh! Mother was the only one who told me the truth!' His tone hardens. 'My father ruined my life.' He stops and glances at the floor.

I sense an opportunity. 'How did he ruin it?'

Reginald's face falls. He suddenly appears ten years older. 'When my father learned Mother was pregnant, he joined the Navy so he wouldn't have to provide for me. He turned up a few times after I was born when his ship docked at Southampton. He would give me a toy, the odd chocolate bar, a few coins, but nothing that would keep me and my mother from starving. She put an end to his pathetic attempts to bond with me before he could let me down again. Mother told me I was worth far more than half a guinea and a toy car.'

I frown. 'But...why would your mother burn your gifts?'

'Mother never burnt my gifts. I did.' Reginald's mouth tweaks up on one side. 'She asked me to take an oath beside the fire. I was to put myself first in all things, take whatever I thought was rightfully mine, and never feel guilty. Those words changed my life, and I treasured them. I dragged myself up from the gutter with them to become the man you see. A man who made something of himself.'

A chill goes through me to hear his terrible life's mantra. Was his mother really so cold and hard, or is it a story he's told himself so often, he believes his own lie? Whatever the reason, he thinks this oath gives him the green light to do anything necessary to achieve his quest for wealth, including murder.

No wonder Reginald refuses to move away from his mother's grave. No one else could possibly understand.

'Nenagh and Delia didn't deserve to die,' I say. 'They did nothing wrong.'

'You mean, they did *nothing!*' Reginald gives an unpleasant smile, showing neat, white teeth. 'My wives were nobodies who never made anything of themselves. They did not deserve their houses or their wealth. Their only duty was to live as kept women. Nenagh, Delia. Pah! No one misses them.'

I fight the urge to call him out on his brutality. The last thing I want is to push him over the edge.

'How did they die?' I ask. 'Did you hit them on the back of the head, too?'

'I am not a monster,' Reginald says in a low, lethal tone. 'An overdose of sleeping tablets did the trick. They died as they lived. Meekly, without leaving a trace.'

'And Colette?' I push. 'Is that what's in store for her?'

'I told you, that's none of your business.' Reginald moves the pistol, aiming at me.

Anger rises deep inside me. I can't believe we got it so wrong. Reginald wasn't traumatised by his mother, or forcefully separated from his loving father.

'René, darling?'

The woman we saw earlier at the window peeks into the room. She clutches the doorframe, wearing a navy wool coat and cream scarf, and shiny patent leather shoes with a low heel. Her face is pale and drawn, with lips pressed in a thin line.

Her eyes widen at the sight of the gun. 'What was that you said about sleeping pills?'

49

Colette's gaze darts from Antony to me, then back to her husband. Her bone-white fingers clutch the doorframe.

'You told me your wives went missing,' she says shakily.

'And I told you to stay upstairs.' Reginald adjusts his aim, pointing the gun at Antony.

'Where did you get the gun?' she asks, eyes wide. 'Please put it down.'

Reginald shakes his head. 'These are the bad people I warned you about. They'll ruin our lives if I don't deal with them. Get back in the bedroom and lock the door.'

'He's an evil bastard, Colette,' Antony says, leaning forward on the sofa. 'He's planning to kill you too and steal your house, just like he did with the others.'

'I told you to shut your mouth, you cocky little sod,' Reginald seethes, all pretence of civility gone.

'You're calling me little? That's rich coming from you.' Antony's tone doesn't match the tightness around his eyes or the sallow cast to his skin. 'What are you, five-foot-six in your mother's heels?'

The pistol shakes in Reginald's hand. 'Don't talk about my mother!'

'René, the man in the hall is a police officer. I saw his badge.'

Colette casts a worried glance down the hall. She clutches her coat at the collar so tight, she looks close to strangling herself. 'Why did you hurt him?'

'I was protecting you.' A muscle twitches in Reginald's cheek. 'He's an imposter, like these two. They broke into our house to set me up and rob us blind. Get back upstairs before you get hurt.'

A glimmer of hope rises inside me at Reg's reluctance to shoot us in front of his wife. His warped and twisted mind probably thinks that would make him look like a monster. Death must be meted out in the correct way, the way he planned it. A bullet for me and Antony, but hopefully not while Colette is watching.

Whatever happens, we can't let her leave.

I grab my police lanyard and flash it in her direction. 'Colette, we're with the police. Your husband's holding us hostage. He's wanted for murder.'

'Be silent!' Reginald's voice is taut with anger. He aims the pistol at my shuddering chest, his last veneer of charm cracking and falling away.

Colette cowers in the doorway with her eyes bulging. 'I won't be part of this,' she says shakily. 'We should call the police.'

'No police!' Reg snaps, 'How many times do I have to tell you! For the love of God, do as I say and go upstairs!'

'Don't leave us!' I yell.

Colette bravely enters the lounge, comes up behind Reginald and tugs at his sleeve. 'Darling, put the gun down and let's talk this through sensibly.'

Reginald attempts to shrug her off, but she refuses to let go.

'Where's my René? Where's the man I married?'

In one swift move, Reginald grabs Colette's arm and pushes her back with surprising strength towards the sofa. She staggers back and cries out as her leg bangs the coffee table.

Antony catches her before she falls and helps her onto the sofa between us.

Tick, tick. The hands on the grandfather clock point upward: eleven fifty-nine.

I put my arm around Colette's shuddering shoulders. Her eyes jitter in their sockets as she stares at the man who duped her.

The clock strikes twelve with melodic, chiming bongs.

Reginald's finger trembles on the trigger, his well-laid plans in shreds, his eyes wild with anger. Muscles tighten in his cheek. My brain slows as his intent becomes sickeningly clear.

Terror claws up my throat. My breath goes in and out in small, strangled heaves.

Antony slips his hand in his pocket. In one smooth move, he hurls a handful of coins at Reginald's face, making him flinch.

CRACK! The muzzle flashes brilliant orange.

Colette screams as a lamp bulb explodes. She drops to the floor with a yelp, her hands clamped over her head. I dive to her side and drag her out of the way as Antony lunges at Reginald in a blur.

A high-pitched wailing sound fills the house and drowns out Colette's whimpers. I wince under the shrieking sound. My heart crashes against my ribs as I try to make sense of what I'm hearing.

Is it a police siren? Let it be the police!

It's the house alarm.

Why is the alarm going off? Has someone set it off?

Through the doorway, Antony tussles with Reginald against the corridor wall. Antony ducks his head and Reginald's punch glances off his brow.

He strikes back, slamming his fist into Reg's gut.

'Oof!' Reginald folds forwards, the wind knocked from him.

Antony grabs Reginald's shirt and drives him hard against the radiator. Glass crunches as Reg's head smashes a framed painting on the wall. A patch of hair shifts on his head, revealing his bald, liver-spotted scalp underneath.

Reginald wildly swings his right arm. It's a lucky haymaker – his fist connects with Antony's face.

Antony shouts out, grabs him by the throat and shakes him like a ragdoll. 'Had enough yet, old man?' he growls.

Reginald flails wildly. He scrabbles at Antony's strong arms, trying to break his grip. Then, he slowly raises the pistol at Antony's unprotected stomach.

Unthinking, I launch myself through the doorway, grab Reginald's wrist, and wrestle his arm away from Antony. The black metal snout points down the corridor. I twist his wrist and yank his fingers, but Reginald retains a super-human grip on the pistol.

To my horror, the gun is now pointing at Henry. He's directly in the line of fire, on his hands and knees on the Persian rug. His arms and legs shake as he attempts to stand, but his leg gives way beneath him and he collapses.

Colette clings to the lounge doorway with tears streaming down her face as Reginald struggles in Antony's grip, flinging me this way and that. He can't be getting any air, yet still he grips the gun.

A primitive urge overtakes me. With a grimace, I lean over and bite down on Reginald's fingers.

Reginald shrieks. The pistol drops from his hand and clatters onto the floor.

CRACK!

Dread grabs my heart at the snap of the pistol, clearly audible against the clamouring alarm. The hall radiator *pings* and the garage doorframe explodes in paint flakes and wood splinters.

Henry cries out, falling onto his back with his hand clapped over his face.

I wipe my mouth. *Please, God, let him be all right!* I kick the pistol away from Reginald. It skitters across the parquet floor, landing near Henry.

Henry reaches for the gun. A shallow score runs across his cheek where the bullet nicked him. He releases the magazine, then pulls back the slide to eject the chambered bullet. Seconds later, he slumps against the hard floor with the weapon and magazine held close to his chest.

A glint of steel catches my eyes. A pair of handcuffs, clipped to Henry's belt.

I rush over to Henry and crouch beside him. I yank off my scarf and scrunch it up, pressing it against his bleeding face.

Colette joins me, kneeling on the hard-floor beside Henry. I grab her hand and direct her to keep the pressure on while I unclip the cuffs.

'Sod this!' says Antony, releasing Reginald. He steps back and lands a beautiful right-cross on his chin.

Reginald drops to the floor like a sack of potatoes.

'I've got cuffs!' I yell, coming up alongside him.

Antony yanks Reginald's arms behind him. With shaking hands, I snap the cuffs around one wrist and then the other.

With his face pressed into the floor, Reginald is no longer the suave, immaculate dandy, but a battered and bruised old man with a toupée.

Antony straightens, breathing heavily. He touches his fingers to his bruised and swollen right eye.

Colette cradles Henry's head, applying gentle pressure to his cheek.

'You okay?' Antony asks, as the sound of the house alarm suddenly cuts out.

I nod and fall into his embrace. The alarm rings on inside my head, joined by the distinctive trill of Henry's mobile phone.

'That was fun.' Antony squeezes me tight. 'I've got a right shiner, haven't I?'

'You need to put some frozen peas on it.' I take in a shuddering breath, checking that all my limbs work. 'I can't believe we're in one piece.'

Colette gently lays Henry down, gets to her feet. Using the wall for support, she staggers over to Reginald as he comes to.

He looks up at her.

Colette leans over her husband, her grey lips pressed together. 'You're a bad man, René Moreau.'

She draws back her foot and gives him a sharp kick in the ribs.

He groans.

'A very, very bad man!'

I say, 'Colette, are you all right?'

Colette raises her chin and sniffs. 'I am now, dear.'

I cast a concerned eye over Henry. 'I can still hear that bloody alarm in my head.'

'That's not the house alarm!' Antony warns, pulling me towards the wall.

Loud thumps make the front door shudder. My heart pounds as the wood splinters, cracks, and smashes open.

50

A police officer wielding a red metal ram steps back from the splintered doorframe. Behind him, blue lights blaze in the dark.

'Armed police! Armed police!' A burly officer in body armour yells through the doorway. 'Stand still and keep your hands visible!'

Officers equipped with bullet-proof vests, visored helmets and rifles tramp through the entrance hall and surround us. The tactical team splits to search the house. An officer pulls on latex gloves, removes the pistol and ejected magazine from Henry's grip, and places the items into an evidence bag.

Police call from various parts of the house: *'Dining room, clear!'*

'Bedrooms, clear!'

'Garage, clear!'

Antony and I stand rooted by the lounge door with our hands in the air. I couldn't move if I wanted to.

'Who are you?' an armed officer confronts me and Antony.

'I'm Alex Martin.' I nod towards Antony and introduce him. 'We're working with DC Henry Longhurst, who's over there.'

The officer examines the lanyards around our necks.

'That guy there tried to shoot us.' I point at Reginald's prone form. 'He hit Henry over the head with a poker in the lounge.' I bite my tongue, realising I sound like I'm playing Cluedo.

'Okay, you can put your hands down.' The officer turns to confer with his team.

Colette stands over Reginald, jabbing her finger, her face white with anger. 'I hope they lock you up and throw away the key!'

A female officer puts an arm around her and guides her towards the front door. 'Come with me. Let's get you checked over.'

Amidst a blur of activity and raised voices, armed officers haul Reginald to his feet.

'Reginald Goddall,' a tall, well-built officer says. 'I'm arresting you on suspicion for murder and attempted murder. You do not have to say anything, but it may harm your defence if you do not mention when questioned something which you later rely on in court. Anything you do say may be given in evidence. Is that clear?'

Reginald sways on his feet, blinking rapidly. 'I was defending my home and property, as is my right. I mistook the officer for an intruder.'

'You'll get your chance to give us your side of the story at interview,' the arresting officer says coolly.

Two female officers drag Reginald past the lounge. He nails Antony and me with a chilling stare.

'Hey, Reg, I hear the food's good in Wormwood Scrubs,' Antony says.

I refuse to drop my gaze or allow Reginald to intimidate me. His cold manner and lack of remorse are infuriating, but there isn't a bluff, con or ploy that can help him now.

Officers assist a scowling Reginald into the back of an armoured van and slam the doors. Once the vehicle has driven away, my breath comes out in a giant rush and my knees go weak. Back on the red sofa, I'd resigned myself to Reginald's face being the last I'd ever see. It's hard to believe the worst is over.

Antony puts his arm around me. 'You okay?'

I nod. 'Just glad he's gone.'

The tactical unit traipses back down the entrance hall and exits the house. A senior officer with a receding hairline, wearing a smart blue suit, approaches.

'Alex Martin? I'm DCI McKee, Henry's boss.' He glances at Antony's battered face. 'I can see you've both had one hell of a night. You'll need to see the medical team and get checked over. We'll do the nitty-gritty later.'

He steps aside to allow a team of paramedics carrying a yellow, lightweight stretcher to pass.

I flash a concerned look in Henry's direction. 'Can I see him?'

'Later. We need to get out of the way and let everyone do their jobs,' McKee says, gesturing us towards the smashed-up doorway.

Antony and I follow the detective outside. An officer on the doorstep glances at my lanyard and gives me a nod.

'You know, there's only one thing I don't get,' Antony says, checking his phone. 'Why the hell did that burglar alarm go off?'

'Y2K,' I say, remembering what Simon told me. 'The clock chip must have malfunctioned and triggered it at midnight.'

Reginald should have had a chat to Simon about upgrades.

Three ambulances and four police cars occupy the drive and muddy verge opposite. The vehicles' flashing lights cast halos against the pitch-black sky.

I shudder in the cold air as we walk past a second team of para-medics pushing a trolley stretcher on wheels towards the house. A forensic team puts on protective gear outside the bay window: white coveralls, gloves, masks, and shoe covers.

'How did you know we were here?' I ask McKee.

McKee pushes his jacket back and puts his hand on his hip. 'We received a tip-off from a concerned party. They told us that you and Henry Longhurst were here and could be in danger.'

'Was it someone called TJ?' I push him.

McKee's eyes widen fractionally. He clears his throat. 'I'm afraid I can't disclose that information. If you'll excuse me.' He heads over to the forensics team.

I smile at Antony. 'The League came through for us.'

'We could have done with their help half an hour earlier,' he mutters, gingerly touching his bruised face.

'The police wouldn't have turned up at all if it wasn't for them. It proves they're the good guys.'

'If you say so.' Antony wraps his arms around me, his right eye swelling shut. He hugs me so tightly I can barely breathe. 'I love you.'

'I love you too.'

Antony kisses me, a brief, intense kiss in front of half the Hertfordshire police force.

I pull away and gently touch his bruised eye. 'You need ice on that.'

We head towards a paramedic, who puts down a clipboard to scrutinise Antony's bashed-up face and says, 'I'd better take a look at you.'

As he clambers into the back of the nearest ambulance, a paramedic escorts Colette to a police car. She's hunched over like an old woman with an NHS blanket wrapped around her head and shoulders.

'Colette.' I step close and touch her shoulder.

'Bless you,' she whispers through cracked lips. She extracts her hand from the blanket and gives my arm a feeble squeeze. 'I want René to face justice for what he's done.'

'He will.' I force a thin smile. 'I promise.'

Two officers assist her into the back of a police car.

The medical team emerges from the house with Henry on the portable stretcher. His arms are strapped to his sides. The team transfers Henry onto the wheeled trolley and support his neck on a foam block.

I rush over. His forehead is slick with sweat and blood. A female paramedic arranges a blanket over him.

Sadness washes over me that I escaped scot-free while he ended up injured.

'Will he be all right?' I ask.

'His signs are stable, but he'll need X-rays and a CAT scan at the hospital,' she says quietly.

I take Henry's hand in mine.

'Alex.' His voice slurs as he squeezes my fingers. His pale blue gaze is unfocused. 'I can't think straight. They gave me something—'

'Don't worry about anything.' I gently stroke his cheek. 'You're going to be fine. This amazing team are going to take care of you.'

Henry whispers something. I lower my head to hear.

'Stay with me.'

My cheeks burn. 'I…I'll come and see you in hospital, I promise.'

'We're ready to move him,' the paramedic says kindly.

I step back, wiping my eyes as she wheels Henry to the ambulance. He and I have seen this case through from beginning to end. He should be taking charge of the final stages and soaking up his great achievement instead of leaving the scene, alone, in the back of an ambulance.

On the skyline, an explosion of brilliantly coloured fireworks lights up the sky. I take deep breaths until Antony returns, holding a cold compress to his swollen eye. He opens his puffa jacket so I can slip my arms inside.

'Happy New Year,' Antony says, as we stare up at the fireworks. 'It's not quite the laser show I promised you.'

'It's perfect.' I smile up at him.

'So, is this your life from now on?' he says. 'Chasing murderers? Calling in hit-squads?'

'As if!' I snort, snuggling against his chest. 'After tonight's madness, I'm looking forward to a quiet life and a load of movie boxsets.'

'You said that last time.'

'Well, this time, I really mean it.'

My phone buzzes in my pocket, the screen flashes green. MUM_AGH!

My thumb hovers over the *Accept Call* button. What the heck, it's the New Year. I press it.

'Alexandra? Are you there?'

A cacophony of whooping, hollering and a succession of bangs in the background make it almost impossible to hear her. Mum's voice could raise the dead, but she's no match for her fellow Irish, especially when they've got something to celebrate.

'I'm here with Antony!' I shout back.

'I called to say *Athbhliain faoi mhaise dhuit* from the top of Benbulbin!' Mum yells.

What am I thinking? I pull the phone away from my ear and snuggle closer to Antony, resting my head on his chest. He puts his arm round me and kisses the top of my head.

'Did you do anything special, the pair of you?' Mum steams on at such volume, officers standing nearby look round. There's no such thing as a private conversation when Mum's involved.

'Well, we saw some fireworks.' I glance around at the haze of blue lights and milling officers. Antony raises his brow and winces.

Mum says, 'Moira and I are frozen solid, but it was worth it for the view. I have to tell you, Alexandra, the strangest thing happened just before midnight. We were passing the Fairy Door when we heard little whistles and flutes. It made the hairs on my neck stand up. Father Egan said it was only the wind playing tricks. Then that eejit Darragh said the spirits were coming and would grab us if we didn't get a move on.' She pauses for breath. 'Moira said he was only after the mulled wine and mince pies at the top. But a terrible fear came over me, and I decided to get down on my knees and say a prayer for the two of you.'

'Thanks, Mum.' Weird shivers go through me, thinking of Mum saying her prayers while we were looking down the barrel of Reginald's pistol.

'I'll leave you now,' Mum says. 'The choir's started singing one of your favourites, Alexandra. How Great Thou Art. I want to sing along.'

Through the phone's tinny speaker, the Sligo faithful, defiant under assault by howling wind, throw themselves into a rousing rendition of a hymn guaranteed to bring tears to my eyes.

For once, Mum's right. I was always a reluctant church-goer, but something about this hymn reaches deep into my soul. The mass of soaring voices has me reaching into my pocket for a tissue.

I pass the phone to Antony and blow my nose. 'I am *not* going to blubber.'

Antony listens on my behalf and shrugs. 'It's hardly Eminem. But it's not bad.'

And that's how we celebrate the Millennium, listening to the church choir singing their hearts out through my tinny Nokia speaker. I can't imagine a more fitting way to mark the fact we made it, into the twenty-first century.

51

— • —

TWO DAYS LATER

Antony and Charlie sit together at the kitchen table, stacking Cheerios. I hold my breath as Charlie's chubby fingers attempt to place a seventh Cheerio atop the stack. Ludo sits at the boy's feet, licking his chops in anticipation of breakfast cereal falling from the table.

The stack topples over. 'Durr!' Charlie claps his hand to his head. 'We'll never do seven!'

'We will this time, short-round,' Antony says, setting a Cheerio down. 'One.'

'Two!' Charlie immediately takes his turn without any sign of a tantrum.

My eyebrows shoot up and my fingers loosen their grip around my coffee mug. Until this morning, I had no idea Antony had a way with kids. He's so good, I bet he could side-hustle as a children's entertainer if his new design business doesn't pan out.

Marcus sets a rack full of toast on the table beside the coffee percolator jug. 'Help yourself.'

'Cheers,' Antony says, topping up his mug. 'This should keep me sharp for the drive home.'

Marcus glances out the window, where brilliant sunlight floods the garden. 'The rain's held off. You should have a clear run back.'

I suspect he can't wait for us to leave after the chaos we brought to his door in the dead of night on New Year's Day.

Olivia's face went paper white when she opened the front door and saw me, Antony, and DCI McKee on the porch. McKee swiftly explained the situation and reassured Marcus and Olivia that Henry was in the best possible hands.

'Things might have turned out very differently had it not been for these two,' McKee said. 'They deserve a medal for bravery.'

'Thank you, for what you did,' Olivia said, giving both of us a hug. Shell-shocked, she ran upstairs to pack an overnight bag and called a taxi to take her straight to the hospital.

Marcus added his thanks, turned to Antony and said, 'I don't remember Henry mentioning you. Are you a plainclothes detective?'

'I'm not with the police.' Antony had put his arm around me. 'I'm with Alex.'

Even though it was a lovely thing to say, I wanted to curl into a ball and disappear.

'Ahh...' Marcus drew out the sound as though he had no clue what to say.

Over forty-eight hours later, Olivia is spending more time at the hospital than at home. The atmosphere has improved considerably, although some of Marcus's breeziness has gone.

Thankfully, we've finished with our interviews, statements, fingerprints and DNA samples. Our duty is done, our bags are packed, and there's only one more port of call before we head back to Birmingham.

'We did it!' Charlie claps, after Antony successfully places the seventh Cheerio on the stack.

Antony high-fives him. 'Right, better grab my stuff.' He takes his plate and mug over to the sink.

Charlie's face falls. 'You going?'

'Soon, but not yet.' Antony smiles.

Charlie clambers off the chair and shoots out the door.

'He's wound up tighter than a Jack-in-the-box,' Marcus says, running hot water into the sink. 'When he finds out Henry's coming to stay, he'll probably explode.'

The hospital has not yet set a date for Henry's discharge, but when he is released, I have no doubt that staying with Marcus and Olivia, eating hearty meals, and having Charlie bouncing around, will be as therapeutic as any prescribed medication.

Charlie hurtles into the kitchen with two Lego mini-figures clutched in his fist. He thrusts one into Antony's hand. It has Lando Calrissian's head stuck on Darth Vader's body.

'I made you, Antony!' Charlie says. 'It's a present!'

'Wow!' Antony's eyes widen as he examines the figure.

He puts out his fist and Charlie presses his knuckles against Antony's with a grin, then hands me a Princess Leia figure carrying Boba Fett's jetpack.

'Thanks!' Grinning, I examine the jet pack. 'Is this so I can fly?'

Charlie shakes his head. 'That's your rucksack. It's where you keep your treasure.'

I lean over for a hug, and Charlie presses his squidgy cheek against mine. I consider the truth in his innocent observation. While the League have the finding machine, I do feel as though I've lost my treasure. Jonathan Prudente-Poulton texted yesterday to say he would be in touch shortly, but I haven't heard back.

I step into the hallway with my mobile phone and dial the League. After five long rings, TJ answers.

'Hello, Alex. Glad to hear you're all right.'

'Not half as much as me,' I say with a shudder. 'Thanks for your help.'

'No problem. Listen, JPP wants to discuss something with you,' TJ says. 'As soon as he's in, I'll get him to contact you.'

'What's it about?' My heart races.

'I can't say.' The silence that follows could mean anything. 'He'll check in with you later.'

TJ ends the call, leaving me pacing the hall with my heart in my mouth.

The doorbell rings. I open the front door, squinting against the brilliant sunshine.

A technician in aquamarine overalls with a *Chips-Away* logo stands on the porch, holding a toolbox.

'Hi, I'm Dave.' He gives me a broad smile and thumbs at the Audi. 'Shall I get started?'

'Please.' I hurry to the kitchen and call Antony. After putting on our shoes, we head outside.

Antony stares dejectedly at the red and green spray-painted words that deface the Audi's driver's side door and rear wing.

HAPPY Y2K, PIGS!

The vandal struck on New Year's Eve while the Audi was in the police car park. We were looking down the barrel of Reginald's pistol around the same time, which only adds insult to injury.

Antony walks around the Audi, inspecting the panels for rogue paint splashes.

'Don't worry,' Dave says chirpily. 'She'll be good as new by the time I'm finished.' He kneels on a foam mat, opens his toolkit, and sprays solvent solution onto a cloth. 'You should have seen the Chief Superintendent's motor. The culprit sprayed fireworks down both sides and then started on the roof. He was still on the roof when they caught him.'

'About bloody time!' I exclaim.

Antony absently massages the spot on his arm where Kaiser latched onto him. 'What does he look like?'

'Tall skinny white kid. Only fifteen.' Dave looks Antony up and down and grins. 'Apart from the hoodie, he looks nothing like you. The Super said his old man got kicked out of the police for fiddling his expenses. The kid reckoned he'd get back at the force on Dad's behalf. Make his feelings known.'

'I'd like to make my feelings known on his thick skull!' Antony growls.

'Come on, grumpy.' I put my arms around him and gaze into his eyes. 'Try and look on the bright side.'

'I'm trying.' Antony pulls me close.

'She's right, you know,' Dave nods sagely, moving the cloth in circles. Red and green paint comes off on his cloth.

'It's a new century and the sun is shining. Things can only get better.'

· · · · · ● · ● · · · ·

Antony parks the gleaming, graffiti-free Audi in a bay in The Queen Elizabeth II Hospital car park, and stretches back in his seat.

'I'll wait here...if that's okay.'

Frowning, I say, 'You're not coming in? Henry wants to thank you.'

'I don't need his thanks.' Antony makes micro-adjustments to the rear-view mirror. 'This is between you and him. I'd be a third wheel. Give him my best.'

Antony has a point. It will be hard enough to face Henry without the additional pressure of my boyfriend hovering in the corner.

'If you're sure.'

'I am.' Antony glances at the hospital entrance, on the far side of the carpark. 'Shouldn't you have brought flowers or something?'

I shrug. 'I don't think flowers are Henry's thing.'

'Fair enough.' Antony shrugs. 'I'll wait here.'

'Thanks.' I lean over for a kiss, then step out of the car and close the door. Moments later, the Audi is booming with bass beats. Thankfully, there's no one around to complain.

The hospital is a plain, brown block standing seven stories high on the southern outskirts of Welwyn Garden City. Statuesque oak trees surround the building, doing their best to soften its edges. The trees thrust their bare branches over swards of soggy grass either side of a wide path leading to the entrance.

I ask for directions to Henry's ward at the reception desk, and run up two flights of stairs with my insides twisting. I follow the signs for Ward G9, then push through the swing doors and approach a stout nurse with grey hair scraped into a bun.

'I'm Alex Martin, here to see Henry Longhurst.'

She raises a brow. 'A police officer is waiting to speak to you. Follow me, please.'

I bite back my questions and follow the nurse to a door with a silver plaque: *Relatives' Room*.

'You can go through,' she says.

Curiosity niggles at me as I step into a grey room with chairs arranged around the walls. Magazines are scattered across a low table. DCI McKee stands in the corner, talking on his mobile.

'She's here,' he says in a low voice before ending the call. He strides over and shakes my hand. 'Alex, good to see you. Take a seat.'

I perch on a grey, plastic chair, my throat suddenly dry. 'Is it Henry? Is he okay?'

'Henry's doing well. Once he's recovered, he's in line for a promotion.' McKee sits in the chair opposite me. 'I want to talk to you about something else.'

My breathing speeds up.

McKee clears his throat. 'Firstly, your contribution to this investigation has not gone unnoticed. I've spent the last few days reading through Henry's reports. They have been eye-opening, to say the least. Your methods are a complete mystery, but no one can doubt they work.' He leans forward and lowers his voice. 'You can tell me in confidence, Alex. I want to know how you do it.'

I duck my head with my cheeks burning. 'I'm sorry. I can't say.'

'Shame.' McKee straightens. 'Henry's unorthodox methods have always raised eyebrows. He used a psychic before, and the results weren't half-bad, but yours are extraordinary.'

'Glad I could help,' I mumble.

'You did more than help.' McKee's eyebrow arches. 'If it weren't for you, we wouldn't have found Delia, Nenagh, or Reginald.' He reaches into his jacket pocket and withdraws a plain, white envelope. 'There's a place for you at Hertfordshire Police. My superiors agree. Inside this envelope is a proposal, approved at the highest level, for a new initiative aimed at finding people. We still have to work out the details, but the long and short of it is, we want you onboard.'

My mouth drops and my heart thunders in my ears. 'Me? Really?'

The idea of using Dad's machine with the police's full support sends thrills shooting up my spine. A rush of unease follows. If McKee's curiosity is any indication, it would be next to impossible to keep the finding machine secret. Word would leak out, sooner or later.

McKee taps the envelope on his hand. 'You'll have access to our systems and files, and back-up in the field when necessary. The pay is performance-related. You could do very well out of it.' He stands and passes me the envelope.

I stare at the blank, white paper, my mind whirling.

'Wouldn't I need police training?'

'We can fast-track you through, if you agree to join us.' He pauses. 'I know this is a lot to take in. I'll give you the rest of the month to think about it, but I need a decision by February.'

'What if I say no?'

McKee releases a slow breath. 'I've worked for the police for nearly thirty years, Alex. During that time, I've seen huge developments in technology and police procedure. But nothing comes close to what you've done. I hope you make the right decision.'

'I'll try.'

'Good. It goes without saying, the proposal is confidential. No one can know about it at this stage, not even Henry.'

'I understand.'

'Then I'll leave you to it.' McKee nods and exits the waiting room, his shoes squeaking on the pale green linoleum floor.

I stare at the envelope, chewing the inside of my cheek.

It should be a dream come true, but the events of the last few weeks have changed me. Reginald aiming a pistol at my head changed me. My stomach cramps every time I realise how close I came to dying.

McKee has promised me a team and backup, so I need never look a killer in the eye again. There's only one problem. Without the finding machine, the proposal is meaningless.

I check my mobile phone. No new messages.

Slipping the Nokia back into my pocket, I put McKee's offer and the League to the back of my mind, leave the waiting room, and head for the door at the end of the ward.

52

The patients recuperating on the ward are dozing, reading, or watching TV in bed, and take little notice of me as I walk past.

The door to Henry's room is ajar. I knock gently and peek through.

'Hello. Is it all right if I come in?'

Olivia looks around from her chair beside Henry's bed. Blue foil balloons float in a column behind her. The windowsill is cluttered with get-well cards, boxes of chocolates, punnets of grapes and bunches of flowers that make me regret arriving empty-handed.

Henry is propped up in bed with his head bandaged and a cannula taped to the back of his hand. A line of neat stitches runs across his cheek.

A monitor at the end of the bed emits regular beeps as it displays his vital signs.

'Alex, come in,' Henry says in a croaky voice, before dissolving into a coughing fit.

Olivia fills a paper cup from the water jug on a side table. She waits for his cough to subside, then places the cup in his hands.

Henry sips the water before sinking into the pillows and rubbing his eyes.

'I think I'll get some fresh air.' Olivia puts the half-empty cup on the table. 'Do you need anything, Henry?'

'I'm fine.' His gaze fixes on me.

'All right. See you in a bit.' Olivia takes her coat from the back of the chair and gives me a wan smile on the way out.

I approach the side-rail, lean over the cold bars and gently squeeze Henry's hand, careful not to disturb any wires or tubes. It's heartening to see the colour returning to his cheeks.

'It's good to see you.' Henry smiles. 'Is Antony here?'

'He's waiting in the car.'

'Ah.' Henry's smile falters. 'I guess you're leaving, then.'

'There's not much for me to do now that Reginald's in custody.' I stare at my hands, realising that's not entirely true, with McKee's offer burning a hole in my pocket.

Monitor beeps fill the silence.

'Marcus tells me you're doing well,' I say.

'So everyone keeps telling me.' Henry shifts position and winces. 'My skull's healing, and the headaches aren't so bad anymore. The issue is my short-term memory. I'm missing chunks of it, and the neurosurgeon can't guarantee I'll get them back.'

'How bad is it? A few days, a week, longer?'

'I can't remember anything after I entered Reg's house, and the weeks before that are a blur.'

'Give it time,' I say gently.

'That's something I have plenty of, stuck in here. Could I have some more water?'

I place the cup in his hand. He sips water and pushes himself upright.

'I lie here day and night, trying to fill in the gaps. It bothers me. I had a theory about how you found Nenagh and Delia, but I'm damned if I can remember it.'

'That's not a memory lapse. I never told you how I found them.'

Henry fixes me with an ice-blue stare. 'There's more to it than that.'

I flush under his scrutiny but remain silent.

Henry sighs and looks at the ceiling. 'McKee came in this morning and read my reports back to me in the hope they would jog something loose. I remember bits and pieces, but when he updated me on the case it was like I wasn't there. It's maddening.'

My ears prick up. 'What updates?'

'Let me think.' Henry pauses, his brow furrowing. 'Reginald's briefcase.'

I think back to the moment Reginald surprised us by the stairs, the black case in his hand. 'You were lying on a Persian rug during that bit.'

'You make it sound like I was taking a nap.' A smile briefly flits across Henry's face. 'The briefcase contained fifty thousand pounds. It was getaway money. Reginald had stashed it at the office in case he couldn't return home.'

'Sounds like he was ready to flee again.'

'Almost certainly. He had a fake passport and driving licence sewn inside the lining of his coat, both under a new name.'

'I'm guessing Colette wasn't invited.'

'Seems not.' Henry's expression turns grim. 'She didn't have a passport. And, because she refused to sign over the house to him, he had no further use for her.'

Goosebumps rise on my arms. Colette had been a hairsbreadth away from becoming victim number three.

'Colette is our star witness,' Henry says. 'She can demonstrate how Reginald isolated his wives from the outside world and how he put pressure on them to sign over their houses.' He swallows. 'By the time this case comes to trial, I intend to be sitting in the front row.'

'I have no doubt you will.'

Silence falls between us. My skin prickles as Henry's gaze locks on mine.

'The hours pass slowly here,' he says. 'I find myself stuck in a loop, running over memories Reginald didn't destroy. Memories of happier times.'

'Does it help?'

The corners of Henry's mouth turn down. 'I keep thinking about the day you stepped off the train at Hertford with that heavy rucksack on your shoulder.'

My heart picks up pace.

'You looked so lost.'

'Henry, I—'

Henry rubs his forehead, lines creasing at the corners of his eyes. 'I'll never forget the moment you waved at me. A ray of sunshine broke through the clouds and fell across you. I thought it was a sign.' He slowly breathes out. 'Foolish of me.'

I bite my lower lip, agonising over what to say.

'I remember that day, too,' I eventually say. 'I'd lost my job, and things at home were a mess. I had no faith in myself, but you did. You gave me the confidence to be brave and trust my instincts. I'll never forget that.'

Henry blinks rapidly. 'Would you pass me a tissue? I have something in my eye.'

I pull one from the box on the side-table and pass it to him.

'I have so much to thank you for,' I say. 'The last thing I wanted was to hurt you. Please, can we part as friends?'

'Of course.' Henry wipes his eyes and gives a rueful smile.

The ward nurse enters the room and checks the readings on the monitor.

'All looks good. I just need to change your dressing,' she tells Henry, reaching for the privacy curtain. She pauses and looks at me. 'I shouldn't be more than a few minutes.'

'You should probably go,' Henry says, reaching for my hand.

I give it to him without thinking. He presses my folded fingers against his cheek before releasing his grip.

'Goodbye, Alex.'

I withdraw my hand and curl it into a ball. I stand and give a wavering smile.

'Goodbye.'

Before my emotions get the better of me, I turn and walk away.

I cross the car park to the Audi, open the passenger door, and sink into the seat. Antony turns off the music and smiles.

'All right?' he asks.

I nod.

We leave the hospital grounds in silence and join the main road. Antony drives more slowly than usual, following signs for the M1, while I try to put my jumbled thoughts into some kind of order.

We pass a pretty red-stone village, and Antony says, 'You want to talk?'

I let another mile pass before saying, 'It shocked me to see Henry in such a bad way, lying in a hospital bed like that. It made me think, if you hadn't followed me to Hertford, I could have ended up dead.'

'Don't go there. It'll only do your head in, thinking about it.' He pauses. 'Henry will get better, don't worry.'

'I hope so. At least he has family around him.' I think of Dad, who I miss every day. And my mother, hundreds of miles away.

'We have each other.' Antony touches his lips to his fingers and presses them to mine, a gesture that melts my heart. 'I was thinking, since we missed out on the New Year's celebrations, why don't we head out tonight for a slap-up meal with fizz? That is if you're up to it.'

'I'd love that,' I say, smiling. 'We could walk down the canal and skim stones, like the good old days.'

I stretch my legs out and let my mind drift, staring at the farmland beyond the window. But I can't stop thinking about the finding machine, my last link to Dad. I miss it.

Antony accelerates and joins a dual carriageway. He glances at me.

'Penny for them?'

'Dad's machine was never meant to be put in a box. It should be used for good.'

Antony cocks a brow. 'Go on.'

'What if there was a way of using the finding machine without any of the danger?'

'If that was true then I wouldn't have a problem with you using it, in principle,' Antony says. 'I've seen the good it can do. The lives it's saved. It'd probably be a crime *not* to use it.'

I shoot round. 'You mean that?'

'Yeah. *In principle.* It's the difference between principle and practice that's the problem.' He takes one hand from the steering wheel and turns on the stereo. 'Do you mind if we have some music?'

'Go for it.'

Antony cranks up the volume. Eminem's tongue-twister lyrics fill the car. 'This is what the homies are listening to these days.'

'Seriously? Homies? You're not in the hood, you're in Hertford-shire.'

My phone buzzes in my pocket. A new voicemail from Jonathan Prudente-Poulton.

I play it as we join the slip road that leads to the motorway.

Alex, Happy New Year to you. I am pleased to say that your machine is ready for collection. Furthermore, the team has made several modifications that have improved its performance. We also have a proposal for you. One, I dare say, you will be unable to refuse.

ALEX MARTIN COZY MYSTERY SERIES:

THE FINDING MACHINE
THE MILLENNIUM AFFAIR

Thank you for reading! Please take a moment to leave me a review - no matter how short - you won't believe the difference it makes, plus, it's so helpful for other readers. If you enjoyed my book, please recommend me to your bookish friends! To keep in the loop about my latest projects, exclusive content, sneak peeks and other random cool stuff, sign up for my newsletter on my website and receive a FREE book.

Come find me at: https://lucylyonswrites.com, on Instagram and Facebook under lucylyonswrites.

ACKNOWLEDGEMENTS

Once again, many amazing people helped knock this book into shape. I owe a great debt to my international critiquers on Scribophile with special mention to Jim Moran, Jed Winter, Eric Diekhans, Sonny Kohet, Robert Parker and Winter Bliss Addison for reading from beginning to end. I am grateful to my Beta readers – Eamon McGing, Peter Berriman, L.N. Hunter and Isobel Peters for giving me a valuable overview on how the book was hanging together. Thank you to Police Officer (Retd) & Police Driving Instructor Mark 'Jack' Russell for ensuring I didn't make too many policing blunders relating to 1999, and relating Y2K anecdotes from his career, some of which made it into the book. Special mention goes to my run group, Any1CanRun – you are awesome. And to Yateley Book Club for welcoming me across the border, the team at Camberley Library and Buzzpodcasts UK. Lastly, thank you to my hubbie Carl, for the final finishing touches and elevating the book to new levels.

"WHY ARE YOU WRITING ABOUT Y2K? NOTHING HAPPENED!"

Friends and family asked me this question so many times, whenever I mentioned the book was set at the turn of the Millennium.

It's a common misconception that nothing happened, or that failures only occurred from midnight 31st December. Things had been going wrong since 1988 and all through 1999, with companies advance-testing for the Millennium far too late. Industries worldwide ran into all kinds of problems. Nuclear shut downs occurred at 15 sites worldwide, and air traffic control issues meant all flights to Scotland were cancelled. The wrong medical results were given to patients, due to hospital computers miscalculating patients' date of birth. VISA glitched, rejecting thousands of card payments. The situation was so bad that the company asked the card producers to stop making cards with 00 as the year date.

Y2K affected millions of independent systems that were vulnerable to failure. It's hard to believe, but the same systems are vulnerable today. Take GPS, for example, the modern world relies upon it, yet the signal is (from my sources) easy to jam and vulnerable to solar storms. A single cyberattack could cause chaos.

An idea for another book, perhaps?

www.ingramcontent.com/pod-product-compliance
Lightning Source LLC
Chambersburg PA
CBHW021246190726
48289CB00005B/1515